Camp Crackers

Published under licence by Brown Dog Books and
The Self-Publishing Partnership, 7 Green Park Station, Bath BA1 1JB

www.selfpublishingpartnership.co.uk

ISBN printed book: 978-1-83952-249-9
ISBN e-book: 978-1-83952-250-5

Cover design by Patrick Knowles
Internal design by Andrew Easton

Printed and bound in the UK

This book is printed on FSC certified paper

Camp Crackers

Lisa Stewart

BROWN
DOG
BOOKS

Chapter 1

I had imagined running my own business in a sleek designer suit and making executive decisions from behind a glossy desk. Not sharing a cheerless café with an awkward teenage couple and their three-legged dog. I sighed, eking out the mug of hot chocolate. Well, I say 'hot' chocolate – the murky brown liquid might once have been stirred in the same annexe as a microwave, but I wasn't about to complain. The pockmarked girl with amber hair and lime dungarees had the sour expression of someone who had been slapped in the face. Hard. She swiped at the tables with a damp sponge, shoving each chair back into place with an irritating grating noise. Granted, this was my second mug and, okay, so I might have been hogging the prime spot in the café, but it was the only table with a view. The nodding masts of the docked yachts took me back to a time of seaside holidays and sand-filled sandwiches. Despite the gloomy grey of a Scottish summer's evening, it was unlikely to get dark until after ten. Clinging to my window seat I passed endless minutes observing the dog-walkers and cyclists criss-crossing the harbour promenade. An impatient child lobbed handfuls of bread to the diving birds, which were expert at snatching crusts mid-air. One greedy gull - swooping too close - was thumped off course by a stale bap.

Despite the frequency of requests for me to chaperone newly

introduced couples of the retired variety, evening dates tended to be uncommon. Just as well, since hanging around cafés after office hours when I could be at home doing … actually, anything else … had rapidly lost its appeal. But I'd got lazy recently with my own business, Do Me A Favour, and over-reliant on the easy money generated by love-seeking pensioners.

My phone pinged, attracting a further glare of disapproval from Happy Hannah. A text: 'help we r stuck'. I snatched up my phone and stepped outside.

'Grace? What do you mean, "stuck"?'

'Oh, Sunny, thank goodness you answered!'

'What's up, Grace? *Where* are you stuck?'

'Well, Stanley and I were just taking a stroll along the esplanade when he offered to give me a wee tour of the old barrack ruins here, so we walked out along the pathway and now we're sort of on an island, but the tide has come in and …'

'What the—?'

'Please don't be angry.'

'Don't be angry? I'm *furious*!' I dodged back into the café, threw a fiver on to the table – that wouldn't have improved Happy Hannah's spirits, as my bill, I realised later, was over six pounds – grabbed my bag and jacket and strode towards the harbour wall. I scanned the khaki water, which had lapped over the Cramond Causeway, leaving the island cut off from the mainland. An event that happened twice every day yet still caught the ignorant off-guard.

'Sunny? Are you still there? What are we going to do?'

'I'm thinking,' I growled, speed-reading the instructions on the public noticeboard. 'I'm going to have to call out the Queensferry lifeboat.'

'Right. So what shall we do?'

'*Do?* There's nothing you *can* do. Just stay in one place and we'll get to you as quickly as possible. Are you warm enough?'

'Not really. I've only got my light jacket that I bought in a Debenhams sale and it's really just meant for when I go out to the club or something and even then I always get the bus. It doesn't even have a proper lining. What's that, Stanley? Oh, Stanley's just given me his blazer. Thank you, love. Now he's in his shirtsleeves. What's that, Stanley?'

'*Grace!* I need to get off the phone so I can call out the lifeboat.'

'Oh, rightio. Stanley's asking if we should build a fire.'

'*No!* The last thing we need is for you to set the island on fire. Hold tight. I'll call you back.'

I too noted the drop in temperature as the wind picked up and the choppy waves slapped at the stone pillars marking the one-mile causeway. I squinted at the island, but it was too far out for me to detect any figures on the rocky bulge.

'Right – the RNLI boat is on its way.'

'That's good. Will it be long? Only Stanley's lips have gone a funny blue colour.'

'I'm sure they'll be as quick as they can.'

'We're thinking of getting married.'

'Really, Grace? That's nice. But this is your first date. I'm not sure you should be rushing into this.'

'No – I mean now. We're thinking of getting married now.'

'Eh?'

'Well, apparently Stanley is ordained and has married quite a few people over the years. He hasn't done one for a while but says it's like riding a bike.'

'Grace – don't be ridiculous. He can't marry you himself. *Can he?* I was on tricky ministerial ground here.

'He says he doesn't want to die a bachelor.'

'No one's dying,' I reassured her. *Not until I get my hands on you both, at any rate.*

'What's that, Stanley? Oh, yes, sorry, I will.'

'Will what?'

'Take him to be my lawful wedded husband.'

'*Grace!* Stop this charade right now. The boat will be here any minute and you'll both be back on dry land before you can toss your bouquet.'

'Hang on a minute, Sunny – my husband wants a word with you.'

'Grace, I— Oh, hello, Stanley, how are you doing?'

'If you're worried about my intentions, they are entirely honourable, I can assure you.'

'No, it's not that.' I groaned. 'I'm just really tired and cold and want to get home. This evening hasn't exactly gone to plan.'

'You're spot on! But isn't that what's so marvellous? You go out for a summer's stroll and you come back a married man!'

'I'm not sure if— *Boat!* There's a boat! Got to go – over and out.'

As the RNLI dinghy bounced over the waves into the harbour I could see Grace and Stanley huddled together on the bench, wrapped in Bacofoil like a couple of doomed turkeys. The two crew members helped the shiny couple to negotiate the stone harbour steps. I thanked them profusely, making a mental note to donate more generously in future. They shook their heads in bemusement as Stanley asked for their blessing, launching into his groom's speech about him and his wife. The boat sped off, leaving a wide foam wake.

'Right, you pair, the taxi's waiting and we're getting you home.'

'Oh, but we've got our bus passes,' Stanley protested. 'And the night is young – we should be out celebrating!'

'I don't care if you've got backstage passes to Holyrood Palace, we're going home – *now*!'

I bustled them into the idling taxi, relieved it would be the last I'd see of this mad pair. As I fastened Grace's seatbelt, she whispered in my ear. 'I don't think I'm going to like being married.'

I patted her knee. 'I wouldn't worry. I don't think that counts.'

'Really? I hope not. I only came out because there's nothing on the telly on a Tuesday.'

Chapter 2

After last night's stress of *Two Get Stranded on Cramond Island* I allowed myself a lie-in. There's nothing like eleven hours of sleep to make me feel perky. Or not. I drifted through to the kitchen, stuck the kettle on and selected my favourite mug. I reached into the fridge for the milk, reading Gil's accusatory note: 'Much as I support all life, spore-formers play havoc with coffee'. Gil's polite way of informing me I'd let the housekeeping side down. Again.

The sun felt surprisingly warm on my freckled face as I returned from the corner shop with a pint of milk. I opened the door to the building's communal hall and browsed the small pile of post and circulars. I had my key poised when, from nowhere, out sprang an anxious-faced youth dressed in a faded grey hoodie and torn jeans. His glasses looked like they'd been cleaned with a discarded chip wrapper.

'You're Gil's sister, right?'

I sighed, my key halfway to the door. *So close!*

'Look, I've told you and your buddies that I'm not passing him any numbers, notes or fan mail.'

'I just think if he could give us five minutes ...' He hopped in agitation.

'Anyway, who let you in here?'

He blushed and mumbled something about the postie. 'It's

really important,' he urged.

'I've told you lot before – he's not interested.'

'But it's not just me – the whole world is waiting to hear his account.' Tears sprang to his eyes.

'And the world sent you?'

He placed his hands together as though praying and I caught a whiff of garlic mixed with petrol. 'Please? Here.' He held out a torn scrap of paper with a mobile number scrawled on it. I let him hold it out.

'Go,' I ordered.

'But—'

'Leave now or I'll call the police.' I tried to look as menacing as possible for a five-foot troll with ginger hair. He sniffed, wiped his nose on his sleeve and sloped off towards the door, which I slammed behind him. *Wait till I get hold of the postman. If I ever give a Christmas tip, his is being withheld.*

These spods were getting crazy. Ever since Gil's testimony in court he had been badgered relentlessly (I know that sounds like a good thing) by super-geeks who believed he'd had a genuine alien encounter. They seemed to miss the actual point that Gil *didn't* have an alien encounter. TD34 was proven to be nothing more than a fraudulent criminal who is now being detained in Winchester prison. However, a small but persistent group has gradually grown and now there's an entire website dedicated to Gil – as if he needed any more disciples. What began as the odd phone call or letter has escalated into full-blown mob mentality. Initially Gil savoured the attention – who wouldn't want to be pursued for an interview by *Clarkesworld Magazine*? – but even he acknowledges it's got out of control. Much to his mortification, he came home last week to find a huddle of identical suited nerds waiting on the pavement. As he pushed past them, he spotted Edith from upstairs asking one of them if he'd mind putting her bucket out. She whirled around in confusion when six Gils sprang forward to help.

'What are you going to do about it?' I quizzed Gil as we tackled our evening meal.

'Eat it, I suppose,' he muttered with his mouth full.

'I mean about these idiot fans.'

'Oh – them. Sorry, what are these?'

'Fish fingers.' I feigned hurt but secretly wondered whether they might make better space shuttle heat shields. 'And butter beans.'

'Anyway, they'll soon get fed up.'

'You think? It seems to be getting worse. Have you seen the ridiculous posts on the website?'

'I don't know what you mean. I never go on it,' he lied. I knew full well that he checked out the Planet Gil site every ten minutes.

'You know they're planning a convention next month?'

'Hmm, I think I might have seen something about that.'

'I mean it, Gil – you need to get them to shut it down. I can't keep having strangers jumping out at me like that.'

'It's not that bad.'

'Gil, last week I was followed all round Lidl by an astronaut. We're living our lives in a goldfish bowl. In fact, I think that's what he had on his head.'

'Okay,' he snapped. 'I'll tell them to remove the site.'

'Good.' I nodded, dishing out the dessert.

'Why does this cream taste weird on the apple pie?'

'Oh, sorry about that. I think it might be goat's cheese.'

Chapter 3

I had finally given in to Berta's incessant nagging about getting fit – not that she was exactly a fundraising triathlete, but she at least participated in dance classes twice a week. I hadn't owned a pair of training shoes since high school. I couldn't understand what we were in training for. Still, I was conscious that although Mathew said he loved me for my personality (which was just as well), I couldn't assume his unconditional acceptance of my less-than-beach-ready body. My low point came last week when I climbed Clermiston Hill to reach one of my clients, who lived in a bungalow affording panoramic views of the city. She answered the door to find me bent double and puffing like Thomas the Tank Engine. As I sucked gratefully on her inhaler I knew I needed to get into better shape. Or at least a shape resembling a twenty-three-year-old female. It was with a heavy, cholesterol-rippled heart that I stuck a zumba DVD into the player and flicked on the TV.

With sweat dripping off my chin, my legs like jelly and my breath rasping, I pressed the pause button. I'd been zumba-dancing for eight and a half minutes. The landline rang, which I took as God's way of telling me I'd done enough for day one.

'Sunny?' accused my mother. *Who else would be answering the phone on a Wednesday afternoon?* 'Are you alright? You sound like you've got a chest infection. Have you been to the doctor?'

'It's just zumba, Mum.'

'Zoomber? You probably caught it off one of those old people you insist on visiting.'

'It's my job, Mum.'

'You sound dreadful.'

'You're right. I better go and lie down.'

'Hang on, Sunny, I need to talk to you about something.'

I flopped on the floor, pressed speakerphone and spread my legs and arms like a starfish, gazing at the ceiling. *Why is there a tea bag stuck to the cornice?*

'What?'

'It's about your uncle Clyde.'

'What about him?'

'He's really in a pretty bad way. He hardly manages to look after himself and he says the house is falling into disrepair. I think the roof has a hole in it.'

'And?'

'Well, you know how much we all enjoyed spending our family holidays at his cottage. You and Gil loved whiling away the summers down there. He just needs a wee hand to get the place a bit more habitable.'

'Why don't *you* go?'

'Don't be ridiculous. You know I'm in plaster.'

'How convenient.'

'Don't be smart, Sunny – it doesn't suit you.' *That's right – Gil's the* smart *one.* I sighed.

'What do you suggest?'

'I thought perhaps you and your little friend Roberta might like to stay for a couple of weeks and give the place a lick of paint or something.'

'Why would Berta want to do that?'

'He says he can pay you. It could be like a working holiday.'

'Clyde's never got any money.'

'He assures me he will pay you.'

'Then why doesn't he just pay a proper DIY person?'

'He doesn't have *that* kind of money!' She tutted.

'The kind of money that might actually pay for things?'

'Look, Sunny, I promised him you'd go and help.'

'*What?* You had no right! Anyway, what about Gil? How come he gets away with it?'

'He's working, as well you know.'

'I'm only going if he goes.'

Silence. *Is that fifteen–love to Sunny?*

'I don't doubt for a minute that Gilbert will offer to assist. He's such a gentleman and cares about people. If you feel you need to take advantage of his kindness, then …'

'I do feel the need, actually.'

'I'm sure I—'

'Gotta go, Mum – need to start making Gil's dinner.'

Berta needed no persuasion whatsoever. Granted, I did suggest it was a holiday in the country with free board and lodgings. She was halfway to biting my arm off when I let slip about our proposed painting and decorating services, but by then it was too late. She knew she was chewing on my hand and couldn't spit it out. I had shattered her dream of lying out in the garden topping up her tan while browsing the gossip mags, but she'd get over it.

I wasn't sure what approach to take with Gil. He and I would never contemplate spending leisure time together so I couldn't dress it up as a holiday. Nope, I had to go in with all guilt-guns blazing. This was about repaying a debt to dear old Uncle Clyde, about thanking him for the years of sun-kissed summer holidays, about doing something good and rewarding for a kind relative going through a rough patch. And about getting Mum off my back.

I took my time planning a sumptuous supper that would woo Gil over to my side. Last month he had hopefully informed me that his current favourite was pork belly – couldn't get enough of it, apparently. I didn't really know which part of the pig a chop came from but surely some of it must come from the fat tummy part? We only owned one steak knife, which I gave to Gil while I hacked away at my chop with a sawing motion that would flare up the average professional's tennis elbow.

'Mum called today,' I dropped into the conversation.

'Mmm?' he murmured, browsing his iPhone. I couldn't really be snippy about his antisocial obsession with world affairs – after all, I found the latest celebrity having a part of their body removed and sewn on elsewhere equally fascinating.

I repeated, 'Mum called today.'

'And?' he answered, not even glancing up.

'Uncle Clyde has a hole.'

'Oh?' He pushed his glasses up the bridge of his nose. 'You mean like an ulcer?'

'Eh?'

'A hole in his stomach or something?'

'Oh, no! Nothing like that. A hole in his roof. It's leaking. And you know how much rain we've had this summer. Seemingly the most rainfall since records began.'

'Uh-huh?'

'Absolutely. Looks like the Scottish reservoirs are good to go for the next five years.'

'So why doesn't he fix it?'

'Good question! Give that man a coconut.'

'Well?'

'Oh, you know Uncle Clyde. He's never got any money. And he's not very well. High blood pressure and low energy.'

'Really?' Even Gil's serrated implement wasn't exactly carving through the tender meat like a butter knife. In fact, his forehead had developed a light sheen as he wrestled the fat off the meat.

'Yep. A worrying combination. So I said to Mum, "If there's anything I can do, nothing's too much trouble". I even offered to go and help him. You know, as a gesture of goodwill.'

'Like Comic Relief?' He was chewing like a cow on leather grass.

'Yes!' I nodded. 'Just like Comic Relief. Except I'm not giving my services for free and there's nothing remotely amusing about Uncle Clyde.'

'How much do you need?'

'*Gil!*' I chastised in mock offence. 'It's not about the money.'

He raised one eyebrow. I *so* wished I could do that. I sighed. 'Look, Berta and I are going down for two weeks to give him a hand. I know it's not what you'd plan for your annual leave, but we would really appreciate your help. Apart from which, I don't know one end of a paintbrush from the other.'

'Well, one end has bristles that are covered in paint,' Gil said smugly.

'You see! I bow to your expertise.'

'And this is ...?' He frowned.

'I opened what I thought was a tin of Black Forest cherries, but it turned out they were olives.'

'An honest mistake.' He scowled. 'But did you need to smother them in Dream Topping?'

So Gil was in. Those in formal employment (Berta and Gil) were required to submit their annual leave requests while I let Mrs Marshall know I was on a summer break. I sensed an element of relief, as she had booked a Mediterranean cruise and probably felt bad passing me a mere handful of clients searching for romance. And as for any of my private 'cleaning' jobs…well – surely nothing that's dirty after two weeks?

Chapter 4

Mathew and I pressed our noses against the grubby glass enclosure as the common squirrel monkey nibbled on grapes and held our gaze with black soulful eyes. Its pal leapt up onto the bench next to him and also stared with no shame. It chattered something and both shrieked in hysterics.

'It's saying, "That ginger one looks tasty"', I commented.

'Nah!' said Mathew. 'Probably wondering why all our hair has dropped off.'

The first monkey selected a slice of orange and rammed it into the mouth of its companion. In response, monkey two angrily plucked a grape and shoved it into his chum's ear. Furious, monkey one snatched a peanut from the shelf and poked it up the nose of its friend, who recoiled in shock.

'Oh, what was that game we used to play?' Mathew laughed. 'Remember – when you had to fit the right shape into the right hole?'

'Uh …' I frowned. 'You mean like snooker?'

'No – oh, that's annoying me now. I'll google it.'

Monkey two wailed, reaching for a banana and thrusting it into his pal's—

'Perfection!' shouted Mathew triumphantly. 'If you didn't get all the pieces in in time the whole board popped up.'

'Well, that one looks like he's about to explode!' The monkeys chased each other around the compound.

Mathew took my hand and we wandered back outside. Struggling up the steep zigzag path, we finally summited at the crest of the zoo. We could see for miles across Edinburgh's rooftops and beyond to the Pentland Hills (might have been the Himalayas). I was sure the air had thinned. We perched on a wall overlooking the rhinos as our oxygen levels stabilised. I waved goodbye to demure composure.

To our left, a face-painting stand attracted a line of expectant children pulling at their parents. A chubby jester was kneeling in front of a toddler, studiously turning the youngster's face into that of a butterfly. I was reminded of my recent visit to the Latvian beauty therapist who had blanched at my self-tanning attempts and corralled me into looking like a cramped tiger.

'So you're okay about me being away for a couple of weeks?' I asked, not trusting myself to look into Mathew's eyes. Unfortunately I couldn't bring myself to be as impassive as our monkey friends.

'Course I am.' He nodded, putting his arm round my shoulders.

'And you won't go off with anyone else?'

'Course I will.' He grinned. I flinched, not quite believing we were still together after four months.

'Besides, we've got a lucrative contract coming up. I'll be putting in some long hours and no doubt I'll be like a bear with a sore head anyway.'

'What are you working on?'

He snorted. 'Och, it's some ridiculous toy for kids, like a trampoline for indoors. They bounce on this mat and it makes a *doing!* sound. It must drive their families nuts. Anyway, it's to be a TV advert too.'

'Sounds like I might be better out in the country.'

'I'm sure.'

'You can always come visit me.'

'Hmm,' he answered without conviction.

'So you *will* still be here when I get back?' God, even I was getting fed up with my clinging whine.

'Well, maybe not quite *here* – but somewhere where my buttocks won't go numb.'

'Point taken. Cup of tea?'

'Why not?' We ambled back down the hill, me still reluctant to let go of his hand as we entered the café.

Chapter 5

So on the last Saturday in June, Gil, Berta and I were shivering in Edinburgh's draughty bus station waiting for the X95 bus to Hawick. Berta and I were creasing up as she replayed her favourite clips of dogs performing acrobatics. Who knew that corgis were so bouncy? Or stretchy?

Gil hovered several feet away and seemed rather on edge. I put this down to his displeasure at having to spend a fortnight sharing DIY duties with his sister, coupled with a germ-associated phobia of public transport. Then, five minutes before our bus was due, his shoulders relaxed and his smile broadened. He jogged towards a mousy-brown-haired girl, her rimless glasses balanced on a pointy nose. She was buttoned into a mustard wool coat and pulled a wheeled case in our direction. I assumed she must be a librarian moving stock from one library to another. As Gil pecked her on the cheek I gripped Berta's arm.

'*Aya!*' she protested. 'What's that for?'

'I've never seen Gil kiss a girl before.'

'Call that a kiss? I've had more intimate relations with a Magnum.'

'But who is she?' I whispered. 'And why is she pulling a case?'

'Maybe she's coming with us.'

'Gil?' I shouted across the station. He blushed and picked up his rucksack, nudging Colman's in our direction. He coughed, flapping his hand towards his companion.

'This is Romilly,' he mumbled. 'That's Sunny, my annoying little sister.'

'Nice to meet you, Romilly.' I nodded. 'And you would be …?'

'Gil's girlfriend.' She scowled, her face gripped in serious concentration. 'Gil, did you not mention I was coming too?'

Gil turned crimson and spluttered, 'I, well, I wasn't sure. You know, if it was definite …'

'Ha! Gil's got a girlfriend!' crowed Berta.

'Gil! You might have said!' I punched him on the arm. 'How rude of you not to prepare us.'

'I don't think that's any way to be speaking to your elder brother,' Romilly remarked.

'He's my *only* brother – I can speak to him any which way I like. Gil, you're a twat. See – the sky hasn't fallen on my head.' Berta slapped me on the back of my head.

'Now, Sunny – watch your language in front of the young lady. So, Romilly,' Berta took a step forward until she was almost touching noses with her, 'what do you do?'

'She's a poet,' answered Gil with pride.

'A poet?' Berta repeated.

'I am.'

'And someone pays for you to do that?'

'I'm freelance.'

'Well, I'm pricey,' Berta quipped.

At that point the bus arrived and Gil assisted the mustard one on board, heaving her case into the storage area below. Berta mounted the steps and paid the driver for a ticket. She stopped in her tracks. Lodged in the front two seats were a couple of rugged young men in matching green baseball caps, fleeces, canvas work trousers and trekking boots. One had what looked like a gun case resting across his lap.

'Whoa,' she breathed. 'Who are you and where are you off to?'

'Jamie.' The guy nearest the aisle smiled.

'Andy,' answered the one pressed against the window, tipping his cap.

'Berta.' She introduced herself coyly. 'And can I ask why you're dressed as Outdoor Action Men?'

'Woodland Commission.' Jamie smiled again. 'We've got a job on down in Hawick. Where are you guys headed?'

'Where is it we're going?' she twittered.

'Bonchester Bridge.'

'What? Are we?' Berta shrugged her shoulders in a hey-I'm-just-such-a-go-with-the-flow-kind-of-person gesture.

'Get a bloody move on!' the man behind me bellowed, shoving my back.

'Come on, Berta. Playtime's over.' I chivvied her along. She gave what she thought was a sultry smile and shuffled towards the rear. I didn't tell her she had black teeth from the wine gums she'd been chewing.

We threw our coats on to the rack and commandeered the back row of the bus. Just like our school days. Up ahead I observed Gil and Romilly deep in conversation.

'Who'd have thought?' I puffed.

'I know – such talent on public transport!' Berta lifted a box of six jam doughnuts from a plastic carrier bag at her feet. She bit into one and red syrup oozed down her chin. 'Doughnut?' she offered with her mouth full.

'No, thanks. I'm going to start with savoury.' I opened a family-sized bag of Cheetos and munched on a handful, wiping the orange cheesy dust on my jeans.

'Don't mind if I do.' Berta smiled, sticking a few Cheetos into the hole vacated by the jam.

'I thought you were on a diet?'

'Am.'

'Really?' I glared at her hamster cheeks.

'The next two weeks are going to be like a crash diet for me.' She sprayed tiny particles of doughnut in my direction. 'It'll be like I'm going in for a marathon, so I need to ensure my body's prepared.'

'So you're telling me you're carb-loading for going on holiday?'

'S'right.'

'Unbelievable.' I shook my head.

'What?' she protested. 'When we get back on this bus in two weeks I'll be a shadow of myself. I'll save money on a bus ticket 'cause you'll be able to store me on that coat rack.'

'Wanna bet?' I scoffed.

'Wait and see.' She winked, reaching for a second doughnut.

The bus rumbled out of the station and soon we were motoring along country roads, heading towards the Scottish Borders.

'*Where* did you say we were going?' Berta licked her fingers.

'Bonchester Bridge.'

'Never heard of it,' she muttered.

'We spent all our holidays there,' I said. 'It was brilliant when we were young. We were allowed to go wherever we wanted. There were fields and hills, woods and rivers. Even an old fort. All you could ever want as a kid.'

'Hmm.' Berta pondered. 'I hated the country as a kid. Nothing to do. *Boring!* I can't say I'm exactly in love with it now. Are there any shops or pubs?'

'We're not even *in* the village. It's a half-hour walk away.'

Berta groaned. 'It'll be good for your diet,' I reminded her. 'And nothing to waste your money on.'

'S'pose.' She grunted, closing her eyes and snoring like a pregnant warthog.

As we weaved deeper into the rolling countryside, the bus swung back and forth. The driver must have been on a mission, taking the corners on eight wheels. As we lurched over a hump in the road Berta's eyes sprang open.

'I don't feel so good,' she complained. Right enough she had a sickly pallor. 'How much longer?'

I peered out of the window. 'Another ten minutes?' I knew it was more like twenty. She groaned loudly.

'Need to get off the bus.' She turned greenish and sweat pricked her forehead.

'Not long now,' I said overcheerfully. Berta had a good BS detector and suddenly stood up. She staggered towards the front, lurching from side to side as she approached the driver.

I heard her mutter, 'Need to get off the bus.' The driver glared over his shoulder.

'Next stop's coming up soon. I can't just pull over in the middle of the road, pal!'

'Need to,' she insisted.

'Sit down!' he barked, slewing round another corner. Berta whipped the baseball cap off Jamie's head and retched mightily.

'*Oy!*' Jamie objected. Berta heaved again. The driver slammed on the brakes and she hurtled towards the front window, landing in a heap at the top of the steps. By some minor miracle she still held the cap aloft, although it sagged with the weight of recycled doughnuts. The driver snapped the door open and Berta rolled on to the grass verge. I trotted off the bus to her aid, noticing Romilly holding a hankie over her nose in distaste.

'Get up, you greedy cow.' I kicked her shoes and laughed. 'That's what you get for eating all those doughnuts.'

'Yeah, but that's how to enjoy them and gain no calories!' She gave a wicked grin at my frown. I heard a thumping noise and looked up to see a row of passengers glowering down at us in disapproval. Offering my hand to Berta, I heaved her on to her feet. We clambered aboard the bus as she wiped her mouth on her sleeve.

'Just delightful,' Jamie muttered under his breath. I pushed Berta up the aisle again as she indicated for Jamie to 'call me!'

On arrival in Hawick we disembarked to a unanimous cheer, the driver blaring his horn in celebration. *You too, mate.* The street was deserted except for an old couple studying the baker's window display, deliberating over the custard slices and iced buns. The four of us stood by the side of the road in awkward silence.

'What do we do now?' wondered Berta, glancing into her carrier bag. 'Must be nearly dinner-time.'

'Is your uncle expecting us?' asked Romilly with concern in her voice.

'Oh, yes.' Gil nodded as he peered in both directions at the empty road.

'So where is he?' she demanded. She gripped the handle of her pull-along case as though a street urchin were about to leap from behind a nearby bush and make off with her Brontë collection. Her whiny voice was beginning to grate and I'd known her for less than two hours. I appreciated that Gil had never exchanged bodily fluids with a member of the opposite sex before but I had credited him with better taste than this. She removed her glasses and polished them in agitation, hoping Uncle Clyde would materialise like a genie. Her staidness reminded me of our old primary school teacher. I nudged Berta.

'Who invited Miss Crompton, eh?'

She giggled. 'Oh, yeah – see what you mean! *"Girls!"*' she screeched. ' *"Con-cen-trate!"*'

'"It's not cool to be a fool!"' we chorused in unison.

'Cut it out,' Gil warned. 'Stop your cackling.'

'If that's a joke at my expense, your efforts are wasted on me,' Romilly retorted.

'I thought you were *free*-lance?' Berta needled.

'Come on, guys. Enough of this bickering.' Gil sighed. 'Finally!' He pointed to a rusted pick-up truck that hiccoughed along the road. The tarnished front bumper hung at an angle and both wing mirrors were missing. The vehicle drew up at the kerb as the exhaust backfired with a *boom!* Gil pulled open the passenger door, which squealed in protest. Clyde's left hand rested on the steering wheel as he took a slug from a hip flask.

'Everybody in,' I instructed, chucking my rucksack into the open bed of the truck. I climbed in and Berta followed. 'You'll have to sit on my lap,' I said, knowing I'd be numb after two minutes. *When did she say the diet was starting?* She perched on my knees, her blonde hair crushed against the roof of the cab. Gil squashed in next to me. Romilly remained on the pavement, her hands on her hips.

'Come on, Romilly.' Gil held out his hand in encouragement.

'I'm not getting in there,' she objected. 'He's *drunk*!'

'If only,' muttered Clyde, glugging away. 'Are you getting in or not?' he shouted over our heads.

'Not.' She crossed her arms in defiance. 'I'll get the next bus.'

'The next bus could be two hours,' Gil informed her.

'Then I'll call a taxi.'

'Aye, you do that, lass.' Clyde smiled. 'Likely as not, Tam will be more "drunk" than me.' He scratched his grey stubble and put the truck into gear. It moved forwards an inch, the door still open.

'Romilly!' Gil cried.

'*Romilly!*' we mimicked. She yanked her case to the back and threw it over the side. Gil hauled her up and tried to close the passenger door as the top half of her body extended out of the open window. She held on to her glasses as Clyde revved the oily engine and we spluttered up the road.

Just at the point when I'd given up hope of ever having full use of my lower limbs again, Clyde turned left on to the familiar rutted single track. Grassy tree-flecked fields extended for miles on either side. I felt every jolt of the bumpy ride that led to Crackers Cottage (this would be an excellent drive for any overdue-and-desperate-to-give-birth mother), which stood alone except for a sagging wooden garage and slanting shed. The once-crisp whitewashed facade looked as though it had been resurfaced with cold porridge. I couldn't help but feel sad as I took in the mottled paint, cracked windows, missing slates and overgrown garden where an upside-down television had been jettisoned. Gil and I exchanged a look. If this was how ruined the cottage looked from the outside, what neglect would we find inside?

As soon as Romilly unleashed the passenger door we all tumbled from the cab in a pile of arms and legs. I felt my hair being nibbled. 'Larry!' I couldn't believe Clyde's pet ram was still alive. His formerly black face had turned grey and his wool hung in bedraggled clumps.

'Poor Larry,' whispered Gil, rubbing its ears. 'You've not been sheared in years.' Larry baaed forlornly, nuzzling against my leg.

'We've known Larry since he was a lamb – *obviously*,' Gil explained to Romilly.

'He smells awful,' she complained, again retreating behind her hankie.

'Better get used to the aromas of the country,' advised Berta, never having stepped beyond the boundaries of a shopping mall in her life.

Clyde lifted a bag of shopping from the back and stomped into the house. 'Welcome to Crackers Cottage,' he announced. Dumping the bag on the kitchen table, he popped open a can of Tennent's. 'There's food there if you want it. I'll be through in the front room.'

'So that'll be your uncle Clyde?' Berta shrugged.

'Yep,' I said. 'He was never one for niceties. I think that's why we liked him so much. He just left us to our own devices, eh, Gil?'

'Well, I think that's serious grounds for child abuse,' Romilly remarked. 'I mean, look at this place. It's a hovel.' Right on cue, a field mouse darted across the kitchen floor, pausing to salute us on the way. Romilly screeched in my ear and leapt on to a chair. 'Gil, we can't stay here if there are vermin. You know about my phobia.'

'It's just a wee mouse. It won't come near us. In fact, that's it gone under the skirting board.'

'But what if it comes back?'

I'm pretty sure I saw the mouse asking for a signed contract clarifying that it can no longer perform its mousely duties after being deafened by a human scream. Which I do believe may be magnified to the smaller animal community. That's why we sing 'see how they run'. Larry sniffed with interest at the hole where said rodent had departed with the letter addressed to its agent.

'You never get mice when sheep are around,' Berta said.

'Really?' asked Romilly in hope. Gil threw Berta a rare look of gratitude.

'Yep,' I concurred. 'Now let's see what's for eating.'

'How can you possibly think about food in this disgusting environment?'

Romilly was bang on. The kitchen looked like it had survived Pompeii; a grainy layer of dust coated every surface. Unit doors dangled at a variety of angles; the mass of dirty dishes in the sink made me marvel at the range of crockery at Clyde's disposal and each of the six kitchen chairs was piled high with newspapers, flyers and yet more remnant-caked plates. Larry persisted in licking a brown stain running down the overflowing rubbish bin.

'If we prepare any food in this house we'll all come down with cholera.' Romilly gagged. This might have been the first thing this girl had uttered that I'd agreed with.

'Sunny, you're the professional cleaner,' Berta pointed out unhelpfully. 'Where shall we start?'

I had that sinking feeling – the one I had most Monday mornings when I was expected to do a week's work in exchange for Scottish pounds. I prised open the cupboard under the sink, a well-known and accepted locality for storing cleaning products. I found a bottle of supermarket-brand bleach and an aged bottle of Ajax cleaning powder and plonked them both on the draining board.

'God, I didn't even know they still made this stuff,' said Gil, recoiling as though I'd just produced a bottle of asbestos hair conditioner.

At the very back of the cupboard hid an unopened box of ten wire wool pot scourers.

'I guess that's it. Come on, guys, roll up your sleeves. Let's get stuck in.'

'Actually, do you mind if I have a lie-down?' Romilly simpered. 'I feel rather nauseated.'

'Jam doughnut?' suggested Berta. Romilly blanched.

'Why don't you rest in the front room with Uncle Clyde,' said Gil. 'We'll let you know when we're finished.'

'Good one, Gil,' Berta snorted.

'She's not used to hard labour,' Gil reasoned. 'She's at the peak of the self-actualisation pyramid. It's all about altruistic realisation for Romilly.'

'*Bullshit!*' Berta coughed. 'Sorry about that. It's the dust catching my throat.'

I chucked them both a scourer for each hand. 'Come on. The sooner we get started, the sooner we can face eating.'

'Baa,' Larry agreed.

Between the undiluted bleach and the toxic powder, our hands were soon raw as we attempted to erase years of domestic idleness. I decided that Clyde's mountain of beer containers represented a homage to laziness rather than climate-control recycling. Clearly he had no concept of the purpose of the wheelie bin that was parked at the back door and was as squeaky clean as the field mouse. I dragged it into the kitchen and we passed a competitive twenty minutes throwing crap into the open bin. The empty beer bottles were the most satisfying, hitting the bottom with a reverberating crash. This was followed by (mostly) empty lager cans and, finally, several years' worth of printed news, including Bonchester's recently formed pipe band and a 'Home-Grown Vegetable Competition' won by Mr Sinclair's beautifully cared-for 42.6 cm courgette.

Berta had discovered a toothless broom and made vague sweeping gestures in an effort to shift the grime from the cracked lino to the back door. Larry was almost swept out to sea but dug his hooves in at the wooden threshold and ducked back under the table. The three of us used damp newspapers to 'skate' over the lino, which left streaky ink marks but at least exposed some of the swirly green 1970s pattern.

Exhausted, we finally sank on to the wooden chairs at the table. Berta rested her head on her folded arms. 'I think I'm dying.' Her voice came out muffled from under her hair. 'I haven't even got the energy to feed myself.'

'At least you can live off your hump,' I moaned. 'My arms are so tired I won't be able to lift a cup of tea.'

'Cup of tea?' Romilly sparkled, heading for the shiny kettle.

'Yes, please,' we chorused. Even Gil slumped to one side. He wasn't exactly conversant with cleaning, either. *Says me, mistress of all domestic talent.*

'Is this all we've got to eat?' Romilly complained, emptying out the brown paper bag Clyde had deposited on to the table. One loaf of sliced white bread, one packet of plain biscuits and one jar of frankfurters. 'Didn't you tell your uncle Clyde I'm a vegetarian?'

'I did, but it wouldn't compute with him.' Gil sighed. 'If it's not processed meat, it's not worth eating.'

'Is it too much to hope the fridge is stocked with eggs and cheese?' she whined. I opened the door to find a six-pack of beer, a tub of margarine, a half-empty pint of milk and something sticky and red congealed in a bowl.

'Biscuit sandwich, anyone?' asked Berta, chomping out loud.

'So it's tea and bread for me, then, Gil? How am I supposed to tune in to my creative genius on such slops?'

'Don't worry.' He rubbed her shoulders. 'First thing tomorrow we'll go shopping and you can buy as many vegetables as you like.'

'Who's making dinner?' demanded Clyde as he reached into the fridge for another can. A cigarette jiggled at the corner of his mouth and ash sprinkled on to the floor. Berta's eyes narrowed.

'We've just cleaned that floor,' she growled. 'And when you say "dinner", are you referring to the jar of sausage-shaped garbage that provides as much nutritional value as that fag?'

'Aye – the very thing. Give's a shout when mine's ready.'

'Uncle Clyde, we haven't been formally introduced yet.' Romilly extended her hand. 'I'm Romilly, Gil's girlfriend.' He let her hand hang mid-air before flicking his cigarette ash into her open palm.

'Urgh! What a foul man you are!'

'Look, hen. I'm not running a youth hostel here. I believe I'm paying your wages. So stop with the hysterics and get my dinner on.'

'Gil?' she demanded. 'Are you going to let him talk to us like that?'

'That's just his way.' Gil shrugged. 'He's lived alone his whole life.'

'Really? You surprise me,' said Berta drily.

'Just ignore him,' I added. 'He's always been a bit of a bugger but he's got worse over the years. That's why we used to take off for the day. Just consider it free bed and breakfast – perhaps without the breakfast.'

'Talking of bed, can we see our room now?' Romilly suggested.

I bowed and waved my hand with a flourish. 'I shall show madam to her room.' I led the way up the twisting wooden stairs.

'Ow!' cried Gil as he cracked his head on the low beam. 'I must have grown since we were last here.'

'Gil, you were about fifteen when we were last here.'

'S'pose.' He rubbed his forehead grumpily.

At the top of the threadbare landing we were faced with four doors, the paint cracked and faded on each. 'That's Clyde's room,' Gil nodded. 'You don't want to go in there.'

'You think?' Berta muttered.

'That's the bathroom over there.'

'I shudder at the thought!' Romilly gasped.

Berta opened the nearest door. 'Bagsy we get this room!' She threw her holdall on to one of the single beds.

'No way,' Gil said. 'That's our room.'

'But I thought you'd want a room with a double bed.' She winked. Gil blushed.

'There is no double room. Yours is next door.'

She moved her bag reluctantly as I held the door open. 'What? Bunk beds!'

'Don't worry, you can have the top bunk.' I smiled sweetly.

'But these aren't even proper-sized beds. They're, like, for midgets!'

'Think of how fit it'll make you climbing up and down the ladders.'

'Sunny, I'm not sleeping up there. Anyway,' she said, playing her ace, 'how could you sleep at night thinking that at any moment I might come crashing down on top of you?' She took another hefty bite of her biscuit sandwich. I sighed.

'Fine by me, but if you hear any scampering along the floor, bottom bunk is nearest shelter.'

'Good point!' said Berta, chucking her stuff on top. 'And don't tell me we're meant to pee in that?' she asked in a horrified voice, pointing at a saucepan in the middle of the floor. I gazed at the ceiling.

'Great! Guess we've got the room with the lousy beds and the hole in the roof.'

'Eh?' Berta asked, open-mouthed. 'I'm not even kidding, Sunny – I can see the sky. We can't sleep in here. What if a raccoon gets in?'

'Raccoon?' I laughed. 'We don't have raccoons in Scotland!' *Do we? Must check with Gil.*

'Come on. Let's just get something to eat and have an early night.'

Berta yawned. 'You're right. All this hard work and country air is knackering.'

We headed back downstairs, where Romilly was sitting at the table cradling a mug of tea. She was using a teaspoon to fish floaters off the surface. We sat eating our hot dogs in regretful silence while Clyde could be heard swearing at the television. By nine p.m. we traipsed back upstairs in muted spirit.

Chapter 6

The flimsy nylon curtains let the bright morning sunshine flood into the room. Where the hell was I? It was echoey, unlike my overstuffed, overheated and cramped bedroom. It didn't smell like Mathew's aftershave-imbued Egyptian cotton bedding. I sat up and smacked my face on the wooden slats of the bed above. Bloody, bloody Clyde and his alcoholic, shambolic life! The distance between my rose-tinted memories of joyous adventure and this shithole would require an ocean liner to traverse. I was having great trouble recalling the bramble-lined open fields, the picnics by the clear burbling stream or the days spent building a campfire by the fort as we protected Bonchester Bridge from the invading English.

I reached for my phone and texted Mathew – Missing you – as the lumpy mattress above bumped up and down a few inches from my face.

'I need a pee but I'm scared to go. Will you come with me?' Berta's voice resounded like a whiny god from the heavens above.

Having spent the minimum time necessary in Clyde's 'bathroom' (council-owned public convenience buildings proffer more luxurious pampering), Berta and I drifted downstairs to the kitchen. An elderly lady in a pale-blue twinset and pearls was parked in a wheelchair at the table. She had neat grey hair, a friendly face and glasses hanging from a chain round her neck. I would have been less surprised to find the kitchen adorned with the Lady Boys of Bangkok.

'Hello,' I stuttered. 'I didn't know Clyde entertained visitors.' *Why would he?*

'Oh, I'm not a visitor.' She smiled, sipping tea from a china cup. 'I live here.'

'Here? Where? Who?' came out in a jumble.

'I'm Clyde's mother, Mavis. I live here.'

'Really?' This was getting surreal. If I turned round and Justin Bieber was grooving in the corner I just prayed I'd wake up in my own bed.

'Yes. My room's through there.' She nodded towards the front room.

Berta appeared at my side. 'Where were you yesterday when we arrived?' she asked with a suspicious frown.

'In my bedroom. I heard a lot of commotion and did wonder why Clyde had locked me in my room with a packet of sandwiches.'

'I didn't *lock* her in her room,' muttered Clyde, stomping into the kitchen. He snatched up his half-full mug and retreated. I tentatively took the seat next to Mavis. I don't know what I expected her to do.

'Any chance I can make some toast?' asked Berta, searching the cupboards for a toaster.

'You need to use that,' Mavis advised, pointing to the gas cooker.

'I don't want to *cook* the bread,' Berta grumbled.

'It's an overhead grill.' I pulled the handle.

'Oh, I've never seen one of those before. Is it like a barbecue?'

'A bit. I don't think they make them any more.'

'No kidding.' Berta leapt back as the grill whooshed into life.

'Would there be any prospect of you preparing a slice of toast for me, please?' requested Mavis. 'I haven't had toast for months.'

'How come?' I asked. She pointed to her wheelchair.

'I can't exactly reach.'

'Why doesn't Clyde make you some?'

'Hmm. He's not best friends with patience. "No kidding", eh?' She winked.

As we ate our breakfast I enquired, '*Where's* your room, Mavis?'

'Clyde converted the dining room.'

'I don't suppose you have an en suite shower, do you?' asked Berta, ever optimistic.

Mavis snorted, wiping her mouth. 'I've got a toilet and a basin in a cupboard.'

'Nice.' I nodded. 'Have you seen my brother Gil yet?'

'Oh, yes! Gilbert is such a delight. He and his lovely friend made me some tea, then they went off to the shops. You're so lucky to have such a fabulous brother.'

'Don't worry – I thank him every day.' I clutched at the hope that one day I could travel to a privately owned port on the remote Cape Verde and I'd bump into someone, *anyone*, who had never met my brother Gil.

'But hang on, then.' Berta crunched with her mouth full. 'If you're Clyde's mum, how come you're not their gran?'

'Clyde's not our real uncle,' I explained. *Thank God.* 'He and Mum were best friends growing up. When he came to Scotland she followed him North and that's why we spent all our holidays here.'

'Didn't your dad think that was a bit odd?'

'To be honest, I think he enjoyed the respite. Wouldn't you be grateful if your spouse took the kids off and left you in peace to watch an any-shaped ball being thrown around a pitch-slash-field?'

'I guess.'

'So how long have you been up here, Mavis?'

Mavis wiped a tear from her eye. 'It's all been a bit of a trial.'

'Should I put more toast on?' Berta offered.

'Please.' She nodded with gratitude. 'You see, everything was going fine. I'd lived in Biggleswade my whole life. Clyde's my only family and I was devastated when he moved up here. But I got on with my life – have worked hard all my life. But then a few months ago I had a stupid fall.' She thumped the table with her fist. Larry jumped and skittered off.

'So stupid. I was just standing on a chair to catch a spider. I overbalanced and went down like a sack of King Edward's. Can I smell burning?'

'Bloody hell!' Berta grabbed the grill, chucking the smoking toast on to our plates.

'Clyde came down and spoke to my doctor. It was all such a shock! I hadn't even done any real damage, although my knee doesn't exactly point in quite the right direction any more. I thought the time had come for me to be with my son. I'm ninety-three, you know? But it was so hard to give up my lovely little flat and all my friends to move up here. And now I'm so lonely I don't know if I've done the right thing. I just sit in that prison all day and read or do my Mensa tests.'

'That's crap.' Berta nodded in sympathy.

'So it's nice to have a bit of company.' Mavis smiled, patting my hand.

'Right – *Woman's Hour* is over,' barked Clyde, chucking his mug into the sink. 'Gil's here. Let's see some action. Come on – chop chop!' Without warning, he grabbed the handles of the wheelchair and manoeuvred Mavis out of the kitchen.

Gil and Romilly struggled through the back door, weighed down with bags bulging with what looked like Bonchester's entire fruit and vegetable stock.

'Been watching *Joseph and the Amazing Technicolor Dreamcoat*?' I asked.

'Sorry?' Romilly snapped.

'You know – seven years of bumper crops, etc. Expecting a famine, are we?'

'Some of us actually respect the public health recommendation for consuming five portions of fruit or veg per day. In fact, if you look at the evidence, we should really be taking nearer seven or even *nine* portions a day.' She denounced our white bread toast.

'*Actually*,' Berta countered, 'I think you'll find the evidence doesn't apply to Scotland, where opting for avocado over cake aggravates our natural constitution.'

'Anyway,' interrupted Gil, unpacking a kilo of curly kale. 'Clyde, your truck has finally given up the ghost.'

'What are you on about?'

'The clutch?' Gil prompted. 'You might have warned me that it was slipping like a nun on skates. I had to come home in second gear!'

'Oh, that.'

'We've had to carry the shopping all the way up the drive. We had to abandon that heap of junk at the turn-off,' Romilly announced.

'Jesus! Can a man not lend a vehicle without having it returned in pieces?'

'You're lucky we're alive! Poor Gil tried to pull out at a junction and the truck stalled in the middle of the road.'

'Funny – I don't *feel* lucky,' said Berta.

'Right, can we please get down to business?' Clyde clapped his hands. 'I know you're only here for a couple of weeks but these are all the jobs that need doing.' He unfurled a crumpled piece of paper covered in scrawled handwriting and slapped it on to the table.

'Perhaps you could summarise?' Romilly suggested.

'Basically, every room's to get painted. The roof needs to be fixed. The outside could do with a wee lick of paint. The windows are cracked. If any of you lassies are good with flowers, the garden could do with a makeover.' *Is he mistaking us for DIY SOS?*

'And can I enquire about remuneration?' asked Romilly.

'*Romilly,*' hissed Gil.

'Aye – all in good time,' muttered Clyde.

'And what resources are at our disposal?' Romilly pressed on.

'You've got a mouth on you, eh? Right, follow me.' Clyde pushed Larry aside and stepped out of the back door as we trooped behind in silence.

'Are we going far?' Berta asked. 'Only it's a bit parky out there and my jacket's upstairs.'

Approaching the decrepit shed adjacent to the house, Clyde rattled a set of keys until he found one that made the rusty padlock spring open. A lock seemed wholly unnecessary when a passing hedgehog could probably storm the door. We lined up in the gloomy interior, daylight straining to perforate the dusty windowpanes. Clyde grunted to a higgledy pile in the corner. 'There are tins of emulsion, gloss for the window frames, some masonry paint.' He kicked a bucket that was piled high with paintbrushes and rollers.

I browsed the paint pots, reading out the colours. 'Carousel pink, calypso blue, evergreen, wild orchid. Clyde, there aren't two pots of paint the same. Where did you buy these?'

'Och, you don't need to buy paint around here. Auld Jock brings in his leftovers to the pub and swaps them for pints.'

Berta sighed. 'Ever heard of Kelly Hoppen?'

'Who?'

'She'd drive a bulldozer through your house if she saw this lot.'

'What do you care? Anyway, that's my workbench by the window. Whatever tools I've got are hanging up over there.' Clyde pointed to a rack that might once have boasted a full set of appliances suitable for the average DIYer but now displayed a hammer, a bent saw and three cracked plastic-handled screwdrivers.

'Not exactly B&Q,' muttered Berta.

'And you'd know, would you?' Clyde leant on the workbench and ran a rough hand fondly over the pitted surface.

'Uncle Clyde, you do know that none of us are experienced in home decorating, don't you?' Gil asked. 'I mean, please don't get your hopes up. I got the impression from Mum we were to give the rooms a coat of paint. Surely you should get a tradesman in for the roof and windows?'

'I'm not made of money!'

'Talking of which—' Romilly began.

'Alright, alright. You're persistent, I'll give you that.' *And as easy to shake off as an STD.*

He shooed us out of the shed and made his way across the small courtyard to the equally dilapidated garage, a larger wooden building on its knees with age and rot. Again he fumbled with his key ring.

'Jesus. It's not as if the crown jewels are stashed in there,' Berta complained as the wind buffeted around the small enclosure.

Clyde left the door wide open and indicated for us to go in. The mishmash of rubbish layered against the walls resembled a car boot sale. Discarded pine furniture, columns of fusty magazines (I won't go into details but they weren't the sort Berta had in mind), misshapen garden implements and cardboard boxes awash with used beer bottles and cans. In the darkness teetered a warped wardrobe and an old Perspex BT phone box.

'What's with the phone box?' Berta giggled. 'Did it come with all the hooker contact numbers?'

Clyde glared at her. 'If you must know, I had plans to sink it into the garden as an ornamental fishpond. Anyway, this is what I wanted to show you.'

In the centre of the garage stood a cloth-covered hump.

'Now I don't have any cash to pay you,' Clyde began.

'Oh, here we go!' cried Berta. 'Why are we not surprised by that?'

'Clyde!' I protested, jabbing him in the chest. 'You told Mum you'd pay us! It's really mean of you getting us all the way down here and then breaking that news—'

'Whoa – hold your horses,' he interrupted. *Did he say horses? Perhaps he's hiding a thoroughbred under the blanket.* I half expected Shergar to canter out and neigh '*Surprise!*'

'Here,' he said, yanking at the dust covers. 'Give me a hand.'

He peeled back the heavy cotton sheet to reveal a sleek racing-green sports car with what had once been shiny chrome wheels and a cream leather interior. I was certainly no expert – to me a car was a metal box with a taxi sign on the roof – but this looked like a costly classic.

'*Wow!*' breathed Gil, running his fingers over the long bonnet and leaving a trail through the grimy surface. 'An E-type Jag, if I know my cars.'

'Aye. A 1974 Roadster,' Clyde boasted as though he'd given birth to it.

'Does it work?' Romilly asked.

'It used to, but it hasn't moved for about thirty years. All the works will be jammed. The battery will be flat, apart from anything else.'

'Is it actually yours?' Gil inspected the car with longing. I swear he drooled over it with more lust than he'd ever had for Romilly, who stood with her arms folded.

'Well, I won it in a bet many years ago. The farmer had no more cash to wager than I did, but he'd traded some land for this beauty. I can't even remember what we were betting about. Probably something to do with football. Mind you, a fat lot of good it's done me! It's been loafing under cover all these years. Anyway, here's the deal. If you get all this work done for me, the car's yours.' He jangled the car keys under my nose.

'Clyde, that's so generous!' Gil gave him a manly hug, lifting him off the ground.

Clyde shook him off. 'Well, who else am I going to give it to? I'll leave it up to you lot to fight it out amongst yourselves – and you'll need to get it towed out of here, but there you go. Satisfied?' He glared at Romilly.

'Very kind.' She dipped her head. 'And I'm sure you'll be willing to sign a contract.'

'Whatever,' he muttered.

Berta made a grab for the keys and opened the driver's door with a loud creak. She eased herself behind the wooden steering wheel and pretended to drive, waving at passers-by. She tooted the horn loudly, startling Larry, who backed on to a rake, smacking Romilly on the side of her head. She screamed in fright and collapsed on to Gil.

'Right, you lot – clear out of here!' Clyde bellowed. 'It's like a bloody pantomime. Come on, hen, get out the car. You don't own it yet.' Romilly rubbed her head angrily as Gil tried to comfort her. *Maybe the bump on her head will kick-start her 'creative genius'?*

Clyde locked the garage behind us, leaving us huddled in the open yard. 'I suppose we'd better get started,' said Gil. 'Do you girls want to paint the bedrooms first? I might try to rub down the outside window frames while it's still dry.'

'Come on, then, Berta,' I sighed. 'Let's choose some paint. I fancy the *carousel pink*. What are you going for, Romilly?'

'Actually, I really need to produce some work today.'

'Uh-huh?' Berta scowled. 'And so do we.'

'I mean something beautiful and poetic. I have a deadline I need to meet.'

'Deadline or dead lazy?'

'Right, that's enough!' Gil snapped. 'Let's give Romilly some peace today. I'm sure she'll feel much more up to helping once she's got this commission out of the way.' He pecked her on the cheek as she smirked and trotted back into the house.

'Let's do our room first, then,' said Berta. 'Maybe it won't look so depressing once we give it a Barbie makeover.'

We stomped back upstairs with the paint, a roller, a brush and two mugs of coffee. Berta flopped on to the floor, reaching for her phone. 'Sunny, why aren't I getting a signal?'

'Don't ask me,' I shrugged, prising the lid off the pot. 'Whoa! Might need sunglasses for this work. You'd be better to ask Gil. Not *now*!' I cried as she headed for the door. 'The sooner we do our room the sooner we can scout for Clyde's vodka collection.'

'Ooh! That's bound to be more impressive than his range of fresh produce.'

'Exactly. Now – take this roller and get going.'

'What about the ceiling? Shall we do that too?'

'Might as well. It's pretty chronic with all those stains on it.'

'What about the hole?' She peered up at the sky.

'Why don't we stick a piece of paper up there, then just paint over it?'

'I like it!' Berta smiled. 'Although it won't keep the raccoons out, will it?'

She fetched a kitchen chair and hopped around the room, swiping at the ceiling. 'Hey – what's with the tent over there?'

'Where?' I pushed her off the chair for a better look. 'What the—?' I tumbled down the stairs in my haste and charged out to the field beside the cottage. I strode over the rough grass to reach a tatty orange two-man tent pitched near the property. I hovered at the zipped entrance. 'Er, hem!' I coughed.

'What?' came a disgruntled voice.

'I need to speak to you.'

The zip slid down and a head popped out. The camper looked younger than me – I'd say not more than twenty. He wore a floppy woollen Rastafarian bonnet with two dirty blonde dreadlocks poking out at his ears. His grey eyes scrutinised me as he blew smoke out of the narrow opening. 'What?' he repeated.

'Are you coming out?' I asked, bending over to make eye contact.

'What do you want?'

'You shouldn't be camping here,' I said with authority. 'This is private land.'

'No such thing in Scotland. Under the Land Reform Scotland Act 2003, you are allowed to camp on most unenclosed land.'

'Really?' *Shit, I think that rings a bell.* 'Well, you shouldn't be here. This is my uncle Clyde's field. It's not for public use.'

'He give me permission.'

'Eh?'

'That's right, Little Miss Hitler Youth. Check your facts before trampling the vulnerable.'

'I ...'

'Yes?'

'I ... I'll be back.'

'You do that.'

'What are you doing here, anyway?' I demanded. 'We're in the middle of nowhere.'

'I'm on a journey.'

'Where are you going?'

'I mean an *emotional* journey, man.'

'*Boring!*' I faked a yawn. 'A victim, are you?'

'Might be,' he muttered. 'Actually I'm searching for my father.'

'Tried the Death Star?'

'He's from the Caribbean.' He took a proud draw on a roll-up before releasing a puff of smoke out of the tent.

'And how are you going to get there?'

'I'm hitch-hiking, man. The lure of the open road.'

'What – to the *Caribbean*? You do know that a free lift will only take you so far? At some point you'll need to cross the Atlantic.'

'I know, Smarty Pants.' He twitched.

'So?'

'I'm saving for my flight. Working the land and all that.'

'I can see that. Well, I'm going to find out from Clyde what's going on, so you better be prepared to pack up your troubles and move on.'

He withdrew his oversized noggin and zipped up the tent.

Clyde was dozing in a threadbare armchair, the one-thirty from Haydock going unwitnessed. I prodded his stomach and he jolted up. 'Eh? What? Just vanilla, please!'

'Clyde.' I positioned myself between him and the horses. 'Who is that young man you've got staying in the field?'

'Och, that's just Ambrose.'

'Uh-huh. And what's he doing there?'

Clyde peered round my torso. I'd like to say he easily had a clear view of the screen but that would be exaggerating.

'He's just staying for a couple of days,' he muttered, scratching his groin. 'Any chance of a coffee?'

'We're painting!'

'Doesn't look like it.'

'So he's moving on? I don't like the idea of some young layabout taking advantage of you.'

'God forbid!' He scowled at my midriff. 'You'd make a better door than a window.'

'As long as you know what you're doing.'

'All the time.'

As I mounted the stairs I could hear Berta's hysterical whine. I opened our bedroom door to find her sitting on the floor cradling her phone. Gil was trying to calm her down, his face flushed.

'What's wrong?' I asked.

'No internet,' Berta wailed. 'What am I going to do?'

'Gil?'

'I just told her that Clyde doesn't have Wi-Fi. As far as I'm concerned, it's a positive thing. We spend far too much time online. It will be good for us to have a break. Get back to nature and all that.'

'Speak for yourself.' I sniffed.

'But what about my Instagram account?' Berta cried. 'It will seize up.'

I sighed. 'Where do you think the nearest place is?'

Gil shrugged. 'I think the Horse and Hound has free Wi-Fi.'

Berta looked up, her face full of expectation. 'A pub?'

'Yeah,' Gil nodded. 'It's about a half-hour walk in that direction.' Berta followed his finger as though he were guiding her to the road to Damascus.

'What are you searching for that's so vital?' I queried.

'Just googling the Woodland Commission. Thought I might take a wee wander after lunch.'

'Oh, aye?' I nodded. 'Thought it had to be something important.'

'You can have a break, but only when you've finished painting,' Gil ordered, leaving the room.

'Come on, then.' I dragged Berta to her feet. 'The Horse and Hound beckons.'

Chapter 7

The next morning, sun streamed through the kitchen window as we sat having breakfast. At least, I thought it was the sun – my eyes might still have been adjusting from being enclosed in a disturbingly pink box overnight. Gil leant against the sink, stretching his back. 'I hope you're not straining yourself, Gil,' Romilly simpered, massaging his shoulders.

'Well, one of you ought to be,' said Berta.

'I'm fine,' Gil answered, rotating his trunk from side to side. 'Think I overreached yesterday but I want to crack on with the painting today.'

'Good man!' Clyde smiled, lifting a piece of toast. 'I'll come and inspect your work when I'm finished.'

'Finished *what*?' demanded Romilly.

'The paper doesn't read itself, you know.'

'Sunny, are you two going to tackle our room today?' asked Gil.

'Huh?' I cried. 'What's wrong with *her* arms? They go up and down, don't they?'

'Mine are ready to fall off,' moaned Berta, who still had a stripe of lurid pink paint down one cheek.

'Painting a room is hardly the best use of my talents,' Romilly said, sipping her lemon tea. 'I can't afford to cripple my assets.'

'What your assets need—'

'I mean, look.' She held out her hands. 'If something were to happen to these, how would I craft a living?'

'Ooh, did you see that guy on the Living Channel who paints all his Christmas cards with his toes?' Berta asked.

'We're not asking you to put your arms through a mangle,' I said, 'but you need to pull your weight.'

'I assure you I'm most definitely not trying to duck out of my responsibilities. It's just that I have a—'

'Yeah, we get it – a deadline. So I guess *we* have to paint your room, then?'

Romilly frowned. 'I'm rather concerned about the long-term impact those paint chemicals might have on my health. Those fumes can be awfully irritating.'

'Just the fumes?'

'I'm particularly susceptible to volatile organic compounds, and who knows what risk that poses to my liver and kidneys?'

'Oh, are we planning lunch already?' Mavis wheeled herself into the kitchen.

'What about *our* health?' Berta demanded. 'We might have sustained all sorts of damage sleeping in Barbie's bloody cave!'

'Exactly,' said Romilly. 'Then again, who would notice?'

Clyde began clanging a metal spoon against a saucepan. 'Right – everyone out of here! Come on – get a move on.' He grasped the handles of the wheelchair and headed for the back door. 'The sun's shining, so let's get you outside for some fresh air.' He wheeled Mavis through the courtyard and parked her at the front gate.

'My book!' she called to his retreating back.

Gil leant the ladder against the cottage and began painting the first floor window frames.

'Let's give her *evergreen*,' Berta said, selecting a tin of paint. 'Any luck she'll be lying on her bed and we can paint right over the top of her.'

'She can be like that Bond girl covered in oil.' I giggled.

'Yeah, I bet that would "irritate" her skin.'

We shifted the furniture into the middle of the room and began transforming the dull, mottled walls into an enchanted forest. Berta warbled along with Taylor Swift as she covered the ceiling, yesterday's revelation being the fastening of the roller to the broomstick. She and I both understood that such zeal was fired only by her desire for the Action Men of Hawick.

'Where *is* the roaming poet, anyway?' asked Berta. 'She better not be bloody lounging in our room.'

'I think I saw her heading for the poppy meadow at the back of the cottage.'

'Poppy meadow?'

'Well, to us commoners it's a grassy field full of cow shite but no doubt her nibs will see it from a much more romantic stance.' I painted over the light switch. 'That'll make it harder for her to find in the night.' I snickered. 'Ready for a coffee?'

'Why are you even asking?'

'Fair enough.' I laid the paintbrush on the pot, wiped my green hands on my jeans and headed downstairs. I bounced through the kitchen door only to hear a thunderous crash from beyond, followed by the sound of a screaming banshee. I pushed against the door, but it wouldn't open.

'*Argh!*' Clyde shouted. 'Help me! I'm on the floor!'

'Oh my God!' I cried. I leant against the door again, but it wouldn't budge.

'Help! I'm dying here!' Clyde bellowed. Shit – Gil was outside up a ladder. Berta came careering down the stairs and barged into my back.

'Oomph!' I groaned, winded.

'What's going on?' she wheezed. 'What's all the ruckus?'

'I think I've killed Clyde,' I wailed. 'He must have been standing behind the door and when I went to open it I think I knocked him over.'

'Ooh,' she gasped. 'You *have* killed Clyde.'

'Don't be so bloody stupid!' he cursed. 'Just get me off the floor. I'm in agony. I've dropped a whole bag of Nik Naks and Larry's eating them all. The last time he went mad on my nuts he had diarrhoea for a week.'

'Berta, call nine-nine-nine!' I instructed.

'What? Don't call the bloody police!' Clyde moaned. 'I owe them some money. Not to mention I think I'm wanted for something to do with the barmaid at the Spinner.'

'It's for an ambulance,' I snapped.

'I don't want an ambulance. Anyway, they'll take about four hours to get here. Just fetch Gil – he'll pull me up.' I entered the living room, but the window was at the back of the cottage.

'Sorry, Mavis.' I apologised under my breath as I opened her bedroom door. I tried not to focus on the line of synthetic off-white drawers drying over the radiator or the spare teeth floating in a glass of water like a rare laboratory specimen. Her room overlooked the front garden and I could see her snoozing in her wheelchair at the end of the lawn. I rammed the window open as wide as it would go, which wasn't far as the frame was clogged with years of hardened paint. I stuck my head out, craning my neck to the right. Gil balanced at the top of the ladder, whistling to himself as he carefully painted the wood.

'Gil!' I shouted as loudly as I could. Nowt.

'*Gil!*' I roared. Mavis jumped to attention.

'Fire? Is there a fire?' She scanned the house for billowing smoke.

'Mavis, it's me, Sunny!' I called.

'Oh, there you are. What are you doing in my room?' she enquired with distrust from the bottom of the garden.

'Can you get Gil's attention, please?'

'Get his what?'

'His attention!'

'His confession? Why, what's he done wrong? I hope it's not drugs, as I don't really approve. I mean, I try my best to abide by the mantra *live and let live* but I *do* get frightfully angry when you hear about pensioners being robbed of ten pounds for a bit of Charlie.'

'Mavis! Please can you tell Gil we need him?'

'Rightio. Gil, dear,' she called. He continued painting. I spotted the earbuds and groaned.

'You might have to get a bit nearer!' I shouted. Mavis nodded her understanding. She grasped the wheel rims and attempted to propel herself over the bumpy uncut grass. Pushing with all her strength, she managed to shift the chair forwards an inch. *Bloody hell!*

'What's keeping you?' Berta demanded, appearing at my side. I withdrew my head.

'Gil's got his music on. No doubt he's chilling to Jethro Tull or some other ageing hippy band. We can't get his attention. Mavis is miles away and has about as much volume as a sparrow with laryngitis.'

'Stand back,' Berta ordered, leaning through the gap.

'*Gilbert McIntosh!*' she bellowed. A minute later, having descended the ladder, he trotted up to the window, white paintbrush in hand.

'What are you pair doing in there? Get out before Mavis sees you.'

'Uncle Clyde's had a fall.'

'What? Where?'

'He didn't exactly *fall*.' I elbowed Berta in the ribs.

'He's in the kitchen, but he's fallen behind the door so we can't get to him.'

'He didn't fall,' Berta repeated. I pulled her hair from behind.

'*Aya!*' she squealed. Gil sprinted to the back door. Mavis was still inching her way over the rough lawn.

'What's going on?'

Berta and I hovered behind the kitchen door. We could hear Clyde crying in pain. 'Mother, I'm ready for my tea,' he was moaning.

'That's not a good sign.' I frowned. 'I wonder what medication he keeps in the cottage. Berta, check out the medicine cabinet in the bathroom.'

'But I might be needed,' she protested.

'What's going on?' I called to Gil.

'It's not looking good,' he muttered. 'The way he's lying with his leg bent I'd say he's broken his hip.'

'It's my arm, ye daft laddie,' wailed Clyde.

'*And* his arm. We shouldn't move him. Have you called an ambulance?'

'He wasn't keen.'

'Well, unless he believes he'll spontaneously recover from a broken hip from the luxury of his kitchen floor, I can't see that he's got a choice. By the way, why is Larry retching under the table?'

Clyde began snivelling. 'Don't tell Father I bunked off school to go tickling trout.'

'Two-man ambulance is on its way,' Berta relayed.

The kitchen door opened a fraction and Gil asked, 'Are you coming in, then?'

'*What?* Sorry, but last time I looked, I wasn't exactly a racing snake. Is that the widest it'll go?' Gil huffed and puffed behind the door, expanding the gap by another couple of inches. I squeezed through, risking a friction burn to my abdomen. Clyde lay crooked on the floor like a transformer halfway between superhero and articulated lorry. I didn't think his limbs were meant to be pointing in opposite directions like that.

'Mother?' he appealed with hope in his eyes.

'Thanks!' I retorted, not exactly magnanimous in a crisis. 'It's Sunny.' I tried to smile with compassion like I'd seen celebrities do when visiting a disaster zone.

'Sunny? Gil's sister, right?'

'Fuck's sake!' I exploded.

'*Sunny,*' Gil reprimanded. 'Poor Clyde is probably delusional with pain.'

'Not enough,' I growled.

Berta compressed her body through the gap and gazed at the patient. 'Oh dear,' was her professional opinion.

'Yeah, thanks for your expertise, but I think we're under control,' I grumbled, putting the kettle on.

'Got anything stronger?' Berta asked, peering into empty cupboards. 'It's been quite a shock for me.'

'Really?' Gil frowned. 'My uncle is lying prostrate in agony and *you're* in shock?'

'No point in us all crying, is there? Ooh, I've found a bottle of gin at the back, behind this box of laxatives. It doesn't go off, does it?' She unscrewed the cap and sniffed with disdain.

'Alcohol doesn't go off, but what are those flakes floating in the bottom?'

'*Oy!* Hands off!' Clyde suddenly seemed to regain lucidity. *Jesus, talk about smelling a drink from a hundred paces.*

'Maybe we should give him some,' Berta suggested. 'Pour some into his mouth.'

'He's not a dumb animal!' said Gil. 'He's right there and he *can* hear you, you know.'

'Tippy tappy raindrops! Tippy tappy raindrops! You love me – so do we,' Clyde sang.

Berta raised her eyebrows at Gil and glugged a generous measure of gin into a glass. 'Sunny?'

'Go on, then – although I shouldn't think he's got any tonic water.'

'There's some organic grape pressing in the fridge,' Gil offered.

'Of course there is,' replied Berta drily.

We were on to our second glass when the paramedics pitched up at the back door. Both were unquestionable contenders for Scottish Borders Gurning Champion and neither was far off claiming their NHS pension, despite the fact that the government insists that citizens enter their seventh decade before accessing it. They mumped and moaned as they stepped around and over Clyde's body. There was much head-scratching and sucking of air through their (probably false) teeth as though they were competing in the regional heats of *The Crystal Maze*. Finally they wheezed back to the ambulance, returning with a stretcher between them. They moved the chairs and asked us to stand aside as if we would compromise their chances of bagging the crystal prize. Funnily enough, neither batted an eyelid at Larry, who surveyed every movement with doleful eyes and orange lips.

Having watched Clyde being strapped on to the stretcher, we were then exposed to a comical half-hour of slapstick. I'd have paid money for a similar skit at the Fringe, were it not a Laurel and Hardy style of old hat. The more Berta tried to suppress her giggles as the paramedics turned this way and that, the more annoyed they got. At one point they rested the stretcher on the kitchen table and swivelled it as though seeking the North Pole. Their parting shot was, 'You do know that one of your other patients has pitched out of her wheelchair?'

'Oh my God – Mavis!' I'd forgotten all about her.

'Don't worry, we put her back in.' They nodded smugly.

'Where is she?'

'Well, we left her out in the garden where we found her. Still, we don't think much of this old folk's home.'

'It's not a—' Gil began, but they were already edging out of the door, the older one stumbling backwards over the threshold.

Despite the uphill gradient Mavis had almost reached the edge of the lawn. 'What's going on?' she cried. 'Oh, my goodness – is that my Clyde? What's happened to him?'

The paramedics halted for a moment, the second-in-command sagging under the weight. *Twenty pounds says he's going to drop Clyde on the grass.*

'Looks like he's broken his hip,' the captain muttered. 'We need to get him to hospital.'

Clyde groaned out loud. 'I'm dying here! Give me something for the pain.'

'Which hospital are you taking him to? I'm his mother. Can I come with him?'

More dubious mutterings from the crew as they pressed the hydraulic lift to enter the waiting ambulance. 'We're taking him to the Borders District General.'

'Where's that?'

'Melrose.' He went to close the door.

'Please?' she begged. 'He can't go on his own.'

'Oh, alright.' Paramedic two sighed. He put the lift down again and his buddy loaded Mavis on board.

'How will you get back?' asked Gil.

'Don't worry about me.' Mavis gripped Clyde's hand. 'I'll get a taxi back later but I'll stay as long as he needs me.'

'I need drugs!' Clyde shouted.

We trudged back into the kitchen and Gil put the kettle on.

'What was that ambulance doing?' Romilly enquired, breezing through the door. 'It just about knocked me into a ditch!'

As Gil recounted the events she glared at me. Berta interspersed the story with unnecessary detail.

'So it's *your* fault?' she accused.

'No!' I objected. 'How was I supposed to know he was languishing behind the door? It's not as if the kitchen's his favourite room in the house—'

'Anyway – changing the subject!' Gil cut in. 'How did you get on today, Romilly?'

'Oh, just wonderful!' she breathed. 'I'm so inspired by being at one with nature. I felt as though I could almost *hear* what the wilderness was saying to me!'

'Please stay off the grass?' suggested Berta.

'So ... Romilly?' I ventured. 'That's an unusual name. Where did your parents get that from?' After all, as far as naming conventions went, surely I was the victim of parental acumen gone wrong.

'Well, I was named after Samuel Romilly, of course!' She preened.

'*Seriously?* The guy who invented sausage rolls?' asked Berta with newfound respect.

Romilly tutted in distaste. 'Samuel Romilly, famous barrister and judicial reformer. You must know him?' She observed Berta's blank expression. 'Fiercely strong opponent of the slave trade?' Nope – nothing.

'Pity, really. Sausage rolls must be one of the key inventions of the last century.' Berta slurped her coffee.

Chapter 8

The following morning we sat in muted pairs glaring at each other across the kitchen table.

'So what now?' Berta demanded, slathering butter on to toast (now she'd perfected the grilling).

'I suppose we should carry on,' said Gil. 'I mean, Clyde's list for renovation was pretty inclusive of every surface inside and out.'

'What if we paint the wrong thing?' Romilly objected.

'A, what would *you* know about painting?' I said. 'And B, Clyde wouldn't care if we laminated the cottage with Christmas wrapping paper. He knows as well as we do that anything would be an improvement.'

'I think now, more than ever, we should try to get everything done on his list,' Gil asserted. 'He's not going to manage any DIY in his current situation.'

'Was he ever?' Romilly's tone was contemptuous. She pecked at her pomegranate and quinoa mix. 'He should be eternally grateful we've arrived here like the cavalry.'

'*We?*' echoed Berta. 'So you're saying Sunny did Clyde a favour?'

'Of course not!'

'What role in the cavalry do *you* play?' I said. 'Fourth Poet From The Rear?'

'Now, girls,' Gil broke in. 'I checked Mavis's bedroom and it looks like she has stayed over at the hospital. I think it will make her feel so much better about Clyde's situation if she can see that we're working together as a team.'

Berta snorted. 'A team where three people have paint on their hands and one has a pencil blister?'

'She's right, Romilly,' Gil nodded. 'We really need you to help out now.'

Romilly glared at him. 'But what can I possibly do? I've never painted anything in my life!'

'And we spent our primary school years learning the trade?' said Berta. 'You dip the brush in the tin and wipe it over the walls.'

Romilly frowned. 'But isn't there, like, a *technique* or something?'

'Yeah – keep it off the square glass things and try not to drip it on the expensive carpets.'

'Okay, well, I'll carry on with outdoors,' said Gil. 'Romilly, could you tackle the living room?'

'What, *all* of it? On my own?' She wrung her hands anxiously.

Berta burst into song. 'All by myself! Don't want to be—'

'Just give it a go and one of us will help out if needed.'

Berta changed tracks. 'One of us is lonely, one of us—'

'Right.' I stood up. I quite fancied transforming Clyde's bathroom with a tin of *corndog yellow* I'd spotted at the back of the shed.

I was locking up the shed and swinging my pot of luminous paint from one hand when I spotted an estate car, roof rack piled high under a tarpaulin cover, jolting over the rough track to the cottage. Strange. I sauntered over to investigate. Maybe Mavis had hitched a lift with passing holidaymakers.

As the vehicle neared I observed a carful, eager parents in front and hostile kids held captive in the rear. The car pulled up and the doors sprang open as all four clambered out, stretching their limbs. I didn't think a car trip from Melrose would be so arduous. Anyway, unless Mavis was holed up in the back of the estate, this wasn't an impromptu taxi.

Each of the four passengers had been modelled from the same block of clay, giving them the appearance of a well-rounded family of grizzly bears awakening from hibernation. They must have shopped in a land where material was a rare, precious commodity – the only possible explanation for wearing shorts in the middle of a Scottish summer. Had they never *heard* of midges? I'd seen enough TV to know what accent they would have before they even opened their mouths to ask for directions – although I wasn't sure why exiting the vehicle had been necessary. The tropical shirts in colours as vivid as Clyde's paint were a giveaway.

'Hey there!' shouted Pop in a broad Texan accent. *Who, me?* The only other person in view within ten miles, assuming they hadn't spied Gil up the ladder.

They approached as a pack and I now understood why salmon leap upstream, desperate to escape those razor claws. I felt myself backing away.

'Hey – you!' he demanded. They were closing in. I checked behind me. Yep, I was the only human on the menu today.

'Is this Crackers Cottage?' Mom enquired. Ah – a tag team.

'Ye-es,' I faltered.

'See, Chuck!' Mom beamed. 'I knew I was right with my directions!'

'Crackers Cottage?' Pop repeated.

'Yes. Why?' I asked, getting ready to wield the tin like a battleaxe.

The kids I estimated to be aged about nine or ten – twin boys with Lego haircuts and brand new trainers. They stood with their hands in their pockets and well-practised scowls.

Mom waved a piece of printed paper in my direction. 'We've got a booking at the campsite here for eight nights.'

'Ah!' I smiled, the light coming on. Lost tourists indeed. Still, I didn't fancy their chances of fitting back into the car again. It would be like trying to stuff four sleeping bags into four condoms. 'You must be looking for a camping site somewhere near Bonchester. Or maybe nearer Hawick?'

'No – it definitely says "Camp Crackers", Crackers Cottage. Here, look at the receipt with the postcode. We've paid for eight nights.' She flapped it in my face, which made it difficult to focus on.

'But there isn't a campsite here – or even near here, as far as I can remember.' Mind you, it had been a good few years since Gil and I had gambolled with Larry in the hay.

'Sorry, lady, but this is it.' Pop poked a chubby finger at the booking document. He almost stamped his foot. 'Do you want to go and find someone in charge?' I could see I was going to have to reach for the tranquilliser gun. The boys began unpacking the car, fetching equipment down from the roof rack and heaping it on the ground like seasoned roadies. Mom and Pop stood their ground, hands on hips.

'Wait there,' I commanded in my most authoritative whimper. I strode over to the ladder, where Gil continued to whistle cheerfully. '*Gil!*' I hissed. He carried on, oblivious. I shook the ladder.

'*Ayee!*' He screamed and grabbed the wooden rungs. '*Sunny!* Are you trying to kill me too?'

'Get down here right now! We have a situation.'

'What's going on?' He slid down the ladder as though responding to an emergency. 'Is Clyde okay?'

'It's nothing to do with Clyde,' I muttered. 'Although I don't *think* it is.' A nasty suspicion was forming in the back of my mind.

Turning round, Gil noticed the bear family for the first time. 'What are they doing here?'

'They think they've booked eight nights at "Camp Crackers",' I said through gritted teeth.

'Eh?' Gil pushed his glasses up his nose, leaving white paint on the bridge. 'Just tell them they're mistaken. It must be somewhere further along the road into Bonchester itself, although I haven't seen a campsite near here. Why don't you tell them to head towards Kielder Forest?'

'*You* tell them. I've *tried* telling them.' I shoved Gil in their direction, taking cover behind his larger frame. Not that I'd wager he'd be much better than me in any type of warfare – the only exception being those bloody war games he plays with his geeky pals.

Chuck's eyes lit up at the sight of a man. Clearly his experience of Scottish females to date was of the empty-headed and obstinate variety. 'Okay, now we're getting somewhere,' he boomed. *Not far enough away.*

'How can I help, sir?' Gil asked. See, he *did* have a way with people. He would have extended his hand, were it not covered in *snow gloss*.

Chuck relaxed a fraction. 'I've been informing this young lady that we have a booking here for eight nights but she is determined we have the wrong place. Now perhaps you can set the record straight?' *Young lady? Well, I've been called worse.*

Gil's forehead creased as he read from the piece of paper. 'I don't understand. There isn't a camping site here.'

'Then please go and fetch Mr Clyde Davidson, because I've already paid him for a week!'

'I'm afraid that's not possible.'

Chuck pulled an iPhone from his pocket as Mommy Bear closed in. 'Here, let's check out his website.'

Gil and I began to laugh. 'Clyde doesn't have a website.'

'Oh, but I can *assure* you he does.' The anger was rising in Chuck's voice.

'There's no connection out here,' said Gil, adding, 'besides, Clyde's never heard of the internet.'

'He doesn't even have a flat-screen TV,' I offered helpfully. '*Or* a mobile.'

'*Look, folks!*' Chuck roared in anger. That's what happens when you poke a bear. 'I have promised my family a camping holiday in your Scat-land and that's what I am going to give them.'

'There's a tent already up in the big field,' one of the twin cubs announced.

'What?' Gil challenged in disbelief.

Mom and Pop gave self-satisfied smiles. 'There we go. So maybe you pair of "can't dos" don't work here but I have a binding contract with the owner. Okay, Jordan, Jayden, let's get this tent up.'

Gil strode round the side of the house where the faded orange tent was still pitched in the middle of the field. I trotted along behind.

'What the—?' Gil exclaimed. He rounded on me. 'Did you know about this?'

'I met him yesterday. He said Clyde was letting him stay here for a couple of nights and when I checked with Clyde he sort of just dismissed it.'

The bears were sprawling the contents of the entire estate car over the grass as Chuck delivered military-style orders. He punctuated instructions with brisk handclaps. I swear he even gripped a stopwatch as he timed the operation.

Gil marched up to the patched ridge tent. Music could be heard from within. 'What's his name?'

I shrugged. 'Can't really remember. Andrew or something.'

'Excuse me, can you come out, please?' Gil demanded. We heard rustling.

'Be cool, man,' a voice answered. The steel drums continued.

Gil tried knocking on the canvas roof. 'Hey! Private property!' the voice protested.

'And talking of private property,' Gil said with authority, 'you shouldn't be camping here. This field belongs to my uncle and—'

The zip flew up and the Rasta bonce poked out. 'As I told that Miss Bossy Boots yesterday, Clyde and I have an arrangement.' I moved into his line of vision.

'Hi.' I smiled. 'Remember me?'

'Can you come out, please?' Gil requested. 'We need to talk to you.'

The camper let out a disgruntled sigh as he unfurled himself from inside the tent. Despite it being early afternoon he was sporting baggy cotton pyjamas and bare feet, the woollen hat still pulled over the knotted dreadlocks. His face was wan and speckled with blond stubble.

'Sorry, what's your name?'

'Ambrose, man.'

'Ambrose Mann?' Gil repeated. 'And what's this arrangement with Clyde to which you are referring?'

'You call the cops on me?' He glared in my direction. 'I'm just passing through and your Clydey let me stay for a couple of days.'

'Did he charge you?' Gil persisted.

'Like I said, we had an—'

'Yes, so you keep saying. Can you be a little more specific?' I could tell Gil was as frustrated with him as I had been.

'Look, all I done was set up this website for him. I said that since he had this big, like, field, he could make some extra dosh by letting people camp here.'

Gil and I exchanged a look of incredulity. 'But people can't camp here!' I objected. 'There aren't any facilities, for a start.'

'Facilities?'

'You know – showers, hot water, toilets,' I listed.

He nodded his oversized head in agreement. 'That's true. So, like, there's an outside toilet in a hut thing round the back.'

'And, of course, a shower block in the garage,' I said sarcastically.

He shrugged, scratching his thigh through a hole in his pyjama bottoms. 'There's an outside tap over there. I just, like, use that. It's okay for drinking from too.'

Gil and I sighed. 'What are we going to do?'

'Can I go now?' Ambrose yawned. 'You Bolshevik types are a real drain on my energy.'

'I need a coffee,' Gil groaned as we retreated to the kitchen. Romilly heard our voices and appeared at the door. She must have found a full set of painter's overalls in the shed; she had tied a towel round her head and was wearing plastic goggles and gardening gloves.

'Did I miss the anthrax warning?' I asked mildly. 'Poor Larry won't stand a chance.' I didn't like to tell her that the only part of her face showing – round her nose, mouth and chin – was dappled with copper paint. I'd allow Berta the satisfaction of letting Gil's girlfriend know that she could easily pass for an Irish leprechaun.

'How are you getting on?' Gil smiled.

'Oh, lovely. I can absolutely relate to how Michelangelo found painting the Sistine Chapel so rewarding.'

'This I must see!' We followed her into the living room, where three square feet of one wall had been painstakingly covered with, according to the tin, *sun dust*. Gil bit his tongue, giving her the thumbs-up sign. I climbed the stairs in search of Berta. I found the pot of *azura's star* congealing, the brush dried hard with paint and Berta spreadeagled on Clyde's bed, snoring, with her entire filling collection on display to the world. I sat on her stomach and she oomphed.

'*Sunny!*' she protested, struggling to sit up.

'Working hard, I see.' Clyde's wall declared, 'Romilee is a lazy cow'. She stretched, rubbing her eyes.

'Yeah, well. Gil better not be giving her a quarter of that car – no way. Anyhoo, how have you been getting on with the bathroom? Is it halfway decent yet? Are we allowed to use it? Only I'm dying for a pee.'

'I haven't started yet.'

'Wha—?! And you've got the cheek to slag me?'

'Come and get a coffee. We need to talk.'

'Uh-oh, that sounds serious. Am I chucked? 'Cause that's actually fine. When's the next bus out of here?'

Gil and I explained the camping crisis to Berta and Romilly as Gil buttered a mountain of bread, slapping in slices of cheese and tomato alternately. No one complained that his hands were still encrusted with gloss.

'Why don't we just tell them that Clyde is in hospital and that they can't possibly stay here?' Romilly suggested, nibbling at a crust.

'We could,' Gil nodded. 'But I feel sorry for anyone who has booked and paid their money. I mean it's not as if we can redirect them anywhere else. If people have travelled a long distance it wouldn't be fair to turn them away.'

'And technically we *do* have a stable at our disposal,' said Berta.

'But as soon as they see there *isn't* a campsite, surely they'll be furious anyway? I mean, if they think they've paid for a fully equipped site and they find it's a shitty field with a tap ... we could have a revolution on our hands.' I bit my nails in agitation.

'Look,' Berta interrupted. 'There may only be this one family and from what you've said, they seem quite happy with what's on offer. I think we bash on with all the DIY and get out of here as quickly as possible.'

'I agree with—'

'Berta?' Berta offered.

'Yes, I agree with Berta.' Romilly's mouth was set in a determined line. 'This is Clyde's doing. I say let *him* sort it out.'

'Not that easy from a hospital bed,' Gil replied. 'And anyway—'

We all froze at the sound of an approaching vehicle. Berta leapt up to peer out of the window. 'Relax, guys. It's a taxi.' We heard a car door slam. I opened the back door to witness the scruffy driver bringing a wheelchair round to the passenger side. He strained to assist Mavis into the chair.

'This yours?' he shouted.

'Hi, Mavis!' I called. She gave a regal wave as the driver attempted to propel the chair across the courtyard. I took the handles from him and without a word he turned the taxi and sped off down the track.

'I don't think he was very happy with the tip I gave him,' Mavis confided.

'Oh?'

'I suggested he might want to purchase one of those air fresheners for the car.'

'So how's Clyde?' I manoeuvred her into the kitchen.

'Mavis! Tea?' Gil offered.

'Yes, please!' Mavis nodded. 'I've got a thirst could choke a horse.'

'And what's the news on Clyde?'

Mavis gave a despondent shake of her head. 'So he's broken his wrist *and* his hip.' She got the expected reaction as we gasped as one. 'He's got a plaster on his left wrist. That'll be on for about six weeks.'

'And the hip?'

'They took him to theatre this morning and apparently they've put a pin and plate in. He's going to need a bit of rehabilitation to get him back on his feet, though.'

'A bit?' Berta snorted. 'He wasn't exactly of Olympian fitness *before* this.'

'I know!' Mavis fretted. 'But I don't understand it. I fall off a chair and more or less bounce. He slips in the kitchen and has *two* broken bones.'

'He didn't exactly *slip*,' Berta started. I jabbed her in the ribs.

'He normally keeps pretty well and he's never broken any bones before. *And* he's thirty years younger than me. The doctors took X-rays and said his bones weren't in great shape.' I couldn't picture what *might* make a great shape for a bone. A star? An igloo? 'They did all these tests and asked if he was dependent on alcohol. The cheek of it! I mean, I told them he liked the odd can of beer.'

'Pfft!' Romilly exclaimed, but stopped as Gil shook his head.

'Anyway, I'm very tired now. I didn't get any sleep last night. I think I'll just retire to my room. Oh, by the way, what are all those fat people doing on the front lawn? Is there some kind of charity event on?'

None of us said a word as Mavis wheeled herself off. 'Night, then.'

Chapter 9

On Wednesday morning Gil stared with exasperation at the gloomy grey sky, buffeting winds and swirling drizzle. 'Looks like we're all on indoor duties today.'

'Oh, goody!' Romilly squealed. 'Can you help me, then?'

'Don't forget to colour in Adam and Eve,' I said as Romilly draped herself around Gil.

'What's that all about?' Berta enquired. 'Toast, anyone?'

Romilly sniffed. 'Do you really have white bread toasted every morning?' she responded with evident distaste.

'Actually, I usually opt for a full Scottish fry-up with a separate portion of chips with curry sauce on the side. Got a problem with that?'

'I'm merely making social comment that one is what one puts into one's body.'

'Well, better than looking like a fruit bat.'

'Ooh, fruit bat,' Mavis said, wheeling into the kitchen. 'That sounds lovely. Is it like a muesli bar or something?'

'Similar,' Berta agreed. 'Both are full of sh—'

'Sugar!' I interrupted.

Gil halted mid-water-pouring at the sound of a loud knock at the back door. We exchanged worried looks.

'I think there might be someone at the back door,' said Mavis.

I groaned, opening the door to the Daddy grizzly, a bear covered in full-length transparent plastic poncho. The water dripped off the plastic in rivulets. 'Morning!' He grinned. He must have mistaken my look of panic for coldness.

'Hey, I'm sorry. I think we must have gotten off on the wrong foot yesterday. I'm Chuck.' He extended a plump hand from under the poncho – no claws. I gave it a limp squeeze.

'Sunny,' I whispered.

'So, Sunny, can you tell us where we can find the shower block? Gloria is still in her nightgown so she sent me to find out. I had a bit of a scout around but couldn't find it. Oh, and …' he looked at his feet in embarrassment, 'your john has run out of paper.'

'My John?' I repeated, suddenly desperately missing Mathew.

'You know – the can. The bathroom?' Referring to the dilapidated outside toilet as a 'bathroom' was almost as far-fetched as referring to Clyde's cottage as Gleneagles. I nodded feebly.

'Shower block?' he asked again. I couldn't blame him for labelling me as retarded. He must have been ready to congratulate Clyde on supporting a local cause by giving challenged youths like me the opportunity for gainful employment. I was sorely tempted to slam the door in his face, praying that when I opened it again he'd have sloped off into the woods.

I was conscious of everyone behind me listening with expectant ears. Everyone except Mavis, who clearly thought she'd been exposed to dangerously high levels of oxygen in the ward that were contributing to these unwanted hallucinations.

'Can you give me a minute?' I mumbled, closing the door on his surprised face. 'What do we do?' I cried. 'Gloria wants a hot shower! And there's no paper in the toilet!' Berta moved to slap my face.

'What's going on?' Mavis asked with suspicion. I would have suggested an in-depth family conference but it was highly likely that Chuck was poised in the rain less than two feet away from the door.

Gil and I blurted out the headlines of the camping crisis as Mavis listened, nodding. Berta twisted her hair into Britney bunches and Romilly sucked on a grapefruit skin while we awaited her response.

Mavis's mouth tightened with purpose. 'Right, we need a plan. We're going to need supplies; bread, milk, toilet rolls, cleaning products, burgers, sausages, matches, toiletries like soap, possibly even charcoal,' she reeled off. 'Is someone jotting this down?' Romilly shimmied off, returning with her writing pad and pen.

'Biscuits?' suggested Berta. 'Everyone needs biscuits. Ketchup?'

'Tea and coffee,' Gil added.

'And a selection of fruit,' Romilly scribbled.

'Now, one of you girls will need to go into Bonchester.'

'But we don't have transport,' I objected.

'What about Clyde's truck?' Mavis asked.

'Gil murdered it.' Berta was always the first to point the finger.

Mavis raised her eyebrows. 'So I suggest you walk to the nearest shop and get what you can there. You'll need to ask Tam to give you a lift back. We don't have time to get a bus into Hawick – maybe one of you can do that tomorrow. Now, do any of you have any spare cash?'

'Don't look at me,' Berta shrugged. 'I was promised paid employment. Last time I looked I couldn't swap tea bags for a steering wheel.'

Gil produced his wallet and laid out a pile of twenties.

'Gil, you shouldn't be dipping into your pocket!' Romilly

griped. 'Doesn't Clyde keep money in the house?'

'Ha!' Gil coughed. 'Your best bet is down the back of the settee. Any local currency is usually exchanged for beer.'

'But what about the shower?' I said. Gloria was bound to send out a search party for Chuck any moment. 'Should we let them use Clyde's bathroom?'

'No!' they chorused.

'Absolutely not!' asserted Mavis. 'Listen, I survived four years at Bletchley Park without a bath or shower and it never did me any harm.'

'Bletchley Park?' Gil echoed in awe. 'Wow! I never knew.'

'I've never heard of that resort but it sounds rubbish,' Berta tutted.

'But if showers are what they've paid for ...' I said.

'Gilbert,' said Mavis. 'Go and check in Clyde's shed and garage. I'm sure he has a hosepipe in there. When we had that dry spell recently he used it to water my tubs.'

'Dry spell?' I asked. 'Wasn't that in the seventies?'

'And what do you propose we do with the hosepipe?'

Mavis sipped her tea. 'The only other hot water sources are in here or the basin in my bedroom. I suggest we run the hose from my tap out the window and they can take a shower in the garden.'

'Eh? In front of the house?'

'Got a better suggestion? All we need to do is rig up a curtain or something. They want the great outdoors – let's give it to them!'

'Hang on a mo,' I said, a thought beginning to form.

'Uh-oh, she's thinking,' Berta remarked.

'What about that old phone box Clyde's got stashed at the back of the garage?'

'What about it?' asked Gil.

'Couldn't we paint it and then poke the hose over the top and – *voilà!* – Clyde's your uncle!'

'That's the spirit!' Mavis smiled. 'But we still need to keep painting the house – we need to finish off the DIY. It would be marvellous if we could get it done before Clyde comes home from hospital. Gil, do you think you can have a go setting up the shower? You'll probably need help. Now, which one of you girls is going to walk to Bonchester?'

'Sunny's a professional shopper!' Berta offered. She really was in a major broadcasting frame of mind. I threw a crust at her head and it caught in her bunches. She removed it, scoffing it in one bite.

A sudden rap at the door interrupted our planning session.

'Only me!' Chuck chortled. 'You were going to show me the shower block.'

'Ah, that!' I tried for a winning smile but he recoiled at my grimace. 'Slight technical problem,' I muttered. 'Just ... er ... just calling our plumbing engineer. Perhaps Gloria won't mind waiting until a little later?'

'I guess.' He frowned. 'Oh, and can you tell me where the camp shop is? I can't seem to find that either.'

'Of course!' I bluffed. 'We tend to operate the shop from our kitchen – feel it has a more homely vibe.'

'So can I come in?' he said, stepping nearer. I pulled the door behind me. 'We really prefer if our campers just ask for what they need and one of us will fetch it for them.'

'We're not allowed in?'

'Definitely not!' I shook my head. 'We have ... er ... cats that we don't want to let out.'

'Cats? In a store? Is that even hygienic?'

'Sorry, did I say cats? I meant bats! Yes, we have rare indigenous bats that can't be allowed out.'

'O-kay,' he conceded. Clearly he was worried about upsetting the locals. 'You got any milk in there? And perhaps a loaf of bread?'

'Sure. Back in a tick.' I shut him out again. 'Quickly!' I hissed. 'Pass me some milk and – how much bread is left?'

Berta threw me the last of the loaf and lifted a half-empty carton of milk from the fridge.

'Is that it?'

'Hey! You're the shopper around here.' I shot her a filthy look and opened the door to Chuck's bemused face. I handed over the groceries. 'So sorry. Our delivery man hasn't been yet this morning!'

He accepted the scraps with a furrowed brow. 'Not really your day, is it? Any chance you'll be getting eggs delivered?'

'Eggs!' I cried, mentally adding them to the list. 'Yes, of course. I'll let you know when they're here.'

'How much do I owe you?'

'Owe me?'

'For the supplies.' Chuck indicated the leftovers.

'Oh – consider that a welcome pack!'

I retreated indoors. He turned and drifted back to his tent in a daze.

The rain was coming down in an obstinate drizzle as I armed myself with Gil's all-weather anorak (again) and my old trainers that let in the water before I'd even turned off Crackers Track. I cursed Berta as she gave a cheerful wave from the kitchen window, third cup of coffee in hand.

I hadn't been into Bonchester Bridge since I was an emerging teenager, when the cool place to hang out was Pepe's Taverna. Coke was served in real glass bottles, milkshakes were properly dense and pizza came with pasta. Despite my already-ignited infatuation with

Mathew, I couldn't help but have my ginger head turned by the local farm boys. Well, when I say 'local', I seem to remember spending a whole summer panting after Pawel, a gangling dweeb who'd been recruited for strawberry picking. He was all teeth and no finesse – says me, queen of intrigue. As far as I recall, our only actual encounter involved a quick fumble in Clyde's garage, resulting in me losing my favourite Beyoncé key ring and having to spend the following day picking strawberry hulls from my braces.

Having confirmed my hunch that no major supermarket had invested in Bonchester Bridge, I settled for McKay's Food Store. Clearly no one shopped for more than was necessary. I settled for two hand-baskets. Working my way through the aggregated list, I headed for the chilled cabinets, but found the aisle blocked by a large-girthed woman encased in a full-length waxed mac. She had her shopping basket hooked over one arm and a bulging canvas bag-for-life over the other. As she trundled towards me, a trail of tins and packets were bumped off the shelves in her wake. We reached the bacon fridge simultaneously. I had one hand on the door but, unless she put her tanker into reverse, I wasn't going to be able to open it.

'New here?' she accused.

'Just visiting,' I mumbled. I tried for another lunge but she was too quick with her riposte.

'Oh, yes? Who're you visiting?'

'My uncle Clyde.'

'Along at Crackers Cottage?'

'That's right.'

'You know he hasn't paid his council tax for over a year?'

'I wouldn't know.'

'Anyway, he's laid up now.'

I tried tugging on the cabinet again but her frame blocked me. I rattled it against her hip as a hint. She probably never felt a thing under her armour. I would have left it, but Mavis had insisted I purchase a range of easy-to-grill products.

'Hang on a minute.' Her eyes narrowed. 'Are you the one that knocked him down?' Jesus, she made it sound like a hit-and-run.

'It was an accident,' I muttered. Without warning she gripped my arm. I let out a strangled cry. *Is she giving me a Chinese burn on his behalf?*

'Don't be saying that!' she hissed, looking behind her.

'Saying what?'

She mouthed the word 'accident'. 'Before you know it he'll be on the phone to them compensation lawyers and you'll be dragged through the courts.'

'Oh, I don't think—'

'You'll end up losing your house, your kids ...'

'I'm *twenty-three*. I barely own my phone.' *In fact, I don't even think I do own my mobile.*

'Knowing Clyde, he'll even get you buying him one of those motor scooters.'

'Look, I just need some sausages.'

She peered into my basket. 'What's with all the milk? One of them vegrants, are you? And why are you buying lots of small packets of tea bags? Just buy one of the mega-packs. Here, *Davey!*' she bellowed. 'Go and chuck over one of those 240-packs of tea bags, would you?' She started scooping the packets out of my basket and restocking the shelves.

'No, really!' I objected, shovelling them back in. 'I need them like that.'

She gave a haughty sniff. 'Just trying to help you. Must be

rolling in spare cash, then. Still, that won't last after Clyde's cleaned you out. Don't say I didn't warn you!' I could see no end to this impasse but to double back on myself and approach the chillers from the rear.

I ducked down the next aisle and almost collided with a young man wearing a faded grey hoodie pulled up over his face. He wore tatty jeans and old Converse boots. There was something familiar about his furtive movement as he scuttled off. I watched him for a couple of minutes as he studiously focused on the Tampax Super Plus Jumbo pack. As I brushed past him, he even *smelt* familiar. The door slammed as Wide-Berth exited.

I heaved my two laden baskets on to the counter.

'Is there any chance of calling a taxi?' I asked as Davey rang through my purchases. He nodded to the left.

'You'll find Tam next door.'

'Is it okay if I leave my shopping here while I go and check?' He shrugged.

I pulled open the heavy door to the Horse and Hound, where the traditional bar was decorated in creams and browns with a mottled chestnut carpet. Paintings of horses leaping over hedges in pursuit of foxes covered the walls, along with a selection of leather and brass bridle parts and dated competition rosettes. A stooped barman was wrestling a pint. I spotted a total of five male pensioners scattered over three tables, all clutching pint glasses. I approached the bar.

'I'm looking for Tam,' I said.

'I'm Tam!' four of the men shouted, followed by raucous laughter. I appealed to the barman, who pointed to the same tired geezer I'd observed hauling Mavis from his taxi. I walked over to him.

'Any chance I can get a lift up the road to Crackers Cottage?'

'*Shh!*' he admonished, flapping at me to sit down.

'Question eight,' a flat-capped man read from a folded paper. 'Who has been awarded the most Oscars?'

'Och! I ken this one!' shouted a toothless punter gripping an unlit pipe between his gums. 'James Bond!'

'Don't be daft.' The barman laughed. 'James Bond isn't a real person.'

'Och – you ken what I mean. That Sean Connery fella.'

'What about John Wayne?' This was met with much neighing.

'Get off your horse and drink your milk,' recited Flat-Cap.

'"You're short on ears and long on mouth,"' Tam added in an American drawl. I sat down in resignation.

'*How* many questions are there in this quiz?'

'Dinnae fash yersel', hen. Just let me finish my pint.'

'Pint?' I echoed.

'Ach, it's mostly water.'

'Oy! I heard that!' the barman objected.

'Must be that American lass,' shouted a man wearing dark glasses.

'You need to be a wee bit more specific, Jim.'

'Her ken that does all thae accents.'

'Nope.'

'She was in that film, mind?'

'*Titanic?*'

'What a pile of shite that was!' said Jim. 'I mean, whose idea was it to make a film where we all ken the ending? It's as bad as making a film aboot the 1966 World Cup!'

'Aye, but that would have a worse ending!' More guffaws.

'You want a drink?' the barman called to me. I shook my head.

'Is she paying?' Jim laughed.

'You mean Mary Street?'

'Who?'

'That wifey you were on about.'

'Eh?'

'God help us.' The barman shook his head. 'You mean *Meryl Streep!*'

'Nuh! It wisnae her. D'you give in?'

'Ask the lassie,' Flat-Cap suggested. I shrugged.

'Tom Cruise?'

'*Who'd* she say?'

'Tom Cruise!' Tam shouted.

'Who's he? Is that the new James Bond? If it is I win as that's what I said hours ago.' *Sure it wasn't days ago?*

'Walt Disney,' Flat-Cap revealed.

'Och, that's not fair. He's a cartoon!'

'No, he's not – you're thinking of Mickey Mouse.'

'I'm not thinking of anything,' Jim protested.

'Come on, then.' Tam stood up, draining his glass. He announced to the bar, 'I'll be back soon. Hold off on question nine.'

'Right, Tam.'

As we drew up to the cottage I could see Gil and Berta finalising their sanitary installation; Berta had almost finished painting the phone box the ubiquitous *evergreen* and Gil was atop the ladder fixing the hose with a twist of wire. In the kitchen I unpacked the supplies under Mavis's watchful eye and began stocking the empty cupboards.

'I wish I could be more help,' Mavis grumbled.

'What? You're the boss – top position in the organisation!' I joked. She slapped the wheels of the chair. 'But this is holding me back.'

'How long have you been in a wheelchair, anyway?' I asked. 'If you don't mind my nosiness.'

'I've never needed a wheelchair!' she protested. 'I'm not an invalid! After my fall, Clyde insisted I use this ancient thing. God knows where he dug it up from.'

'You mean you can walk?'

'Well, I'm not exactly about to do a twenty-mile charity trek dressed as a giraffe, if that's what you're hoping for. But Clyde said he didn't want me falling again so it would be safer if I didn't walk at all.'

'Clyde doesn't half talk a load of bollocks!'

'The thing is, I haven't walked on my own for a few months now. I only go from this on to my bed or on to the … you know. I don't know how well my legs will support me.'

'Wait here!' I said.

'I think we've established I don't have much choice.'

I entered the living room – *by the way, where's Romilly?* – and returned with Clyde's wooden tea trolley. I removed the empty beer cans, chucked the mountain of curled newspapers into the bin, wiped down the surfaces with a damp cloth and checked the wheels ran smoothly. 'Right, Mavis, let's try this. I've visited tons of old people recently—'

'Pardon!'

'—and lots of them have walkers just like this. Come on.' I bent to unhook the footplates, placing her slippered feet on to the lino. 'I'll help you. Right, on three we'll stand you up.'

'Are you sure?'

'Quite. One, two, *three*.' I heaved her up and she stood, gripping the arms of the wheelchair. 'Now hold on to the trolley handle.'

'Sure it won't skite away?'

'I'll brace it.'

First one hand, then the other was transferred on to the handle, her knuckles white.

'It's pretty solid,' I nodded. 'They don't make wooden battering rams like these any more.'

'Yes, that feels satisfactory.' She moved it back and forth a few inches.

'Okay, let's attempt a tour of the kitchen. Larry – skedaddle!' I pushed him under the table, to which he objected with a disgruntled 'Baa!' I walked backwards, guiding the trolley towards me as Mavis followed, step by cautious step.

'Right, I'm going for a corner,' I announced, manoeuvring the trolley. Mavis's face was taut with concentration as though she were negotiating a moon landing. After the second tour of the kitchen her shoulders relaxed a fraction. I pulled up a kitchen chair behind her. 'Right, have a wee seat now, Mavis.' She collapsed back in relief.

'Golly, I've never walked in Scotland before!'

'Yes – it's very different from south of the Border.' I laughed. 'When you're ready, John O'Groats is in that direction.' I pointed out of the window.

She patted my hand. 'Thank you, Sunny,' she said, with tears in her eyes.

'Now don't go all flaky on me.'

Gil burst into the kitchen, beaming. 'Right – prepared for a test run? Mavis! What are you doing sitting at the table?'

'Feeling like a human being.' She smiled.

Gil looked confused. 'Long story,' I said. 'So what do you need us to do?'

'When I say "go", turn the tap on.' He ran out of the kitchen.

'Right.' I headed to Mavis's room.

'What about me?' she wailed. 'Wait for me!'

'If you're up to it?'

'It was my idea, wasn't it?' She pushed herself up from the table as I held the trolley in front of her.

'Take your time,' I advised.

'Hurry up!' Gil shouted from outside.

Our little procession, with Larry following out of curiosity, entered Mavis's bedroom. I placed a chair at her basin, where Gil had fastened the other end of the hose to her hot tap. I squinted out of the open window, where the 'shower cubicle' partially eclipsed the view of the garden. Berta stood to one side, waiting in anticipation. Her fair hair and face had a *Wicked* green tinge.

'Ready?' Gil checked. I turned to Mavis, who gave the thumbs-up.

'Ready!' I echoed.

'Go, go, go!' he commanded. Mavis turned on the tap with both hands. After a couple of seconds hot water came pouring out of the hose into the *evergreen* phone box. Berta cracked open the cubicle door.

'Ha!' she cried, holding her hand under the stream of water.

I yelled to Mavis, 'Houston – we have lift-off!' She cheered, waving her pink facecloth above her head in celebration.

Gil spoke through the window opening. 'No wonder you were snatched up by Bletchley Park!'

'What's all the commotion?' asked Romilly, crowding into the room. Ah – there she was! I proudly pointed to the Tardis outside the window.

'Welcome to our newest facility.'

She sniffed. 'Well, I've been busy too. I've nearly painted one wall of the bathroom.'

'I thought you were doing the living room?'

'I was, but Gil said he'd help me with that and suggested I tackle the bathroom as the ceiling's not so high.'

'Fair enough. Well, Mavis, are you ready for me to send Gloria over?'

'Ready as I'll ever be.'

Chapter 10

There was no mistaking Chuck and Gloria's open-air construction. Near the stream that ran alongside the cottage two imposing green tents had been erected side by side. Between the two tents an awning had been fixed, affording a covered outdoor space. Chuck and Gloria were wedged into folding chairs that leaned back at a precarious angle. Plastic mugs of steaming coffee sat on a rickety occasional table. They reclined in their matching ponchos, taking in the views of the rolling hills. There was no sign of the cubs. Chuck was sporting a pair of binoculars and jotting down the names of birds as they darted overhead. 'I'm sure that's another sedge warbler, honey,' I heard him say.

'Hey, Sunny!' he called on my approach. 'Are there any marsh tits near here?' I blinked, not able to come up with a straight-faced answer.

'I just wanted to let you know that the shower is now operational.'

'You hear that, honey? The shower is now operational.' *Of course she heard it – I just said it.*

'Oh, marvellous! I'm still sitting here in my nightclothes under this mac thing.' Gloria made an attempt to stand but the chair remained jammed round her rear. I extended my hand, which she dragged on (don't worry, I didn't actually *need* that socket) as

Chuck gripped the chair from behind. She eventually catapulted free of the chair, nearly taking me down with her.

'Shall I follow you?' she asked, regaining her composure.

'Sure,' I nodded.

'Just be a tick, hon.' She ducked into one of the tents and could be heard trampling around on the plastic groundsheet like a buffalo escaping its gift-wrapping.

'So the rain's stopped,' I said. And my mother wondered why I never went to university.

Chuck nodded in agreement. 'Hooded crow!' he exclaimed.

'Oh, I'm sure she's not that bad.'

'Excuse me?'

'Gloria.'

'What about Gloria? I'm trying to spot rare birds here.'

Yeah – so am I. How long does it take to grab a toilet bag? Finally she emerged with a bulging rucksack.

'Bye, Chuck. Keep an eye on the boys, remember.' I wasn't sure how he was going to manage that unless grizzlies had X-ray vision.

Gloria's face was a picture as I provided a demonstration of the shower. I explained it slowly for a second time. 'So you knock once on the window to start the shower. Then knock again when you're finished.' Her mouth remained open for the duration of my presentation.

'But it's just a ...'

'A ...?'

'Is that a *phone booth*?'

'We're very strong on recycling in Scotland. Now, in you go.' I nudged her in, jamming the door closed. I had no idea how she was going to remove her many layers. If I stuck around I might be treated to a Houdini-type show – a five-minute frantic wrestle followed by a naked Gloria shouting, '*Ta da!*'

I was trying to erase that particular image from my mind when I heard Gil shouting from above. He was back up the ladder with his *snow gloss*. 'Sunny!' he yelled. 'Car!' He was transforming into a proper ship's lookout up there. I turned to see a compact silver car bumping up the track. *Shit!* Who was this? The car parked parallel to Chuck's large estate, which looked like it had had a baby.

The driver eased out of the vehicle, leaving his door open. He looked to be in his mid-twenties, with sandy curls, wearing a checked shirt, jeans and boots. Bloody hell – I'd better keep him away from Berta! He approached, his round face arranged in a friendly smile. 'Is this Crackers Cottage?' He scrutinised the shabby building, his gaze halting at the dark green phone box as water gushed from underneath and Gloria's hand appeared over the top. 'I'm looking for Camp Crackers,' he faltered.

I sighed in resignation. *If you build it, they will come.* 'Round the back there.' I pointed to the side of the house. 'There's a field. Take your pick of pitches. Have you paid already?'

'Three nights.' He nodded back at the car. 'Am I alright to park there?' The passenger door opened and a dark-haired young man emerged, smartly dressed in black shirt, chinos and designer glasses. 'That's Jason,' the driver said. 'I'm George, by the way.'

'Sunny.' I glowered. Well, it usually worked. I left them to it as they unpacked the car.

The next morning I sat across the kitchen table from Berta, who had her head resting on her folded arms, her eyes closed. 'Wonder how much we'll get for that old car?' she mumbled to herself. I reached past her head for the butter. Mavis stood – yes, I said *stood* – at the sink, leaning against the worktop for support as she washed her breakfast dishes.

'I don't know why we didn't get you upright before now,' I said.

'Chuck said he wanted to be first in the shower so I thought I ought to be at the ready.'

'Quite right. Where are the other pair?'

'Young Gilbert is up on the roof.' Mavis pointed with the washing-up brush. 'He found a Reader's Digest DIY manual and is convinced he can replace the broken slates. I've no idea where Romilly went but she disappeared clutching her writing pad and said something about tapping into her creative seam.'

'I'll tap my foot up her—' Berta announced.

'Oh, my word – here comes Chuck now,' Mavis said. 'But I'm not ready!'

There was a sharp rap at the back door. 'Yes?' I asked without enthusiasm.

'Morning!' Chuck greeted me with a jolly wave, wearing oversized paisley pattern pyjamas and boots.

'You're too early!' I complained.

'Oh, I'm not here for my shower! I haven't had my breakfast yet. Just wanted to check where and when we rendezvous for the Crackers Hike.'

'The what?'

'Crackers Hike,' he repeated.

'Just saying random words doesn't help me,' I snapped.

He waved a piece of paper in my face. 'We're all booked up for the outdoor hike this morning, but it doesn't say when or where we're meeting. It just says, "Packed lunch will be provided".'

'Right,' I said faintly. 'Excuse me, will you?' I stormed past Chuck's baffled face, leaving him dangling the paper in one hand. I marched through the wet grass and slapped my hand hard against Ambrose's tent. 'Wakey wakey!' I barked. I was met with his usual stony silence. 'Ambrose, if you don't come out this *instant*, I'm coming in!' I heard a low grumble. 'Right.' I bent down and yanked the zip up with a satisfying buzz. Ambrose remained cocooned in his sleeping bag like a skinny maggot. I tugged on the nylon material, dragging it towards me. His legs were out of the tent before he came to.

'What the—!' he protested. 'Not cool, Miss HY!' He attempted to wriggle back under the canvas but I held fast as though landing a giant fish. Believe me, I was prepared to whack this fish against something solid.

'Ambrose, what have you done?'

He opened one eye and squinted into the morning light. 'Your knickers are well and truly twisted. Chill, man.'

'I'll "chill" when you tell me why Chuck says he's booked on a hike today and what you're going to do about it.'

'Oh, that,' he mumbled, wiping his nose on his pyjama sleeve. 'I just thought I'd ...'

'What?'

'Jazz things up a bit. I mean, Clyde wasn't that impressed when I said I'd set up this field as a campsite. He thought we could make extra dough by sort of exaggerating what was on offer.'

'What? *How?*'

'So, like, saying how that stream over there had "youthful properties" and that we can supply "free-range organic home produce".'

'Okay,' I growled. 'I'll allow some stretching of the truth.'

'So maybe I got a tad carried away.' He couldn't look me in the eye.

'*Ambrose?*'

'Uh ... I might have booked some people on some activities

...' I waited for him to continue. 'A historic hike around the hill and fort. What else? Er ... a survival afternoon, Pets' Corner, jungle adventure, outdoor yoga ...' he mumbled. 'Oh, and maybe a cookout.'

'*What were you thinking?*' I bellowed, kicking his sleeping bag in fury.

'I was thinking I'd be long gone out of here, man,' he confessed.

'And leaving Clyde to guide a hike round the countryside? How would that work?'

'I thought he'd have staff he could pull in – and he has.' He gave an indignant sniff.

'We're not staff! We're not even getting paid to do the naffing painting.'

'Aren't you?'

'No! So, if you want to stay here, you can bloody well start pulling your weight. Get up, get dressed and get painting in that house!'

'Harsh words.'

'I seem to remember you said something about "working the land". Well, it's time you earned your keep.' He grunted under his breath.

'Sorry?'

'Got any coffee?'

'If you do some painting I might allow you some coffee and toast.'

'Truly?' His expression brightened.

'Don't you have any coffee in there?' I peered into his sparse tent.

'Been living off rice for the last ten days.'

'Good enough reason to get handy with the paintbrush. Oh – and while you're at it, have a bloody shower!'

I was heading back to the cottage when the bright yellow dome tent behind Ambrose caught my eye. The two young guys, who were sitting in stripy chairs and sipping from steaming mugs, had witnessed our shouting match. They grinned and held up their mugs. 'Morning!' George called. 'You tell him!' I turned and stomped back over the field.

'Be ready in an hour!' I barked at Chuck, who saluted as I brushed past him.

'Right, we need five packed lunches,' I said to the top of Berta's head as I grabbed the loaf of bread.

'Sleeping,' she replied. I flicked her exposed ear. 'Aya! What's that for?'

'Bloody Ambrose!'

'S'not my fault!'

'Okay, I'm going to give you a choice here. We need more supplies – more than what we can get from the poxy shop along the road. So you can either get the bus to Hawick and tap Gil for a taxi back or you can take the flipping Brady family for a hike around Bonchester Hill.'

'You're kidding!' she laughed. 'Is that what they've signed up for?'

'Yep,' I grunted, slapping spread on to slices of bread.

'Where do I get the bus from?'

'It goes along the bottom of the road. There's usually one gets you into Hawick for about twelve. Sure you wouldn't rather go on a hike?'

'Quite sure.'

I shook the ladder again, much to Gil's irritation. I filled him in on Ambrose's imaginative range of activities and insisted that he appoint him to a useful duty in my absence.

'I haven't got the first clue about history around here,' I grumbled.

'Nothing to it,' Gil said. 'Just tell them what they want to hear.'

'I don't even know who built the fort.'

'I think it was the Romans. They built everything.'

'Sure you wouldn't rather take them?'

'Sure you wouldn't rather be up on the roof replacing the slates?'

'Might need to borrow your anorak again.'

'Why don't you just buy your own?' he objected.

'I don't normally need a coat like that.'

'What – in Scotland?' He snorted.

'Well, I don't usually go outside if I can help it,' I moaned. 'Can I borrow your boots too?'

'They won't fit you.'

'I'll just put on a few pairs of extra socks.'

'Looks like it might rain soon.' Gil smiled, climbing back up the ladder. I stuck my two fingers up at his ascending back.

I loitered at the back door like Scott of the Antarctic, parcelled up in Gil's waterproofs and boots, rucksack on my back. Chuck and Gloria ambled closer, only their eager faces visible beneath the various layers of waterproof clothing. I wasn't even sure I could name any of the garments. They seemed to be wearing things that went over, round and through their limbs. I wondered if I got to remove a layer when the music stopped. The twins had also been mummified, their not-so-eager mushes poking out.

'Rightio, follow me,' I instructed, striding with purpose through the camping field to reach the foot of the first hill. George and Jason gave us friendly waves as we passed. What *were* they doing with those branches?

'We're so excited,' gabbled Gloria. 'This is my first trip to Scat-land. Chuck has been before but that was before we were married. I can't believe I'm going on my first hike outdoors!'

'Yes,' was all I could muster. I led the way up over the grassy track through clumps of wild heather and boggy peat.

'Is it true that the Scot's men don't wear anything under their kilt?' she asked.

'That's right.' I nodded. 'Only their manhood.' Gloria giggled. And where was my man when I needed him? I had texted Mathew that morning to find out how his contract was going and whether he missed me. It didn't go unnoticed by my ego that his response pinged back: 'contract is proving to be a right bugger'. I found myself flanked by Gloria and Chuck, the boys trudging along behind us in resentful silence.

'So who put this hill here?' Chuck asked as we began the slow climb.

'What?'

'You know, when they were building Bon-*Chester*. Whose idea was it to put the hill here?'

'The Romans,' I answered flatly.

'And the river? Was that them too?'

'Yep.'

Chuck stopped to regain his breath as Gloria puffed to catch us up. 'You'd think they would have put a rail up or something,' Gloria moaned. When I gave her a blank look she continued, 'You know, so that old people could pull themselves up the hill. My mom is just gone sixty and there's no way she could get up here without a lift.'

'Don't they ever put those tow-lift things in nowadays?' Chuck asked.

'Hmm, not so much.' I shrugged.

'Come on, boys!' Chuck yelled over my head. 'They're about a quarter my age and I'm still beating them up this hill.' The twins glared at him. 'You know,' he said, 'if there was a games console at the top, they'd sprint right on past me. Isn't that right, honey?'

'But I told them,' said Gloria, 'they don't have the internet in Scat-land. At least, we haven't found it yet.'

'Yes, that was a huge oversight they had when they were building the village. They should have moved it nearer a hub.'

We kept climbing higher and higher as rainfall began again. First a light drizzle, then heavy drumming on to our hoods. I had to turn my entire body whenever I needed to look to either side.

'When's lunch?' one of the boys whined. *He speaks!*

'I think we should keep going until we reach the fort.' *After all, that's what you bloody well came to see, isn't it?*

'Does it have a café?' Gloria enquired.

'Can we get a hot chocolate? *Please!*' whined Boy Two. I turned my body round.

'It's an old ruin.' I tutted.

'But it'll have a gift shop at least?' Gloria asked. 'I'd love to get a gift for Mom. Do you think they sell teaspoons with this hill on it? What about a toilet?'

'A teaspoon with a toilet?' I puzzled. 'Or a toilet with a hill on it?'

'Either would be just dandy.' She smiled.

I didn't remember the hill being this steep. It felt as though someone had humped another hill on top of the original. Mind you, in my younger days I had probably thought nothing of skipping up to the top just for the fun of it. Those were the giddy days before physical activity incurred torture.

'How much further?' a voice protested.

'Now, Jayden,' Gloria panted. 'Just think of the appetite you'll have for your lunch.' Oh yes, about that lunch ... if they knew what delicacies I'd prepared they might be tempted to chew on a handful of wild grass.

When the incline flattened out I extended my arms in a Julie Andrews spin as I announced, 'Here we are!' Chuck's face had the strained flush of a man about to succumb to a heart attack. He wiped the sweat, or it could have been rain, from his face and grinned like a triumphant Tour de France champion.

'Wow-ee!' Gloria puffed. 'Gee, I've never been up a mountain before. Don't they give out certificates or something for climbing one of your Scottish mountains?'

'You mean for bagging a Munro?' I asked, shaking my head. 'Technically, this isn't—'

'Is this *it*?' fumed J-boy. 'I thought we were getting to see a castle.'

'Well, it used to be,' I offered, indicating the stone outline of the fort.

'This sucks,' complained his brother.

'"This ancient hill fort was once occupied by the Romans under the name Bonna Castra: *Good Camp,*"' Chuck read from the small plaque fixed to one of the crumbling stones. *I knew that.* We stood within the circular ruin and would have marvelled at the view were we not surrounded by heavy cloud and zero visibility.

'Why did they build it way up here?' Gloria enquired. 'I mean, it's such a long walk to get here.'

'Well, honey,' Chuck explained. 'It's so they could see the enemy.'

'That's right – so they could see the English army approaching,' I said.

'*Who* could see?' J-boy asked.

'Er ... Robert the Bruce.'

'Hear that, honey – this was Robert the Bruce's castle.'

'See the English army?' Gloria repeated. 'But I thought we *were* in England?'

'This is *Scotland,*' I said tightly. *Look, are you going to force me to bring out my bagpipes?*

'But isn't Scat-land *in* England?'

'Right, who's for lunch?' I removed my rucksack and glanced up at the grey sky, grateful for a temporary reprieve. 'Let's sit here.' I pointed to a row of stones. The Brady Bunch perched in a line as I dished out a plastic bag to each podgy hand. Their disappointment as they clocked the contents can have been no more acute than mine as I wished the unappetising cheese sandwiches had somehow transformed into Greggs sausage rolls. The trek hadn't enhanced lunch's appearance. Gloria held her limp sandwich between finger and thumb as though I'd picked up a cowpat and slapped it between two slices of bread. Perhaps it hadn't been the wisest decision to throw an apple into each picnic. From my bag I withdrew an apple sandwich as the two had fused – but reminded myself that some of the best culinary inventions were the consequence of accidental collaboration.

'Is there a choice?' J-boy whinged.

'Yes, there is.' His face brightened. 'You can take it or you can leave it.'

'Eat up, son,' said Chuck before I whipped the bag away.

'Mmm,' I munched, convincing no one. The twins glowered at me through their waterlogged fringes. *Hey, you guys paid for this! Don't blame me if your folks didn't take you to Disney World.*

'So where are you from?' I asked, hoping that polite conversation would distract them.

'Austin, Texas,' Chuck bragged.

'Where everything is huge?' I said, trawling my sparse memory bank for US facts.

'You got it, lady. Everything is oversized. We have a massive villa in the Cedar Park district.' Well, it would need to be large to house a family of wild bears.

'Have you heard of it?' asked Gloria.

'Can't say I have.'

'Oh, you'd love it over there. We've got such a delightful neighbourhood – restaurants and beauty salons and a bowling alley. *Three* shopping malls.'

'Great school for the kids,' Chuck added.

'So lots of families like yours?' I said.

'I guess.'

'Sounds wonderful. Jaffa cake, anyone?' I passed round the packet.

'*These aren't cakes!*' the twins protested. 'They're like the tiniest bite-size pieces going!'

'Hmm, depends how big your mouth is.' I gathered up the remnants of the picnic. *Picnic? Ha – who am I kidding?*

We trundled back down the hill, me thinking that it would be much easier to roll them down as though Easter had come early. On our return to the campsite (again – who was I kidding?) we parted company, Chuck calling out, 'The boys can't wait for the "Jungle Adventure" tomorrow!' I groaned.

'Rough day?' George beamed. He looked like he hadn't moved since we set off up the hill – still reclining in his chair with a mug of something hot. Smelt like Bovril. His pitch, however, had been remodelled. An inventive circular windbreak surrounded their dome tent – a series of wooden branches hammered into the ground and armfuls of lush green ferns and wild grasses woven in and out of the improvised stakes.

'Wow!' I said. Their little camping area had an enclosed

perimeter, with an opening facing the site so George could observe the comings and goings.

'I know, right.' He smiled, taking a sip. 'That's Jason for you. He's an interior designer and just can't help himself. I keep telling him he's meant to be on holiday but he never stops. Watch this.' He reached over and flicked a switch. A string of fairy lights threaded along the top of the windbreak suddenly danced in pink and white.

'What? How?' I laughed.

'Battery-operated. You looked like you needed cheering up.'

'I did. Thank you.'

'No problem. So what's on the activity programme tomorrow? I love it when a site lays on entertainment.'

'I will need to consult my team of experts. Right now, I need a coffee.'

My legs had no idea they moved up and down like that and now they were lodging a formal complaint.

'You look like hell.' Berta grinned as I nudged the kitchen door open. I slumped on to the nearest chair.

'Is there the remotest possibility that Clyde's bath could be used for actually having a bath?' Last time I looked it had resembled a garden pond, complete with foamy sludge and natural wildlife.

'Depends.'

'On what?'

'Whether you mind sharing it with the local fauna.'

I sighed, weighing up whether having a hot, bubble-filled heaven would be worth the exertion of fumigating the bath. 'If you were my best friend, you'd offer to clean it for me.'

'I can do better than that!' Berta beamed. She reached into the fridge and withdrew two bottles. 'Vodka coke anyone?'

'You are a lifesaver!'

'Bit early for that, isn't it?' sneered Romilly, breezing into the kitchen.

'Depends whose watch you're checking.'

'I don't go for all that "five o'clock somewhere" nonsense,' she retorted.

'And what exactly have *you* been up to all day?' I accused, spoiling for a fight.

'If you *must* know, I've been holding Gil's ladder for him.'

'Eh?'

'It's been raining here all day.'

'Uh-huh. I had noticed. *And?*'

'The ground has been very soft underfoot,' she simpered.

'And I'll tell you what else is going to be very soft under *my* foot if you don't get out of my way!'

'You can't hold me responsible for your foul mood, Sunny. And I strongly disapprove of compounding such ill temper with alcohol.'

'Berta?' I appealed. Berta stood up and held her arms out in front of me.

'It's for your own protection, Romilly – best you run. *Now!*' She scuttled past as I made a lunge for her.

Chapter 11

The following morning I woke to find someone had spent the night dropping heavy rocks on my legs. I thought I was getting out of bed but it turns out I couldn't actually move. That same inconsiderate person had been dropping similar boulders on my head. I groaned out loud. 'How many did I have?'

'Five, I think,' Berta mumbled from above.

'How many did you have?'

'I lost count. I might have had about six before I fell off my chair.'

'Can you please send my apologies?'

'What for?'

'I'm not going to make it today. Just wake me up tomorrow. By the way, what's that smell?'

'I think it might be you.'

'Oh, right. The bath that never happened.'

Mavis handed me back my phone as though it were about to explode. 'I hate these things,' she grumbled.

'Well, you don't have a lot of choice since Clyde's landline has been cut off.'

'No wonder I never got any calls from my pals down south.'

'Anyway, how is the patient?'

'Seemingly the physios have had him up with some sort of a

hoist. He's a bit anaemic and they've picked up on him being low on vitamin B12.'

'What do we need that for?' I asked.

'Must be something to do with "B" for blood,' suggested Berta.

'Makes sense,' I nodded. 'Hey, Mavis, maybe you should ask if he can bring a spare walking frame home for you!'

'Good idea. And maybe Social Services will put up some handrails too.'

'Talking of Social Services, here's Ambrose.'

He tapped at the door before skulking in. He still paraded the Rasta beanie but had swapped his pyjamas for a ragged Superdry T-shirt and a pair of blue cotton shorts, a tear through one leg. 'Whoa – full house, man!' he muttered, edging towards the kettle. 'Any chance of that coffee and toast?'

I blocked his path. 'Mavis?' I asked. 'How did he do yesterday?'

'I sent him to pick up where Berta left off in Clyde's bedroom.'

'And I done all the first coat of paint like you asked!' he said.

'*Did*,' she corrected.

'Who's "Romilee", by the way?'

'I am.' Romilly squeezed into the kitchen. 'Why?' He looked at her slyly from under his hat.

'Go on, then,' I said. 'Dig in.'

'And that is what I's doing today, Missy. We need a firepit for the cookout so I'll get to that after some yum yums.'

Mavis pulled out her list and tapped her pen on the table. 'Right, folks. What's the plan of attack for today? Young Ambrose is on to the firepit.'

'I could crack on with the second coat in Clyde's room,' offered Gil.

'Good man. Berta?'

'You said you needed a Pets' Corner. I'll see what I can rustle up.'

'And what do *you* know about livestock?' Romilly smirked.

'She works at Pet City,' Gil whispered into her ear. Romilly flounced towards the fridge, retrieving a covered bowl of figs.

'Sunny?'

I groaned. 'Chuck tells me the twin cubs are booked into a "Jungle Adventure". What am I meant to do for that?'

'Just take them over the stream and up into the woods. They're boys. They'll love it,' said Gil.

'Why don't *you*?'

'He's already said,' snapped Romilly. 'He's finishing Clyde's room. And that will be *so* important for convalescence when the invalid comes home.'

I folded my arms in case one of them accidentally shot out and whacked her in the face.

'Don't look at me,' said Mavis. 'I'm on shower duty. And we'll need someone here to man the shop. I think we should limit the opening hours, otherwise I'll be on beck and call all day. I do need my afternoon nap. I'm ninety-three, you know.'

'Respect,' Ambrose nodded, attempting a fist-bump. Mavis frowned as his hand hovered mid-air.

Romilly piped up. 'I'm rather talented at calligraphy, Mavis. Would you like me to create a sign for the door with the shop opening times?'

'Oh, thank you, dear. That would be lovely.'

'Want to join my corner?' Berta asked.

'But that's not fair!' I whined. 'I'm babysitting the Bozo clowns while she's here writing bloody opening times.'

'Sunny, there's no "I" in team,' Romilly said, smoothing her skirt. I had my mouth open for a witty retort when a knock at the kitchen door caught us all by surprise.

'If it's Gloria, tell her I'm finishing my tea first,' said Mavis. I opened the door and stepped outside to find a trio of stringy student-types, all greasy hair, thick-rimmed glasses and barely enough facial hair to produce one moustache between the three of them.

'Camp Crackers?' the one in front asked in a squeaky voice. I hoped for his sake he was a late developer and wasn't going to be saddled with a lifetime of Mickey Mouse jibes. And then the penny dropped. Grey hoodie, tatty jeans, Converse boots and that oh-so-memorable eau de cologne – garlic mixed with petrol.

'*You!*' I accused. 'I thought I told you to stay away from Gil?' I said in a loud voice, but the chatter coming from the kitchen indicated the close of the meeting and attention moved to the day's tasks. The lad shuffled his feet, retreating to stand between his pals. I probably could have flattened all three in one swipe. Even a mild flu virus could take them out.

'You said to stay away from your flat.' His voice wavered. 'You didn't mention anything about Bonchester.'

'How did you find us?' I asked. 'Have you been following us?'

'It's a free country.'

'Well, it's not free to stay here, matey! It's fifteen pounds per tent per night to stay here.' How do you like *them* apples?

'Website says twenty.'

'That's what I meant. So clear off.'

He dug into his hoodie pocket and retrieved a handful of paper. I needn't have worried about requesting used notes.

'We've got two tents. There's two hundred and eighty quid for the week.' He held out the wedge at arm's length. I snatched it before it could be withdrawn.

'Round the side there. I want you at the furthest point away from the house, do you hear me? And if you so much as try to speak to Gil or go anywhere near him I will take your tent pole and erect it somewhere that sounds like grass but isn't!'

I decided to tackle Gil later. Right now my priority was going on a bear hunt. I dawdled towards the campers. At least it had stopped raining, but it would be an exaggeration to suggest the sun was attempting a breakthrough. I spied George at the entrance to his enclosure. 'Morning!' He grinned, mug of coffee ever-present in his hand.

'Where's your pal?' I enquired.

'Oh, he's off picking some wildflowers or something. I heard him telling Gloria the types growing in the woods and before I knew it the pair are off with a plastic bag. What's on the agenda for you today?'

I pointed darkly at the conglomeration by the water. 'Jungle adventure with the boys. God knows they're about as enthusiastic as I am. Can I tempt you to join us?'

'Ha! No – I'm just enjoying watching the Rasta chap with that spade. Dare I ask?'

'Firepit.' I shrugged, no longer able to put off the inevitable.

'Morning!' I shouted to Chuck. He jumped, lowering the binoculars. The boys were lying on their stomachs on the grass and they scowled at the sound of my voice. 'Who's ready for a jungle adventure?' I twittered. One picked at a blade of grass as the other rolled on to his back, gazing up at the awning.

'They sure are!' Chuck beamed. 'We had a super day yesterday, didn't we, boys? I can't believe we were in Robert the Bruce's castle.'

'Yes, well, maybe don't tell everybody or they'll all want to go!'

He tapped the side of his nose. 'I hear ya!'

'Right, follow me, then, boys. Let's go have fun!' Without a sound, they hauled themselves up and dragged their feet through the rough grass.

Chuck stood to wave us off. Nodding at Ambrose he asked, 'What's the young fella up to?' Ambrose's skinny legs paced out a circle as he marked his territory in the centre of the field.

'He's building a firepit.'

'Really?' Chuck puffed out his chest, adjusting his baggy chino shorts. 'I might just give him a hand. I do know a thing or two about the building industry.'

'I'm sure he'd appreciate your advice.'

As he marched with purpose towards Ambrose I swear I saw George rubbing his hands in glee.

I hadn't walked along the stream in years but knew it was easier to cross here at the cottage before it got too wide further into the woods. 'This water starts at the top of the hill we climbed yesterday,' I informed the boys. 'It eventually joins the River Rule, where there's a bridge. That's why the village is called Bonchester Bridge.' They exchanged a bored look from under their solid fringes (must have been easier for the barber to whizz across with the shears in a single flourish).

'I can't keep calling you J-boy. Which is which?'

They were kitted out in matching grey shorts but one wore a fawn Knott's Berry Farm T-shirt and the other advertised with a white tick. 'Okay,' I said, pointing at the first. 'You're Berry and you – you're Nike.' They seemed to like that and nodded in agreement.

'Our dad can't tell us apart.'

'I'm not surprised. How does your mum tell which is which?'

'I've got a scar on my chin,' answered Nike, pointing to a pale mark on his tanned face. 'I fell off my bike when I first started going without training wheels. I took off from the top of our street and crashed into our neighbour's van at the bottom.'

'So why doesn't your dad use that to remind him?'

'Because he can never remember which of us fell off our bike.' Nike shrugged.

We traipsed in silence for a while, our feet suckering into the boggy terrain. I picked up a large stick and began sweeping the long grass as we picked our way along the water's edge. When they gave me curious looks I confided '*Snakes*,' in a whisper. I smiled to myself as they did the same, slashing the ferns as we passed through. On reaching a clearing I stopped to admire the magnificent willow that leant out over the bank, its long fronds dipping into the water. This was the broadest segment, where the dark brown pool ran at its deepest. The stream gurgled in a foamy froth at the entrance and fell away in a lazy tumble as it headed down to the Rule. 'My brother and I used to swing across this part of the river. Well, we called it a river. It felt like that when we were your age.'

'How did you swing over it?' Berry asked, poking the marshy reeds.

'I think we must have found someone to sling a rope over one of those branches.' I had no idea. It must have been Clyde in a rare burst of energy.

'Can we?' they asked in unison.

'No! I can't reach those branches and I'm not climbing up a tree!'

'We could, though, couldn't we, Jordan?'

'I don't think your folks would approve. What if you fell in?'

'We do stuff like this at home all the time, don't we, Jayden?' He nudged his brother.

'All the time.' Berry nodded with serious eyes.

I sighed. 'I suppose we could check in Clyde's shed for any rope. But if we can't find any, that's the end of it!'

'Sure.'

What were the chances of us finding a length of rope hooked over the back of the shed door the moment we opened it? I know! Bloody Clyde. The twins grabbed it between them and headed back to the stream. They skirted the rear of the site to avoid attracting any attention. We needn't have worried, as Chuck and Ambrose were having some type of altercation, each tugging the opposite end of a spade.

I held my breath as both boys inched their way along the solid bough that extended over the water. As Nike jolted to regain his balance, I could hear the lawsuit dropping through the letterbox. He crawled along, his knees hugging the worn bark. One hand gripped a knobbly branch that was to serve as a seat. Wriggling into position, he reached back as Berry fed him the end of the rope.

'Make sure it's secure!' I shouted from the sidelines. Nike's tongue protruded in concentration as he passed the rope under and round the bough several times before tying it tightly. 'What knot are you using?' I called. Like I knew one end of a cow hitch from a sheepshank.

'Dad says always use a reef knot.'

'Rightio. Now make sure the stick is clear of the water.'

Nike glared at me and shook his head. He wound the rope round the bough until the seat hung a few inches above the deepest part of the water.

'Okay, you need to catch this!' he commanded as he moved the swing back and forth until it gained momentum. As it neared my side I made a grab for the seat, missing as it veered away. He pulled back on the rope and this time I was ready. I seized the wood with both hands.

'Dibs on first go!' they shouted.

'Careful coming down,' I instructed. They slithered down the trunk, landing on the bank with a thump. I tried not to freak at the bark-stained clothes and grubby knees.

Nike went first. He drew the swing back several feet before leaping on to the branch with both feet. He arced majestically across the water, bending his knees again to keep the momentum going. 'Yee-ha!' he cheered, punching one hand in the air.

'My turn!' Berry clamoured, hopping from foot to foot. Nike reluctantly passed the branch to his brother.

'That was *so* cool!' he beamed.

'So I take it you've *never* made a rope swing before?' I asked. They looked bashful.

'We don't really go outside much,' admitted Nike. 'That's why Dad wanted us to do this dumb camping trip.'

Berry sat astride the branch, keeping one foot on the bank. 'Give me a push, then!' Nike used both hands to launch his brother over the water. He spun like a top as he leant back and gazed up at the sky. As he neared our side we grabbed his T-shirt and pushed again. I lost count of how many times they swung back and forth – enough for my caffeine level to need a serious top-up.

'Right, guys, we better head back to camp.'

'Aw!' Berry objected.

'Why don't you have a go?' said Nike.

'Oh, I'm a bit old for that carry-on.'

'Is it because you're a girl? You *are* a girl, aren't you?'

'Yes!' I replied indignantly. 'I mean, no, it's not why.'

'Chicken!' Nike goaded. Berry joined in, clucking up and

down the bank, flapping his arms. Something deep in my psyche must have snapped. What other plausible explanation was there for me snatching the rope and mounting one foot on the branch? I was preparing for take-off when the twins gave me a mighty shove. Gyrating at speed, my sweaty hands lost their grip and I felt myself orbiting backwards. The torpedoing of my body into the pool was drowned out by their guffaws of laughter. My head submerged in the murky water and I came up spluttering. Attempting the breaststroke in jacket and jeans – not to be recommended. Now I know exactly what is meant by 'doubled up laughing'. The lads gripped their sides in mirth as I hauled myself to the edge, humiliated, on the boggy embankment.

As the story was recounted for *at least* the fourth time, Chuck thought it hilarious to complete each version with, 'and that's what we call a "slam dunk"!' Yeah – once is funny. Except it's not.

I trudged back to the cottage, my saturated attire drooping with each soggy step. I intended leaving my clothes to fester at the back door, and shouted for help. Where the hell was Gil when I actually needed him? Berta had performed an amazing disappearing act too. I schlepped back round to Mavis's room and peered through her window. She was dozing on top of her bed covers, doing a convincing impression of a body laid to rest. I gave a gentle tap on the pane. Not so much as a grunt. 'Mavis!' I called through the hosepipe gap. I hated to disturb a woman in slumber but I feared a clump of algae had colonised my bra. I thumped my fist against the glass. Mavis sat bolt upright with a shriek, her teeth landing in the middle of the floor. She screamed again at the vision of me pressed up against her window. The creature from the black lagoon – only not as attractive. She took a good few seconds to come to before reaching for her glasses.

'Oh, Sunny, it's you! What are you doing out there? Is it raining?'

'I made the mistake of rising to the bait.'

'Were you fishing, then?'

'Sort of. Without a boat. Listen, I need to leave my wet clothes out here. Is there any chance you can turn the shower on for me? And maybe pass out some shampoo and a towel? No one seems to be around.'

'Rightio.' She shook herself awake and got her balance before leaning on the trolley, taking her time to collect items from around her bedroom. I reached through the gap as she handed out each item.

'Thanks, Mavis. You're a star.'

'And one good turn deserves another?'

'Sure – but can I get out of these clothes first?'

The shower was surprisingly effective, although I found it rather disconcerting that the cubicle had no roof. I hoped Gil wasn't lingering nearby up a ladder. I towelled my hair dry and entered the kitchen as Mavis poured from the kettle. 'Coffee?'

'Yes, please! Now, what was this favour?'

'Well, you know I can't manage the stairs to the bathroom?'

'Don't worry – we don't expect you to finish the painting!'

'It's just that I haven't had a shower since leaving my lovely flat in Biggleswade. So I wondered ...'

'Uh-huh?'

'Could you help me have a shower outside?'

'In the phone box?'

'Please?'

'It's not exactly the Hilton.'

'I understand, but short of taking a dip in the river – which I gather is not to be recommended,' she smiled, 'I don't have a lot of choice.'

'Okay, then. Let's give it a whirl.'

'Only thing is, my balance isn't so good.'

'Hang on a tick.' I left her open-mouthed as I crossed the courtyard to the shed. I half expected to find Berta asleep on the mountain of rubbish but there was no sign of her there either. I pushed aside the furniture until I found what I was looking for.

Mavis greeted me with an expectant smile. 'Are we ready? Can you fetch my toiletry bag, a towel and my dressing gown? I don't mind using the wheelchair to get round the side.'

I pushed the wheelchair up to the open door of the phone box. She glanced inside, where I had placed one of Clyde's plastic garden chairs. 'Bingo!' she cried. 'That's just perfect.' I helped her on to the chair, closed the door and she threw her clothes out over the top like a seasoned stripper.

'Are you ready?' I shouted out of her bedroom window. I heard a faint affirmation and turned on the hot water tap. I trotted back to the phone box, where I could hear her splashing around with joy. 'Okay in there?' I checked.

'I'm in heaven!' she exclaimed. I definitely needed to lower my expectations of the afterlife.

Having changed into fresh clothes, I continued my search for Berta. Instead I found Gloria and Jason lounging on the grass outside the yellow dome tent, George looking on in amusement from his throne.

'Are you actually doing what I think you're doing?' I asked.

'Jason and I are flower-arranging,' Gloria confirmed.

'How?' I said. 'Why?'

'Good point, caller,' George smirked.

'These are so pretty,' said Gloria. 'What did you say they were?'

'So the white flowers are wild garlic. The yellow is cowslip.'

'And I know this is ivy.'

'What have you got there?' I pointed to a pile of stones.

'You make a wee circle of stones, push a plastic bag into the centre, pull it up like a vase, then fill it with water. Easy!' Jason smiled, pinching the end off a stem.

'Oh, we've got it all going on here!' George laughed. 'Tips for outdoor home-making.'

'Will you make one for our front door too?' Gloria begged.

'Of course.'

'He's my new best friend,' Gloria confided. 'And so full of interesting information about Scat-land. Jason was telling me that we're here just in time for the start of the haggis season and maybe, if you have time, Sunny, you could take us on a haggis hunt?' George snorted into his tea.

'Maybe,' I said, catching Jason's wink.

'And I never knew that Scat-land is named after Mary Queen of Scats. Or that the new Queen of England has a castle up north in – where did you say, Jason? Balamory?'

'Exactly so.'

'Anyway, have any of you seen Berta?' I asked.

'Now which one is she?' Gloria pursed her lips.

'A wee bit taller than me –' *wouldn't be hard* – 'and she has blonde shoulder-length hair.'

'Oh, the *cute* one.' Gloria nodded. 'Sorry, we've been over in the woods all morning.'

'You didn't hear it from me but I did spot her heading into the village earlier this morning,' George reported.

'Tell me she looked like she was gathering animals for a Pets' Corner.'

'Again, not from me, but there was definitely a wee bit of lippy on the go. Not to mention heels.'

'Right.' I stood fuming.

Our conversation was interrupted by raised voices from across the campsite. I excused myself and stalked towards the frustrated, 'Just listen to me, son!' from Chuck as he stood with his chubby legs apart, fists on hips. Ambrose was holding the spade above his head.

'But Miss HY told me to—'

'Told you what?' I demanded.

'That I needed to earn my keep,' he muttered.

'So what's the problem here?'

They both began shouting at the same time. 'Whoa!' I held up my hands. 'One at a time. Ambrose?'

Ambrose snivelled in defiance. 'I got my own pace for doing stuff, man. I like to think before I leaps in, like. I was marking out the circle over there and he keeps trying to move it.' Chuck raised his hand to speak. 'I'm trying to tell him that he's digging it too near the tents. If it's windy and there's a whole lotta smoke, no one wants that blowing in their faces. *He* wants to get stuck in with digging a hole. *I* suggested we mark out the circle with rocks first, then we can see how it's gonna look.' Ambrose took a draw on a roll-up.

'Hey, dude, I have dug many a firepit and I bin telling you, it's best to dig first. You'll regret it, man – trying to stick a spade in where the rocks are already there.'

I sighed. 'Look, I have no view on the construction of a firepit but Ambrose is right in that I did ask him to pay his way.'

'Thank you, Miss.' He bowed and blew smoke into the air.

'And what are you smoking?' I accused.

'It's only my holy herb, Miss.'

'I'm not a bloody teacher, Ambrose, so stop calling me "Miss".'

'He's outta his tree,' Chuck muttered, shaking his head.

'Well, let's just leave him to it,' I said.

'Fine. I'll get back to my birdwatching.' Chuck marched off in a huff.

I made my way over to the edge of the field near the outside toilet, where we had agreed 'Pets' Corner' would be located. I discovered Larry with a rope looped round his neck, the other end attached to a metal ring on the wall. He greeted me with an abundance of gratitude, not understanding what mischief had led to this punishment. I untied him and he scampered off without a backward glance. 'You're welcome!' I called after his woolly bottom.

'What the—?' In the furthest recess of the field, at the foot of the hill, the Planet Gil geeks had pitched their tents in succession as directed. I couldn't fault them on that point, although their presence was as welcome as itching powder at a psoriasis convention. No, what I objected to was the ten-foot-high white flagpole rising from the perimeter, a black flag fluttering like a Jolly Roger from the mast. I marched across as quickly as my stumpy legs allowed. Both tents were zipped shut but I heard muttering from behind the canvas.

'Who's in charge here?' I demanded. The muttering stopped and furious whispering commenced.

'I can hear you, you know. Come out right now.'

The zip wavered up and a greasy-haired head popped out. I indicated for him to exit the tent. He crawled out, followed closely by his two pals, as though they only came in packs of three. Never to be sold separately. All three wore identical black T-shirts with 'OOOWU Summit 2013' printed in white.

'What's going on?'

'We're just talking,' mumbled the ringleader. *Barely, I'd say.*

'What's your name?' Okay, so I *was* starting to sound like a teacher.

'Duncan.'

'So, Duncan, what were you talking about?'

'Stuff.' He avoided eye contact.

'Stuff that warrants a flagpole?'

'That's for the others.' This comment generated a sharp jab to his ribs from his pal.

'What *others*?' I interrogated.

He fingered his T-shirt. 'The summit.'

'You're going to have to help me out here, Duncan. What does the OOOWU stand for?'

'Out Of Our World Ufologists.'

'And, funnily enough, I'm no further forward.'

'We study UFOs.'

'Of course you do.' I scowled. 'So,' I glared at his chums, 'are you all part of the Planet Gil club?'

They nodded mutely. 'And you're holding some kind of summit *here*? In this *field*?'

'It's a sign,' Duncan announced.

'It's not a bloody sign! It's where our uncle Clyde lives. Now, I've already laid down the house rules but you're pushing your luck with this.'

'You never mentioned "no flagpoles".'

I tried for my scariest grimace. 'And it hadn't crossed my mind to say "no advertising" but that doesn't mean I expect to find a billboard erected by the roadside.'

'Ooh – billboard! Good idea!' His friend looked enthusiastic until he saw my face. I gave the flagpole a departing kick, which I immediately regretted as, for a temporary installation, it was surprisingly sturdy.

I felt a nagging headache pulsing at my temples as I wandered back indoors. And there, like the Pope waiting to receive his audience, sat Berta with Mavis, sharing an iced bun.

'I greeted you yesterday with "you look like hell", quipped Berta. 'I don't suppose I can use that line two days in a row? Even if it *is* true,' she whispered to Mavis.

'Nothing that a nice cup of tea won't improve,' said Mavis.

'Good idea. Stick the kettle on while you're up.' Berta grinned.

'Sorry, but has anyone seen my best friend?' I asked. 'She was meant to be making a Pets' Corner while I've been working my backside off.'

'Oh, I know the answer to that one! Here I am and how do you know I haven't?'

'Because I found Larry tied to a ring-pull and have released him into the wild.'

'Wha—? But kids love a sheep – get it?'

''Scuse the pun.' Mavis nodded in appreciation.

'You're thinking of goats,' I objected.

'No, I'm not. I'm imagining a nice hot mug of coffee. Now guess what Mavis is thinking?'

'Have you been drinking?' I asked, sniffing her breath.

'I have one or two pints of lager in the course of my duty and suddenly I've got a drink problem?'

'You've never had a problem drinking.'

'Correct.'

'So?'

'Okay, truth is I met up with Jamie and Andy.' Blank looks from Mavis and me. 'From the Woodland Commission,' she prompted.

'How? We have no connection here.'

'Well, I'm not just a pretty face.' I poked both her cheeks with my fingers. 'Ow! I texted Michelle at work, she googled the Woodland folk, got their mobile number and there you have it.'

'And you arranged to go for a drink without me?' I asked, incredulous.

'You'd never have allowed it, would you?'

'Of course not! We're here to work.'

'All work and no play …'

'Pays the bills!'

She shrugged, stirring her coffee.

'And were you intending to keep them both for yourself?' I demanded.

'You've got Mathew. Don't be greedy.'

'Says you with two blokes on the go.'

'Keeping my options open.'

'We used to call them tarts,' said Mavis.

'Thanks, Mavis.'

'Just saying.'

'And the fact that you barfed into Jamie's hat hasn't deterred him at all?'

'I told him I worked at the hospital and had picked up a virus.'

'Unbelievable!'

'It's only what they want to hear.'

Not long after, Gil and Romilly returned from Hawick, where

they'd apparently gone on a shopping trip. *Shopping? While I was risking life and limb entertaining the young uns – not to mention exposing my lungs to potentially lethal pond life?* As though justifying his jolly, Gil produced an electric drill and basic toolkit. I prayed Romilly's bag contained something more enticing. Even I had a limit to how many days I could survive on toast.

'What've you got there?' I quizzed.

Unpacking her bag, Romilly answered, 'Butternut squash, garlic, onions, bulgur wheat, et cetera.'

'"Et cetera" – does that include a cut of steak?'

'Romilly has kindly offered to cook supper for us all tonight.' Gil smiled at her.

'I like mine well done,' Berta said.

'I'll eat anything.' Mavis smiled. 'One winter during the war I remember we ate little else but cabbage for an entire month.'

'That must have had its consequences in such close living quarters,' commented Gil, tightening a drill bit.

'I should say!' Mavis nodded. 'One of my chums, Martha Greenbank, could clear a room quicker than a live grenade without a pin.'

'Why was that, then?' asked Romilly. 'Did she have a temper on her?'

Mavis rolled her eyes. 'That's right, dear. Anyway, I'd have gnawed off my own fingers if they came with gravy. So butternut whatever is just grand.'

'But the shops *do* stock meat these days? I can feel myself becoming anaemic with all this outdoor living.'

'Actually,' Gil spoke up, 'it's pretty tasty fare and better than what we normally have …' He trailed off as he caught my eye.

Romilly was serving up her hippy casserole when we heard a tap at the back door. Ambrose stuck his Rasta-hatted head in. 'Just to say that I done nearly all the digging for yo' hole.'

'Good-oh,' I replied, forking a mouthful of what I presumed to be a chunk of the butternut squash but, quite frankly, could have been a bar of soap.

'So I was wondering …' He loitered in the doorway.

'Uh-huh? Whether you should get it finished tomorrow?'

'Well, that stew smells so lush, man.'

'Hmm, it's not so much a stew as what you might use to—'

'Sunny,' growled Gil.

'Is there any, like, going spare?' asked Ambrose.

I sighed. 'Pull up a seat. If there isn't any left in the pot, there's plenty on my plate looking for a good home.'

'Sweet!' He beamed, grabbing a chair and squeezing his way next to the crowded kitchen table.

'You certainly look like you could do with being a bit fed up, young man.' Mavis frowned at his skinny arms.

'Oh, I'm not bored. I quite like having a job to do, man. It's just that crazy cowboy dude who keeps getting in my face.'

'So Sunny tells me you're on your way to the Caribbean,' said Gil.

'Sure thing.'

'And do you mind us asking a bit about that?'

Ambrose scooped in forkfuls of veg. 'No worries, man. S'all cool with me. I'm trying to track down my dad.'

'How are you going to do that?' asked Berta. 'Where will you start?'

Ambrose suppressed a burp. ''Scuse me. Well, I know he comes from St Martin originally. He came over to Leicester in the nineties, looking for work. That's where he met my mum – she was working in a garage. They had a brief fling, like. When she found out she was pregnant he didn't want nothing to do with that and said she should get rid of me.'

'Harsh,' I muttered.

'I know, right? She moved all the ways up to Elgin 'cause that's where my two aunties live. Just after I was born, she wrote to my dad and told him I was a boy.' He gave a fleeting grin. 'She got just the one letter back from him saying more or less he had no money for her and he had already gone back to St Martin.'

'Must have been tough on her,' Romilly said. 'A single mother and all.'

''Tis so. She hooked up with my stepdad for a few years but he was pretty handy with his hands, if you know what I mean.'

'Like craftwork?' Romilly asked. We all glared at her as she shrugged.

'But if you don't mind me saying,' Gil began, 'you're not exactly … I mean, was he …?'

'African–Caribbean? No, mate, I don't believe he was.'

'But you feel an affinity for Rastafarianism?'

'I am definitely keeping the Rasta alive for him. Yes, that's the case. Even though I been brought up in Scotland, I have to be true to my roots. So when I'm back with my brothers, man,' he thumped his chest, 'I will feel at home straight away. And that is some mighty tasty scran, lady.'

Romilly beamed. 'I'm so pleased. Now would you care for some yuzu organic curd?'

'Not really, Miss. I'll be brewing my ganja tea back in my tent. Night, all.'

'And good luck with your venture!' Berta called.

'You mean with, like, my dad and all?'

'Actually I meant your hole.' Berta blushed. 'But hope you find him too.'

Chapter 12

The following morning I was prodded awake by sunlight streaming through the nylon curtains and on to my face. You can understand my initial confusion and all, what with sunbeams being as rare as dentists partial to combining molar removal with aromatherapy.

My good humour, brought on by the warmth emanating from the sky, was short-lived as I spotted two unfamiliar vehicles parked next to Chuck's. Mavis followed my scowl. 'Eight of them came knocking on the door this morning before I'd even put the kettle on. I told them they needed to come back later when you were up. Said something strange about "woo-woo".'

'Where's Gil?' I asked through gritted teeth.

'I do believe he mentioned something about getting an early start on the painting. He's just desperate to move on to using that new toy of his.'

'And I've got some pretty good ideas for how we can use it too.'

I barged into Clyde's bedroom and found Gil and Romilly snogging by the window. 'Ow! My eyes!' I cried. 'You might have warned me. I may never recover from this! Jesus! Maybe I'll need laser surgery.'

'Stop exaggerating, Sunny,' Gil chastised, keeping his arms round Romilly's waist.

'Okay, put her down then. Bloody hell – I haven't even had breakfast!'

'Well, you should respect people's privacy,' argued Romilly. 'Gil and I need our *us* time.'

'Now I actually feel quite nauseous.'

'What do you want?' Gil sighed.

'Well, you can't have failed to noticed the ruddy great flagpole sticking out the corner of the field.'

Romilly giggled. 'Gil has his own flagpole, don't you, sweetie?' He blushed the colour of our Barbie bedroom.

'You promised!' I said, thumping his arm.

'Promised what?'

'You – promised – me,' I said, giving him a punch with each word, 'that you would get them to shut down Planet Gil.'

'Sunny, I won't allow you to abuse your brother like this,' said Romilly.

Gil rubbed his arm. 'I meant to …'

'But?' I prepared to take another swipe but Romilly blocked my target.

'I just forgot, what with coming away and everything.'

'And now we have a bloody OOOWU convention on our hands.'

'Really?' He peered out of the window.

'Yesterday three of your disciples arrived and raised a flag. Today Mavis tells me there are another eight.'

'But they're not doing any harm, are they?'

'So you're not the least bit freaked out that they've followed us here and now they're planning to hold a *convention* in the field?'

'Gil, who are these people?' Romilly demanded.

He shrugged. 'It's a bit of a misunderstanding, that's all. Remember I told you about that fraudster who convinced me he was an alien? Well, this group seems to think I actually did have an extraterrestrial encounter and they want me to do an interview

– to talk to them, at least.'

'They're following him around as though he has some kind of special insight,' I complained. 'We were under twenty-four-hour surveillance at our flat!'

'But he *is* special,' Romilly said dreamily, rubbing his arm.

'Oh, please. Save it for someone who hasn't seen him parading around the house in our mother's Betty Boop dressing gown.'

'I was *being* Obi-Wan Kenobi!' he protested.

'With her rolling pin?'

'Right, you two!' Romilly stood between us. 'So is there a problem now?'

'There will be if tons of people turn up and we don't have the facilities to cope with that. Besides which, we have genuine campers like George and Jason, who are trying to have a proper break in the country. It's not fair on them. It'll be the wankers versus the campers!'

'Maybe I should speak to them,' said Gil.

'Oh, no, you won't! Talk about throwing petrol on to a fire. No – you keep away from them. But we need a plan, and fast. Before the lunatics take over the asylum!' I slammed the door and charged straight into Berta.

'Hey! Trying to put me in hospital too?' she complained. 'I don't mind you shoving me down the stairs but do you think I can grab a coffee first?'

I growled something indecipherable.

'Good morning to you too,' she chirped.

I stomped across the courtyard, sensing the anxiety in their eyes as I approached. I rapped on the nearest window and waited as the driver wound it down an inch.

'I'm giving you the same rules as the rest of your mob. You

don't go near Gil, you don't speak to Gil and if you've any sense you'll steer clear of me too. Understand?' Frantic nods from four members of the IT crowd.

'How long are you staying?' I barked.

'Erm ... depends.'

'On what?'

'At least a week,' one answered from the back seat. 'We can pay, if that's what you're worried about.'

'Do I look worried?'

The driver found his voice again. 'The girls in the other car have the money.' The girls? Oh, this was going to be interesting. I couldn't wait to break it to Romilly that she might have competition.

I gave the first car a lingering glare before moving on to car two. As I approached, four girls sprang out simultaneously as though the Fiat Panda had given birth. Not that pandas were prone to spontaneous birth. The girls, in their early twenties, wore a uniform of sorts: sloppy sweatshirts, skinny jeans and canvas pumps. All four had long, straight hair in a range of colours as though they'd taken delivery of Cher's Variety Wig Pack. The girl who had been front passenger held out a brown envelope.

'We tried to book online but the site wouldn't accept our payment,' she said with a Highland twang. 'Here's the money for two pitches for a week. It's all there.'

'Hmm.' I accepted the envelope like a repugnant bribe. 'Where are you from?'

'Inverness.' She preened.

'Bloody hell! That's a long drive down.'

'Not for an OOOWU conference,' her pal chipped in. 'Last year it was in York. Anyway, this year will be special.'

'Oh, yes?' I asked with suspicion. 'Why would that be?'

'*Because of Gil!*' they squealed in unison. Fuck's sake. Bad enough I've had to endure years of Gil-adulation from people who *know* Gil, but to have perfect strangers falling over themselves to get near him was a right pisser.

I threw the money on to the kitchen table.

'What's that?' asked Berta.

'Apparently another two hundred and eighty pounds.'

She whistled. 'Maybe your uncle Clyde did have the right idea using the old field to make some money.'

'My Clyde has never been good with money,' Mavis said, shaking her head. 'If he was here that money wouldn't even have landed on the table.'

'But technically it's not the campers who are bringing it in, it's those bloody nutters!'

'True. Is that more of them, then?'

'Another eight – four girls and four lads.'

'I hope there won't be any hanky-panky.' Mavis frowned. 'You know how giddy young people can be when they're let loose.'

'If only,' I muttered. 'This bunch aren't like us normal folk. *What now?*' I exclaimed at a knock on the door.

'Only me,' Chuck beamed. 'Gloria's asking what time is the Heritage Walk?'

'I don't even know what that is!' I cried.

'But we're all booked up on it for today. The boys are particularly excited, especially after the whole jungle adventure.'

'I think you'll find it's a historical or cultural tour,' Mavis offered.

'Yes – thank you,' I replied over my shoulder.

'So?' Chuck waited expectantly.

'Eleven o'clock do?'

'Perfecto!' he said, saluting. 'And packed lunch?'

'Oh, it's the whole caboodle included.'

I sighed, reaching for the sliced loaf. Why ever did I let my mother talk me into this? Slapping a coat of paint up and down a wall was one thing, but running Center Parcs was not in the brief.

'Where will you take them?' Mavis asked. 'I can't really help you as I don't know anything about this area. Clyde has only taken me into the village a few times by taxi, as I can't get into his truck. And when I do try to chat to the locals I can't understand a word they say.'

'Right, Berta,' I said. 'Get on to your pal Michelle and ask her to google some useful info for me. It's the least you can do to help.'

'The least I can do would be to sit here enjoying my breakfast.'

'And don't think you've been let off the hook with the Pets' Corner either.'

She held her hands up in protest. 'Hey, don't take your mood out on me! It's not my fault Clyde let a Rasta loose on the internet.'

'Every day it's another bloody absurd activity! I'm scared to ask what else they've booked.'

'Trapeze performance?' Berta giggled.

'Dressage for beginners?' Mavis lobbed in.

'Or,' Berta laughed, 'what about sky-diving? I can just see Chuck shoving Gloria out of a plane!'

'Just get texting,' I muttered, flicking marmalade in her face.

And so it was, dear readers, that a merry band of four Texans and I set off down the road to Bonchester Bridge. There wasn't a proper pavement – why would there be? Who in their right mind would walk when actual motor transport had been invented? I mean, we no longer witness ponies trotting around the streets of Edinburgh pulling traps, with coachmen declaring, 'Taxis? What is all this nonsense? My faithful carriage will get one to one's destination.' Or transatlantic airline pilots who turn their backs on air travel, favouring a three-week passage via boat.

I was aware of Chuck speaking to me. 'Sorry?'

'Can you tell us a bit more about our Heritage Tour?' he repeated.

'Sure,' I nodded, reading from Berta's prepared script, scribbled hurriedly as I attempted to cobble together something other than a cheese sandwich. 'We will be taking a fascinating tour through the highways and byways of the local area, known as Bonchester Bridge. The countryside we pass through is some of the most beautiful in the Scottish area. Historic landmarks include the birthplace of Rabbie Burns, the mill with the first tartan ever invented and the site where Bonnie Prince Charlie fought the Vikings. In the village we will pass a monument to soldiers that fought in a war. There is also some artwork on display near the river, which people think is what gave Banksy his name.'

'Wow! Hear that, Gloria?' Chuck shouted behind him. We were walking in single file, trudging along the grass verge. 'This is going to be fascinating. I never knew there was so much history crammed into one place.'

'Yep,' I nodded. 'They tried to do that to make it easier for tourists. Saves a lot of travel time.'

'Wonderful,' Gloria beamed. 'Will there be any chance of seeing Andy Murray, do you think? The boys are big tennis fans and it would just tickle them if we could get his autograph.'

'No problem. Let's knock on his door on the way past.'

Warmth radiated from the speckled blue sky as our tour party crossed the humped stone bridge over the Rule Water. As for generations before us, we felt compelled to lean over the ancient stone parapet to inspect the rushing brown water below.

'Where does it come from and where does it go?' one of the boys asked.

I began to jig up and down. 'Where did you come from, Cotton Eye Joe!' I sang, trailing off as I received blank looks all round. 'Oh … er … well, it comes from up that hill we climbed behind the campsite.'

'You mean *mountain*,' Gloria corrected me.

'That's right – Ben Bonchester.' I coughed. 'And it goes right out to the North Sea, which is over there.' I waved in the opposite direction.

'What's the biggest fish that lives in the river?' his brother asked.

I inspected his chin for the telltale scar. 'Well, Jordan,' I answered in smug certainty. 'We do get the—'

'I'm *Jayden*,' he interrupted.

'Sorry, Jayden.'

'Don't listen to them, honey, they're winding you up,' Gloria clucked.

'Right.' I pointed to the twin wearing a Mustang T-shirt. 'Today you're Thing 1 and,' pointing to the other, 'you're Thing 2.'

'I hear you!' Gloria laughed. 'However much I try to change their hair or whatever, they do this deliberately to fool me.'

'To answer your question, the biggest fish would be a shark, which is why you should be so grateful I wasn't attacked yesterday in that deep pool.'

We continued on our way, receiving stares from local shoppers, who must have wondered why I was parading through the village with a family of grizzly bears in T-shirts and shorts. A runt of a lad with a thatch of matted blond hair was shimmying up the lamp post outside McKay's Foodstore. The only unstained area on his grubby, mischievous face was above his top lip, where a clear line of snot dripped from his nose. He brightened at the sight of two like-minded fellows under duress and slid back down to pavement level. Trotting alongside, he asked, 'Where you lot going?' I ignored him and kept walking. He dropped back to keep pace with Chuck. 'Where are you off to?' he persisted.

'This right here is a Heritage Tour of the local area,' said Chuck.

'What's that, then?' He sniffed.

'We're getting to find out all about the local history and culture,' Gloria joined in.

'Ha! That'll be quick.' He laughed. 'Ain't nothing of no interest around here.'

'There's plenty to see,' I objected. Didn't want him raining on my parade.

'Can I come?' he asked.

'No. Get lost,' I said.

'Please?'

I looked him in the eye. 'Shouldn't you be at school?'

'I'm off sick.'

'No, you're not, you bloody skiver.'

'I am!' he protested.

'Then we don't want your germs.'

'Ah, but you can't catch what I've got,' he retorted.

'What's that, then? Terminal laziness? Bath allergy? Incurable stupidity?'

'Eh? What're you on about? My mum says it's my wisdom teeth coming through.'

'You're kidding me.' I guffawed. 'Well, I won't hold my breath for them to make an appearance.'

'Anyway, it's the last day of school today. So can I come?'

'No. *Piss off!* These good folks have paid for this tour. It's not a freebie.'

'Ah, but I've got something I can show you that's cool.' He touched his nose. 'Only I know about it, right. But it's worth seeing. I can show you if you like.'

'What is it?' I asked, curious.

'I'll need to come with you first – then I'll show you.'

'What's your name?'

'Archie.'

'Look, Archie, I'm not interested.'

'You'll be sorry.'

'I'm sorry already.'

We trundled past a row of neat terraced houses and I gave a vague sweep of my arm. Reading from Berta's notes I announced, 'And now we're passing the miners' cottages where miners had to get up really, really early to work a full shift down the mines. They were so poor they sometimes added coal to their porridge to make a decent meal.'

'I guess that would have been good for their bones,' Gloria tutted. 'We're so lucky we don't need to eat coal, eh, boys?'

'Or porridge!' Archie sniggered. I snapped my head round and he shrank back, following up at the rear.

We meandered through the village and eventually reached the outskirts. Gardens and houses expanded in size and opulence. We neared an impressive property protected by towering iron gates and an impenetrable brick wall. 'So we've now arrived at Andy Murray's residence.' I halted the tour.

'But—' Archie interrupted. I shot him a Sunny grimace. As the group huddled around I made a show of testing the gate handle. It opened. *Shit!*

'Right, you lot – wait here,' I instructed.

'Oh, how exciting!' squealed Gloria, clapping her hands. 'I wonder if he'll come out to speak to us?'

'He's probably practising,' said Chuck.

'Is this where Andy Murray lives?' Thing 1 whined. 'Why can't we go in?'

I took my time tramping up the straight gravel drive, past two gleaming Mercedes sports cars to the imposing front door. I counted at least six Georgian windows on each of the first and second floors. There might even have been a third level. I congratulated myself on selecting a country mansion that could well have accommodated at least four tennis courts to the rear. The wood-panelled door was painted a regal green, the brass fittings polished to the point where my rosy cheeks were reflected back at me. I took a deep breath and pressed the surprisingly unimposing button of a doorbell. Behind me I glimpsed the five faces pressed against the iron bars. All they needed was a Get Out of Jail Free card.

I was about to press the bell again when a classy silver-haired woman wearing what Mother would call a housecoat answered the door. 'Can I help you?' she asked, looking me up and down before scrutinising the fanbase at the foot of the drive.

I gave what I hoped was a winning smile. 'Can you do me a *huge* favour?'

'Sorry, we don't allow the public to use our facilities,' she said with snooty disregard.

'Oh, it's not that,' I said. *Actually I could do with using her facilities. I bet they're larger than Clyde's entire cottage.* 'I know this sounds really weird, but I'm working with a special needs class – that's why we have one adult for each child.' She frowned at the motley party. As if to prove my point, Archie attempted to scale the gate, slipping to the ground and squawking in pain as his knees hit the gravel.

'He's got that attention disorder,' I confided. 'Never had enough as a baby.'

She glared at me with distaste. 'Anyway,' I continued in a rush, 'please don't ask me why, but this is a bit of a test of their initiative.' Silence. She was obviously saving her words for a more interesting conversation. 'It would be *brilliant* if you could please write on a piece of paper "All the best – Andy Murray". Then that just leaves us to find a bus ticket and a photo of the Prime Minister.'

A look of incredulity flashed across her posh mush. 'You want me to write that on a piece of paper?'

'Thank you *so* much! You'll make a group of exceptional children very happy.'

She left me standing on the doorstep as she retreated into the marble-pillared vestibule. A few minutes later she returned with a substantial sheet of ivory writing paper, *Cockdown House* ornately embossed at the top. Using a fountain pen – the ink had barely dried – she had inscribed, All the best Andy Murray! as though we would be hand-delivering a goodwill message for Wimbledon. 'Please send him our good wishes.' She curtsied, closing the door in my face. Ha – result! I hurried back to the disappointed faces.

'Where's Andy Murray?' Thing 2 complained.

I sighed, closing the gate behind me. 'Unfortunately, he's training hard for Wimbledon.'

'I told you, guys,' Chuck nodded.

'But,' I said, producing the prized document, 'he stopped for one minute to give you boys his autograph.'

'Wow-wee!' crowed Gloria. 'Aren't you boys just the luckiest?'

'*Cool!*' they chorused.

'Now let Mom keep it safe in her bag,' Chuck said. 'Thanks, Sunny!' He patted me on the back as Archie shook his head in disbelief.

We took the path down to the river and followed the slow-moving fudge-coloured water as it curved away from the village. As the twins moaned about 'dying of hunger' I selected a flatter area of the grassy bank where we could relax and dine on our magnificent lunch. Sadly we only had sandwiches. I dished out a foil-wrapped pack to each hopeful hand – none more expectant than Archie. Luckily I'd made extra. He could thank me later.

'*What's* this?' Thing 1 asked, opening up the bread.

'It's what we in Scotland call a "Mar-Mar" sandwich,' I bluffed.

'What's that, honey?' Gloria asked.

'So in America I believe you like your peanut butter and jelly sandwiches?'

'Sure do!' Thing 2 said in excited anticipation. 'Is that what we've got?'

'No – this is the Scottish equivalent. Marmite and marmalade,' I said, hardly daring to eat them myself. Still, needs must. 'Down the hatch!'

We ate in bewildered silence, interrupted only by the slurping of orange juice through straws, followed by the noisy draining of the last remnants.

'Dessert, anyone?' I offered, passing round Romilly's bag of dried apricots. I considered it my contribution to tackling obesity. As I packed away the rubbish, Archie leapt ahead.

'Can I show you my discovery now?'

'Well?' I relented, rather glad of the distraction.

'This way!' he grinned. Like an eager sheepdog he ran ahead, doubled back on himself, nipped at our heels and generally herded us across a fenced field.

'We need to cross this stile,' he said, clambering over the top and prancing into the next field. Things 1 and 2 attempted to replicate Archie's agility, wrestling themselves over the obstacle.

Chuck eyed the rickety construction with doubt. The three narrow wooden steps up, the crossbar over the fence, followed by the three planks at the other side did not look sufficiently robust to support a runaway badger. Each step creaked under Chuck's weight as he straddled the fence uncomfortably; he sweated and strained trying to maintain his composure. From behind he looked like he was trying to shag a picnic table. Finally he flopped over and landed in the next field. Gloria and I were left behind.

'Oh, I just don't know about this,' she said anxiously. 'I'm not very good with climbing frames.'

'Throw your bag over,' Chuck shouted from beyond. She swung it around her head and hurled it like a Commonwealth hammer.

'Got it! Now you, honey!'

Gloria gripped the fence and placed a tentative foot on each bar. At the top she performed the same awkward balancing act as Chuck, riding the bar like a broomstick.

'Help me, Sunny!' she cried, flapping her hand in my face.

'I'm here.' She pressed down on my head.

'Take my hand,' said Chuck.

'I can't!' she wailed. 'I'm stuck.'

'No, you're not,' I said, shoving her fleshy rear. I plunged in up to my elbows in an effort to force her over.

'*Oh, Lord!*' she yelled, dropping anchor in Chuck's ample arms. He buckled momentarily before they both sank to the ground. The twins whooped in celebration as the brawling sumos untangled themselves.

'My word!' Gloria panted, rising to her feet. 'We don't have anything as complicated as that in the States. What are they thinking?'

'It's to keep the animals out,' I said, thinking that Larry could negotiate the stile while juggling a small selection of turnips.

'Where are we going now?' Thing 1 moaned. 'Are we nearly there?' Damn, I should have been playing cliché bingo.

'It's over here.' Archie beckoned us across to a gap in the hedge that ran between the field and Rule Water. All along the waterside, raspberry bushes were sprouting in wild thickets. Their stems were laden with ruby-red fruit that dangled in pendulous bunches. The twins grabbed handfuls and scoffed until they looked like Hannibal Lecter. Archie feasted in triumph. 'See?' he declared. 'Cool or what?'

'They're so juicy!' Gloria exclaimed, plucking away.

'I've never tasted anything quite like them,' agreed Chuck. So much nicer than Romilly's dried fruit. And her apricots.

'Shall we take some back with us?' Thing 2 asked.

'I don't see why not,' I said. Judging by the fruit rotting on the ground, few locals were aware of the hidden bounty.

We were still gorging when we were interrupted by a keening noise. 'Is that someone *crying*?' said Gloria.

'Sure sounds like it, honey.'

'It's coming from the river.' Archie plunged through the long grass at the edge of the water. We heard more urgent wailing.

'Look!' cried Thing 1. 'There's something floating in the water.'

'*There!*' I pointed to a rotting grey suitcase bobbing along at a leisurely pace. It waltzed in a slow circle towards the bank. Archie grabbed a stick and tried to guide it ashore. The mewing increased. Oh dear, not good; this wasn't part of the Heritage Tour. The case rotated again and drifted out of reach. Without thinking, Archie waded in, slipping on the mossy rocks. He snatched at the case but it slid from his fingertips.

'Careful, boy!' Chuck called.

Archie ploughed in deeper, lunging at the case with both hands. He dragged it back to shore and hauled it up on to the bank, the shabby case collapsing open. Inside the waterlogged coffin were two wretched almost-drowned black kittens, each with a blob of white nose and cute white socks. They appealed to us with big gold eyes and wailed in pitiful whimpers.

'What in the world …?' Gloria gasped, tears springing to her eyes. 'Who would do this to such defenceless creatures?' She reached down to rescue the castaways, looking as though she had scooped a handful of prunes into her plump palms. We crowded round, distressed by their tiny pink mouths gaping for food.

'Chuck, pass your sweater and let's get these babies dried off.'

'Can we keep them?' begged Thing 1.

'Can we?' repeated Thing 2. '*Please?*'

'Boys, we can't take them home with us,' Gloria said, patting the fur like a BFG.

'But we can take them back to camp, can't we?' The boys gazed at me with the same appeal as the abandoned kittens.

'I suppose we can ask Berta what we should do with them. She does work in a pet shop, after all.' I knew there was little correlation between working in Pet City and having any useful insight into or expertise on the management of animals. It merely indicated that she received a wage for wearing drab dungarees and drinking coffee from an *I Brake For Snakes* mug.

The twins were desperate to find some suitable food for our miniature survivors. I can't say I was disappointed at cutting short the tour. During lunch I had glanced at Berta's tour guide notes and wasn't convinced I'd be able to pull off a battle re-enactment or demonstrate how to weave tartan from a handful of river reeds and frog spit.

As we arrived back at the campsite the first thing we noticed was the number of additional tents pitched in the OOOWU sector. I ground my teeth but decided to tackle that later. Chuck and Gloria collapsed gratefully into their folding chairs as the three boys and I went in search of Berta. We passed Ambrose's firepit, which had one solitary stone placed on its outer rim. Cradling the mewing kittens, I didn't have to go far to find Ambrose and Berta's stockinged feet sticking out of his tent. Mavis needn't have worried about any 'hanky-panky' as the canvas vibrated with their cumulative snoring.

I kicked their feet. 'Oy! You pair! Enough with the napping. We've got a proper animal rescue on our hands.' Well, in my hands to be exact. No reaction. I gave the twins permission to pull two feet each. Berta came out kicking and fighting.

'What's the problem? Can't a girl get any peace around here?'

'You're not meant to be getting peace. You're meant to be working, remember? A quarter of a classic car and all that?'

'Humpf.' She rubbed her eyes blearily.

'What's all da commotion?' Ambrose climbed out of the tent, still wearing his Desmond Dekker pyjamas. 'Oh, cutie pie!' he grinned.

'Thanks, but I— oh, you mean the kittens?'

'What else?'

'So since I'm naming and shaming the lazy bastards of the day – 'scuse my French, boys – why have you only managed to add *one* stone to the firepit ring?'

'They're well heavy. Might need some help,' he mumbled.

'Whatever. In the meantime what are we supposed to do with these?' I passed the two hysterical kittens over to Berta, who looked like I'd just placed a turd in each of her hands.

'Why are you giving these to me?' she asked, holding each one up for closer inspection.

'Contribution to your Pets' Corner.'

'Can we give them some milk?' the twins pleaded. She sighed.

'Come on, then, let's see what we've got in the kitchen.' They scampered after her, leaving Archie loitering with his hands in his pockets, his jeans and trainers still dripping.

'Off you go, then. Tour over,' I said.

'Ain't you got any work for me here, then?'

'Work?' I echoed. 'How old are you?'

'Thirteen next birthday.'

'But won't your mum be wondering where you are?'

'She mostly plays online bingo,' he muttered.

'Your dad?'

'He lives somewhere near Glasgow with a girl dog.'

'A what?'

'That's what my mum calls her.' He sniffed loudly.

'Well, I think you should head home now. We've rescued enough waifs and strays for the day.'

He shrugged and wandered back across the field just as Gloria came panting up. 'Oooh, Sunny, I'm glad I caught you. I forgot to ask this morning. Where's the campsite launderette? The website said something about being able to get your laundry done.'

'Really?' Uncle Clyde was going to get such a kicking when he came home.

'We got a whole heap of clothes could do with washing.'

'Yo! Archie!' I shouted. '*Archie!*' He turned and came jogging back. 'Did you say you wanted a job?'

'I'll do anything to make a bit of money.'

'Right – you're in charge of laundry. Go with Gloria, then take her washing into the cottage. Ask for Mavis and she'll keep you right.'

'Awesome.'

'Righty, young man.' Gloria beamed. 'Come with me.'

I entered the kitchen to find Berta, Things 1 and 2 and the kittens sprawled on the floor. The boys were trying to spoon milk into the kittens' gaping mouths.

'They haven't quite got the hang of feeding themselves,' Berta explained. 'Oh, are you making coffee? Give mine two scoops. I'm still half asleep.'

I took my coffee upstairs to find Gil completing the gloss woodwork in Clyde's room with meticulous concentration. The room was looking good, even if it felt like standing in the yellow submarine. 'I hope this doesn't make him feel too bilious,' I said.

Gil frowned. 'I've done my best with what he's given us. It's not my fault he's too tight to pay for decent paint.'

I held my hands up. 'Hey! Don't shoot the messenger. I could quite happily feed what's left of Clyde to the Bonchester Zombie Association.'

'What's he done now? Or not done?'

'Apparently the campsite has a launderette.'

'Nice one.'

'I've recruited some child labour for that, but we're going to need a super-long washing line put up if we're going to get any of it dry. Assuming Clyde doesn't have a tumble dryer secreted in the shed.'

'Can't say I've seen one.'

'Right. Well, I'll leave that one to you.'

'Fine. I'll get to it after this.'

'Where's your devoted girlfriend, by the way?'

'Oh, she had to nip into Hawick library to do some research.'

'Hmm. You do know that "research" is an anagram of c-her-arse?'

'See her arse?' repeated Gil. 'That's not bad for you, Sunny.'

'And what happened to the Sistine Chapel? She's barely covered the first half hour of the world's creation.'

'Now, now. Play nice.'

Chapter 13

I drained my coffee cup and braced myself for conflict. The earlier sunshine of the day had retreated behind heavy slate storm clouds. How appropriate. The hotchpotch of tents was pitched close together in military fashion. I glanced up at the mocking black flag that danced in the gathering wind. An army-provision marquee had been erected, the front flaps tied back to allow the free coming and going of the OOOWU attendees. Each participating twat had been provided with a lanyard and plastic-covered conference badge, and at least three clipboard-wielding supervisors directed foot traffic.

I hovered just inside the marquee until the activity slowed and came to a grinding halt. If we'd been playing musical statues I'd have had a hard time eliminating anyone. Finally an older guy sporting an ugly beard and glasses approached me. He wore military fatigues and was bald except for a tangle of brown hair that started just above his ears and grew down towards his yellow-starred epaulettes. I was pretty sure he'd get drummed out for parading that hairstyle, never mind his metallic laced boots. 'Can I help you?' he asked in an English accent. I'm guessing the Midlands

'This is just getting way out of hand,' I growled. Someone's mobile went off, the ringtone sounding suspiciously like the Star Wars theme tune.

'Sorry, who are you?' he queried, stepping forward. Not only a lanyard but a whistle also hung round his neck. Maybe he had plans to enter the local sheepdog trials. I was sure Larry would have something to say about that.

'I'm Sunny McIntosh. This is my uncle Clyde's field. He didn't mind opening up his spare land for campers on holiday, but this,' I waved my hands around me, 'is not what he planned.'

'Sunny? Gil's sister, right?'

Oh, I swear I'm going to shove that whistle where no alien will dare trespass. He broke into an ingratiating smile. 'My name is Paul Crank. I'm Director of OOOWU – that stands for—'

'I know what it stands for and I've no interest in the slightest what this bloody convention is all about. What *you* need to know is that I'm going to mark off this corner of the field and I insist that you stay absolutely within the confines of this area. There will be no access to our facilities. You can get to the main drive round the back of the cottage.'

'So you don't mind if we expand up the hill?'

'I don't care if you camp up Ben Nevis – just stay away from us.'

'But we have paid for this pitch. Don't we have a contractual right to any other facilities?'

'No.'

'What about the shop?' he persisted. 'We can get to that round the back and wouldn't be crossing the field.' The prospect of charging a captive audience triple for a sliced sausage appealed to my business acumen, otherwise known as inner greed.

'You know what? I *will* allow you to access the shop. Just stick to the opening times.'

'Agreed,' he replied mildly, holding out his hand. I grunted, glaring at the members as they lowered their eyes in embarrassment.

As I exited the marquee I spotted Ambrose lugging another stone from the stream across the field.

'Hey, Ambrose, I need to move you on to another job.'

'What, lady?' he puffed, dropping the stone on to the grass.

I pointed to the convention tents in the corner. 'I need you to rope off this area so that no more of their tents can be put up in this field.'

'Rope it off? What with, like?'

'I don't know. Find something in the garage or shed.'

'What if I can't find nothing?'

'Then you can ask next door at the farm. Mr Struthers is usually happy to help out with stuff like that.'

'But I thought you was banging on about getting this firepit done.' He scratched his hair under his hat.

'It's called prioritising, Ambrose. If you don't cordon off this area, they'll be bloody camping *in* your firepit.'

'Who's Gordon?'

'Just do it.'

'Hey, what's for tea tonight? I'm starving already.'

As I stomped back over the grass, I felt the first plop of rain against my face.

'Afternoon!' George called from his arena. 'How do you like our gazebo?' He smiled. 'Jason's been cribbing from our US friends over there. He couldn't be outshone by their canopy. Here, have a seat.' He patted the empty chair next to him.

'Fair play,' I said. Jason had rigged a length of plastic from one side of the windbreak, over the low tent and on to the other side.

'Cosy, eh?' he nodded, drinking his tea. 'Want a cuppa? You look like you need it. I've even got chocolate biscuits!'

'Go on, then.' Since Romilly had voted herself chief shopper we'd been denied anything other than root vegetables and bland pulses. The idea of indulging in a chocolate treat would be like smack to her. I gazed up at the awning, where the rain drummed steadily. 'What's he used?'

'Och, it's just an old groundsheet we keep in the car. Handy, though.'

'Where is Jason, anyway?'

'I sent him along the road to buy something decent for dinner. I fancy a curry. We can heat it up on the stove.'

'I'd kill for a curry!'

'By the looks of your wee dispute with the students over there I'd say you'd kill for a lot less. What's going on, anyway? It looks like a girl guide or scouting camp.'

I explained about Gil's followers and their misguided faith in him.

'Gil? That's the tall one with dark hair who spends most of his time up a ladder?'

'That's him.'

'And you're his sister?'

'That's about it.'

'Interesting.' He dunked the digestive into his tea. 'You know, we had only planned to stay for a few nights but this is the most fun we've ever had camping. We might stay on.'

'I'm so pleased,' I muttered.

'Don't worry, we'll give you a good rating.' He winked. 'Jason was in the village yesterday and checked out the Camp Crackers website. Apparently one of your "geeks", as you call them, put a one-star rating and posted, "Is this the worst campsite in Scotland?". Unfortunately I think it might actually have the opposite effect.'

'How do you mean?'

'Well,' he grinned wickedly, 'some campers like to think they're a bit hardcore. You know? To say how tough they are camping in the wild.'

'We're not exactly in the wilderness.'

'But you might be getting a reputation already.'

'Great.' I sighed. 'Right, I better make a move. Enjoy your curry.'

'Will do.' He saluted.

I think I was on to my second vodka as I slumped at the kitchen table. It wasn't that I particularly enjoyed being exposed to Romilly's rear as she commandeered the cooker concocting God knows what, but I hadn't the energy to move. On the plus side, it was near the vodka. Mavis was sipping a dry sherry that Romilly had brought back from Hawick having been persuaded that it was for medicinal purposes only. Even Gil was swigging from a bottle of beer. Living under Clyde's leaky roof had driven us all to seek solace in alcohol.

The kittens had been housed in a cardboard shoebox behind the back door, where Larry was overseeing them with paternal interest, perhaps wondering if he'd been responsible in some way. The new Pets' Corner. I'd allowed Jayden and Jordan to name the kittens. Fantastic – another set of twins I won't be able to tell apart.

Mavis handed me back my mobile. 'How's he doing?' I asked.

'He's making progress.' Mavis nodded. 'Apparently he's now up walking short distances with a gutter frame, whatever that is.'

'Clyde was never far from the gutter.'

'And he could certainly do with someone looking at his gutters here,' Gil added. 'They're chock-a-block with leaves and crap.'

'Hmm, I'll be sure to pass that on.'

'Any word of when he's getting home?' I asked, ever hopeful

that he would take over the role of circus master.

Mavis tutted. 'Ooh, it'll be a while, I should think. He's got to be able to get up and down those stairs, and they're not easy. Not that I'd know, of course, being grounded down here.'

'You're not missing anything, Mavis,' Berta chipped in. 'It's not as if there's an infinity pool on the roof or anything. What'll happen when we go home, though?' She voiced what we'd all been thinking.

Mavis shook her head. 'I've no idea. I can't look after him.'

'You'll need to get some help,' I suggested.

'I might ask Tam to take me up to the hospital in the next day or so. I'll speak to the doctor and see what he says.'

'Anyone for chilli con courgette?' Romilly asked. 'I'm about ready to serve up.'

As though he'd been listening at the keyhole, Ambrose stuck in his mighty bonce. 'Did I hear chilli, like? I could well eat a horse.' He snuck in and pulled up a chair.

'There's no one serving horsemeat here,' said Romilly scornfully.

'Just hold your horses – or not!' I grabbed Ambrose by the arm. 'There will be no food for you, young man, until you've shown me that you've roped off the loons.'

'Oh, my days!' he protested. 'I couldn't find no rope.'

'Any,' Mavis sighed.

'So I did what you told me.'

'Told.'

'And that old boy gave me somefink else to use.'

'Some*thing*.'

'Uh-huh?' I prompted.

'I blocked 'em off with hay bales.'

'But if you struggled with lifting stones, how did you manage to shift hay bales?'

He grinned. 'Ah, well, clever farmer-man borrowed me a wheelbarrow thing, like, for carrying, so I done it with that.'

'Okay, I officially give up!' Mavis exclaimed. 'Don't they teach you grammar up here?'

'Oh, she died years ago, Miss.' Ba-dum-bum-*ching*!

I dragged him outside. 'Show me.'

'Help! You's hurting my weak arms.' Ambrose wrestled free and lumbered around the side of the cottage. 'See!' As the rain had retreated over the hills, the happy campers were enjoying the long summer light and were cooking outdoors – Chuck mastering burger-flipping on a camping cooker and George studiously reheating his lamb jalfrezi. The enticing smells wafted in our direction. Beyond the idyllic picture the view could only be described as the rural version of the Berlin Wall. Ambrose had stacked hay bales across the field in a semicircle from the stream on the left to the foot of the hill on the right, effectively quarantining the OOOWU crowd. They'd be forced to use the back of the cottage to access the main drive.

Ambrose sensed a thaw. 'So do I get some scran?'

'Absolutely. Good job, Ambrose.'

'Wicked.' He beamed and went to give me a high five.

'Let's not get carried away.'

I, too, felt I could consume a large Shetland pony as Romilly served up the chilli in bowls.

'So these are the new rules,' I shared. 'The OOOWU weirdos are fenced off from the rest of the campsite. They can't use the toilet or shower facilities or go anywhere near the front of the cottage.'

'How grim,' said Romilly. 'They'll be living like peasants.'

'Well, in case you missed the brochure, we're not exactly

marketed as an International Conference Centre.'

'Probably going to ship in those Portaloos like at T in the Park,' Berta commented.

'But we're still charging them the same price?' said Gil in surprise.

'That's right. If they don't like it they know what they can do. Anyway, I'm letting them use the shop since they can get round the side.'

'That's fair, I reckon,' Ambrose mused. 'I had to queue, like, ages for the shower this morning.'

'And that would be why you were still wearing pyjamas this afternoon?'

'Kinda. I'm running out of clean clothes.'

'Funny you should mention that. We now have a new laundry service, care of Archie, who followed us home like the abandoned kittens.'

Gil sighed. 'Now I know why it's referred to as a cottage industry.'

'Sorry to change the subject,' Berta said, 'but *what* are we eating?'

'Chilli con courgette,' Romilly retorted.

'*Why?*' Berta muttered. She plopped a forkful of mush back into her bowl.

'Have you got any better ideas? I mean, I find it stressful enough trying to meet my literary deadlines without the additional pressure of being head chef.'

'Couldn't we have a barbecue tomorrow? At least it's easy to chuck on a few burgers and sausages.'

'S'pose,' Romilly agreed. 'I like halloumi.'

'I like me-me.'

'By the way, George and Jason are staying on for a few more days. What about you, Ambrose?' I said.

'Me? Oh, man, I'm always up for a barbecue. My brothers are well into jerk chicken and them charred plantains.'

'I meant how long are you staying?' I asked. 'I thought you were just passing through on your way down south.'

''Tis true, sister. I can hitch a lift down to Eng-er-land but I was hoping to save a bit more money to cover my fare, like.'

'How can you save money if you're not working?' asked Romilly.

'Ah, the old conundrum of life.' He shrugged.

'How much do you think you'll need?' Gil said.

Ambrose scratched at his stubble. 'I reckon the flight's going to set me back 'bout eight hundred nickers. Once I get there I hope to live off the bountiful land.'

'Hmm, it's a bit of a vague plan,' I said. 'How much have you got so far?'

'Not that much, for sure. I spent most of it getting my camping gear together.'

'I see many of the local fruit farms are advertising for labour,' Romilly advised.

Ambrose thought about her words. 'I see what you're hinting at. You mean get a job?'

'Hold the front page!' Berta exclaimed. 'Unemployed youth discovers work exchanged for cash!'

'And is this what yous all think?' he said, taken aback.

'*Yes!*' we chorused.

Chapter 14

I lay in bed, scrolling through my gallery in search of a precious glimpse of Mathew. Photos of him were rarer than the four-legged wild haggis, what with his antipathy towards the camera and his loathing of selfies. Most of the photos taken in his company were either of me or of half his frowning face. I'd like to say that I missed his winning smile and sense of humour (apparently the two attributes most sought-after by the average singleton), but that would be a stretch of the imagination even for J. K. Rowling. I found his constant grumbling and belief that he wasn't really needed quite adorable. Now I thought about it, he had more in common with an inflamed appendix. I missed him desperately and found his casual approach to our relationship more than alarming. I still had to pinch myself to remind me that I was actually going out with Mathew Vanguard! I'd been carrying a torch for him for so long I was surprised I hadn't given him permanent retinal damage. I was about to kiss my screen when Berta's sagging bottom dipped perilously close to my face. I shoved it back up. 'Oy!' I protested.

'Sorry,' she said, not in the least bit.

'You know what?'

'What?'

'I think I'm just going to have a day indoors. I'm not going to scale any mountains, ford any rivers or tramp through the countryside. Outside is just going to have to take care of itself today.'

'Right on, sister.'

'S'all very well for you,' I ranted. 'I don't see why I'm getting landed with all the bloody activities. It's about time Gil took a turn.'

'So tell him.'

'I will.'

'Right, Gil,' I warned. 'It's my turn to stay at home today. Whatever cock-a-hoop bloody notion that Chuck comes up with this morning, it's your turn to deal with,' I raved, munching on my burnt toast.

'Fine,' he agreed.

'Is that it?' I challenged.

'Mmm hmm.'

'Even if it's a quad-biking safari or North Sea scuba diving, you'll do the family outing?'

'Don't forget the dressage,' Mavis added.

'No problem,' Gil nodded.

'He's such a dreamboat, isn't he?' Romilly murmured, stroking his arm.

I smiled sweetly. 'We'll see.'

I jumped up in a flash to answer the knock at the door. Chuck stood outside expectantly, baseball cap in hand. 'Morning, Sunny!' He bowed.

'How can I help you today?' I grinned.

'Well, Gloria and I are having ourselves a little grown-ups time.' He winked. 'We're heading off on an open-top bus tour we've booked.' He scanned the leaflet in his hand, reading out,

'"Abbotsford House, Melrose and Dryburgh Abbey, William Wallace Statue and Scott's View". Awesome, eh?'

'Uh-huh.'

'So the boys are all booked in for the "Survival Skills" training and they're mighty excited about that.'

'Gil,' I said. 'This one's for you.'

'Hey, Chuck. So today I'm building a barbecue. That do?'

'Absolutely!' Chuck gave the thumbs-up. 'I'll send them over after breakfast.'

I slammed the door.

'What?' Gil smiled.

Gil had turned all macho, sporting a tool belt and wielding his electric drill like 007. When the twins appeared they were allowed five minutes to feed the kittens before being ushered towards the shed. Ambrose downed his coffee and dashed out of the back door, toast in hand – probably concerned I'd add more duties to his workload. Romilly wittered something about 'finding a local reflexologist to manipulate her vertical zone'. I didn't think that warranted a response and ignored her as she floated out of the door.

'Where's Berta?' I turned to Mavis, who shrugged.

'Don't look at me. I've two hours turning a tap on and off while tuned to Radio Four. No doubt there's some mutinous Maori protesting against the excessive subsidising of the *kapa haka*.' She nudged her trolley out of the kitchen, shuffling along behind.

So I guessed I was on shop duty. I cleared away the breakfast dishes, which felt surprisingly comforting as this was the nearest I'd come to my usual routine. That is, lounging about the flat while Gil hammered out a respectable living.

Before long, Archie appeared. He might even have wiped

his face and brushed his hair. 'Hello, Miss. That's me got them foreigners' washing. Yesterday the old lady—'

'Mavis.'

'She showed me what to do. Plus I have to do it at home anyway.'

'Really? What about your mum?'

'Who?'

'Your mother. Doesn't she do the laundry?'

'She's got a thing about appliances – thinks they're all trying to brainwash us so she won't touch 'em.'

'How convenient.'

He began loading up the washing machine, a right little Hattie Housewife with his own Persil and fabric softener. He withdrew a receipt book from his rear pocket and scribbled 'USA', tearing out the tab and placing it on top of the empty bin bag. 'I'll be back in an hour,' he chirped. 'Off to get the next loads.'

It would have been easier to install a revolving door to the kitchen for the continuous flow of OOOWU followers. I counted a further ten groups of devotees. None of them were on good terms with personal hygiene. It was only a matter of time before their corner would take on the fester of Edinburgh's Old Town slums. We'd smoke 'em out like rats. Mavis had been using one of the kitchen drawers for the float and it was now stuffed with cash and cheques. This was way more than Clyde could have dreamed of and I knew we'd have to hide it before he got home and blew it on whisky and beer. The original *wild rover*.

The only happy camper not part of the conference fiasco stuck her blonde wavy-haired head round the door. She was wearing a pink-and-white candy-striped poncho and lilac wellies. If her overexcited boobs hadn't been trying to escape I'd have passed her off as a nine-year-old. '*Hiya!*' she gushed, all blue eyes and blusher.

'I'm Blossom! I'm here to do some camping.' *Never!*

'I tried to book a week but the website wouldn't let me. "*Computer says no!*"' She collapsed in a giggling fit.

'Yeah, we don't really have a connection here.'

'Oh? I thought that was the whole point of it being a *World Wide* Web – that you could get it anywhere. Even up the Khyber Pass.' More hysterical laughter. 'Ooh, I love your jumper!'

'What, this?' I wasn't being modest – I was actually wearing a skanky week-worn University of Dundee sweatshirt that Mathew had donated.

'The detail is gorgeous! Anyway, I've got a cheque here for Mr Davidson. Do you work for him?'

'Something like that,' I muttered.

'Ah, is he not a very good boss?' she fished. 'I've had a terrible one where I've been working. Mr Grosvenor's his name. Every time I go into the treatment cupboard he follows me in and shuts the door. I can always tell when he's up to no good as he pops a Polo mint into his mouth. Last week when I was raking around for some crepe bandage he came right up behind me and offered to massage my shoulders. Can you believe the cheek of it?'

'Mmm.'

'So I gave him a swift karate chop into his stomach and when he was catching his breath – and let me tell you he *needed* that Polo – I ran back out. Unfortunately I think I may have overreacted.'

'Anyway …' I said, needing another cup of coffee.

'Oh, yes. Listen to me rabbiting on. What am I like? Well, how would you know what I'm like? You've only just met me! So, my name's Blossom.'

'At least we both agree on that.'

'Doh!' She slapped her forehead.

'So just pitch your tent wherever you like in the field – this side of the hay bales.'

'You know, I had a quick recce at the site and it's not all that bad.'

'Sorry?'

'Well, the website says, "Is this the worst campsite in Scotland?" but I can't see how it's that bad. I mean, you're lovely!'

'I ... er ...'

Gil appeared behind her. 'Excuse me,' he said, squeezing past.

Blossom put one hand round her mouth and said in a loud whisper, 'Is that your boss?'

'No – that's just Gil.'

'Oooh, I love your tool belt! What I wouldn't give to have a handyman in my flat. I don't suppose you're for hire? Anyways, this tent isn't going to put itself up. Cheery-bye!'

Gil looked nonplussed as she scurried off. 'And you think my lot are bad?' he remarked. 'Who was that?'

'Someone on medication.'

As the sun glowed in the cobalt sky – it had been a most unusual summer in more ways than one – I lifted my chair outside in a bid to do nothing. There was something very relaxing about watching other people beavering away. I couldn't figure out why Archie was dragging a mini stepladder behind him until I observed that he was hanging out the washing. Gil had overestimated the height of our workforce and created a washing line about six feet off the ground. Poor Archie was up and down that ladder like a Victorian chimney sweep. He had procured the wheelbarrow from Ambrose to collect and deliver laundry around the campsite. I kindly ignored the fact that he was providing a service to the OOOWU gurus – after all, I was the last person to stand in the way of a fellow business entrepreneur making a quick buck. In fact, if I hadn't been taking a break from Do Me A Favour, I might have tendered a competitive bid. Give the lad his due, he also had the savvy to gather a shopping list from the Wanker Campers and had distributed valued commodities *en route* from home.

Ambrose persevered with the painstaking task of transferring rocks from the stream to the firepit, working under pressure to get it finished for this evening's much-anticipated barbecue. Since Romilly was taking the road most travelled – that is, by bus – we voted (much to her horror) that she be hunter and gatherer for the day. We assured her that no actual viscera need touch her delicate skin but if we didn't get meat there would be a riot. *Who knows, even Ambrose's Berlin Wall might be at risk of collapse.*

Jayden and Jordan each transported a kitten in the front pocket of their hoodies. The little mites were perfectly at home snuggled into the womb-like pouches. Berta hadn't been entirely sure of their sex so the twins had opted for 'Bugs' and 'Bunny' in the hope that no offence would be caused. I thought the only likely offence would be when the boys left camp and I threw the orphans back into the river. *I'm joking.*

After lunch there was still no sign of the slippery Berta, and Mavis had retired for her afternoon nap. It seemed to me that there were countless years between infancy and old age when taking an afternoon siesta was frowned upon in Britain and I wondered whether I could lodge a motion to reduce the period of unacceptability by about fifty years.

George had positioned his chair to soak up maximum sunrays and was just pouring from the kettle.

'Time for a brew, Missus?' he smiled.

'What the hell—?' I exclaimed. Beyond the Hay-dried Wall (okay, that *nearly* worked) it appeared that Glastonbury had temporarily relocated. Some of the marquees would be commonplace at a royal wedding and I realised the schoolboy error in charging per tent. However, it wasn't so much the patchwork of corporate canvas that freaked me out but what I can only describe as the parcelling of Bonchester Hill. For some bizarre reason, the grassy slope had been carpeted with hundreds of silver squares. I stood there gaping like an oxygen-deprived barracuda.

'Don't ask me,' George shrugged, whipping out the tea bag. 'They've been at it all morning.'

'But what's it for?' I asked.

'I've no idea what it's meant to be or its purpose,' he said. 'But it looks to me like they've been pegging foil blankets on to the ground. You know, the emergency blankets they wrap round marathon runners.'

'How would I know that?' I snapped.

'Just saying.'

'Sorry.' I collapsed on to one of their camping chairs. 'This is all a bit beyond me.'

George patted my knee. 'Caramel log?'

I unwrapped one in silence and chewed thoughtfully. 'What do you and Jason make of all this?'

'They're nuts,' he proposed. 'These people are fanatics. It's their life. It's what drives them. You'll probably find they go from site to site in the vague hope of snatching a glimpse of something weird and wonderful.'

'But I don't understand why they've latched on to Gil.'

'Desperation?'

'I guess.' I dunked my biscuit. 'Where is Jason, anyway?'

'Oh, Gloria talked him into going on the bus tour.'

'I thought they wanted some "grown-up" time together?'

'Jason most definitely isn't into a three-way, but he *is* partial to a warmed scone and I think afternoon tea was part of the deal.'

'And you're not?'

'I'm surrounded by kids all day. Sometimes it's just nice to sit here and let the world go round without you.'

'What do you do?'

'I'm a classroom assistant in a primary school.'

'Uh-huh?'

'Basically I pass the day wiping noses, telling the kids to sit down and getting them dressed for outside. I honestly spend most of my day kneeling in front of kids and zipping up their coats.'

'Okay – gotcha.'

'So sitting in a chair in a field drinking tea is heaven. Throw in the weirdest live show I've ever seen and this is camping gold!'

'Fair enough. I'm just not sure what lengths they'll be willing to go to.'

'How do you mean?'

'To get a piece of Gil.'

Chapter 15

As I neared the hay bales I took a deep breath and counted to ten. I was gobsmacked to find a registration desk had been set up between two Portaloos at the entrance to their village, where a scholarly girl with grey skin and lanky hair was ticking names off a clipboard. She barely glanced up. 'Name?'

'Sunny McIntosh.'

She scanned the page. 'No – your name's not on the list.'

'Really? I'm surprised. I go to all the Boo-hoo gigs.'

'It's OOOWU, actually,' she sneered.

'Can I speak to Paul Crank, please?'

'He's busy.'

'What – preparing to roast the biggest turkey in the world?'

'I'm not with you.'

'Please tell Paul Crank I'd like a word with him.'

'And I said he's otherwise occupied. This has been the most popular convention we've had in years.' She sighed, her two-hour customer-service training kicking in. 'If you like, I'll take a message. Who did you say you were?'

'Sunny,' I said with deliberation. '*McIntosh.*'

'McIntosh?' She paled. Her sweaty hand dropped the pen. I nodded.

'As in *Gil* McIntosh?' she gibbered.

'Correct.'

'So you'd be Gil's sister, right?' Oh, she was *so* lucky to be beyond cuffing distance. She leapt up, the chair falling over in her wake, and sprinted for the most imposing marquee. Two spindly teenagers locked in serious debate were bowled over as she barged past. Almost as soon as she had ducked into the tent she reappeared with Paul Crank striding behind. I didn't think it was possible for him to look any more ridiculous than he had done yesterday, but I stand corrected. Not only did his bald head have an overexposed sheen, but he had opted to braid the remaining hair into two plaits. He still boasted the sergeant major jacket, having replaced the trousers with camouflage shorts and shin-high silver boots. I had no idea why this bunch was fixated on extraterrestrials when there were clearly more peculiar beings at large much closer to home.

'Sunny,' he greeted me, his hand extended. I ignored this.

'What's going on?' I demanded.

'I thought I explained. We're holding our annual OOOWU convention. And, once again, I'd like to offer my gratitude to you for allowing us to host it on your land.'

'Not that,' I growled. '*That!*' I indicated the hill, where dozens of anaemic labourers were tapping pegs into the tufty grass as the silver blanket expanded.

'Ah, that would be our communication platform,' he declared. 'It's a little bit of experimentation I'm fostering this year.'

'For?'

'We're trying to create the optimal conditions to facilitate communication between our planet and any other form of living existence. This reflective shield offers the perfect opportunity to diffuse energy or sound – possibly even gamma radiation. I can see now why Gil chose this spot in the Scottish Borders – it's exquisite. There's a basin within which we sit that allows the harvesting of power. And then, of course, there are the ruins of the ancient fort on top of the hill, which enables the mathematical calculation of grid coordinates. Ha! He's a genius.' He clapped his hands together.

'Are you mad?' I accused.

'Sorry?'

'No, seriously, have you actually got a medical condition that we should know about? I mean, if you're leading these poor deluded randoms into believing they're on to some type of quest ...'

'I can assure you that I'm perfectly sane,' he spluttered. 'You know, I don't expect *you* to understand. *Gil* would understand.'

My fist clenched as the registration girl took a step backwards.

'What I mean,' he rushed on, 'is that this is all very technical. I can appreciate it's not everyone's area of expertise.'

'Yeah, hammering Bacofoil on to the grass is *way* too complex for me.'

'So, now might not be the best time to ask, but I was wondering when it might suit Gil for the interview ...?'

I turned, tossing the table over as I passed. Where was that brother of mine?

I found him hiding in the garage, sitting at the wheel of Clyde's car – or should I say *our* car. He wasn't aware I'd slipped into the garage and was spinning the steering wheel and making 'brrm brrm' noises.

'Entering the Monaco Grand Prix, are you?'

His head whacked the roof of the car as he jolted, sounding the horn at the same time.

'*Jesus, Sunny!* Don't go sneaking up on people like that!'

I leant in the window. 'So this is where you skulk while I'm entertaining the masses.'

'I've been here five minutes. Can't a man take some time to himself?'

'Like I do, you mean?'

'No, I didn't mean.'

'Anyway, how were the boys today?'

'Grand. How do you tell them apart?'

'I don't know. How *do* you tell them apart?' I said, waiting for the punchline.

'No, I'm asking.'

'Oh, well, then the answer is I can't. And what about the barbecue?'

'All ready to go.'

'So what do you make of all that bloody aluminium nonsense on the hill?' I demanded. Gil climbed out of the car, closing the driver's door with a bang. He shrugged.

'What are we going to do about it?' I nagged.

'What do you *want* me to do?' He rubbed his eyes under his glasses.

'Ought we to stop them or something? It feels like they're losing the plot.'

Gil turned to me in anger. 'Isn't this just you interfering like last time?'

'*I'm* not interfering. They're the ones who keep approaching me,' I lied.

'Who is?'

'Well, their ringleader seems to be this weirdo called Paul Crank.'

'Paul Crank's here!' he exclaimed, whirling around as though Baldy-Boots might pop out of the bonnet. 'Why didn't you say so?'

'Is he a big cheese?'

'He's the bloody editor of *Your UFO*. Yes, he's a big flipping block of cheese.'

'How was I supposed to know? Anyway, he wants to interview you.'

'Really?' Gil grinned, smoothing down his hair.

I glowered at him. 'Don't even think about it. I thought you were still trying to regain your reputation at work without feeding the beast?'

'Ah, but *Your UFO* is a prestigious science-fiction publication.'

'Isn't that an oxymoron?'

'Sunny, *you're* being a moron.'

I sighed. 'Gil, you know this is dangerous territory for you. My job is to keep you grounded, if you recall. If you start believing all their crap, who knows where you'll end up? You need to hang on to the fact that these geeks are there to exploit your vulnerability. Remember the *Evening News* headline? "Gullible Travels"?'

Gil grunted. 'You're right. I need to stay strong. I need to protect Romilly.'

'From what?' Romilly asked, bouncing into the garage. 'That nasty infection hasn't reappeared, has it?'

'What? Oh, no – nothing like that.' He tried to smile. 'How did you get on with the reflexology?'

'Fabulous!' she breathed. 'I feel like he released something in my inner ring.'

'Right. I'll see you two later,' I snorted and exited the garage.

We kicked off the barbecue early in the evening while there was still some heat left in the sun and the midges weren't yet sharpening their fangs. Ambrose had spent the entire day finalising his firepit and revelled in the role of fire-master, adeptly poking the bonfire with a handy branch. He nodded his head in time to the sound of steel-drum reggae booming from a portable speaker the size of an egg.

Archie, being two years their senior, had taken charge of Jayden and Jordan, overseeing their collection of firewood. I got the impression that they'd never actually built a bonfire before. Chuck and Gloria, in fleeces and baseball caps, were encased in their folding chairs, both swigging from bottles of Budweiser. George and Jason were sitting next to them, a bottle of white wine in a chiller with ice nabbed from our freezer. Accustomed to Scottish evenings, they had gone one step further by wearing North Face winter jackets.

Berta had returned from Hawick pissed – I'd be having words with her later. She'd borrowed Ambrose's sleeping bag and was dozing in an old deckchair rescued from the garage. Next to her, Mavis was tucked into her wheelchair under a tartan blanket. She and I had started on the jug of Pimm's that I'd rustled up using Romilly's cucumber and apple. Romilly informed us that she was staying in the cottage until we'd finished eating, as she couldn't tolerate the 'foul smell of burning flesh'.

Gil's barbecue invention transpired to be a wooden frame covered in chicken wire, which he and Ambrose lifted so that it sat above the flames. He placed a sheet of metal over one side that he greased like a griddle, then threw on a smattering of burgers.

Gil had donned a spare apron and was wielding a fish slice in one hand and tongs in the other.

'Hey, man!' Ambrose said. 'Yous look like a short-order cook.'

'I do my best,' Gil responded, flipping the burgers.

'I don't care what Romilly thinks,' I said, raising my voice over the tortured singer lamenting over 'living in a concrete situation'. 'They smell delicious. Sorry, *what* are we listening to here?'

'It's my top band, dude – Aswad,' Ambrose replied, offended.

We heard a tent zip up, then down, as Blossom trotted over to our group, a folding chair in one hand and a picnic hamper in the other. She was wearing a flowery onesie and her lilac wellies.

'Oh, wow! Look at you all. This is just wonderful! Where will *I* sit?'

'Anywhere,' I said. She plonked herself next to Gloria, who patted her hand in welcome. I wafted my hand at the group. 'Everyone, this is Blossom.'

'This is so exciting!' she squealed. 'My name's Blossom.' *Already established!* 'Can you all tell me your names?' Everyone introduced themselves and Blossom gave each one a cheery wave. 'You know, I just love barbecues, but I haven't been to one in years. I don't really know anyone with a garden. Well, at my flat there's a communal garden but we're not allowed open fires. Not since someone set light to the wheelie bins and our whole tenement had to be evacuated. Or fouling dogs. And there's something else we're not allowed ... oh, I know! Ball games. So no football, tennis, rugby, cricket, golf, volleyball, hockey, *table* tennis, baseball, I expect ...' She nodded at Gloria and Chuck.

'Anything with a ball – we get it,' I interrupted. 'Would you like some Pimm's?'

'I'd love to! I haven't had one in years as I don't really know anyone—'

'With Pimm's?' I offered.

'Exactly right!' She opened up her picnic hamper and retrieved a bag of sweets. 'Sour Haribo, anyone?' There were shakes of the head as she gobbled down a handful. 'Oooh! *Sour!*' She scrunched up her face.

'So, Gloria, how did you enjoy your bus tour?' I asked.

'It was fabulous.' She glowed. 'We got an awesome trip through the countryside and on such a fantastic day. We didn't know there was a sun in Scat-land.'

'There isn't,' George said. 'I'm sure normal service will resume tomorrow.'

'That Abbotsford House is just terrific,' Chuck said. 'All that art and stuff. We don't have anything like that near us, do we, hon?'

'That's for sure. Although there is a Burger King castle in the next town.'

'So, this dude Sir Walter Scott,' Chuck continued. 'I've never heard of him. I didn't recognise any of the books he wrote.'

'I asked the tour guide. When I heard he'd written a book called *The Black Dwarf* I wondered if it was the same as *Red Dwarf*. We like that, Chuck, don't we?'

'And I suggested that the tour should go to famous people's houses that we have actually heard of. I told him he ought to go past Andy Murray's house.'

'But—' said Jason.

'More Pimm's, anyone?' I called out.

'There is a gorgeous garden, where he grew all his vegetables. And the inside of the house is so cool. There were turrets and statues and knights' armour and a stone fireplace even bigger than Chuck,' Gloria continued. 'You must have loved it, Jason, with you being an interior designer and all.' He raised his glass. 'I just couldn't work out where he bought all that stuff. I mean before they had Amazon. And it's such a shame he never got to go *up* the actual Scott Monument.'

'That must be *amazing*, being an interior designer.' Blossom turned to Jason. 'I'd love a job like that, making everyone's house so magical. I bet your home is really arty.'

'I live in a small flat so there's not much opportunity to do all that I'd like to do.'

'And it's all white,' George added.

'Och, I'm sure it's more than alright. I bet it's *wonderful*.'

'Burgers are ready!' Gil announced. That woke Berta up.

'Now, we have the rolls and all the condiments over here.' I pointed to Mavis's laden trolley. I fetched a roll for Mavis as Gil tossed in a burger. 'Cheese?' I asked. She gave me the thumbs-up. 'There you go.' I handed her the burger in a napkin. As everyone helped themselves to a burger Gil tipped a load of sausages on to the griddle.

As Blossom sat down, she announced, 'I'd like to say grace before we eat, if you don't mind.'

George and Jason lowered their buns in respectful silence. Berta spat out the mouthful she'd already taken.

'God is great, God is good. Let us thank Him for our food. By his hands we all are fed. Thank you for our daily bread. Amen.'

'Not exactly the Selkirk Grace,' George noted, taking a huge bite. 'And what's your work, Blossom?'

'Did I tell you I've been working in an old people's care home? Anyway, I've been working in a care home and nearly everyone drives to work. I don't drive because it seems so strict – all those rules and regulations. So no one is allowed to drink. I don't mean at work – of course we're not allowed to drink *at* work. That would be a terrible idea. Can you imagine? We'd be dropping residents all over the place! So even after work there's no point suggesting we go out for a drink or a bite to eat – and I like, for example, scampi. Well, no one ever wants to go out because they all drive.'

I topped up her glass, hoping she couldn't drink and talk at the same time.

'So, do you like your work, Blossom?' Gloria asked. *Bloody hell, don't encourage her!*

'Why, yes, Ma'am, I do indeedy,' Blossom chortled, going for a Texan accent. 'I've worked with older people my whole life. I just love them – don't you? I mean, they have so many enriched memories. It's really something I feel so *passionate* about – helping other people. I just *love* helping people. It's my "thing". You know, sometimes at work I see an elderly gentleman and I just want to hold him. Like my beating heart is close to his beating heart. It almost *breaks* my heart. It's just a pity the whole incident with Mr Grosvenor—'

'Sausage, anyone?' Gil asked.

We all leapt in with a chorus of, 'Yes, please!' which was Scottish for, 'Shut the fuck up.'

We scrabbled out of our chairs to fill the hotdog rolls, squirting lines of yellow mustard and red ketchup. Anything to distract Blossom from her over-sharing.

'Hey, boys – come grab a sausage,' Chuck shouted. But by then the lads had found suitable sticks and were dangling marshmallows in the embers, laughing and burning their mouths on the flaming sugar.

'Anyone want to play a game?' Blossom giggled, the Pimm's kicking in.

'Not really,' Jason murmured.

'I *love* games!' Blossom beamed. 'What's your favourite game, Sunny?'

'Er, strip poker,' I proposed.

She tutted. 'I meant a family game, silly. Like "I Spy" or "Who Am I?"'

'I hate I Spy,' George frowned. 'It reminds me of the hours spent driving from Bonnyrigg to Wales in the back of a Ford Focus with my two wee sisters, one of whom used to throw up the minute we passed Scotch Corner.'

'I spy with my little eye something beginning with V,' Berta slurred.

'Vodka?' I suggested.

'Thank you very much. I'll have a double!'

'Has anyone ever played that game where one of you has to—?'

'*Shit!*' I exclaimed. Immediately behind the Berlin Wall I spied with my little eye scores of lights. 'Sorry, folks, but I think we're being filmed.'

'What?' Chuck demanded, following my gaze. 'What the hell?' He stood up, prepared for battle. All along the hay bales were pinpricks of light, which I assumed to be mobile phones held while recording our gathering.

'Right,' I fumed, storming across the field. With every step I took, the number of dotted lights reduced. By the time I reached the hay bales the OOOWU contingency had scattered into the dark. I hissed like a snake, 'Stay away from us! *I mean it!*'

On my return, Gil was packing away the barbecue and Berta was attempting to wheel Mavis home, for some reason pulling the chair backwards. Ambrose threw water over the fire, and Chuck and Gloria were herding the twins back to their tent. I'd allowed them to take responsibility for the kittens' shoebox. Larry kept trampling over the box and it was only a matter of time before he crushed either Bugs or Bunny underhoof.

'Show's over,' I said to a bewildered Blossom.
'Was it something I said?' she asked, worried.
'Actually, no. It wasn't anything you said.'

Chapter 16

Breakfast time had become a scramble – not of eggs, but of bleary-eyed bodies bumping around the kitchen table as coffee and toast were shared out. Mavis tapped her knife against her plate.

'Okay, people, we need to keep focused on the work plan. Tam's picking me up shortly, so someone will need to take a turn of shower duty. Berta?'

'Does that mean I'm exempt from painting?'

'Naturally,' Mavis agreed.

'*Yes!*' Berta raised a celebratory fist.

'I'm still on laundry all day,' Archie spoke out.

'Starchy Archie!' Gil jested, punching him in the arm.

'How come you're here so early, anyway?' I enquired. 'It's not a breakfast club.'

Archie looked down at his feet. 'I never went home.'

'What?' demanded Gil. 'Your mum will be worried sick about you.'

'Nah – I told her I was staying at a pal's for a while. She didn't even notice I'd gone.'

'But where did you sleep last night?'

'I found this old truck down the bottom of the drive. I think it's been abandoned. Anyway, I brought my duvet and it's quite cosy in there.'

'Clyde's truck?' Mavis said in surprise.

'Dunno, Missus. There are cars parked all the way along the grass verge from here nearly to the village,' Archie said. 'But that was the only one open.'

'Gil, did you leave it open?'

Gil shrugged. 'Well, it's not going anywhere, is it?'

'Also, we need to decide what to do with all this money,' I said, opening the cash-stuffed drawer.

'*That's* not very secure,' Romilly remarked. 'Especially with all these Voodoo people around.'

'OOOWU,' Gil corrected. *Bless you!*

'Anyway, lady,' Ambrose frowned, 'Voodoo is my brothers' way for summoning the god from our hearts.' He patted his chest. 'The spirits can bring protection, like, and bring love.'

Romilly held up her hands. 'Well, sorry if it's only me who has concerns about the number of strangers wandering around the grounds.'

Gil took her hand. 'You're quite right, Rom. We do need to be more careful.'

'Might need a different kind of protection,' Berta sniggered.

'So, any ideas for how we use the money?' Mavis continued.

'Well, Clyde lives for the TV,' I said. 'Why don't we buy him one of those big flat-screen TVs for the living room? He'd love that for when he comes home from hospital, especially if he can't get out as much.'

'That's a super idea,' Mavis nodded. 'So, Gil, are you able to carry on with decorating the living room?'

'Sure.'

'I could take a stroll into the village, like, and get online to order one,' Ambrose offered.

'Hmm, your history with going online has led us to the chaos we have now,' I grumbled.

'Fair play, Miss. But I's good with knowing a bargain, like. I done my homework for knowing who's the best.'

'*Did!*' Mavis exclaimed.

I knew he was right. Expecting someone like me to procure an appropriate TV would be like asking Romilly to write a dissertation on the Scottish Professional Football League. I sighed. 'What does anyone else think?'

'As long as you stick to our budget,' Gil said. 'And don't go ordering some high-whizz technical sound system or games console.'

'No, man – I promise. Just a TV, right?'

I cringed as Chuck's notable knock reverberated at the door. I absolutely could not face the prospect of doing anything more energetic than lifting a mug of coffee. In fact, if I could have paid a servant to do this for me, I'd have been in heaven. Chuck had a perplexed expression as he waved a sheet of paper under my nose.

'How can I help you, Chuck?' I asked, bracing myself for the day's torment.

'So today Gloria tells me this was *her* choice.' He scratched his head. 'I guess I was getting a little too carried away with all the hills and rivers and walking and suchlike. She's more in mind of always trying to better herself. Between you and me, yesterday's history lesson was her idea.' He harrumphed. 'Anyway, it says here something about a creative writing class.'

'Really?' I perked up. As in *poetry*? 'Hang on a moment.' I returned to the kitchen, where Gil and Romilly were getting it on at the kitchen sink – she with rubber gloves on and her hands in soapy water. 'Romilly.' I smiled sweetly. 'How do you feel about sharing your extensive wisdom and creativity regarding poetry?'

'Well, I consider it a vital element of my art. Educating people about the meritoriousness of versification and rhythmical composition is key to enlightenment.'

'That's what I thought,' I said. 'So you won't mind taking a poetry class this morning?'

'With whom? Marge and Homer?'

'If you're referring to Gloria and Chuck, then yes – for a start. Probably Blossom. Maybe even George and Jason could be persuaded.'

'Hmm, they're not exactly Rosencrantz and Guildenstern.'

'And you're not exactly Shakespeare.'

She exhaled. 'I really have much better things to do with my time.'

'What about the key to enlightenment?'

'Well, for some people you're better to leave the door locked.'

'Good. I'll take that as a yes. It's still dry out there, so I'll get them to gather round the firepit.' She flounced out of the kitchen, throwing the rubber gloves on to the floor.

As I made my way round to the field, three vehicles crept up the bumpy drive. We'd allowed the campers to unload their equipment in front of the cottage but then asked them to park somewhere back along the road. I didn't even bother to ask this lot which side of the wanker/camper site they were looking for, just took their cash and directed them round the back. Of course, the fact they each wore T-shirts emblazoned with Gil's face was a bit of a clue. One tubster with a square head and buzz cut was sporting an XXL T-shirt. Gil's unbecoming face was stretched to its limit, which could provide a sobering prompt to stay off the doughnuts.

I found Blossom, clad in a cerise leotard, lying on her back on a towel in front of her tent. She was attempting to use her hands and feet to push her body off the ground. At least that's what it looked like. She could have been trying to screw a ghost for all I knew. I bent my head down.

'Morning, Blossom.' Her eyes flicked to the side and she gasped in effort, finally relenting and crashing back down on to the towel.

'I just love my morning yoga!' She sat up, cross-legged.

Okay, if you say so. No sign of Patrick Swayze, then. 'I've come to ask if you'd like to participate in a poetry class this morning. We are so blessed with having a poet-in-residence this year at Camp Crackers.'

'Oh, yes, please!' she beamed, sweeping her blonde hair off her shoulders. 'I would find that *so* rewarding. I definitely feel like I have something inside me that needs to get drawn out.' I winced. Nothing that a nimble-fingered doctor couldn't help with.

'So they'll be gathering by the firepit.'

'Fabulous. I'll just have some ginger tea to clean out my bowels.'

'Blossom!'

'By the way, I love that outfit you're wearing.'

'These are the same clothes I had on yesterday.'

George was drinking his coffee and holding a slice of bread over the camping stove with a toasting fork. 'There's nothing quite like it,' he declared.

'I can't disagree there, George. So, this morning we're hosting a poetry session.'

'Oh, aye?'

'Our poet-in-residence is going to share her creativity.'

'Is that the one that swans around like she's got a quill up her arse?'

'That's the one,' I nodded.

'Oh, this should be hilarious.' George whisked the toast on to a plastic plate.

'So you'll be there? You and Jason?'

'Wouldn't miss it for the world.' He winked.

I crossed the field to find the Grizzlies perched at their table under the awning. In the centre was a plate piled high with pancakes, surrounded by bacon, fruit and maple syrup.

'Morning!' I said, my mouth watering. 'So we're on for the poetry class today – over by the firepit. We're delighted to announce that our poet-in-residence will be hosting a session today.'

'Honestly?' Chuck groaned. 'I kind of thought we were pushing the boat out a bit with that one.'

'Oh, no. Here at Camp Crackers we aim to meet all your needs, including promoting your free expression.'

'How exciting!' Gloria said, licking her fingers. 'I find being here amongst so much history really invigorating.'

'You could have fooled me, honey,' Chuck moaned. 'Last night you were snoring like a dragon.'

'So – over by the firepit!' I said, ducking back to the cottage. There, I'd done my bit. Romilly couldn't accuse me of not bigging her up.

On my return, I couldn't help but notice the silver 'communication platform' had extended up and round the side of the hill like a lustrous crust. I was sure it wouldn't be long before some irate member of the local council protested about destruction of the native habitat. Would it not come under Prince Charles's very definition of a monstrous carbuncle? And surely, by touting a landing pad that could be seen from orbit, there was a risk of a

Boeing 737 landing in Bonchester?

I found Archie on the front lawn attempting to teach the twins how to play football. It didn't go down well that one of them picked up the ball and ran with it. As I approached, Archie jogged over. 'Hey, Miss! Is it okay if we all go back to that place I took you with the raspberries? I've got some boxes and I reckon we can sell them over at the detention centre for a quid each.'

'Detention centre?'

'That place over there with all the nerdys.'

'You mean convention?'

'Dunno, Miss.'

'Anyway, it's not up to me whether the boys go with you. You need to check with their parents.'

'Oh.'

The one that had scarpered with the ball lumbered over. 'Archie says we're not allowed to pick up the ball. Why not?'

'Because it's dirty,' I said. 'Now skedaddle.' I spotted the surprised face of one of the kittens popping out from his hoodie – this time snuggling in his actual hood.

I passed Ambrose in the shower – at least I assumed those were his pyjamas in a crumpled pile beside the phone booth. 'Hey, Berta, get some heat on, will you?' he shouted.

I made myself a milky coffee and counted out the site money. The cheques were no good to us until Clyde came home, but I counted out £980. Hubba hubba! That would get him up close and personal with Harry Kane. Maybe we could even buy him a new recliner chair and beer table – he was going nowhere else once he got home.

I kept the back door open for shoppers but had remarkably

few customers. I was congratulating myself on my exceptional delegation when a head appeared at the open door. A beanie-covered head followed by a skinny body dressed in a limp white T-shirt and frayed jeans. He had damp patches under his arms and a scrawny face flecked with reddish stubble. It wasn't clear whether he was attempting a beard but I wouldn't have put money on him passing for Gandalf in the next decade. He jerked his head in acknowledgement. 'Have you got any eggs?'

'We do indeed,' I answered, reluctant to part with the comfort of my chair.

'Have you got organic or farm-reared or barn eggs?' he challenged, hands deep in his pockets.

'I've got eggs in a box.'

'Alright,' he nodded. 'How much is that?'

'Two pounds, please.'

'What? That's robbery!'

'Very possibly. But I've got eggs and you want eggs – so what are we to do?'

His eyes scanned the kitchen, focusing on the door to the hall. He hesitated.

'So?'

He slapped two coins on the table. I picked up the eggs.

'Anything else?'

'Er ...' he muttered, feet shuffling.

'Please tell me you're not looking for condoms.' Although Berta probably had a box stashed in her rucksack. 'We're not *that* kind of shop.'

He turned crimson. 'No! I was just going to say ... er ... do you work here?'

Aw! He was trying to chat me up. *Bless!*

'Kind of,' I breezed. *Leave them wanting more.*

'So you know Gil?'

'What about Gil? Yes, I know Gil. Do I know that he still sleeps with a battered Eeyore? Yes, I do. Am I aware that Gil believed the tooth fairy used his old teeth to build false teeth? Yes, I am. Did Gil throw a mega-tantrum aged six when we attended a wedding at Cramond Kirk as he thought Mother had said we were visiting *Captain* Kirk? Yes, he did. So, yes, I know *a bit* about Gil.'

'Then you must be Sandy?'

'Sunny.' I sighed, still holding the eggbox.

'Gil's sister, right?'

My grip tightened and my eyes narrowed. He reached for the box but I was still clinging on.

'I mean,' he stammered, 'nice to meet you.'

I relaxed my grip.

'Is there any chance he might come over and speak to us?'

I gave the box an air-hockey shove across the table and he blocked it with both hands. 'No,' I said. 'Now scramble!'

He scarpered out of the door just as Gil appeared, paintbrush in hand. 'Did I hear you say Captain Kirk?' he asked.

I had no further visitors to the camp shop. Perhaps Gil's Brigade had got themselves organised and dropped by the cash and carry. What did I care? I was gutted that Gil was hard at work painting the living room or I'd have snapped on Clyde's ancient TV set and tuned into *This Morning.* I was fair missing my morning rendezvous with Phillip and Holly. How else would I find out which high-street bikini would make the other sun-loving globetrotters mistake me for Emily Blunt?

So, more out of boredom than anything else, I wandered past

Romilly's poetry class. I pretended to be raking over the ashes from last night's bonfire and tidying up the area.

'Come and join us if you want,' Romilly invited. She was delighting in having a captive audience. Chuck, Gloria, George, Jason and Blossom sat in a semicircle in front of her. Larry hovered with one ear cocked, listening out for an offer of lush treats. 'We're almost finished,' she crowed. 'Everyone is going to share their wonderful piece of creativity.' Fair enough. Let's see what they've learnt from the Meister.

'Who wants to go first?' Her fixed grin slipped as the scrubby grass suddenly held a fascination for each pupil. 'Anyone? Come on,' she encouraged. 'You've been working away for at least half an hour.'

Blossom coughed. 'I suppose I don't mind reading mine out,' she offered.

'Splendid!' Romilly clapped her hands in anticipation.

Blossom fingered her paper, nerves kicking in. 'I loved your poetry class!' she gushed. 'I just hope I've done you justice.'

Romilly waved her on, her eyes shut as she prepared to listen.

'My poem is called "In This Wild Field",' Blossom murmured. She took a deep breath and focused on her words.

My life is blessed,
I dream of sharing.
I cannot rest,
I must be caring.

I want to roam
But wonder why
I'm all alone
Beneath the sky.

CAMP CRACKERS

I said I'd wait,
I will not yield,
By this old gate,
In this wild field

To make me whole,
My person kind,
My thoughtful soul
Our hearts to bind.

To share my life,
Rain for my sun,
Be someone's wife,
Be someone's fun.

No, I won't move,
I will not drift,
I need to prove
He will exist.

In this wild field,
By this old gate,
I will not yield,
He'll be my mate.

In this wild field,
By this old gate,
Our fate is sealed,
I said I'd wait.

There was a stunned silence. No one uttered a sound. A gust of wind blew a tuft of heather past our feet. Romilly said quietly, 'Blossom, that was just *beautiful*.'

Blossom wiped a tear from her eye. 'I knew I had something I needed to say.' She hugged a surprised Larry, burying her face in his thick wool.

Romilly gathered herself together and applauded as we joined in with vigour. 'Now, can anyone follow that?'

'Not me!' George shook his head.

'I wish I could,' Gloria said, squeezing Blossom's hand.

'What about you, Chuck?' Romilly insisted. 'Let's hear from one of you menfolk.'

Chuck shrugged. 'Oh, man, I'm really not cut out for this fancy stuff.'

Romilly gave him a winning smile. 'We're amongst friends here, Chuck. Blossom was so very generous in opening up her heart to us. The least we can do is share another personal journey.'

'I guess,' he relented. Romilly sat back once more and closed her eyes.

Chuck cleared his throat. 'Okay, here goes.'

There was a wise Texan named Chuck,
Who camped near the broken-down truck,
He pitched in a field,
At the campfire he kneeled,
And shouted, 'God help me I'm stuck!'

'I told you I wasn't no poet!' he blustered as George rolled off his chair in silent mirth.

'Oh, Chuck, Rabbie Burns will be smiling down on you!'

Romilly clapped lightly. 'Even so, we must acknowledge Chuck's bravery in speaking out. Now does anyone else want to share his or her morning's learning? No? Well, I myself have found this session absolutely uplifting and know that in each and every one of you there is a laureate straining to get out.' More stifled giggling from George. She continued, undeterred. 'Now, I'm heading into Hawick this afternoon, so if you like, I'd be more than happy to get your poems laminated and perhaps we can display them for the other campers to admire.'

'What about putting them up in the outside toilet?' George suggested.

'Good idea,' Chuck said, poker-faced. 'It would be a great chance to ponder while we—'

'Oh, I don't think so!' Romilly cried. 'I was thinking more about mounting them near the back door for people to peruse at their leisure.'

'That's what I said!' Chuck objected. 'To poop at their leisure.'

In a fluster, Romilly gathered up her paper and pens and snatched the poems back from the group. 'Well, if you aren't going to take this seriously ...' She flounced off.

Chapter 17

My attention was distracted by a shout from Ambrose, who, like Chicken Licken, was jabbing his finger up at the sky. A black helium-filled blimp bobbed towards the grey clouds as it tugged against its leash. It had a white 'OOOWU' daubed on the side and looked like a floating killer whale. This wasn't simply nonsense, it was positively surreal. Just when I thought the scenario couldn't possibly get any more bizarre, the wind blew the giant balloon and it rotated slowly, revealing a planet-sized photo of Gil's face. If any poor child in Bonchester had nightmares about being watched by an almighty being, he or she would be sleeping with their eyes open tonight. I stared in disbelief as the summit-busters whooped with joy. When they came up with the name 'out of our world' I wondered whether they had actually meant 'out of our minds'. This was a crusade gone Camp Crackers whacko!

'Just ignore them,' George advised, placing a restraining hand on my shoulder. 'We know they're mad. Just leave them to it.' The sensible part of my brain knew he was right, but the majority wanted to blast their side of the field with napalm.

'Hey, guys, we're walking into the village for lunch,' Gloria announced. 'Anyone is welcome to join us. We're going to round up the boys on our way.'

'Oh, that's so kind of you!' Blossom beamed. 'I'd *love* to. I'll just get my purse and poncho.'

'Any chance someone can borrow me a tenner?' Ambrose pleaded.

'Of course, sweetie!' said Blossom. 'I wouldn't see a fellow camper starve.'

'Nice one.' He grinned, pulling his hat over his ears.

George and Jason made polite excuses and headed back to their tent, leaving me seething on the spot.

I spent most of the afternoon in grumpy solitude stirring my coffee first one way, then the other. By the time Berta sauntered in I was almost stir-crazy.

'What's up?' she asked, flopping on to a chair and kicking off her trainers. 'I swear that bloody village moves further away every time I walk it. And it's started raining again.'

'How did you manage to sneak out of the compound?'

'Well, I spent hours turning that bloody tap off and on. I'm surprised my hand hasn't fallen off. I came looking for you but you were raking out the firepit or something. Jesus, Sunny, you've turned into a right little homemaker.'

'And what have *you* been up to?'

'Och, I went looking for Jamie but he couldn't leave his site – he was meant to be carving up some fusty old trees but a local twat had parked their car underneath them so he had to wait. I popped into the Horse and Hound for a quick pint. No law against that, is there?'

'Thought it was full of old men?'

'Was a bit, but then they started up a pub quiz and I got quite into it. Did you know that the only mammal that can't jump is an elephant?'

'Really? You don't exactly see many sumo skipping competitions.'

'What's up with you, Crabby Cathy?' Berta jibed, pouring herself a coffee.

'Did you see that frigging massive balloon floating over the hill?' I demanded.

'Sorry, are we still talking sumos? You've lost me.'

'The bloody geeks! Didn't you spot their latest tribute to Gil?'

'Oh – the hot air thingy? You know *your* problem?'

'What?' I scowled.

'You're not getting it.'

'And *you* are?'

'Might be!' She grinned. 'Why don't you ask Mathew to come down for a couple of days?'

'I've already tried that, but he's not taking the hint. Anyway, I'd be asking him to come down here and sleep where, exactly? I think we've already exceeded the weight limit in the bunk beds. And then what? Get up and shower in a phone booth followed by a candlelit dinner of roast falafel turds with six randoms?'

'I'm not a random!'

I sighed. 'I know you're right. The sooner we get this house finished the better. I just can't wait to get back into my own bed and shower without the possibility of a rain storm or passing pigeon crap.'

'I'm with you there, pal. When we get back let's head straight to Willie's, then go up town and get pissed.'

We clunked our mugs together as Blossom burst through the door, swathed in a wet cagoule. 'Ah, there you are, Sunny!' she gasped as though I had been missing in action for the last six months.

'How can I help you?' I hoped she wasn't about to demand

anything more energetic than a thumbs-up. She unzipped her jacket and flipped down her hood.

'It's Ambrose.'

'What about him? Is he stinking up the field again?'

'Oh, no! You're on the wrong track there, although I do believe he has a rather relaxed approach to personal hygiene. No, he's been telling me all about his astonishing and *actual* journey to discover his father. Such a sad story. When he was telling me how he was brought up I nearly dissolved into my scampi – which, by the way, was *delish*!' She shuffled her chair closer to us and lowered her voice. 'Thing is, you two and I know he's never going to afford to pay for a flight to the Caribbean.'

'Wouldn't have thought so,' I concurred.

'He doesn't even have enough money for a razor,' she continued. 'Although he made up some excuse about it being against his religion.' She took a deep breath. 'Anyway, on our way back I had this *amazing* idea. Why don't we do a fundraiser for Ambrose? You know, like an appeal? They're always doing those charity things on the telly and he is a bit like one of those … you know?'

'Lazy bastards?'

'I meant asylum-seeker people. He is in truth displaced and should be repatriated to St Martin.'

'Hmm, I'm not sure we could class him as a charity cause,' I said.

'Lost cause, more like,' Berta muttered.

'Oh, but he is,' Blossom insisted. 'At my work we do fundraisers all the time and for a lot less deserving people than dear Ambrose.' *Dear* Ambrose? 'One year we raised five hundred pounds just so the care home manager could get a garden makeover as she'd hurt her back and the garden getting overgrown was compounding her stress. I made flipping hundreds of cupcakes for her bake sale and she didn't even say thank you. In fact, she resigned a few weeks after that and even had the cheek to send us the bill for her bush-trimming.'

'What did you have in mind?'

'Well, I think she had allowed it to grow over into her neighbour's territory, so had to do something PDQ.'

'I meant about Ambrose?'

'Oh, that! So one of my cousins on my mother's side, Hammy, owns that Cine-Me. Have you seen it? It's absolutely super! He can set up a movie theatre wherever you want. So one year we raised money by showing *Grease* at the local high school and everyone paid for a ticket. He does me one free event each year and I haven't claimed one for this year yet. If I could get him to come down here and show a film, we could charge people ten pounds each – maybe throw in a glass of wine or beer and some crisps. What do you think?' She looked at us both expectantly. Berta shrugged, making a 'Don't ask me' face.

'But who would come?' I asked.

'The weirdos behind the hay wall, of course! There are tons of them and if we show a geeky film,' she snorted, 'we could make enough money for Ambrose's flight.'

'I'm not sure that's a good idea. They're a pretty freaky bunch. In any case, I've been telling them to keep away from us and now you're asking me to schmooze with them?'

'If you can get Gil to go, you'll have to hold back the rush,' said Berta. 'So why shouldn't we take advantage of their fanaticism?'

'I suppose we *could* exploit their ridiculous fixation,' I mused. 'I bet Gil wouldn't need much persuasion to put in a royal appearance. In fact, I'm surprised it hasn't occurred to him before now that he could be making money out of them. Not like him to pass up a business opportunity.'

'So is that a yes?' Blossom held her breath.

'If you can be bothered organising it,' I agreed.

'*Fabby!*' She hugged me tightly in a sweet-smelling frothy embrace.

As Blossom was leaving the kitchen Romilly arrived, dripping wet and laden with brown paper bags stuffed with fruit and veg. At least I presumed the leafy sprouts protruding from the top were not concealing chicken wings.

'How *are* you, Blossom?' she enquired with a patronising smile. 'Many participants find my soul-searching poetry classes pierce their very innermost spirit.'

Blossom nodded eagerly. 'Funny you should mention that – I *have* had a burning in my chest since lunchtime, but I put it down to being heavy-handed with the tartar. Right, I best be away – calls to make, films to organise!' She winked as she skipped off.

'You know, I *try* to elevate the creative mind but there is just no helping some people.' Romilly rolled her eyes and began unpacking her groceries under Berta's scrutiny.

'Just looking at all that fibre makes my bowels recoil. Think I'll have a lie-down before dinner. Unless you think I ought to contribute in some way?' Berta asked without enthusiasm.

'Oh, well, you could core and slice the savoy.'

'Actually, I've just remembered I need to ... er ... trim my toenails. They're really giving me gyp.'

'Sunny, what about you? How do you feel about tackling the vegetables?'

'I'm fine about it,' I answered, reaching for the campsite log. 'They don't scare me in the least. In fact I get great satisfaction from demanding their money.'

I picked up the cash box, pulled on my jacket and made my way over to the dark side.

To my surprise, the chair usually occupied by an unhelpful receptionist lay vacant. There was no queue at the Portaloos. No armed guards prevented me from wandering into the belly of the canvassed convention. The place was deserted except for Larry, who looked very pleased with himself as he chewed on a length of guy rope.

I approached the largest marquee, where the flaps, generally tied back, were hanging closed. I cleared my throat. No sign of movement. 'Anyone around?' I listened outside the entrance but could hear only a distant clinking sound. Maybe they were taking a communal nap. 'Excuse me – it's Sunny here.' I pushed the tent flap aside and entered.

I found two circles of gormless geeks, one inner and one outer circle, sitting cross-legged on the groundsheet. They each had their eyes closed, frowning in deep concentration. In the centre of the inner circle, Paul Crank relaxed with a glass nestled between his crossed legs. He wore a battered cycle helmet and what looked like a pale-blue hospital gown. Every few seconds his hand rose and he tapped a spoon against the glass. He gave a low hum, to which the group responded with a longer 'mmmm'.

'Sorry to bother you,' I interrupted. Sorry *schmorry*! Several pairs of eyes sprang open, while Paul's remained locked. 'Only I've come to collect the day's site fees.' A few more individuals risked a sideways glance, but quickly resumed their sleeping faces as Paul continued with the humming. *Ting!* went the glass. *Hummm. Mmmm.*

'I'm not coming back later,' I persisted. 'I've got better things to do than stand here watching you … well, watching you do whatever it is you're doing.'

Paul's hand dropped mid-ping. He slowly opened his eyes.

'Sunny,' he growled. 'So pleased you could join us.'

'I'm not exactly *joining* you.'

'Please feel free.' He gestured to his fellow drowsy companions. 'Have a seat.'

'What are you doing?' I asked, not because I was interested but more in an effort to engage him in wallet-finding activity.

'Duncan,' Paul said in an even voice. 'What are we doing?'

'Er … we're … er,' garbled Duncan in a high-pitched yawp as all eyes flew open in his direction. 'Mr Crank is leading us in contact meditation. We're practising for this evening.'

'Ah, that explains it,' I said, tapping the cash box. 'So I've come to collect your dues.'

'Now isn't a good time,' Paul replied, stroking his glass. At least, I assumed it was his glass – it was difficult to discern from the folds of his gown. 'Duncan, tell Sunny why our meditation is so important to get right.'

'We're hoping to unite our hearts and send a healing light around the planet to enfold all of humanity in grace and peace,' he squawked, reading my glare.

'And I need a piece of your cash.'

'Patience,' Paul whispered. 'Can't you feel the golden light of our loving energy?'

'Not really,' I said, checking my watch as though I had an extremely important business meeting to attend.

'Well, maybe you should come back tonight when we will be practising our meditation outdoors – won't we, Duncan?'

'Yes, sir.'

'Explain why,' he encouraged.

Duncan coughed. 'We're going to use this same energy to create a wave into space, reaching out in the spirit of brotherhood to connect with those ET civilisations our group chooses to invite in for communications.'

'Yeah, that's what I thought,' I nodded. 'Did I mention we charge double for having overnight guests? Look,' I said, stepping into the circle, drawing a collective gasp from the group. I remained rooted to the spot as an eerie silence followed. Duncan gulped. I dared not move. For all I knew my action would spark a mob mentality, the set stampeding me like a herd of infiltrated cows.

The seconds ticked by. Finally the hand rose to the glass. *Ting!* The group released its breath, and shoulders relaxed. I eased into reverse. 'I think we agreed that you'd pay five pounds per head per night as a simpler way to cover your site fees. So – ' I totted up the greasy heads – 'that's two hundred and sixty-five pounds, by my calculation. Actually, it's really quite handy having you all together like this – makes it much easier to work out what's owed.'

'Duncan, fetch the cheque, please,' Paul instructed. 'But Sunny, I must object to your timing. We would appreciate not being interrupted again. It's practically impossible for me to arouse my karma once disturbed.' *I bet it is, especially sitting on solid ground.*

I whipped the cheque from Duncan's trembling fingers. 'Till tomorrow, then!' I chirped, wondering if I ought to report the Crank for cult grooming. Mind you, what else would these losers be doing on a Monday evening that could be more stimulating than humming to the sick beat of a cracked tumbler?

I found Gil in the bathroom, using a scrubbing brush to remove splatters of paint from his hands. I perched on the edge of the bath. 'You know, your loony pals have just taken one step closer to a galaxy far, far away.'

'They're not my pals.'

'Only because I won't let you play with them.'

'What have they done now?'

'Aside from floating an airship with your mug on it for all the Scottish Borders to gawp at?'

'Eh?'

'And now they're running some kind of Hare Krishna outer-space meditation crap.'

'Sunny, you're not making any sense.'

'*I'm* not making sense? They're the ones who are chanting and pinging and praying for some ET visitor.'

Gil dried his hands and pushed past me. 'Just leave them alone. They're not doing any harm, are they?'

'They smell pretty offensive.'

'Then stay away from them.'

'*Someone* needs to collect their money. I wouldn't trust Berta with a fiver and *you* couldn't step beyond the first hay bale. You *have* seen *The Wicker Man*?'

'Och, you're just exaggerating as usual. That's the end of it. Now, I'm getting a cold beer. And don't go into the living room. The paint's still wet and I don't want you bumbling around making a mess of it.'

'*As if.*'

Chapter 18

Ambrose shovelled in the cauliflower and fennel bake as though it was, well, as though it wasn't cauliflower and fennel bake. I wished I knew his secret. Despite being starving I couldn't quite reconcile myself with the chunky casserole. I never thought I'd fantasise about a cheeseburger or hotdog but I'd made a pact with my stomach that as soon as the bus pulled into St Andrew's Square, I'd walk – nay, *sprint* – to the nearest McDonald's.

'So I hear Blossom's got you down as a charity case,' Berta remarked, tucking into her cheese on toast. I eyed her plate with envy, wishing I had the courage to offend Romilly so blatantly.

'Yeah, it's well cool, innit?' He grinned. 'I'll be limboing my ways over before the end of summer, I reckon.'

'The end of summer?' Romilly moaned. 'Please do let me know when summer has started.'

'We used to get lovely long summers at Bletchley,' Mavis reminisced. 'Course, we never got much chance to enjoy it, what with the bombing and all. The huts used to get so hot; one year, when the captain had to go to London for a pow-wow, we spent the entire week working in our underwear.'

'I'm surprised anyone got any work done at all,' said Gil.

'Oh, I'm not talking about the kind of underwear you girls go jaunting around in nowadays! You see more cloth in a pair of laces than you do on a bikini now. No, in my day underwear started at your neck and went down to your knees. Why does the sauce taste of liquorice?'

'That's the fennel, Mavis,' Romilly said. 'Fennel is an excellent source of vitamin C, iron, calcium and pantothenic acid.'

'Huh?' I said. 'What's that when it's at home?'

'Pantothenic acid? It's one of our essential elements for building protein.'

'Really? I'm not quite sure how I've managed without it all these years.'

'Maybe that's why you've got a flabby—'

'Flabby what?' I demanded.

'Anyway,' Gil interrupted. 'How did you get on with ordering the TV, Ambrose?'

'Well sound.' He nodded. 'Actually, surround sound.' He smiled at his own joke. 'I went for an ultra-cool flat-screen LG TV. Man, I wish I had a bedroom wall.'

'Excellent,' said Gil. 'Then that's the living room all finished. When's it getting delivered?'

'I do believe it will be tomorrow, my good friend.'

'Clyde will be made up!' Mavis smiled. 'He used to curse his old TV, especially when the screen had that black line down the middle.'

'How's he getting on?' I asked.

'I met his doctor this afternoon and apparently he's making excellent progress,' said Mavis. 'Considering it's only been a week. He's getting really fed up with the food – says it's worse than school dinners. He told me they tried to serve him mince cooked in water, then he found out later it was actually minestrone soup!'

'How's his walking?'

'Not too bad. He's on a Zimmer frame. But if I know my Clyde, he'll be just desperate to come home and have a whisky.'

'Do you think he'll be pleased with the decorating?' I asked. 'After all, that's the main reason we're here.'

'He'll be delighted,' Mavis nodded. 'It'll be like one of those makeover programmes, you know? We'll tell him to close his eyes and when he opens them he'll start crying with joy.' Or not, as I thought of his yellow submarine bedroom.

We had progressed to tea, coffee and I'd like to say chocolate biscuits, but apparently such indulgence wasn't to feature in Romilly's menu, as she handed around a packet of nuts and raisins. *Bloody hell – what I'd give for a Mars Bar! Even a fun-sized one.*

We heard a knock at the door and Blossom poked her head in. 'Am I interrupting?' I spied a duty-free-sized bar of Toblerone in one hand.

'Not at all! Come in; have a seat!' I jumped up. 'Would you like a coffee?'

'Oh, yes, please. That'll be quicker than me waiting for my wee camping kettle to boil.'

'Is that for us?' I asked rather too eagerly.

'Of course!' Blossom laid the bar on the table and four pairs of hands made a grab for it. Berta, victorious, broke off two triangles and passed one to Ambrose.

'Yum!' he beamed. 'Sugar is good for the soul.'

Mavis took a piece and began sawing it with a knife.

'I expect you're wondering why I'm calling at this late hour,' said Blossom. We shook our heads. Nope. If someone had wanted to break in at midnight we wouldn't have had so much as a smidgen of objection. Not while said interloper was the bearer of chocolate, never mind nougat. Romilly's abandoned bag of nuts fell to the floor and Larry began crunching in delight.

'I'm just giving you a wee update on the fundraiser.' She grinned at Ambrose, whose cheek looked strangely extended. 'My cousin Hammy,' she began. *Wasn't that a film starring Joe Pesci?* 'He's come through for me. I knew he would. Well, I hoped he would, but sometimes you never know.' She waggled her hand backwards and forwards. 'To be honest, he's got a bit of a drink habit and now and then he goes AWOL. There's been more than one Christmas that the mountain rescue team has had to bring him down from some precipice when he's taken off with a rucksack filled with Jack Daniel's.'

'Jack Daniel's what?' Mavis enquired.

'His bourbon, Mavis, that's what,' Berta said.

'So Hammy will drive across from Ecclefechan whenever we need him. Sooner rather than later, as he's heading off to Skegness for a week in a borrowed motor home.'

'Why is he called Hammy?' I asked.

Blossom pondered the question. 'You know I really have no idea. I used to think it was because he loved ham as a kid. He was certainly always eating ham. But then again, who doesn't love ham?'

'Me, for a start!' protested Romilly.

'Ah, but that's because you're a vegetarian, isn't it, Romilly? Not because you don't like the *taste* of ham.' Who could argue with that logic?

'Anyways,' she said, standing up, 'I'll pop over tomorrow and we can clarify the ins and outs. Thanks for the coffee – it was lovely!'

'Are you leaving?' I asked, meaning, *Please don't take away my Toblerone.*

'I'm having an early night tonight, because I thought I'd try my frog pose as the sun comes up. It's my way of commemorating the beginning of the pastoral summer season.'

'Of course,' I said, one eye still on the chocolate.

'By the way, have you seen what's going on at the other side of the field?'

'No.'

'There's a big circle of light on the hill.'

I sighed. 'They said something about meditating and making contact with some guests they've invited over.'

'It's just that at first I thought I could see torches, but I think they might actually be using, like, proper *fire* torches. At my work we'd never be allowed to parade around like that unless we'd done a full health and safety risk assessment. Especially with all that hay and stuff.'

'I'm not going back out there,' I objected. 'Surely the rain will drive them under cover?'

'I expect so,' agreed Blossom. 'Thought it was my citizenly responsibility to report it. Still, we don't want to upset them – not if we're going to fleece them, eh?' She winked and turned to go, shrugging in bemusement as the chocolate had mysteriously vanished from the table.

Chapter 19

Archie appeared the next morning wearing a black bin liner. 'Still raining, then?' Berta observed as he pulled it over his head.

'Yeah,' he muttered. 'Not sure how I'm meant to get all that laundry done when it's pissing down.' He made a cup of tea and pinched a piece of toast from Berta's plate.

'Oy! Cheeky!' She made a swipe at his retreating rear.

I checked my watch. 'Gil and Romilly are late this morning.'

'Maybe they're having a wee extracurricular social?' Berta suggested. 'Gil McIntosh: Undercover Lover?'

'Please, I'm trying to eat.'

'Oh, no,' Mavis piped up. 'They were up and out hours ago. Gilbert said he needed some plumbing fixtures, so they caught the early bus. Since he discovered that DIY manual he's been zapping everything with his drill. He mentioned something about fancying a bash at re-enamelling the bath. He's such a helpful young man to have about the house.'

'Is he?' I said. 'Can't say I've noticed.'

When Chuck's familiar knock came at the door my heart sank. I opened it, mug in hand.

'Morning, Chuck!'

'Hey there, Sunny. Fine day for the ducks,' he chortled. The water ran down his plastic poncho, pooling at his boots. 'I have an apology to make.'

'It's not the outside toilet again, is it? Only Gil's just left for the morning.'

'Oh, no.' He shook his head. 'Although, if truth be told, he might as well leave the plunger out there. No, it's just that we know we have an activity booked for today. The animal husbandry class. But, well, George and Jason are travelling into Hawick today to visit the glassblowing centre. When Gloria heard about it she just about went nuts! She *loves* all that arty-crafty stuff – particularly glassware. Could fill a room with it. Anyway, I feel real bad cancelling at the last minute, but I hope you're okay with that.'

I pursed my lips. 'Well, if you're sure …'

'Perhaps we can do it another time?'

'Possibly,' I nodded.

'Oh, and I hope you don't mind me asking another favour.'

'Uh-huh?'

He removed a box from under the poncho, where Bugs and Bunny were tightly curled into a sleeping furry ball. 'Would you mind keeping an eye on these little fellas today? The boys would use these as an excuse to get out of anything but Gloria is determined they're coming with us. She promised them they'd get a shot at glassblowing too. Do you think they'll get the chance?'

'Sure!' I gave a thumbs-up. Why wouldn't a couple of ten-year-old lads be let loose with a bucket of molten glass and a blowpipe?

I carried the box into the kitchen and placed it on Archie's lap. 'Congratulations, Daddy.'

'Cool.' He smiled, stroking their furry noses. 'I'll take them with me.'

I began clearing the table and was wiping the crumbs on to the floor when Blossom arrived. 'Yoo-hoo!' she called, opening the door. She removed her lilac wellies and hung up her cagoule.

'Nearly done,' I said. 'Make yourself a coffee.'

'You know, I think I will. I couldn't be bothered fetching clean water and I've no milk so I just had handfuls of dry cereal for breakfast. Oh, I love your hair like that!'

'Like what?' Was she being funny? I checked out my reflection in the kettle but all I could see was a blurry orange mass.

'You're so natural with your curls.'

'I have curly hair.'

'But the colour is so vibrant!'

'Yes, I have ginger curly hair. Sorry, I'm not sure what's to love about it.'

Blossom wagged her finger at me. 'You need to love yourself before you can expect anyone else to love you.'

'Says who?'

'Oh, it's well documented.' She nodded, stirring her coffee. *Did she just add* three *sweeteners?* 'Mmm-hmm. Yes sir-ree. Metaphysically you attract people similar to yourself.' *Really? Mathew wasn't ginger last time I checked.* She was on a roll. 'You know, Sunny, we each have a unique belief system and we need to search the world for romantic compatibility. That's why I've been single for so long. I'm still wandering this planet in search of the ideal partner who is tuned to the same wavelength as me.'

Not just because you never let anyone get a word in, then?

'Right.' I made another cup of coffee and sat down at the table.

'Sorry – I could have made you one too.' She slapped her own wrist. 'Selfish Blossom!'

Berta sashayed into the kitchen wearing a scarlet dress and full make-up, her bag slung over her shoulder and jacket in hand.

'Oh, I love your outfit!' Blossom squealed. I rolled my eyes. It was going to be a *long* cup of coffee.

'Where are you off to?' I demanded.

'Jamie's going to pick me up. Think we're heading into Melrose.'

'Thanks for telling me.'

'I *am* telling you.'

'So you're away for the whole day?'

'Might be. It's my day off.'

'How romantic.' Blossom sighed. 'Is he handsome?'

'Er ... he's a bloke with a borrowed car,' Berta replied, adjusting her dress.

'Are you in love?'

Berta scrunched up her face. 'No offence, Blossom, but I'm not fourteen. We'll grab a pub lunch; have a few pints, a few laughs. If he's lucky I might let him park in a lay-by. Put it this way, I won't be coming back engaged.'

'Ah – shame. He sounds nice.'

Berta grinned at me over Blossom's head and teetered out of the door. *Yes, she's for real*, I thought.

'So, I've made a list,' Blossom began. 'At work I was always making lists. I was the Social Convener, the Fire Marshal, Continence Facilitator *and* the Health and Safety Lead. Oh, and the Hand Hygiene Champion! Gosh, come to think of it, no wonder I was always writing lists.'

'What's on your list?' I asked, hoping that being kidnapped by pirates was somewhere near the top.

'I love that you're so direct! You'd never get in trouble at work for dilly-dallying, would you? What is your job, Sunny? No – wait!' she cried. 'Let me guess. I'm a bit of a Psychic Sally, actually.' She closed her eyes and thought for a moment. 'Beauty therapist?'

I guffawed. 'Do you really think I'd choose to have a face like this if I was a beauty therapist? It wouldn't be much of an advert for the customers, would it?'

'Oh, but I was coming from the point of view of *"the cobbler's bairns are the worst shod"*.'

'Cheers, Blossom. Who needs friends, eh?'

She blushed, gasping. 'I didn't mean to be rude! Let me try again.' Once more she closed her eyes tightly in concentration. 'Are you a cook?'

'Based on what? My *cordon bleu* hospitality?'

'Based on you seem to like food?' she suggested meekly.

'You know what, I've had enough of this nonsense! Read out your flipping list.'

'You're right. Let's crack on, as the hen said to the cock! Now, I've done a few of these fundraisers before and I know that Hammy will bring everything he needs. He has an inflatable screen, which is wowza. He brings the projector, the generator, sound system, all that jazz. Not that I'm suggesting that's what we show, of course!' She chortled. 'We can pick any film – and he has *tons*. It's a bit like when you get the karaoke book, you know? He has everything you can imagine. So I'm not worried about that side of things.' She pretended to wipe her forehead. 'But we will need a venue and also catering. Now that I know you're not a cook, maybe we just go for wine, beer and nibbles – food, that is. I can't bear people that chew their fingernails!'

'Yeah. I've been thinking about where we can host it and I thought maybe we could pop round to speak to Mr Struthers. He owns the farm behind and has loads of space.'

'Good-oh,' Blossom said, writing it down. 'How are you spelling Struthers? Is it like "others" but with an S?'

'It's whatever you want it to be,' I said.

'Now, in my experience, people like to get top-ups of wine and beer.'

'*Away!*' I said. 'Who'd have thought?'

'I know.' She giggled. 'Apparently there's a cash and carry in Chesters, so maybe one of us could take a taxi there and stock up. Perhaps we could also pick up some nuts and crisps while we're at it.'

'Sure.'

'Now, in terms of tickets, I would normally charge ten pounds a head. That way they get a film, a drink or two and some snacks.'

'Hey, Blossom, if you can deliver that for a tenner, I think you'll be on to a winner.'

'How many Christians do you think will come?'

'Sorry?'

'You know – from the Scripture Union camp.'

'What makes you think they're Christians?'

'Oh, it was just something you said about them not having a prayer of getting near Gil. I suppose I just assumed they were the praying type. Plus, they do behave as though they are on some type of pilgrimage. What's with all the meditation malarkey? I popped my head into their big marquee yesterday to see if anyone wanted to join me for a cuppa and they definitely looked like they were in some kind of spiritual nucleus.'

'They're more into sci-fi than God, I believe.'

'Oh? Not so much waiting for the return of Jesus to Earth as the Return of the Jedi?'

'Something like that.'

'Then that's just great. Let's hook them in with one of their favourites, shall we? *Star Trek? Star Wars? Blade Runner? Alien?*'

'Any of those will get them salivating.'

'Rightio,' she nodded.

Ambrose appeared at the door and she covered the list with her hand as though he were about to cheat at an exam. 'Morning, ladies.' He bowed, his Rasta bonnet almost touching the floor. 'I done all my duties, so I'm here to wait for the TV delivery man.'

'Excellent,' I said. 'Help yourself to breakfast but don't make a mess in the living room – Gil will go mad. And keep your feet off the furniture.'

'My days! I'm not an animal,' he complained. 'You're worse than my mum.'

'You better believe it!' I said. 'Now, we're off to the farm, so you might need to cover the shop too.'

'Oh, man!'

I poked him in his skinny chest. 'And *do not* let anyone go wandering around the house, understand?'

'Yes, Miss HY.'

'What did Ambrose mean by that?' Blossom asked as we trudged through the mud towards the farm.

'Oh, he has some notion that I held a high-ranking position in Berlin during the forties.'

'Then he's about as good at guessing careers as me!'

Mr Struthers had lived alone at the farm for as long as I could remember – ever since inheriting the farm from his father. Seemingly he had two brothers, but the elder married a pushy Fifer who'd made a fortune in Highland toffee and they had retired to Guernsey, hopefully with their teeth intact. The younger brother developed a wheat allergy early in life and was sent packing to the Royal Navy. So poor old Mr Struthers was left to run the farm largely on his own. However, I do remember having a fearful crush on Billy, one of his occasional farmhands. I followed moody dark-haired, dungareed Billy around for years until he eventually left to start up his own jacuzzi business. At the time – aged about eleven – I was devastated that he never even gave me so much as a fleeting glance. Years later I was comforted by the sight of him in Galashiels, standing outside Aldi, hand in hand with a clown. And I don't mean to be rude about his partner's competencies. No – the guy was fully kitted out in white jumpsuit, frizzy blue wig and squeezable red nose. Despite Billy replacing the dungarees with a three-piece pinstriped suit, he didn't look any less ridiculous.

'Sunny?'

'Sorry, I was miles away.' *I wish.*

'I was just asking what kind of farm this is.'

'Eh? How should I know? Mr Struthers is either on a tractor or a combine harvester or he's sitting in his kitchen drinking whisky.'

'So that makes him an arable farmer, then.' She smiled knowledgeably.

'Does it?'

We approached the farmhouse, which was in a worse state of repair than Clyde's had been prior to Gil's sensible investment in an electric drill. I knocked on the door, half expecting that we'd have to go traipsing around the fields in search of Farmer Struthers, but was surprised to hear a voice shout, '*What now?*'

I pushed open the unlocked door and we wiped our feet on the mud-caked doormat, stepping over a pair of abandoned wellies. Mr Struthers – a wild-haired, wild-eyed, creased man of seventy-plus – was slouched at the kitchen table drinking what smelt suspiciously like Famous Grouse from a cracked mug. On the scarred wooden table half a tractor engine tilted to one side, oil dripping from the internal mechanics on to the floor. He waved us in.

'Who are you pair of lovelies?' he asked, wiping his mouth on a grubby sleeve.

'It's me – Sunny,' I said, risking a step closer. 'Clyde's niece from Crackers Cottage.'

I waited patiently during the inevitable pause while the cogs turned and finally slumped into place. 'Sunny? You mean *Gil's sister*?' he asked in a puzzled voice.

'Yes,' I grumped, telling myself that we needed a favour or I might have been tempted to rearrange his tractor parts.

'You're *Gil's sister*?' Blossom repeated with incredulity. *Now her I could take down with one punch.*

'Yes,' I glowered. 'Why the big surprise?'

'Well,' she faltered. 'He's so ...'

'Uh-huh?'

'And you're so ...'

'Shall we leave it at that, Blossom?'

She nodded with fervour.

'Don't just stand around, then,' Mr Struthers blustered. 'Have a seat, why don't you?'

We perched side by side, facing him over the dismantled machine.

'Can I offer you ladies some refreshment?' he asked, waggling an almost-empty bottle in our faces. I surmised that he was permanently refreshed.

'No, I'm fine.'

'Me too,' Blossom nodded.

Mr Struthers inhaled a deep breath and gave a toothless

smile. 'Which one of you lassies smells like a fresh punnet of strawberries?'

I shrugged as Blossom blushed. 'I do love my matching shower gel and shampoo!' There were two words alien to the Struthers vocabulary.

'Anyway,' I said, before he started sniffing her like a dog, 'we were wondering if we could ask you a favour.'

'What's that, then?'

'Well, we're planning a bit of a fundraiser and we wondered if you minded us borrowing one of your barns.'

'What's that, then?' he asked again.

'A barn?'

'No – a whatsit fun-thingy.'

'A fundraiser? Well, we have a young chap staying at our campsite.'

'A what site?'

'Oh, yes, you're probably wondering why there are so many tents up in Clyde's field.'

'I don't give a stuff what he has up where.'

'Well, he decided to make a bit of extra cash by using his spare field as a campsite.'

'Did he now? The wily old fox!' He took a generous slug from his mug. 'Not that clever, though. I heard old Clyde got pushed down the stairs by his— Hang on a damned minute! Was that you?'

'What? No!' I protested. 'It was an accident.'

He scowled. 'I'm only passing on what I've heard from the townies. Seems he's in hospital with a busted hip or something.'

'Anyway,' I said over-cheerfully. 'I was telling you about—'

'Some young chap?'

'That's right,' I nodded. Maybe he wasn't as daft as he looked.

'Ambrose is his name. He's trying to save up for a flight to the Caribbean so he can track down his birth father.'

'Black fella, is he?'

'Who?'

'This young Ambrose.'

'No. In fact, he's very white.'

'But he *is* a Rastafarian,' Blossom added.

'What's that, then?' Mr Struthers asked.

'Look,' I said. 'That's not really important right now.'

'Might be to me,' he mused.

'Ambrose has his Twelve Tribes of Israel Church and follows the Nazarites,' Blossom piped up. Mr Struthers shifted his gaze … I'd like to say to her face, but it was clear his eyes were focused much lower. 'A Rastafarian, eh?'

'Yes. He drinks a lot of the holy herb.'

'I bet he does! I'm a bit partial to it myself. Does he have any ganja?'

'I wouldn't know!' Blossom replied.

'So we wondered whether we could use one of your barns to show a film and charge people an entry fee,' I asked, feeling a tension headache creeping across my forehead.

'A what?'

'A film – a movie,' Blossom said. 'My cousin runs an outdoor cinema company.'

Mr Struthers scratched his white stubble. 'What people?'

'From the campsite.' I sighed. The bottle of whisky looked mighty tempting apart from the fusty crust round the glass lip.

'Would you mind us having a look at your barn?' Blossom tried.

'My what?'

'Your *barn* – somewhere we can show a film.'

213

'If you want.' He shrugged.

'Don't you want to show us it?'

'Could do, I suppose. Will there be drink?'

'What, now?' I asked.

'No – at your fun-thingy. Is it like a bouncy castle? I saw one once when the shows came to Bonchester. The kids loved it.'

'We'll be having beer and wine on the evening,' I offered. 'Of course, as host, you won't need to pay a penny.'

'I'm boracic lint,' he complained, rising from his chair.

'Ah, but that's what all farmers say!' Blossom said playfully.

'What's that, then?'

'You know – about never having any money.'

'Eh?'

'Brass lint – skint.'

'No, I mean I am boracic lint – look.' He lifted his trouser legs to reveal dirty bandages wrapped round his legs. 'I'm terrible with ulcers. You lassies can't change them, can you?'

Blossom extended herself to her full height. 'Actually, I can,' she announced with pride. 'But that's not why we're here. Don't you have a District Nurse?'

He muttered something incomprehensible.

'Shall we follow you, then?' I suggested as he shuffled towards his wellies. He thrust a brown liver-spotted hand on to each of our shoulders and balanced on one leg as he wrestled with the rubber boots. The fumes from his breath could have powered a wind turbine for at least a week. He yanked on a holey anorak and limped towards his largest barn.

Mr Struthers owned three barns: the blue one, which we were allowed to play in (fantastic opportunities to build any kind of structure using the hay bales); the green one, which was pretty much derelict as the roof sagged under the relentless Scottish weather; and the red one. We were never allowed near the red barn and I had grown up with images of it being crammed full of pumping machinery and factory-type conveyor belts whisking sacks of grain from the field to a purring lorry. As Mr Struthers unbolted the red barn door with a rusty screech, we looked into a deserted cavernous space. At one end a few pieces of ironmongery reclined against the rusted aluminium walls. To our immediate right I could see why, as children, we were banned from access as we gazed upon what I assumed to be some sort of still.

'Any good, is it?' I asked, nodding towards the dilapidated apparatus.

'What's that, then?' he grumbled. 'Not going to shop an old man, are you?'

'By the looks of it you'd do better pouring that over your leg ulcers than down your neck.' Blossom frowned.

He pondered her words. 'Hmm – that's what my doctor told me too. So do you want it or what?'

'Yes, please – this is a wonderful space!' Blossom cried. 'Thank you so much, Mr Struthers.' She went to hug him, but thought better of it.

'When's all this happening?'

'If we can get it organised, maybe tomorrow night. Would that be okay?'

'Makes no odds to me. Did you say you were showing a *film*?' His mouth was obviously catching up with his ears.

'That's right.'

'Any chance it'll be a Western?'

'More like science fiction,' said Blossom, turning in a circle.

'What's that, then?'

'You know,' I said. 'Stories set in the future. Sometimes about different worlds.'

'Sounds like a load of crap,' he muttered. 'My telly's on the blink so I could do with seeing a decent film.'

'You never know,' Blossom smiled. 'You might like it!'

He harrumphed, shoving his hands deep into his pockets. 'The last film I saw at the pictures was *The French Connection* in nineteen seventy-one. I remember seeing Gene Hackman driving a car at high speed, then next thing I knew my pal was telling me it was time to go to the pub.' He puffed as his legs buckled.

'Let's get you over to your house,' offered Blossom. She took his arm and led him back over the muddy trench, just about making it to the door before he collapsed against the stone wall. We dragged him to his chair, where he resumed his slouching position.

'How do you manage your farm?' Blossom asked, concern in her voice.

'Eh?'

'You know – keeping your farm going?'

He grunted, reaching for the bottle. 'Every morning I wake up it's actually a surprise to me. And then I think – *shite!*'

Blossom and I exchanged a look. Mine said, *Let's get out of here.* Hers said, *Aw, poor Mr Struthers.*

He laid his head on his folded arms as I nodded to the door. 'Okay, Mr Struthers – we might see you tomorrow evening, then? We'll knock on your door to let you know when the film's starting,' Blossom said in a loud voice.

His eyes were closed as we tiptoed out of his kitchen.

'Do you think he'll be alright?' Blossom fretted as we headed back to the cottage.

'Och aye – he's probably been like that for years.' *As long as he lasts until tomorrow evening we'll be cooking with gas.*

'How exciting!' Blossom squealed, checking the list gripped in her hand. 'I'm going to start designing some flyers and I'll hand them round the Choo-Choo folks. Do you mind if I sit in your kitchen? It'll be so much easier writing at the table. I love doing stuff like this. I'm actually very arty. I remember my art teacher at high school once said to me ...' *Shut up?* '... he said, "Blossom, you have more creative talent in that one plook than some people have in their entire body; you just need to learn how to squeeze it out".'

'Eugh!'

'I know, right? But he had a point. It's like with that poetry class yesterday. I have all these thoughts and feelings inside me but I just need to learn how to liberate them. Like, you know, when priests hire those people to get rid of the devil.'

'You've lost me, Blossom.' We crossed the muddy courtyard.

'Exorcists! That's what I mean. To get the stuff out of me.'

'That seems a little extreme.'

Chapter 20

We arrived back at the kitchen to hear raised voices and to find Ambrose in an altercation with a young girl. I say 'girl', but the person standing with her hands on her slim hips had a boyish figure, a plain face and cropped mousy hair. She held a razor blade above her head and I prayed she wasn't about to slit her throat as a result of the dire camping conditions.

'Give it *back*!' Ambrose insisted. I knew it didn't belong to him, so I wasn't sure why he was getting so heated.

'S'mine!' she retorted. 'Finders keepers!'

'You didn't find it and it don't count if you go stealing stuff,' he replied in desperation.

'*Ding ding!* Time out!' I said, stepping between them. 'What's going on here?' They both began shouting at the same time. 'Whoa! One at a time. Ambrose?'

Tears sprang to his eyes as he explained. 'I was just letting yo' TV man in and we was in the living room when this *thief –*' she hissed in response but he kept going – 'this thief snuck up to Gil's room and stole that razor from his washbag.'

Wishing to grant an equal opportunity for her to tell her side of the story while simultaneously wanting to slap her face, I snipped, '*So?*'

'I'm having Gil's baby,' she announced, rubbing her stomach proudly.

Now *that* I did not expect.

'Oh, how lovely!' Blossom cooed.

'*No, it's not!*' I roared. 'Why would it be? He's going out with Romilly.'

'Oh, yes, so he is. Oops!'

'What makes you so sure of that, anyway?' I demanded as the hobgoblin scowled at us.

'Gil and I are in love,' she asserted. 'I have a special relationship with him and now we're having a baby together.' *Cuckoo!* I wondered whether we ought to enclose her in a sealed box and pack her off to some institution. There was a silence as she defied us with a smug expression.

'What's with the razor blade?' Blossom queried. *Good point, well made.*

She fidgeted with the plastic. 'I sensed there may be a certain level of denial so I wanted to prove my point.'

'What, by shaving your legs?' I asked, incredulous.

'By comparing his DNA.'

'Are you saying that Gil might contest this? I thought you two were supposed to be lovebirds?'

'Gil is such a strikingly gorgeous guy. I have to accept that there are countless women gasping for his body and I might not be his single love interest.'

'Are you accusing my brother of being a whore?'

'His seeds *should* be spread far and wide,' she proclaimed. 'Think of all the wonderful little Gilberts populating the earth!'

'But in the end it comes down to maintenance payments. Is that what you're digging for?' I snarled, snatching the razor from her hand. I manhandled her out of the door with a shove. 'You and your embryo can get stuffed!' I shouted as she retreated indignantly.

'I'm so sorry, Miss!' Ambrose mumbled. 'Man, she was stronger than me.'

I filled the kettle with water. 'Don't worry about it, Ambrose. I reckon I'm getting used to the range of obsessional weirdos that Gil attracts.' He crumpled on to a chair.

'She was a scary one, though. My days!' I patted his shoulder.

'Good news, though,' Blossom said brightly. 'We've got the fundraiser organised for tomorrow evening. You'll be winging your way to the Caribbean in no time!'

Poor Ambrose looked rather shell-shocked as I pushed a mug of coffee across the table. He didn't look like he'd make it much further than the other side of his duvet.

After Blossom had busied herself in the kitchen making us a French toast lunch – she was hired! – we had cheered up somewhat. It was agreed that Blossom and Ambrose would attempt to decorate the barn (Blossom's idea) and arrange the hay bales into a temporary seating arrangement. Somewhere along the line Archie had latched on to the barn as an indoor drying arena and persuaded them to help him rig up a number of laundry ropes. I took responsibility for the cash and carry visit, not trusting Ambrose with the float and not trusting Blossom to come back with anything stronger than cherryade. We made an executive decision that Clyde wouldn't mind us dipping into his camping stash to pay for the drinks and we'd pay him back out of the ticket sales. I rang Tam, who was as disgruntled as ever at being separated from his pint, and asked him to take me to Chesters and wait while I stocked our bar. His key motivation was the promise of payment in whisky. Who said the art of bartering was lost?

Tam and I passed the return journey in frosty silence. I had made the mistake of initiating jolly conversation about life in

Bonchester but was swiftly told to shut my cakehole while he listened to the horse-racing results. I didn't even know you *could* listen to race commentary on the radio. Why would I? To be fair, we'd got off to an unhelpful start when I asked him to reverse his car up to the packing bay in order to load the two kegs of beer and two kegs of cider I'd shrewdly purchased. He verbalised something about 'not offering a frigging delivery service', his anger rising when turning up the bumpy track to the cottage with the kegs chiming together like Big Ben. I was so relieved to spot Gil up his ladder (they were now inseparable) scooping gunge from the front guttering. I wouldn't have put any money on Tam and I being able to hoist the booze out of the boot. He wasn't exactly your classic World's Strongest Man material. I had visions of Tam spending the next month cruising around the Borders with his car smelling like a brewery. Then again, maybe he'd like that.

'Jesus, Sunny, we're not hosting *Oktoberfest*!' Gil objected as he heaved the kegs out of the boot. He manoeuvred them up against the back door. 'By the time we roll these to the barn they'll be frothing like a rabid hound.'

'I couldn't risk running out of alcohol. They might turn nasty.'

He snorted. 'Yeah, and they might throw down the gauntlet and challenge you to a chess play-off.'

'Just saying,' I muttered, hoping he hadn't twigged my strategy of having at least one barrel left over for us to enjoy at our leisure, a simple perk of being on the fundraising committee. Talking of which, Blossom burst out of the cottage waving a handful of flyers.

'Finished!' she cried. 'Romilly let me loose with her felt pens and I'm really pleased with the effect. What do you think?'

What I think is that I can't remember the last time I witnessed an adult colouring a red barn filled with stick people. 'Lovely.' I smiled.

'Oh, I'm so pleased. I really hope this fundraiser goes with a bang!'

'Well, this should help.' I kicked the kegs.

'Golly! Is that full of beer?'

No, warm cocoa. I'm anticipating a barnful of insomniacs.

'Half beer and half cider.'

She frowned. 'I've never heard of that before. Is it nice? What's it called? Beerder?'

I ignored her and handed Tam his whisky. 'I'd like to say it's a pleasure doing business with you but my mother taught me never to lie,' Tam grumbled.

'Or visit a dentist,' I quipped.

'Eh?'

'Thank you!' I said.

'Shall we hand out these flyers?' Blossom suggested, hopping from foot to foot.

'Might as well,' I said. 'Let's get this over and done with.'

We picked our way over the still-soggy grass. 'Why do they bug you so much, then?' Blossom asked.

'Who?'

'Those.' She nodded towards the Glastonbury camp.

'They're just pretty relentless. The twits haven't left us alone since Gil got into a bit of bother earlier this year.' I frowned. 'They've gone from setting up the Planet Gil website to following us down here, and now – well, you saw today how unhinged some of them are.'

'But why are they so besotted with Gil?'

I sighed. 'Gil believed that he was assisting a being from another galaxy. But, hey, big surprise! He was hoodwinked. This lot are obsessed with the notion that Gil is covering something up – that he *did* have a form of encounter. Didn't you read *Being Gil's Sister*?'

'Sorry. Should I have done?'

'Part of me is reluctant to encourage them. On the other hand, if we can make an easy buck out of them and send Ambrose on his way I'll feel their painful presence has been worthwhile.'

We were halted at the entrance by the customary sap at the front desk. She made a show of leaping to her feet in an attempt to herd us out of the camp but was no match for us – particularly Blossom. Who knew what armoury she concealed beneath that poncho? In an effort at damage limitation the receptionist darted into the marquee town hall, crying out for Mr Crank. *Take us to your leader!*

I was relieved to observe Paul Crank back in his army fatigues and silver boots. His hair was drawn back in a bun. There was just no need.

'Oh, I love your boots!' Blossom enthused. I gave her a hearty dig in the ribs.

'How can I help you?' he enquired, with the least helpful expression he could muster.

Blossom flapped the flyers in his face. 'We're having a fundraiser tomorrow evening. We're showing a film up in Mr Struthers' barn behind the campsite. There'll be plenty of beer and snacks. Everyone's invited!' she announced rather too loudly. Crank winced.

'Excuse us if we seem rather preoccupied here, but we're currently in the midst of running our UFO Fieldwork Investigation course. Some of the students are actually completing their written assessment.' He indicated the far end, where an exam area had been set up with desks and chairs arranged in rows.

'Sorry,' whispered Blossom. 'What are *they* doing?' She pointed to a small group huddled in a circle. In the centre sat a lad wearing a pair of giant headphones, holding a microphone out to a plump long-haired girl perched on a chair opposite. She was wringing a damp hankie in her hands. Paul motioned for us to follow.

'You can listen in if you like,' he said in quiet tones. 'Richard here is practising for his Investigation of Witness Testimony module. It's vital that we can accurately record and interpret a witness's statement. You wouldn't believe the number of nutjobs we encounter.'

'Really? I am surprised.'

'We find role play is an effective approach to developing the appropriate skill set. In any case, we have so few witnesses we can call upon.' Bloody hell – no wonder Britain gets a reputation for eccentrics.

'So perhaps you can tell me a little more about what happened after the being put his tendrils round your neck?' the lad asked, checking his script. The girl began wailing as though Paul Crank represented the entire Academy Award committee.

'He tried … he tried … to … strangle me!' she bawled. Several members of the circle collapsed in tears.

'Come on.' I tugged Blossom away. 'I think we're intruding on something very personal.' Or a lot of bollocks.

'Ooh! What are *they* up to?' Blossom trotted over to another group. Four students, their faces covered by paper masks, were crouched over a table. Each held a small trowel and appeared to be raking through a shallow box of brown soil. As we neared, I could smell why they had their noses covered. '*Eugh!* What is *that?*'

Paul gave the question consideration as though Blossom were prompting the most searching debate. 'A key aspect of the Field Investigation training is the analysis of the surrounding soil and the identification of any abnormal deposits. It is essential the students learn to distinguish local soil and geology from something alien to the area.'

'So you've got them raking through a pile of shit?' I said.

Paul shrugged. 'You never know what material you might have to sift through. It's not always pleasant.'

Blossom pinched her nose. 'And what is that group up to?' We wandered over to another batch of scholars who were crowded around a long table. Paul tapped one on the shoulder and he moved aside to let us through. On the counter lay a skinny, hairless male wearing nothing but a pair of bleached Y-fronts. His eyes were closed and he remained motionless. What appeared to be a pathologist clothed in a set of blue surgical scrubs, facemask and clear goggles hovered over his midriff, scalpel in hand.

'Oh, my God!' screamed Blossom. The surgeon jolted sideways, almost taking out an observer. 'You've killed someone!'

Paul ushered us away from the production. 'Don't be ridiculous,' he snapped. 'We're merely replicating a post-mortem to help the students understand the difference between us and other life forms.'

'A difference like having a brain or not?' I said. 'Come on, Blossom. Let's get out of here before one of us ends up as liver casserole.'

'Yes, I think it would be wise if you left now,' Paul agreed coldly.

'But we need to sell some tickets,' objected Blossom. 'I'm not leaving until we find out how many tickets they want to buy.' Unyielding, she held up the flyers.

I sighed. 'Okay, Mr Crank, the tickets are ten pounds each. For that you will receive an evening's entertainment – a sci-fi film on a decent-sized cinema screen, beer or cider and a choice of snacks.'

He frowned. 'And for what are you fundraising, may I ask?'

'It's a really good cause,' said Blossom. 'We've stumbled on a young man who has sadly become separated from his natural heritage and we're aiming to reunite him with his long-lost father. It's desperately tragic.'

'Hmm, that's not exactly a principle close to my heart. But I can't speak for everyone, so what I'll do is mention it at this evening's after-dinner notices.'

His enthusiasm would hardly have sparked a petrol-doused firework factory. I sensed Blossom's shoulders slump as she let the flyers fall to the ground. We made a reluctant move towards the exit as the rumble of activity returned to normal.

'Unless ...' I began.

Paul raised his eyebrows in question.

'Gilbert.'

'*Gilbert?*' he repeated sharply. A hush fell across the entire tent. I nodded.

'What about him?' Paul probed.

'You can have three questions.'

A look of disbelief flashed across his beardy face.

'Yes,' I announced in a loud voice for all to hear. 'Anyone who buys a ticket for tomorrow's fundraiser will have the opportunity *as a group* to put three – and only three – questions to Gil McIntosh.' The marquee erupted in exhilarated commotion. Even Paul wore a thrilled grin as he hushed the crowd.

'Are you being serious?'

'Yep,' I nodded. 'After the film is finished you can put your questions to Gil. So how many people want a ticket?' Each and every clammy hand shot in the air.

'Oh, how marvellous!' Blossom grinned, clapping in excitement.

'Tell you what, Mr Crank,' I said. 'You drum up their ticket money and we'll pop by after your dinner to collect it.'

'Sure.' He nodded. I could see his mind revving up for overdrive.

Chapter 21

'You did *what*?' Gil raged. 'You've set me up to be slaughtered!'

'Now, now, dear brother, don't exaggerate.'

He gesticulated with the TV remote control as though brandishing a weapon; no doubt one he'd love to turn on me.

'They could ask me anything and when I don't know the answer I'll look a complete idiot.'

'Let's put some perspective on this,' I said. 'All they really want to know is whether you've had an extraterrestrial encounter.'

'And when I say no – what then? Have you seen what an angry mob can do to someone like me? They'll tear me apart!'

'Come off it. Most of them would have trouble tearing open a bag of ready salted.'

'Nuts?' asked Romilly, entering the living room.

'Yes, she is!' Gil declared. 'Barmy.'

'Oh, dear. Do I detect trouble in the McIntosh family?' she smirked. Gil continued to snatch at the cables and sockets attached to the supersonic TV.

'Trouble?' I laughed. 'You've obviously never witnessed Gil in a mood. This is Gil with a wee bee in his bonnet. Just you wait until you experience what happens when you let a hornet in.'

Furious, Gil shook the control at me again.

'Well, I think my work here is done.' I sidled back to the kitchen.

I systematically opened each cupboard in search of a chocolate biscuit to go with my coffee but was faced with one insulting bag of dried fruit after the other. I didn't know that such a thing as dried cranberries or pear existed. Bloody hell, if Romilly tucked into these and washed them down with a pint of water, surely she'd balloon like a walrus?

My choco-radar led me out to the field. The Grizzlies had returned from their glassblowing adventure with George and Jason and were gathered under Chuck's awning gripping plastic mugs of tea.

'Are you looking for decent dunking material?' George asked, holding out a packet of chocolate digestives.

'You're a lifesaver!' I grinned, taking three and slumping on to the groundsheet.

'Oh, Sunny, we had the most fabulous day out at the glassblowing centre today. The crystal was just *gorgeous*. I bought my mom the most delightful little vase. Well, you call it a "varse", I know.'

'And those craftsmen!' Chuck whistled. 'Oh, boy, can they blow!'

'You should have seen them when both the operatives were making a matching pair of goblets – ain't that right, George?' Gloria said. 'They were such geniuses.'

'Gen*ii*,' George corrected.

'You are what?' asked Gloria, confused. 'Anyway, I'm *Gloria*.'

'And it was all going so well.' George smiled. 'Until one of the blowers decided the best way to engage with the twins was to let them have a go.'

'Now don't you go blaming Jayden or Jordan for that,' Chuck warned. 'The boys were just doing as instructed.'

'And who knew they possessed such lung capacity?' George sniggered.

An uncomfortable silence followed. 'What am I missing?' I asked.

'You should ask the glassblower,' George said, no longer able to contain his laughter.

'What?'

'Oh, phooey!' Gloria frowned. 'Little Jordan couldn't help it. When the guy said "start blowing" he obviously meant "take it easy".'

'Yeah,' George chortled. 'How was he supposed to know that Jordan is pea-shooting champion in his class!'

'I still blame the centre,' Gloria sniffed. 'No way should they have had that valuable display right next to the demonstration area. It's not our fault they were showcasing such a brittle display.'

'Honey, it was made of *glass*,' Chuck reminded her. 'What did you think was going to happen when Jordan fired off a bauble like a baseball?'

'Anyways, they soon got it tidied up,' Gloria concluded. 'And the boys had fun. So?'

'So we're banned for life,' Chuck sighed.

'That's no biggy,' dismissed Gloria. 'When are we ever gonna be back in Har-wick?'

'Uh-oh!' Chuck said in a jokey voice. 'Don't look now.'

'*Hiya!*' Blossom cried, bounding into our circle. 'Oh, I love your jumpsuit, Gloria! What colour would you say that is?'

'Blue?' Gloria offered.

'It matches your eyes!'

'But my eyes are brown.'

'Are they? Oh, well! Listen, have you heard about the fundraiser we're having tomorrow night?' She handed her flyers to George and Jason. 'Are you lovely boys coming to the movies?'

George read the flyer. 'Beer or cider. Why, yes! I do believe we'll be there.'

'Fabby!'

'Gloria?'

'Most definitely, Ma'am. The boys will just be over the moon. Imagine – a movie in a barn. Wonder what they're showing?'

'*Chicken Run?*' George suggested.

'*Barn of the Dead?*' Jason threw in.

'Ooh! I know!' Blossom squealed. '*No Poultry For Old Men.*'

'Sunny, what do you think?'

'Hmm, what about *Slumpig Millionaire*? Chuck?'

'Er, man. Okay, what about *The Maize Runner*?'

'Good one!' George chortled. 'Gloria?'

'I'm no good at these things. Let me think. Alrighty – how about *Citizen Corn*? Or *Singin' in the Barn*?'

'Here's one for you,' said Chuck. '*Pork By Porkwest* – get it?' He fell about laughing. 'Or *Harry Trotter*?'

Ambrose appeared, yawning, with hands in pockets. 'Hey, dudes, why the jollies?'

'I'm so sorry – did we wake you?' I said sarcastically.

'Long day, sister. All them hay bales to shift.'

'Fabulous!' Blossom smiled. 'Do we have a movie theatre?'

'It's well cool,' Ambrose nodded, his hat wavering like a stripy blancmange.

I spied Berta in the distance clambering out of a taxi backwards. 'Right, folks, see you later. Thanks for the biccies!'

I followed Berta as she blundered into the kitchen, collapsing on to the nearest chair, which was unfortunate, as someone had carelessly left a box of eggs on the seat. Might have been me. 'What the hell?' Berta exclaimed as yolk ran down the chair legs. Larry was quick to lap it up.

'How did you get on, then?' I asked, trying not to sound like a pint of John Smith's.

'What a laugh, Sunny. You should have been there!' She grinned.

'I don't actually remember being invited.'

'No? Ah, well. You missed a great day. I got picked up by Jamie this morning and we had lunch at some country inn he knows – all Barbour and Hunter wellies. But then he had to go and collect some gadget to do with a band he plays in – a wah pedal or something. So, then Andy pitches up and he was out for a bit of a session. We played this brilliant drinking game,' she slurred. 'Hell, I'm starving. When's dinner?'

'I thought you had a pub lunch?'

'S'was ages ago. Anyway, I didn't want to look like a greedy cow so I only ordered a tuna wrap. What's Rom-Com cooking this evening?'

'She mentioned something about making stuffed marrows.'

'Stuffed with what? Please tell me lasagna.'

'What was the game?'

'You'd love it, Sunny! Any time one of you hesitates, like says, "er" or "um", you have to drink a shot. The trick is to throw in random questions that you wouldn't expect, like, "What's your favourite Christmas song?" or "Which would you rather eat – the exact same meal every day for the rest of your life or only food you hate?". What a hoot! Honestly, I lost count of the shots he made me down.'

'Sounds hilarious. So what's the score? Are you dating them *both*?'

'God, you're so uptight these days, Sunny. *Chill!* I'm just having fun.'

'So I see.'

'And when did you become head teacher?'

'When bloody Clyde abandoned us!'

'Then why did you push him over, dafty? Anyway, I'm knackered. I'm going for a lie-down. Give me a shout when dinner's ready but don't bother if it's cack.'

'Charming,' I muttered. As it was, I didn't bother waking her and she slept through till morning, blissfully unaware of the vegfest we endured.

I shuddered awake on Wednesday morning with Berta's snores reverberating through the bunk-bed frame. I had no sympathy for her missed meal. I suspected she was hoarding a supply of sausage-based products in her rucksack, as she'd been discovered wolfing down Scotch eggs while the rest of us housemates were wrestling with celery and beetroot tapas.

I pulled the duvet over my head and stuck my fingers in my ears. What a bloody awful summer this had been. Apart from the dreadful but entirely predictable weather, I'd sell Blossom for body parts in exchange for a night in my own bed. And when had I become a raging carnivore? Probably the moment Romilly enforced butternut squash as a core ingredient. Was she not aware that as a population we were not genetically designed to digest fibre? Had it not occurred to her that our national diet comprised food best supped by spoon? Haggis, mince, stovies, porridge, Scotch broth. Bloody hell – had Scotland never heard of knives and forks (or mastication for that matter)? We were only just allowing such fanciful terms as *tortellini* and *tikka masala* to creep into our conversations. *Amuse bouche* and *cavolo nero* were just taking the piss. And, according to Lorraine Kelly, the latest culinary delight was eating insects. Jesus, we had container ships of midges. Who needed to fund free school dinners when there were bucketfuls of biting insects to be had? I could feel my irritability flashing like nettle rash and almost relished the prospect of someone daring to push my button.

'Fancy bringing me breakfast in bed?' Berta yawned.

I raised my feet and gave her a swift boot up the jacksie.

'Hey! Bucking broncos! I was only asking.' She sniffed. 'Actually, I think that has helped my back. It's been doing something weird for the last few days. I think I might have put something out.'

'Yes – me!' I grumbled.

'Enjoying your holiday yet?' she sniggered. 'I haven't seen you write any postcards to poor Mathew, who's slaving away at home earning a living.'

'He'd most likely look at it and wonder who sent it. "Sunny? Who's that?" The chances are he's bloody engaged to someone by now.'

'It's only been ten days. It took him ten *years* to ask you out. He's not exactly going to spring a surprise on anyone. His idea of foreplay is to draw up a project plan with six-month milestones aiming to realise benefits over the oncoming decade.'

'Yeah, I suppose you're right. Being stuck in the middle of nowhere is not good for paranoia.'

'Saying that, he must be missing you *and* Gil. Who knows what loneliness does to a man?' I kicked the mattress again.

'Come on, let's get up.'

Gil's anxiety about the upcoming 'interview' (although three questions would hardly make him the victim of radical interrogation) had put him into a drilling frenzy. Sagging curtain rails, wobbly door handles, creaky hinges – nothing was safe from his cordless wonder. Romilly followed two paces behind, carrying his toolbox like a bride's posy, ever eager to supply a Rawlplug or tapered shank. Concealed in the kitchen, I could hear him stalk from room to room, the telltale vibration emanating through the stone walls.

'He's so obliging, Gilbert,' Mavis smiled, sipping her morning tea.

I snorted something.

'How you ended up so different, I can't imagine.'

'Thanks, Mavis.'

'I only meant … by the way, Bugs and Bunny appear to have taken up residency in my bedroom.'

'I thought Archie had taken control?'

'Oh, well, the lad is providing a relentless laundry service to the wankers.'

'Mavis!'

'That's what *you* call them,' she accused. 'Anyway, I'm not very happy about them putting unnecessary pressure on dear Gil. He is meant to be on holiday, after all. Let's hope the DIY jobs are almost finished. I rang the hospital this morning and Clyde is threatening to self-discharge if they don't let him out soon.'

'But what about the stairs?'

'Says he's going to go up and down them on his bottom. Mind you, I believe he's done *that* more than once following a session! He's going to be so pleased with all the decorating and Gil's repairs and the new TV.'

'Where are you off to now?' I demanded as Berta tried to sneak out of the back door.

'I'm not needed, am I?' she asked, slinging on her jacket. 'Ooh, it's freezing out there. No danger of skin cancer today.'

'But we're setting up the fundraiser.'

'I'll be back ages before that. Anyway, here's Blossom. You surely don't need both of us. I'll only get in the way.'

'The way of what? We're working in a barn – it's hardly the control room in a submarine.'

'Can I bring a date?'

'As long as he pays.'

'Want me to get one for you too?'

'Why? Are you off to a Tinder sale?'

'That's the last thing you should be bringing to a hay barn,' Mavis admonished. 'The whole thing will go up like the Great Fire of London.'

I nodded. 'Like I said – *Wicker Man*.'

'Want a date, Mavis?' offered Berta.

'No, thanks, love, I've had some of Romilly's sultanas. I can't risk a roughage overdose.'

'Morning!' Blossom bumbled past Berta. 'I love your hair like that.'

'Thanks. I love your … well, I'll see you all later!'

'Hammy's here,' Blossom announced. 'He left super early as he likes to make sure everything is set up before he goes fishing.'

'Fishing?'

'Yes, he's a proper angler dangler! He's very excited about what he's going to pull out of the Rule.'

'Into shopping trolleys, is he?'

'How long does he take to go fishing?' asked Mavis. 'Won't he be away for hours?'

'Probably,' said Blossom. 'It's a bit of a ritual. He uses it as a way to calm himself down before each performance.'

'He does know he's not playing Caesar's Palace tonight?' I said.

'Oh, Hammy takes his voluntary work *very* seriously. Everything has to go like clockswork.'

'You mean clockwork,' Mavis corrected.

Blossom frowned. 'Like clocks work – you know. Tickety-boo!'

Mavis stood up with a sigh, wheeling her trolley out of the kitchen. The little black ears of Bugs and Bunny poked up from their box on an open-top bus tour.

'Right, well, I better get my fleece on, then,' I said. 'Can't be doing keeping a man away from his carp.' I followed Blossom round to the field as we went in search of Ambrose. 'Knock knock!' I shouted outside his tent.

'Oh, *man.*' We heard him rustling around beneath the canvas.

'There are two gorgeous ladies waiting to escort you on the beginning of your epic journey!' Blossom grinned.

'Steady! Nothing like overselling a product,' I muttered.

'I ain't had no breakfast yet.'

'Come on, Ambrose. Hammy needs you to help set up.'

He waited for us to leave. Finally the zip slid down and he crawled on to the grass. 'But I'm so weak. I needs my yum yums.'

'You need a kick up the arse!' I said. 'Look, if you get started I'll bring you some coffee and toast.'

'Promise? I don't usually get dressed for anything less than a cup of ganja.'

Blossom dragged him up by his pyjama sleeve. 'You'll need something warmer than that, Ambrose.'

He scrabbled around inside and returned wearing a faded hoodie and boots. We each took a skinny arm and frogmarched him towards Mr Struthers' farm. A beaten-up Transit van, which I took to be Hammy's wheels, was parked outside the red barn. Blossom knocked on the driver's window and the door popped open. Hammy flopped out of his seat and stretched. He must have been at least six foot four, with long sandy hair and beard. He was built like a wrestler and covered in tattoos from his neck to the tips of his fingers. In fact, with his greenish hue I was reminded of the Incredible Hulk. He wore a large set of headphones and bobbed his head in time to a rocking beat. Blossom hugged him round his expansive girth (possibly related to his affinity for ham), the top of her head barely reaching his chest. 'Morning, Hammy!' He merely nodded.

'This is Sunny and Ambrose.'

Again with the silent nods. 'Doesn't he talk?' I asked.

'Not really,' Blossom acknowledged.

'*Can* he talk?'

'Oh, yes. He just likes to get on with things. He's got a heart of gold.'

Just as well – he had the body of an oak and the conversation of a wall. He ambled round to the back of the van and began hoisting out the equipment. He handed a coil of cables to Ambrose, whose legs buckled as he dragged it towards the barn. 'Coffee?' he whined.

'I might see if Mr Struthers has any coffee I can nab – it'll be nearer,' I said.

'Rightio,' Blossom nodded, lifting out a folding chair in an effort to assist.

Knocking on the closed front door brought no response. I pumped the handle and the hinges protested with an obstinate creak. 'Hello?' I called. Mr Struthers was sleeping with his head on the kitchen table nestled against the engine. 'Mr Struthers?' He gave a cantankerous snort.

'Who's that?' he muttered with his head down and eyes still closed.

'It's me, Mr Struthers.' I thought I'd save him the rigmarole. 'Gil's sister, Sunny.'

'*Who?*'

'Sunny,' I repeated.

'Sunny? You mean Gil's sister?'

'Yes.' I cursed under my breath.

'Well, why didn't you say so,' he moaned.

'I did!' I snapped. Two can play at grumpy.

He looked up. 'Alright, keep your ginger hair on!' He chuckled to himself. 'What do you want?' He tried to unfurl his bent torso.

'I'm just letting you know we're setting up in the barn.'

'What barn? Setting up what?'

'Remember yesterday we were here and you said we could use your barn to show a film this evening.'

'Don't think so.'

'Yes, you did,' I insisted. I folded my arms as he screwed his face up in concentration.

'Nope, I didn't. I think I'd remember if I had.'

'But you did.'

'Are you calling me a liar?' He attempted to stand but began a coughing fit, culminating in his spitting into a nearby mug.

I attempted an alternative tack. 'I wondered if you had any coffee.'

'Oh, yes, please.' He nodded. 'Milk and two sugars.' I scanned the dirt-ingrained worktops and the sink piled with greasy crockery. A dented kettle stood in the corner, its flex exposed near the plug. I carried it over to the taps. They appeared to be smeared with something brown. I convinced myself it had to be freshly dug earth from the fields. *Yeah, right.* As the kettle boiled I located the fridge, which had a large rusted strip down its front. I cracked it open an inch and four bluebottles flew out like World War Two bombers in formation.

'You know what, Mr Struthers? I don't think I'll—' I turned round but his head was back on the table as he dreamt of brand-new combine harvesters.

By the time I'd delivered three mugs of coffee and several rounds of toast to the barn, I needed to get back to the kitchen to man the shop. McKay's Foodstore had been transporting regular supplies to us via the post van, which was doing its rounds anyway. Adding bacon, eggs, bread and milk to the letters and parcels didn't seem to faze the postie in the least. His obliging nature bloomed when rewarded with hot coffee and Lorne sausage rolls. Like all of us, he had observed the gradual expansion of the OOOWU convention from one insignificant tent and flagpole to a sprawling canvas borough including the silver lining of the hill and the quivering blimp. He shook his head in disbelief, muttering something along the lines of 'Bonchester never having seen the like'. We were the talk of the village. I knew it was only a matter of time before some officious health and safety bureaucrat shut us down. And I couldn't bloody wait. The sooner Paul Crank and the Crankettes were told to pack up their gig and move on, the better. Once we'd raised Ambrose's airfare I thought we'd breathe a sigh of relief.

I spotted Hammy's van bumping off down the track and assumed he was on his way to a riverbank nearby. I closed up the shop and checked out the cine-barn.

'Hey, Sunny! What do you think?' Blossom beamed. She

twirled in a circle as though on stage.

'Impressive,' I nodded. A huge inflatable screen stood against one wall, held in place by guy ropes. Ambrose had manhandled the bales of hay to form lines of seats, imaginatively cordoned off with strands of fairy lights. Blossom's handiwork from the previous day included bespoke bunting strung across the bar area – constructed from yet more hay bales. Who'd have imagined that blocks of cow feed had so many diverse applications? The beer and cider kegs were installed next to columns of plastic cups. Above the drinks, Blossom had painted a banner declaring GRAND SHOW FOR AMBROSE!!! which kind of worked. The boxes of crisps from the cash and carry were stacked behind the bar. A cable ran from a generator outside to the projector inside. It genuinely felt like we were standing in a movie theatre. One that inherently smelt like shite, but who was complaining?

'Hammy can work his magic anywhere,' Blossom said, thrilled with the effect.

'Where's Ambrose?'

'He was *exhausted*. I think he's gone for a snooze.'

'Never!'

'I'm so pleased we've managed to get everything ready for this evening,' Blossom said, slouching on a nearby seat. 'I feel a bit dodgy myself.' She rubbed her stomach under her poncho. 'Think I'm having *women's* troubles. It might just be my time of the month, but I'm pretty damn regular and currently I'm not menstruating so I'm just wondering whether my fibroids have reappeared.'

'Blossom!' I protested. 'Need-to-know basis, please!'

'Sorry. I thought with you being a doctor and everything you might have a medical opinion.'

'What makes you think I'm a doctor?' I frowned.

'Well, you mentioned something yesterday about wishing you had more patients.'

'*Patience!*' I barked, without any.

'Yes, that's what you said. Mind you, I'm jumping to conclusions, of course. When I think about it, you could be a heart surgeon or a psychiatrist and then that wouldn't be much use, would it? Not if I've got fibroids. Unless you could help me with how depressed I get about them. They *do* get me down, especially when I'm trying to wear a slinky outfit and I look like a bloated humpback.'

'Are you finished?' I asked. 'I am *not* a doctor, mental or otherwise. I run my own business.'

'Ooh, exciting! Like a madam? Does Berta work for you? Is that why she's always going out and picking up all these men? That's quite tragic, actually.' She pulled a sad face. Then she clapped her hand to her mouth. 'I should never have made that comment about her being in love! Poor Berta. She's trying to earn a living and I'm romanticising her life like a Mills and Boon classic. Is she crying on the inside?'

'I doubt it. She's pretty tough.'

Blossom nodded knowingly. 'I understand you need to build yourself some armour. That's what I had to do – especially when Mr Grosvenor was on duty. "Mr Groper" we used to call him. I had to steel myself against his advances.' She flicked her blonde hair off her shoulders. 'Mind you, I've grown up with this type of unwanted attention. Perhaps it's all a bit too raw for Berta. I must reach out to her.'

'Yeah, you do that,' I smirked. 'Anyway, cup of tea?'

'Ooh, lovely! Just what the doctor ordered. Not you, of course – *another* doctor.'

I rolled my eyes, stomping out of the door.

Chapter 22

At six p.m. Blossom and I positioned ourselves behind a sagging table at the entrance to the barn, prepared to sell tickets and welcome the patrons. Ambrose, self-appointed Keg Master, plied the guests with booze as they arrived. I couldn't believe that was the best outfit he could summon for *his* event – a bleached, bobbled navy Adidas tracksuit. He was still wearing his Rasta woolly hat and looked like he was representing St Martin's athletic team in the Commonwealth Games.

Berta pitched up with a square-jawed stubbled hunky Woodland Commission bloke casually dressed in lumberjack shirt and jeans. I couldn't remember if it was Jamie or Andy, and judging by the way Berta clung to his arm I guessed she didn't give a damn. As Blossom gave Berta's hand a supportive squeeze and mouthed 'Take care', Berta threw me a quizzical look, but I shrugged innocently.

Chuck, Gloria and the boys arrived in matching sweatshirts and chinos, hair slicked down. 'Oh, my!' exclaimed Gloria. 'I can't believe we're going to see a movie in a barn. It's just like when I was a teenager growing up in Fort Worth, where we had the only drive-through in a hundred-mile radius. I just loved those outdoor dates! But isn't this just the quaintest movie theatre we've ever frequented?'

'Sure is, honey,' Chuck agreed. 'Say, is that beer?'

Romilly appeared, pushing Mavis in her wheelchair. 'Golly, what a delightful space you've created! When I was at Bletchley it was just the same – we had to mend and make do. I remember one summer we converted a room in the big house into a modest theatre where we ran an amateur production of *Salad Days*, which was quite ironic, actually, as we never saw a cucumber for two years.' Romilly steered her towards the seating area; Mavis swiped a cup of cider in passing.

George and Jason wandered in, bundled up in their North Face jackets, George remarking, 'We assumed there was no central heating.'

'Here are your tickets,' said Blossom. 'I love your coats. So cosy!'

'*Close Encounters of the Third Kind*,' George read over Jason's shoulder. 'Would it be hoping for too much for this film to be a sequel to *Brief Encounter*?'

'Oh, George, you're such a hoot!' Blossom giggled.

'I try my best,' he answered drily.

'You might want alcohol,' I advised, pointing them in the direction of Ambrose's bar.

And then the OOOWU wankers landed. If Steven Spielberg had been perched on a nearby hay bale, he would have squawked in delight. First we had Daleks, followed by several Jedi, a handful of Dr Whos (Tom Baker featuring strongly), one Chewbacca (there's always one), a couple of robots, a Storm Trooper, at least three Captain Kirks and a Spock. The girls included an Ellen Ripley (plus cat), two Princess Leias, one Lieutenant Uhura, one scarily similar Sarah Connor, two Storms and one Nightcrawler. There was even a fairly convincing Agent Scully. Don't ask me how I recognised this lunatic parade.

One of the Princess Leias stopped to adjust her buns. 'Where did you find all these costumes in the middle of a field?' I asked in amazement.

'Oh, we always have a fancy-dress parade. It's normally one of the highlights of the convention.' *Of course it is.* 'But this,' she grinned, 'this beats anything we've ever done before.'

Blossom counted them in as Paul Crank had paid in advance. Talking of Paul 'Screw Loose' Crank, he hovered at the door, clearly hoping to make an impact with his entrance. At least I assumed it was Cranky-Panky under the Darth Vader ensemble. The only clue to his identity was the telltale silver boots. I waited eagerly to see if, when he finally removed the helmet, his minions would gasp in horror at his character's distorted face. Blossom handed him his ticket with trembling fingers as he strode over to the bar, sounding like an asthmatic android. He helped himself to a flagon of beer but as he went to quaff the drink, the tankard ricocheted off his helmet. Oh, dear. Ambrose stifled a guffaw.

As Hammy dimmed the lights and prepared to launch the film, the audience's agitation wound up a notch. I knew they were waiting for Gil. 'Maybe you should say something,' I whispered to Blossom.

'Oh, right!' She leapt to her feet, taking centre stage.

'Ladies, gentlemen and *others*.' She giggled. 'I would like to warmly welcome you to Mr Struthers' farm and to Ambrose's fundraiser – "Grand Show for Ambrose".'

Romilly clapped heartily until she realised she was on her own. Not so much a round of applause as a single *put*.

'You've been most generous in helping us reach Ambrose's target and after the film he'll say a few words of thanks.' Ambrose's face screwed up into a *Will I?* glare. 'Now I absolutely love all your costumes – yes, even that terrifying lady with the machine gun! I expect we will be offering a prize to the winner?' Blossom looked at me for confirmation. A wave of excitement rippled through the barn. If only we hadn't polished off Blossom's king-sized Toblerone bar. And where the hell had Gil got to? I would kick his arse all the way home if he stood us up. I didn't fancy my chances against this lot, armed or otherwise.

'Anyway,' Blossom continued, playing for time as she kept her eye on the barn door. 'I am so pleased to introduce my cousin Hammy, who has very kindly donated his time and resource to this evening. Take a bow!' A cheer echoed around the theatre as Hammy saluted silently from the back. 'So, without further ado,' she said, with plenty of ado, 'let's crack on with the film. Now we can sit back and enjoy Hollywood's most famous and popular sci-fi classic *Close Encounters of the Third Kind*. Woo hoo!' Blossom collapsed on to the hay while a rumble of dissatisfaction swept around the audience. And then, thank fuck, the door opened a chink and Gil slipped in. He slithered on to a bale between us.

'Where have you been?' I growled under my breath.

'Just leave it, Sunny. I'm here, aren't I?'

Hammy lowered the lights completely and the opening scene was drowned out by a grateful cheer. I fidgeted throughout the entire two hours and twelve minutes. Our genius idea to sit on bales of hay in place of theatre seats quickly lost its cleverness. Despite wearing jeans, several stalks had wormed their way somewhere between my buttocks. It was a sensation unfortunately not dulled by copious cups of cider. Would it never end? The retreating figure of Richard Dreyfuss on the screen sparked a wave of snivelling – mostly from the distraught OOOWUs. As the credits rolled, the occasional sniff and nose-blowing rose to a crescendo of hysteria.

I must admit, if I didn't get off this pincushion soon I'd be reduced to tears too.

Hammy flicking on the fairy lights was Blossom's cue to advance the evening. 'Thank you, Hammy. That was wonderful! I love that film! Can we please show our appreciation?' Undeterred by her previous experience, Romilly again led the way with exuberant applause. 'So this event has all been in aid of our new friend Ambrose, who, as you know, is on a life-changing endeavour to connect with his father. The money you have so kindly raised this evening will see him well on his way to the Caribbean. Come up here, Ambrose!' He shuffled across to her as she held out a package. She put her arm round his slight shoulders and posed with a benevolent smile as several members of the audience stood to take their photo.

'Speech!' more than one person shouted. Blossom stood to the side as Ambrose coughed self-consciously.

'Oh, my days!' he muttered.

'Speak up!'

'Okay, so I just wanted to, like, thank you all for this. It was well good of you to pay my airfare. Er ... I ... er ... you probably know that my dad hasn't been part of my life and even though he said he wanted nothink to do with me, I know in his heart he don't mean it.' He reached into his pocket and held up a crumpled envelope. 'I been carrying around this letter my whole life. It's, like, my only, like, connection with him. He wrote this to my mum when I was born and it's all I've got to go on. Anyway, I'm sure my genes will, like, guide me to him. So cheers, mate. Good one.' He raised his arms, the letter in one hand and the cash in the other.

'Thank you, Ambrose. We wish you well,' Blossom said, wiping a tear from her eye. 'Now, next up, we promised a very special opportunity.' The barn fell into a hush. 'Who is going to lead this?' *Who does she think?* There was a better chance of Mavis performing a solo act from *Swan Lake* than Mr Shiny Shoes relinquishing his power.

Darth Vader strode to the front and removed his helmet. Actually, there *was* a bit of a disgusted gasp, since his head being enclosed in non-breathable plastic for several hours had given his face a blotched sheen. I felt Gil stiffen next to me as he was summoned to the front like a defiant teenager. He stood to attention, his arms crossed, willing this to be over as quickly as possible. Paul Crank, however, was relishing the spotlight and stroked his beard in contemplation. 'Question one,' Blossom announced as though refereeing a boxing match.

'Well, firstly I would like to say how much we,' Crank indicated his posse, 'appreciate you offering this one-on-one conversation. I do know that you have been approached by a number of competing organisations and we acknowledge your willingness.' Gil gave a curt nod.

'So, our first question is this, Mr McIntosh. Have you ever had an extraterrestrial experience?' The audience held its breath.

Gil shook his head. 'I have repeated this on numerous occasions before but will emphasise it again. I have *never* had an encounter of the first, second and most definitely not the third kind.' A disappointed sigh echoed around the barn, followed by furious mutterings. Crank gazed up at the rafters, appearing to be regrouping his thoughts.

'Question two,' Blossom instructed.

'Do you believe that alien life forms exist?' Crank posed, his face eager with anticipation.

'Of course!' Gil answered. Excited chatter broke out in the

Wanker Camp. He continued. 'Ever since our P2 class project focused on outer space I have believed wholeheartedly that we're not alone in this universe. The view that we share our universe with an estimated two trillion galaxies makes it utterly improbable that we are solitary beings. It is only a matter of time – and what *is* time? That's a dialogue for another day – before we make meaningful contact.'

'I agree!' Paul Crank grinned in triumph as though Gil had suggested it was reasonable to make topknots mandatory.

'Question three.'

Crank pursed his lips, considering the final question. I had no doubt that his crew had debated this for hours. 'Are you sure we can only have three questions?' he pleaded. 'Only there's so much we'd like to discuss.' Gil assuredly held up three fingers.

'Pity, but I accept your decision. So our final question is this ...' Dramatic pause. 'Do you believe that any of the sightings, experiences or evidence collected to date indicating that beings from another planet or galaxy have visited us on Earth are legitimate?'

To give Gil his due, he appeared to be seriously considering the question. 'No,' he replied. This created uproar within the barn as threats, accusations and denials were hurled in Gil's direction. Someone chucked a cup at his feet. Another bounced off his head. Agent Scully screamed and ran out of the barn in tears. Mind you, she *had* forged a lifetime career out of proving the existence of aliens. Crank waved his arms to quieten the mob. Gil attempted to leave the stage but Crank blocked his exit.

'Just "no"? Care to explain yourself?'

Gil sighed. 'It's really only my opinion. Clearly you are within your rights to believe whatever you want. But my view is this: yes, I believe that other life forms exist. Do I want to experience an extraterrestrial encounter? Of course I do, *desperately*. That's what got me into trouble before. But you can spend your entire life chasing a sighting here or a deposit there. You can waste weeks, months, years, trying to grapple with a spectre that doesn't exist. And before you know it, you've forgotten about the people around you who *do* exist – who *do* matter. It's good to keep your mind open to the possibilities, but don't spend so long searching the skies that you forget to look at what's around you. And that's all I have to say. I haven't met an alien and I have no special insight or connection. So please, please just leave me alone.' Gil walked in a determined line to Romilly and hugged her as the audience applauded his every step.

'Well,' Blossom declared. 'That concludes our evening. I hope you enjoyed it as much as I did. Now there is plenty of beer and cider to be finished off, so please help yourself.' What? *No!* That was my supply, required to dull the pain.

Gil looked mightily relieved as he accepted a large beaker of beer from Ambrose. He had finally drawn a line in the barn floor. He kept himself busy helping Hammy dismantle the theatre as an excuse to keep the Wookiees at bay.

Chapter 23

Without warning, over the rabble, we heard what sounded like a shotgun firing outside the barn, followed by another loud *bang!* We froze as the barn door creaked open. In hobbled Mr Struthers, shotgun in wavering hands. He swung it in an arc, demanding, 'What are you lot doing in my barn? Get out of here. *Now!*'

I approached him with care. 'But Mr Struthers – you know we spoke to you about this yesterday. Remember? Blossom and I visited you in your kitchen.'

He pointed the barrel at my thumping chest. 'Who are you?' he barked. The barrel shook in his unsteady clutch.

'I'm Sunny – Clyde's niece.' I curtsied like a right prat.

'*Who?*' Again he arced the shotgun in a semicircle as the audience backed away in terror.

Gil stepped out from the darkness, cool as one of Mavis's long-lost cucumbers. 'Hey there, Mr Struthers. It's me – Gil.' He gave a winning smile.

'Gil? What are you doing here?'

'We're having a fundraiser. I know Sunny came to speak to you.' '*Who?*'

'Me,' I offered helpfully. He eyed me with suspicion.

'Now, we're all friends here,' Gil soothed. 'Why don't you put the gun down?'

Mr Struthers continued to jab it in the air. 'What are you lot up to, anyway? Why is there a hairy giant over there? What's that robot doing?' He took aim at one of the Daleks, whose sucker arm swivelled in panic. 'You shouldn't be in my barn!'

Gil took another step closer. 'I know this looks very strange but we're really just a gathering of friends.'

'Friends?' he repeated, looking at them askance. 'Then why is *she* carrying a shotgun?' He pointed at Sarah Connor, who immediately let go of her weapon and began sobbing.

'It's not real.' Gil smiled. 'It's just plastic. It's fancy dress.'

'Fancy dress? On my farm? Bollocks! Have you come from Galashiels?'

'No,' Gil said calmly, taking another step forward. 'We've come from Clyde's cottage. We've been helping him.'

'*She* hasn't!' he accused, pointing again at me. '*She* pushed him down the stairs!'

'No, I didn't!' I protested.

'Hey, Mr Struthers – look over here!' We all turned to Blossom, who was energetically performing star jumps with her blouse undone. Her boobs frolicked freely as she puffed for breath. Mr Struthers' jaw fell open and he released the shotgun, which dropped to the floor with a clatter. Gil swooped to pick it up and Mr Struthers continued to gawp at Blossom as she rebuttoned her blouse.

'You're the girl who smells of strawberries,' he recalled.

'Yes, I am!' She hooked her arm round Mr Struthers' waist and led him back out of the barn. 'Let's get you home now, shall we?' He nodded mutely.

'Bloody hell,' I breathed. 'He's as mad as a hatter.'

Gil held the shotgun at arm's length. 'I think we'll just leave this over here.' The party dispersed in silence as we filed out of the door. 'I think we can leave the clearing-up until tomorrow,' he said. 'Come on, let's get to bed.'

Which was a great sentiment, but it never happened. Not for hours, anyway. The OOOWU brigade trundled along behind the cottage, the rest of the campers filing after them. Romilly steered Mavis across the courtyard, Gil and I at the rear. I assumed Berta was cosied up with Jamie/Andy somewhere. As long as it wasn't on our bunk beds.

'That was a super night,' Mavis said. 'Apart from the psychopathic trigger-happy farmer, of course.'

'I thought I was a goner for sure,' I agreed, hopelessly missing Mathew's kind smile and grudging embrace.

'But Hammy did a marvellous—' Romilly never finished her sentence. She stopped in her tracks. Gil and I ploughed into the back of the wheelchair.

'What the—?' Gil sprinted to the open garage door. '*No!*' he cried. 'Not the Jaguar!' We followed him into the garage. There was a big gaping hole where Clyde's classic car had been resting for years.

Gil fell to his knees. '*No!*' he repeated in despair. 'Some bastard's stolen our car!'

I moaned out loud. 'Well, there goes our money. *Shit!*' We circled the garage in misery as though we had somehow overlooked the car's presence. Gil kicked the wall with his boot.

'*Fuck!*' he exclaimed. 'Fuckity fuck fuck! Sorry, Mavis.'

'Don't worry.' She shrugged. 'We were all thinking it.'

'Let's call the police,' Romilly said, pushing the chair towards the back door.

We trudged into the kitchen. I put on the kettle as Gil dialled 999. Wretched, despite the late hour, we hugged cups of coffee round the table. Berta stumbled in and glanced from one glum face to the other.

'He's just a mad old farmer,' she said. 'Was it really that bad?'

'Someone has stolen Clyde's car,' I said.

'*What?*' she raged. 'Clyde's car? That was our bloody car! That was our money that we've been working so hard for!' Gil raised his eyebrows.

'Okay,' she conceded. 'That *you've* been working hard for. But it hasn't exactly been a picnic for me either. I'm sleeping in a child's bunk bed, living off flipping cabbage, have hardly any connection to the outside world and now I think I've got a sheep tick stuck on my arm.'

'Let's have a look,' Mavis offered.

Berta rolled up her sleeve. 'Oh, yes,' Mavis agreed. 'You'll need to make sure you get the whole head out or it'll be feeding off your blood for weeks.'

'Fantastic!' Berta growled. 'Now I'm infested with livestock.'

'What did the police say?' I asked Gil, ignoring Berta's tantrum.

He gave a heavy sigh, running his hands through his neat hair. 'Well, there isn't a police presence in Bonchester. They put my call through to Hawick and someone may or may not turn up tomorrow to take a statement.'

'By which time some unholy thief could be sweeping along the coast in the south of France with the roof down!'

'Someone knew,' Gil said.

'Eh?'

'Someone knew that we'd all be away from the cottage tonight,' Gil fumed.

'But who?' Mavis asked. 'Who would want to steal my Clyde's car?'

'And it doesn't even drive,' I protested. 'Someone must have known it was there and known that it would need to be towed.'

'Everyone on the campsite knew we'd be occupied this evening,' Berta said. 'Maybe someone said something to someone in town.'

'Well, *you're* the only one who has been talking to anyone in town or otherwise,' Romilly accused.

'Hey – hold your horses, Missy, before you go round making those types of allegations!'

'Just pointing out the obvious,' Romilly murmured.

'We had a saying during the war,' Mavis said quietly. '"Loose lips sink ships." How true that is. Idle chatter overheard by no-gooders.'

'What if it was one of the wankers?' I suggested. 'Maybe they hung back until we were all out of the way.'

'And where would they have put it?' Romilly asked. 'I mean, I know that marquee is pretty monstrous but big enough to hide a car?'

'No.' Gil shook his head. 'It must have been someone with a tow truck. I expect the police will want to take casts of the area outside the garage. And maybe rule out any of our footprints.'

'Steady, Mr CSI Miami,' I warned. 'Anyway, we've just trampled all over the crime scene.'

'Do you think there's any CCTV in Bonchester?' Berta asked. 'Maybe the police could scan for pick-up trucks driving in the area this evening.'

'CCTV?' I repeated. 'Bonchester's answer to a smartphone is one that records a message. Locals still think Wi-Fi is the woman you're married to and the garage had to resume pump assistance due to the chaos caused by self-service.'

'Then we're screwed,' Berta groaned. 'We might as well pack up and go home.'

'And tomorrow I had better break the bad news to Clyde,' said Mavis, edging out of the kitchen.

I tutted. 'I doubt Clyde will be bothered. It's *our* loss.'

'Let's get to bed,' Gil said. 'Maybe things will look better in the morning.'

'The only thing that will make that hole in the garage look better is if someone on this site has a 3D scanner,' I said – not that I'd know a scanner if it appeared under my pillow and offered to generate a life-sized Tom Hardy for me.

Chapter 24

The only difference between our five mournful faces last night and the five the next morning was that we'd swapped seats. Oh, and maybe our hair was more mussed up. I recognised Chuck's knock at the door but could not face his summons to the Great Outdoors, cultural enlightenment or open-water survival venture.

'Hey, Sunny!' Chuck greeted me. Even *he* looked a tad mournful.

'Morning, Chuck. Look, if it's about today's activity—'

'Actually, I just came to say we're heading off today.'

'Oh?'

'Yes,' he confirmed, downhearted. 'We have just loved every minute of this camping trip and, truth be told, we were only planning to stay a week, but the boys were so excited about the movie and all. Still, we ought to get to the next site we've booked. According to their bumf it genuinely does have a shower block, camping shop and café.' He winked.

'Ah! They'll be spoiling you, then?'

'Apparently so. Anyways, Gloria wanted you to come say goodbye.'

'Of course.' I nodded, shoved on my wellies, grabbed my coat and followed him over the dewy grass. Larry trotted along excitedly as though we were off on a wild grass-foraging trip. I felt a pang of sadness as we approached their estate car, roof rack piled high under the tarpaulin. The twins were trying to maintain keepy-uppy with a flabby football as Gloria shoved their folding chairs into the boot.

'So where are you headed?' I asked lightly.

'Hiya, Sunny. We are driving up to a little bitty place called Mall-aig. I'm hoping it *will* have a mall as I'm dying to do some shopping while we're here.'

'Hmm,' I said. 'I'm sure it will have all the shops you need.'

'Fabulous! As long as it's got a Walmart I'll be fine.'

'Say,' said Chuck, 'Google Maps reckons it'll take about four and a half hours, but surely if I take the freeway we'll get there quicker? We usually only stop for about an hour for a comfort break. Should be there by lunch, you think?'

'Absolutely,' I fibbed.

'Oh, come here, honey!' Gloria hugged me tightly. Her voice cracked. 'We have just had such an adventure – haven't we, boys?'

They nodded while keeping the ball airborne. 'Now make sure the old lady ...'

'Mavis?'

'Yeah – make sure Mavis takes good care of Bugs and Bunny. They've fairly come on since the boys have been hand-rearing them.'

'They certainly feel at home in her room.'

Chuck threw his coat on to the back seat and gave me a big grizzly bear hug. 'You keep in touch, now, you hear?' he said. 'And any time you find yourself in the best state in the US, you come look us up.' He handed me a business card with his details: *Charles Boner – Corporate Taxation Accountant*. Ah, well – that would explain his desire to put four thousand miles between himself and his calculator. I waved them off as they bumped down the track in the early grey light.

'I'm afraid we're heading too,' George announced behind me.

'Bloody hell, George! You shouldn't be sneaking up on people like that!'

'Sorry.'

'And where are *you* away to?' I accused.

'Need to get back home,' George said, pulling a grim face. 'Not for me, you understand. I'm on leave for another six weeks! But poor old Jase has to get back to work. Those throw rugs don't weave themselves!'

'Gosh, the site will be so empty without you guys,' I moaned. 'Who's going to keep me sane and make me cups of tea?'

'There's always Blossom!' George smiled. 'You really don't need anyone else in a field that size when you've got Blossom.'

'And Ambrose,' added Jason. He held out a well-manicured hand. 'Thanks for everything, Sunny.'

George went in for the hug, although he wasn't as brawny as Chuck. 'I can, hand on heart, say I've never laughed as much on a camping trip as this one. Last year we went to Magaluf and it was *so* dull in comparison.'

'Well – we aim to please,' I said. 'But thanks, guys.'

They lobbed their remaining bags into the car boot and carried out a three-point-turn before disappearing on to the main road.

Despite asking Ambrose to close down the website, it was a pity to be winding up the legitimate campers. Clyde would be in no position to support a campsite, whether the worst in Scotland or not. Since Ambrose had his dosh, he'd soon be off. And now that some complete bastard had stolen our money, there was little to keep Berta's interest in Crackers Cottage. Or mine, for that matter. I returned to the steamy kitchen where Gil was churning out rounds of toast. 'Police'll be here soon,' he announced.

'Does anyone mind if I travel to Hawick?' asked Romilly, sipping on a lemon tea. 'A senior lecturer from one of the Oxbridge universities wants to interview me for their "Featured Poet" slot and he's piqued my interest.'

'I bet he has,' Berta said, her mouth full of toast.

'Will you be alright, Gil, darling?' she simpered. 'I do hate leaving you when you're so Doleful Dennis.'

'I'll be fine,' he said. 'I'll need to be here for the police.'

'Don't let them get away with doing nothing,' she instructed. 'If Daddy were here he'd have them pooling all their resources.'

'That'll be both coppers, then,' said Berta.

Romilly ignored the comment. 'So will I bring something back for supper?'

'A cow?' I suggested. 'I swear that teaspoon has more iron in it than I have.'

'You don't need to get iron from meat,' Romilly tutted. 'I'll make sure I add plenty of pumpkin seeds to this evening's stir-fry.'

'I'm not a bloody pigeon.'

'If you were I'd debone you and pan-fry your breasts,' said Berta.

'Charming!'

Romilly had barely closed the door before Blossom's head appeared. 'Good morning!' she crowed, marching in.

'S'not really,' muttered Berta.

'Oh, how so?' She pulled up a chair and helped herself to coffee.

I explained how someone had effortlessly negotiated the garage lock and made off with our property.

'How awful!' said Blossom 'And here I was coming to complain about how dreadful *my* evening turned out with Mr Struthers.'

'Yeah, sorry about that,' I said guiltily. 'You did get landed with accompanying him home.'

'It wouldn't have been so bad if my escorting duties had ended at his front door but no, he *insisted* I have a whisky.'

'What's so terrible about that?' said Berta.

'Well, aside from the floaters—'

'Don't!' I held up my hand.

'Then he began unpeeling his leg dressings for me to have a look.'

'Sorry, Blossom, it's just too early in the morning for all this.'

'Fine,' she conceded. 'But I reckon it's probably been *months* since he's had those dressings changed. Let's just say I can see where someone got the idea for maggot therapy from. That's all I'm saying.'

'Ambrose!' I cried, welcoming him in. 'Please do come in and change the subject.'

'Morning, one and all,' he said with a jaunty grin. 'Mind if I grab a coffee? What's with the rope across the courtyard?'

We recounted the story for his benefit.

'Oh, but that's hideous, man!' He scratched at his blonde stubble.

'We agree.'

'I feel, like, *really* bad, like it's all my fault.'

'Not at all,' Gil reassured, placing his hands on Ambrose's slight shoulders. 'It's not your fault there are shameless, unscrupulous, filthy bandits in the world.'

Blossom patted his knee. 'Anyway, it was an amazing evening for you and we raised all that money.'

'Yeah, Gil, my man. I wanted to say thank you for putting yourself under the glare of the bright lights. Can't have been pleasant for you. Respect.' He doffed his beanie.

'It was nothing really,' said Gil. 'In a way you did me a favour.

Sunny'll tell you they've been hounding me for months. I'm kind of glad I had a chance to say my piece. Because of you it's probably got them off my back.'

'Cool.'

'So do you think you have enough for your transatlantic flight? So exciting!' Blossom clapped her hands.

'For sure.' He nodded. Removing the crumpled letter from his jacket he held it aloft. 'I'm on my way, Dad!'

'Do you mind me asking what's in the letter?' Blossom said coyly.

Ambrose laid the envelope on the table, attempting to smooth it with his hands. 'You know, it don't really say nothing 'cept that he's sorry for what happened but he had no way to support me and had to go home. Maybe it was easier for him to put an ocean between us.'

Blossom scrutinised the envelope. Turning it towards her, she read, '"Cornwall". Why do you think the envelope is postmarked *Cornwall*?'

'What do you mean?' Ambrose asked, doubt in his voice.

'Well, the letter must have been posted in Cornwall. It gets postmarked in the mail. Plus it's a British stamp.'

'But my mum always told me he sent this letter when he got home – back to the Caribbean. I don't understand.'

'You *do* know that there's a St Martin in Cornwall?' Gil asked gently. 'Are you *sure* that your father is from the Caribbean?'

'*Yes!*' Ambrose said emphatically. 'It's what my mum always told me.'

Blossom took Ambrose's hand. 'But do you think she might have just made that assumption? If he told her he was from St Martin – maybe he didn't exactly say *which* St Martin?'

'But ...' Ambrose faltered, his eyes watering. 'But that means ... that means ...' He frantically wiped his eyes. 'If he lives in England, then why didn't he come visit me? I mean, it isn't that far away. We could have met in the middle, like.' He jumped to his feet, his chair tipping backwards. 'I don't even know where the middle is! London? Manchester?' he shouted, thumping the table. 'How hard is it to get a frigging train to London?'

'Come on, Ambrose, take it easy,' Gil said, picking up the chair.

'All these years!' Ambrose raved. 'All these years I thought I was a fucking Rastafarian! And now you're telling me I'm *English*? Christ, man!' He grabbed his letter and ran out of the kitchen, slamming the door behind him.

'Oh, poor Ambrose,' said Blossom. 'What do you think? Do you think we've got it wrong? Do you think he could be from St Martin in the Caribbean?'

Gil shrugged. 'If that's the sole communication from his father then I'd say there's been a huge misunderstanding. That's not airmail.'

'But you'd think his mother would know better,' I said. 'Wouldn't she have noticed the postmark?'

'Maybe it's partly what she wanted to believe, too,' said Blossom. 'It's a bit more romantic to think you've had a tryst with a mysterious stranger from the other side of the world. Perhaps that made a more interesting story for her son. And she probably never imagined Ambrose would go looking for him.'

Chapter 25

'Hello, hello!' a woman's voice called as the door opened.

'What *now*?' I groaned.

A squat middle-aged woman wearing a short-sleeved black shirt and bulging black trousers waddled into the kitchen. It was only the checked epaulettes and handcuffs clipped to her straining belt that gave any indication she wasn't a stray bouncer. Her tightly curled grey hair had been rammed into place under a black checked cap – available in all good toy stores.

'You missed off an "hello", Berta commented drily.

'Ha! Good one,' the visitor replied. 'Police Constable Payne.' She nodded at each one of us. 'Pleased to be of service.'

'Good morning,' Gil said. 'I'm Gilbert McIntosh. I reported the theft last night. Please, have a seat. Would you like a coffee?'

'Would I like a coffee?' She pondered his question. 'I always have to weigh up the benefit with the risk – you know, when you first enter a victim's house. The thing is, what they teach you in training is to balance the accepting of a hot beverage and the fostering of that awkward relationship with offending a potentially violent client by refusing their hospitality.'

'So is that a yes or a no?' Gil asked, the kettle poised under the tap.

'Well, I don't suppose I'll die of anything dreadful here.' She chortled. 'Although I *am* slightly perplexed as to why you have a ram in your food preparation area.'

'Oh, that's just Larry,' I said, ruffling his woolly face.

'*Baaa,*' Larry added.

'So,' she pulled out a small notebook and flicked it open to a blank page. 'Now ... pen, pen, pen. I know I've got one somewhere.' She rummaged in her two prominent breast pockets, retrieving a tin opener from one. 'Oh, I wondered what that was rubbing against my—'

'Here's your coffee,' said Gil. 'Milk?'

'World of Jugs!' she declared, holding up a green biro. 'Have you ever been there?' We stared at her in bewilderment.

'It's fabulous! You really wouldn't think there was that much to know about jugs, but you'd be surprised. Last year I brought back at least five Toby jugs for Christmas presents. Mind you, my cousin Jessie must think I'm daft as she regifted hers to me for my birthday. As if I wouldn't recognise my own jugs—'

'So about our stolen car,' Gil interrupted.

'Uh-huh?'

'I expect you'll want to know all the details?'

'If you insist.' She shrugged, clicking several Sweetex tablets into her coffee and giving a vigorous stir.

As Gil recounted last night's events, PC Payne nodded and mm-hmed while she jotted down notes. When Gil mentioned the OOOWU camp she drew a sharp breath. '*Ooliu?*' she queried. 'As in the organised crime family from Newcastle? They're a deadly lot! You do *not* want to be crossing swords with *them*. If I'm entirely honest, even I'd be cautious about approaching them with anything less than a semi-automatic weapon and a bullet-proof vest.'

'I'm thinking not,' said Gil. 'It stands for Out of our World Ufologists.'

'And what's that when it's at home? Is it like a euphonium? Because they can be a bloody nuisance too! I had a lad next door to me who played with his trombone all night. Just as I was about to drop off he'd be giving it laldy. It got so bad that one day I "accidentally" reversed over his trombone case and soon after that he took up FIFA Manager, so everyone's a winner!'

'Would you like to see the garage?' Gil suggested. 'The scene of the crime?'

'Better had – although not much point. That car's long gone.'

We all trooped out to the garage, where the door remained ajar, the padlock hanging loosely.

'After we discovered the theft we tried not to disturb anything,' said Gil.

'Why's that, then?' she asked, peering into the gloom.

'Well, in case you wanted to take fingerprints or anything.'

'Wouldn't have thought so.'

We ducked under the rope and stood forlornly in the empty space.

'Oh, I remember those!' PC Payne cried, bumbling over to Clyde's shelving. 'We had this same yoghurt maker when I was a teenager. My parents thought they were so hip!'

'Why would you make yoghurt?' Berta asked.

PC Payne tutted, running her fingers over the dusty machine. 'It was in the days before you could buy yoghurt – in the days before we had pizza or lattes or even cupcakes. Imagine a world where the only way to get a curry was to buy a packet and add boiling water!'

'How old *are* you?' Blossom enquired.

'It's not so much my age as the fact that we lived in the Windmill.'

'In a windmill?' Blossom said. 'How romantic!'

'No, that was the name of our house – "The Windmill". It was pretty basic. My father had once been a monk up in Moray somewhere but he felt the cold terribly, so moved down here, where at least they had a coal fire.'

'But no yoghurt?'

'That's right.' She smiled ruefully. 'Or Bird's Instant Whip – God forbid!'

'So will you be wanting to make casts of the footprints?' Gil suggested. 'We're happy to let you rule out ours.'

'Shouldn't think so.' She shook her head. 'Frank's off for two weeks in Butlin's Ayr and he's the only one who knows where we keep the plaster.'

'Will you be wanting statements from everyone?' Blossom persisted, keen to have her moment. PC Payne puffed out her cheeks.

'I've really only got this teensy notepad they've given me. It's not like on the telly when they tell people to go to the station and make a statement. Bob would kill me if a whole bunch of folk showed up to make a statement. What day is it today?'

'Thursday,' I offered.

'Thursday,' she mused. 'Yeah, well, Thursday is the day the Sausage Van parks outside. The last thing he wants when he's tucking into a double sausage roll is a whole lot of dafties who think they can save the world.'

'But what about the convention lot?' I said. 'Will you be wanting to speak to them?'

'And you're *sure* they're not gangsters?' She frowned.

'Do you want me to come with you? I can introduce you to the organiser.'

'But you said—'

'Sorry!' I apologised. 'I meant the convention leader.'

'And why are they having a convention in a field?'

'I'll explain it on the way.'

'Is it far?' She stretched her back while grimacing. 'My hip doesn't half play up when I walk any distance.'

'It's just round the side of the cottage,' I said. 'Five minutes, tops.'

'Should I bring the patrol car round?'

'Honestly – it wouldn't be worth it.' Gil intervened. 'Plus you might churn up my uncle's field.'

'You're sure? I'd hate to hit you with a compensation claim for injuries sustained in the line of duty. You seem like you're a nice couple.'

'Oh, we're not a couple!' I protested.

'No?' She raised her eyebrows.

'That's my brother,' I informed her.

'So you're Gil's sister, right?'

I wondered how many years I'd get for assaulting a police officer.

'Correct,' Gil stated as I cursed under my breath.

Berta murmured in my ear, 'Want me to take her out?'

PC Payne huffed grumpily as we made our way over the field to the OOOWU encampment. 'Whoa, is this even within the law?' she demanded, spotting the foil-wrapped hill, flagpole and floating blimp.

'Well, I'd hate to get in the way of any legal procedures.' I smiled. My smile faded as we neared a troubling rectangle of flattened, bleached grass where Ambrose's tent had been pitched. 'Hang on a mo,' I instructed.

'Oh, don't mind me. I'm glad of the respite.'

I dashed back to the kitchen, where Blossom appeared to be doing something strange with a spatula. 'Blossom,' I panted. 'Ambrose has gone! Can you go and look for him?'

'What?' she gasped. 'I hope he hasn't gone and done something stupid!'

'Like set up a fake website?' said Berta.

Blossom, Berta and Gil followed me out of the cottage. 'I need to deal with PC Plod,' I said. 'Blossom, can you check the river?'

'I'll go through the woods,' Gil said grimly.

'Yeah, maybe I ought to head back to the kitchen,' Berta said. 'One of us should be here in case he returns.'

PC Payne stood rooted where I left her. 'Crisis averted?'

'Not really. One of our campers has gone missing.'

'You lot are a bit careless with your belongings, aren't you?'

'He's young and pretty upset,' I said, scouring the horizon for a Rasta hat.

'Should I report him as a missing person?' she offered, flipping her radio mic on.

'Would you be able to alert all police in the area? That would be great!'

'I'll let Bob know,' she said, barking into her lapel. I waited quietly. 'No response,' she muttered, checking her watch. 'Must be away for his tea break early. Sometimes I think I'm the only one doing any crime-fighting!'

The usual lank-haired anaemic lass sat studying a manual at reception. She eyed PC Payne anxiously.

'Can we have a word with Mr Crank, please?'

'Is this about the post-mortem?' she asked, gripping her

textbook. 'How did *you* hear about it?'

'Post-mortem?' PC Payne spluttered. 'Has there been a serious incident that you've failed to report?'

'I … er … I …' She burst into tears, ducking into the nearest Portaloo.

'Come on, I know where to find him,' I said. We entered the communal marquee, where rows of plastic-covered tables were filled with breakfasting nerds, no doubt still reeling from actual contact with Gil. I spotted Archie munching through a mound of toast – must have wangled sleeping and eating rights in exchange for the personal laundry service. He held up his thumb as we passed and I nodded in return.

Crank lounged at the head of one table, tucking into a plate of scrambled eggs. He had ditched his Darth Vader outfit for his usual army fatigues; his hair was dragged into a rat's ponytail.

'What is this place?' PC Payne frowned as the prattling simmered down with each step we took. Crank glanced up in surprise as we approached. He took his time standing up, wiping his eggy beard with a napkin.

'PC Payne, Police Scotland,' she snapped, adjusting her hat. 'And you are?'

'Paul Crank. Enchanted, I'm sure.' He held out his hand. She giggled like a schoolgirl, holding his hairy hand a few seconds longer than necessary.

'Shall we go to my office?' he suggested as sixty pairs of eyes followed us to the rear of the tent, where a small desk and two folding chairs were positioned. He eased himself behind the desk and indicated for PC Payne to take a seat.

'Don't mind me, then,' I complained, standing with my hands in my pockets.

'What's all this about a post-mortem?'

Crank's brow furrowed but he quickly regained his composure. 'Oh, that was just a slight misunderstanding,' he answered, waving his hand as though the subject were dismissed.

'But the girl on reception,' PC Payne persisted. 'She seemed rather uptight about it all.'

He rubbed his hands together. 'Myriam's just a bit highly strung.'

'Like a violin?'

'Exactly!' He winked.

'What was the misunderstanding?' I said from the sidelines.

Crank glared at me sourly. *Yes, I'm still here.* 'Well, one of the trainees got a bit carried away with a sliding-head machine. To be fair, he hadn't been properly apprised of the scenario and should never have used a turret-mounted probe. Not without Vaseline in any case.'

PC Payne squirmed in her plastic seat, which creaked under her weight. 'So nothing I should be concerned about?'

'Nothing at all.' He beamed, opening his arms widely. 'Anyway, how can I assist you, officer? I know your time is *absolutely* precious and I cannot think why someone as talented as yourself would be diverted from the coalface of serious crime.'

PC Payne glowered at me as though I had manufactured grounds for her to be rerouted to this marquee when dangerous offenders were on the loose. She tossed open her notebook and concentrated on her scrawl. 'So ... apparently a very expensive classic car was stolen from the garage of Crackers Cottage last night. I don't suppose you know anything about that?'

'I don't.' He shook his head.

'Okay, well, I apologise for taking up your time.' She stood up.

'Hey, hang on a minute!' I protested. 'Is that all you're going to ask him? Why don't you ask him where everyone was last night at the time the crime took place?'

'But you know where we were,' he said.

'Ah, but not everyone. What if someone stayed behind to give the nod that we were all in the barn?'

'What are you implying?' Crank said, irritated.

'That there is a tent full of potential thieves looking to top up their student loans.'

'I think you should leave.'

'You heard the man,' grunted PC Payne, tugging my sleeve.

'But ... but we haven't even asked if anyone saw anything.'

Crank smirked. 'How could we have? You know perfectly well that we were all occupied with your little "fundraiser",' he said, making air quotes.

'Let's go,' PC Payne commanded. 'Thank you for your time, sir.'

He bowed graciously. 'Thank you for your courtesy in handling such a delicate matter.'

'We haven't checked if anyone knew about the car!' I fumed.

'Car? What car?' she said.

'The stolen *Jaguar*,' I replied through gritted teeth.

'Oh, that, yes. Well, it seems like you're losing things left, right and centre. Anyway, I need to be off.'

She shuffled over the uneven flooring, emerging into the damp field. I stormed ahead and waited by her vehicle. Eventually she puffed to a halt and leant against the car door. 'So I think I've got all the information I need,' she wheezed, slumping behind the wheel.

'Really? I am surprised. You must have amazing powers of deduction.'

'That *has* been commented on by my superiors,' she nodded. 'In fact, only last month I was invited as the guest speaker at a local psychic supper. Yes, I went down very well after the plum crêpes. And talking of nourishment, if I put my foot down, I might just make it back in time to catch the Sausage Van.'

'Don't let me keep you,' I scowled, slamming her door. She gave a cheerful wave as the car bounced down the muddy track.

Chapter 26

'She was just hopeless!' I despaired, back in the kitchen.

'She didn't exactly strike me as carving out a career in criminology,' Berta agreed.

'The only thing she was interested in carving was a bloody Sunday roast!'

'Oooh, that sounds nice,' Berta said. 'I'm not half missing Willie's. I wonder who he's serving up our Specials to this week?'

'I think I must be getting MSG withdrawal symptoms.'

'You know, there is a Chinese takeaway in Bonchester,' Berta said, brightening up. 'Why don't we go out this afternoon?'

'I'm so depressed!' I moaned. 'I can't believe we're not getting paid for all this frigging strife.'

'Come on, Sunny, let's wander along and get a few pints. Cheer ourselves up a bit?'

'I suppose so. Not much point in hanging around here.'

We were up in our bedroom getting changed when we heard Gil and Blossom returning from their search. 'Any sign?' I asked, slipping on my jacket.

'I can see you're really cut up about it,' commented Gil. 'But no – nothing.'

'I walked along both sides of the water and shouted over the hill,' said Blossom. 'Oh, I love your trousers!'

'They're jeans.'

'Are you going somewhere special?'

'Berta and I are pretty hacked off about everything – thought we'd walk into the village for a few drinks and maybe grab a takeaway.'

'Can I come too?' Blossom pleaded.

I heard Berta mutter, '*Damn!*' as she came down the stairs.

'Of course. But we're heading off soon. It looks like it might piss with rain and we don't want to get soaked on the way.'

'Righty-tighty! I'll be back in two shakes of Larry's tail!'

'*She's* cheered up,' Gil observed.

'Well, *she* hasn't been robbed of her cash. At least you still get paid for your holidays, Gil. *I* don't. I'm losing two weeks' pay to host this bloody charade!'

'One word, two syllables,' Berta quipped. 'Sounds like "shitemare".'

'Spot on!' I agreed. 'Come on, Berta; let's chase Blossom out of her tent. How long can it take her to throw a poncho over her head?'

We hobbled along the road towards Bonchester. Blossom insisted on walking between us, looping an arm through Berta's on one side and mine on the other. She clearly hadn't studied Berta's policy on unnecessary physical contact. Of course, if Blossom had a penis, it would be an entirely different matter. Berta's constant pulling-away made progression as awkward as competing in a three-legged race. 'Shall we sing a song?' Blossom suggested, bursting into:

I love to go a-wandering
Along the mountain track,
And as I go, I love to sing,
My knapsack on my back!

As she took a deep breath for the chorus Berta announced, 'Did I tell you, Blossom, that I'm a distant relative of Florence Nightingale?'

'*No!* Do tell!' Blossom gasped. 'How exciting. Is that why you have an affinity with young men? You know, because she helped all those poor injured soldiers?'

'Must be,' Berta said, winking at me. *Anything to stop that dreadful singing.*

The Horse and Hound hosted its regular Thursday afternoon clientele. Seemed like we'd missed the pub quiz and now they'd progressed to dominoes. We selected a table furthest from the locals and I scooped up three pints from the bar.

'Ooh, I don't normally drink pints,' Blossom confessed. 'Won't I be needing the toilet all evening?'

'What's your usual, then?' I asked, taking a long sup.

'Well, I don't really get out of the house much so "my usual" is tea with milk. But if you mean alcohol, well, I suppose I sometimes take the odd sherry.'

'Odd being the word I'd use,' said Berta.

'But on special occasions I would partake of a cocktail.'

'Oh, would you now?' Berta smiled. 'That's more like it! What's your favourite?'

'You know, I've only tried a couple. But I *do* love a margarita. I have it in my head that one day I might be swept off my feet by a swarthy Mexican.'

'That's not very likely in Bonchester Bridge,' I said.

'I once shagged a doctor from Honduras – does that count?' Berta bragged.

'No – but it would be a great name for a song!' Blossom giggled. She began singing, '*I once shagged a doctor from Honduras! He looked just like Antonio Banderas!*' We fell about laughing.

'Right, you lassies! Keep it down over there!' the barman shouted. After three pints Blossom had trouble focusing so we staggered to the Chinese takeaway two doors down. We reclined on the plastic bench in front of the plastic counter, which had been decorated with plastic pot plants.

'What are you girls having?' slurred Blossom.

'We're having our usual,' replied Berta.

'What's your usual?'

'I've no idea! We always just ask Willie for our usual,' Berta said despondently. 'Sunny, what are we doing here? We need to go home.'

'I know,' I said. 'We will.'

'When?'

'I don't know. Do we need to wait until Clyde comes home?'

'That could be weeks!' Berta protested.

'Not if Clyde signs himself out.'

'I'm not one for praying – but please, God!'

'I know. Let's ask Gil when we get back.'

'Gil – he's so *dreamy*!' Blossom swooned.

'Well, you've clearly had enough alcohol for one day!' I said. 'What are you ordering?'

'Why don't we get a banquet?' Berta suggested.

'A blanket? Are you feeling the cold?' Blossom asked, snuggling against Berta. Berta stood up abruptly, leaving Blossom slumped against the wall.

'If we order a blanket – I mean a banquet – can we eat it here?' Berta asked the dour woman behind the counter.

'No.' She gave a severe shake of her head. 'Take it next door.'

'Bloody hell,' Blossom complained. 'Are they *trying* to force us into alcoholism?'

'It's just good business,' I said. 'One scratches their back ...'

'Okay – one banquet for three, please,' Berta ordered, rummaging for her purse.

Chapter 27

I've a feeling we got a taxi home eventually. I can't quite remember – the details are a little fuzzy. I *do* know that Blossom started ordering margaritas, which threw the barman. Then a girl came on duty who'd done a stint in the metropolis that is Melrose and she at least had *heard* of a margarita. Then the bar took a crazy turn when a group of birdwatchers from Oslo arrived and it was as if they were discovering tequila for the first time. I had flashbacks of Blossom belting out '*Val-deri val-dera, val-deri, val-dera, val-der ha ha ha ha ha!*' and the Norwegians joining in as though it were their National Constitution Day. But today, Friday, I'd really rather stay in bed and sleep. The only way I knew that Berta had also made it home was by the constant lorry engine that rumbled above. A feeling of paranoia crept over me as memories of sending a stream of drunken, sentimental messages to Mathew came flooding back. I cringed as I tried to recall the content. I may even have proposed something as ridiculous as getting a puppy. How would *that* help anything?

It was hunger that finally drove us downstairs. Most of our banquet had been seized upon by the regulars, leaving us to nibble on the sesame toast and prawn crackers.

Berta crashed in a chair with her eyes closed, a mug of coffee untouched.

'Is she alright?' Mavis enquired.

'Who knows?' I said. 'She's one of these people who talk a good talk when it comes to cocktails, but actually she's a bit of a ...'

'Lightweight?' Mavis offered.

'Indeed.'

'And how are *you* feeling?' Mavis asked. 'Only you do know that one side of your face looks like a braille version of the Bible?'

'Must have slept soundly.'

'Any news of Ambrose?' Mavis wondered.

'Why is she shouting?' Berta asked, her eyes still closed.

'You'd know as much as we would. What happened yesterday evening?'

'Oh, it was all very civil here,' Mavis said. 'Romilly made a *lovely* mushroom risotto.'

'*Shit!*' Berta coughed.

'Actually, it was all right. Then we had some peppermint tea and I retired to my room to immerse myself in the latest Dan Brown yarn.'

'So, no word of—'

We were interrupted by a formal knock at the door. Mavis and I exchanged a puzzled look. 'Where's Gil?' I whispered, concerned that PC Payne was back on the case.

'He and Romilly walked into Bonchester to get some *real* coffee – whatever that is.'

The knock sounded again more urgently.

'Someone answer the door!' Berta instructed, still apparently dozing.

I opened the door to a serious young moustachioed gent in a charcoal grey suit and polished black shoes.

'Good morning,' he said. 'My name is Oily McOiliness.'

Actually that's not what he said, but I didn't quite catch his name.

'Sunny,' I said, my mouth still dry as a budgie's sand sheet.

'I'm looking for a Mr Davidson.'

'I'm Mavis Davidson, his mother. Can I be of assistance?'

The suit stepped into the kitchen and shook hands with Mavis and me. He hovered uncertainly in front of Berta, whose jaw hung open in a most unappealing manner.

'What's this all about?' Mavis asked in a clipped tone.

'I'm here to carry out the survey and valuation of the property,' Oily said. Right enough, he *did* carry a clipboard and expensive-looking biro. No World of Jugs freebie for him.

'I think you must be mistaken,' Mavis said. 'This property is not for sale. I live here with my son, Mr Clyde Davidson.'

'And it is Mr Davidson who commissioned our services at Oil, Oil and Even-Oilier.'

'Then you must be mistaken,' Mavis repeated. 'Why would Clyde be selling his house? Oh, hang on a minute – is this because of his accident? Fair enough, I see where this might have come from. You see, my son had a fall a couple of weeks ago. He's probably worried that he won't manage the stairs. I'm sure it's just an overreaction on his part.'

'Of course.' I joined in. 'He's probably panicking that he won't be able to return home. But we're confident that, after he's had some rehabilitation, he will soon manage here fine.'

'Hmm.' The suit hesitated.

'What, you don't think he'll manage at home? Then you don't know my Clyde! He may be in hospital now but it won't be for long,' Mavis declared.

'I didn't actually know he was in hospital. But I *can* tell you that Mr Davidson engaged our services about a month ago.'

'What?' I objected. 'But that's impossible. He only fell a week past Monday. He wouldn't have known about not managing the stairs and stuff.'

'Look,' Mr Oilcloth insisted, 'I have specific instructions to record all the cottage details for the sale and to take photos of the property. Now, I do have one concern about the debris at the front of the cottage – what appears to be a discarded telephone booth – and would request that you please remove it for the purposes of the sales schedule.'

'But I don't understand,' Mavis said, tears welling up. 'I've only just moved here. I gave up my home to be with Clyde. It was *his* suggestion. Why would he put his house up for sale?'

Oily sighed. 'I really can't comment on your specific circumstances. All I know is what I've been told.'

'Which is?' I demanded.

'That this property is to go on sale in the next ten days.'

'You've got it all wrong,' Mavis protested. 'Sunny, lend me your phone. Let's talk to Clyde and he'll sort it all out.'

'Fine,' the gent agreed. 'And in the meantime I'll continue with my valuation.'

'The ward number's engaged. This can't be right. Sunny, why don't you call Gil and get him to come back?'

I sighed. 'Will do.'

'Mind if I …?' Oily indicated the rest of the cottage.

'Go ahead, if you insist,' I said. 'Come on, Berta, help me shift the shower.'

'But that's such a pity!' Mavis said tearfully. 'It's been such a success.'

'It has,' I agreed. 'But Blossom is the only one left and she can use our bathroom if she wants.'

'I suppose,' Mavis said mournfully. 'If you need me I'll be in my room – packing.'

I gave her a hug. 'I'm sure it won't come to that.'

'*Berta!*' I snapped.

'Wha—?' she mumbled.

'Move it.'

I found Gil's ladder and climbed up to unfasten the shower hose, winding it in from Mavis's window. I noticed that she was lying on her bed with the duvet drawn over her head. '*What* are we doing?' Berta grumped.

'We need to put the phone box back in the shed.'

'Why?'

'Well, mostly because Mr Smooth wants to take photos of the cottage He says Uncle Clyde is putting it up for sale.'

'What? After all your work?'

And then the penny dropped with a clang. 'The scheming bloody bastard! He intended to sell the cottage months ago! All that crap about not being well enough to do it and having no money – it was all just a ruse to get us down here and do it on the cheap! What a scumbag!'

I gave the phone booth an almighty shove in anger. It keeled to one side like Pisa.

'Whoa!' Berta cried. 'Remind me never to get on your wrong side.'

I kicked the box and it crashed to the ground, the Perspex splitting in half. 'Right – you grab one end,' I instructed.

'Sir, yes, sir!' She saluted.

We manoeuvred it back into a corner of the crowded shed. Just as we were locking the door, we heard a ruckus from the front drive.

'Hey, Miss!' Ambrose shouted, flapping his arms like an emu

preparing for take-off. 'Miss Sunny!' He jogged towards us, his bulging beanie flopping to one side. On reaching us he was bent double, rasping for breath.

'Hey, Ambrose!' I smiled. 'Good to see you. Are you okay?'

He held up his hand as we waited patiently. Finally his breathing resumed and he grinned. 'I know where your car is!'

'*What?*'

'I know where your car is,' he repeated, nodding frantically.

'Where?' Berta demanded, suddenly alert.

'It's in an outhouse at Hawthornyden Farm.'

'Hawthornden Farm?' I checked.

'That's it!' he cried, holding a stitch in his side.

'How do you know?'

'Well, I was camped out behind a massive, like, hedge near the village. I was well upset after ... after ... you know. I didn't know what to do or where to go.'

'Oh, Ambrose!'

He shrugged. 'So I just camped out in some field but I didn't know it was behind this pub – the Oak. Anyways, I was lying in bed and folks kept coming outside for a smoke. I could hear all their chatter 'n' stuff. Late on, it was dark. I heard these two geezers. One was asking whether he got the job done, like. He was saying, "How did you get on with the truck and all?" And the other said, "Piece of cake". He said he drove up, there was no one about, he busted the lock and towed the car away.'

'You'd better come into the kitchen,' I said. 'Let's get this right.'

Oily was measuring up the kitchen when we walked in. He quickly retracted his tape as though caught with his hand down his trousers and muttered, 'Think that's me got all I need.'

'Yeah, well, you can snap away outside,' I said grumpily. 'We've cleared the "debris".

'Jolly good,' he said, slicking back his hair. 'I'll be in touch.'

'Can't wait,' I snarled.

We waited until Ambrose had been supplied with coffee, toast and peanut butter. Mavis, on hearing Ambrose's voice, had surfaced from isolation. 'Oh, Ambrose!' she cried, hugging him to her bosom. 'I was so worried about you.'

'Thank you kindly.' He blushed.

'Where have you been?'

'Sleeping in a field.'

'What? How awful,' Mavis said, squeezing his hand.

'Mavis, he's been sleeping in a field for weeks,' I pointed out. 'It's not like he was exactly glamping it up here.'

The back door banged open and Gil and Romilly bustled in, both clasping brown paper bags of veg. I swear Bonchester must have thought there was a Green Party conference on the go.

'Ambrose!' Gil cried in relief, punching him on the arm. 'Are you back?'

'Well, only to share some good news.' Ambrose grinned.

'He knows where the Jaguar is!' I crowed.

Gil dropped the bag on to the counter and pulled up a chair. 'Go on.'

Ambrose provided the background to his intel.

'I know that farm,' Gil nodded. 'It's about five miles from here towards Denholm. Sunny, remember there was always a really good fruit-picking farm there?'

'That's right – big fat strawberries. Shame hardly any of them made it back home.'

'Fine work, Ambrose.' Gil smiled. 'Quite the detective. I'll give

PC Payne a call straight away.'

'Hang on,' said Ambrose, munching on a crust. 'There's more. When the old boy asked if he still had the tow truck, like, his mate said there was no point because it was getting moved again on Saturday.'

'But that's tomorrow,' said Berta. She always was a whizz at school.

'Are you absolutely positive?' Gil asked in a serious tone. 'He *definitely* said it was getting moved tomorrow?'

'For sure, man.' Ambrose gave an animated nod. 'Which is why I just about busted my gut running up the road today.'

'Okay. Thanks, Ambrose. Good job.' Gil pulled out his mobile and explained the situation. We listened to one half of the conversation until he hung up.

'So?' Berta prompted.

Gil shook his head in frustration. 'She says she'll look into it on Monday.'

'But Monday's no good!'

'Her words were, "Unfortunately, current resources will not make it possible to progress the situation until next week."' Gil thumped the table with his fist.

Romilly placed her hand over his. 'I knew we should have got Daddy involved.'

'And where is Daddy when you need him?' I demanded.

'Actually he's golfing in Lake Garda this weekend.'

'Hmm, let's hope not golfing *in* the lake,' I said, at which she twittered something into her hot water.

'Great, so what do we do now?' Berta huffed.

I shoved an entire slice of toast into my mouth and chomped, deep in thought. The tick of the kitchen clock echoed. Larry clopped around the table, bumping into our legs. The tap drip-dripped into the sink. Eventually Mavis broke the ice. 'Why don't you just go and bring it back yourselves?'

'What do you mean?' I asked.

'I mean, you know where the car is. Go over there and bring it back here.'

'Isn't that stealing?' Berta said.

'How can it be stealing if you're just retrieving what is rightfully yours? I mean, if you kicked a football into your neighbour's garden and went to fetch it back, that wouldn't be stealing, would it?'

'She's got a point,' Romilly conceded.

'But how do we know it's not locked away or guarded by psychopathic Alsatians?' I said.

'You won't until you get there, but at least you'll have tried.'

'Won't we need reinforcements?' Berta frowned. 'We don't exactly have any weapons. What if they're *armed*?'

Mavis tutted. 'It's hardly the Crown Jewels. Some bugger, 'scuse my French, has stolen your car. He'll be a local low life trying to make a quick buck. It's not likely he's part of some international drugs consortium.'

'Mavis is right,' Gil agreed. 'We only want what belongs to us. Okay, let's make a plan.'

'We're going to need more toast.'

'I'll make some notes,' Mavis offered, retrieving a pen and a copy of this week's *Radio Times* from her trolley. 'Firstly, how will you move the car?'

Gil thought out loud. 'We can't rely on any of the mechanisms to be in working order – like the brakes. So towing's no good. If we have enough people, we should be able to push it. There's no way we're going to be able to get our hands on a tow truck – and what would we say to the driver, anyway?'

'I agree,' I said. 'It has to be done on the quiet. When it's dark.'

'We're not going to be able to manage this on our own,' Gil mused. 'There are only five of us.'

'Don't you think I ought to stay with Mavis?' said Romilly. 'We shouldn't leave her on her own out here. As we've already seen, this is cowboy territory.'

'Hardly!' I snorted.

'So that leaves four of us. That's not enough to push a car five miles up and down these winding roads,' Gil pondered.

'Then we have no choice,' I said. 'We're going to have to ask the Wanker Campers for help.'

'Shall I minute that?' Mavis asked, pen poised.

'Of course!' Berta exclaimed. 'There are bloody hundreds of them.'

'But they won't want to help us.' Gil shook his head. 'Not after I dissed their entire *raison d'être*.'

'That's as may be – you're entitled to your opinion. But they've hounded you for months. I think it's very unlikely they'll turn their backs on you entirely. Even if you differ in your views, at the end of the day you're all frigging sci-fi buffs.'

'I don't know.' Gil chewed his nails.

'If you don't ask you won't get,' Berta prompted.

'*I* don't mind asking,' I offered. 'They can't possibly think any worse of me than they already do.'

'No, I'll come with you,' said Gil, picking up his jacket. 'Come on – before I change my mind.'

Chapter 28

We left the kitchen and made for the camp. Blossom's tent stood alone as though quarantined.

'And as we're walking I must tell you about our other visitor we had this morning.'

'Oh? It's been busy, then.'

'While you were sipping on your macchiato we've been grappling with a slimy estate agent sent by Clyde to put the cottage up for sale. Hence the removal of home-made communal shower.' I indicated the foamy brown soil under Mavis's window.

'What? What do you mean?'

'Yep, our dear, darling Uncle Clyde apparently instructed a company from Hawick to put the cottage on the market.'

'But we've only just finished it! All that work we did for him just so he could— *hell*!'

'Yep,' I nodded.

'Have we all been played?'

'Looks like it.'

'The conniving old sod,' Gil muttered. 'Give him his due, his dirty plan worked.'

At the entrance to the camp I was surprised to find that the reception desk had been removed and there was no sign of any border control.

'See?' Gil groaned. 'They're done with me. I've destroyed everything they believed in.'

'Pfft! You're impressive, but don't credit yourself with such almighty power.'

Uninvited, we entered the large marquee, where batches of OOOWU delegates knelt together in concentrating huddles. Paul Crank, dressed in an unflattering tight-fitting red tracksuit, wandered from group to group, hands behind his back, supervising their activity. He glanced across with a *Who let you in?* frown.

'What do *you* want?' he demanded from afar. 'Come here to throw more scorn on our faith?'

A hush seeped across the tent as Crank strode towards us in his stretchy pants. Gil raised his hands in surrender. 'Mr Crank, sir, I've come here to apologise,' Gil began. He announced in a loud voice, 'In fact I've come to apologise to you all.' The huddles crawled nearer to listen, with eager expressions. I had the sensation of wandering into Lilliput. Gulliver – I mean Gil – gave an awkward smile. 'I appreciate how I must have come across the other evening. I'm not normally so negative regarding the subject on which I'm most passionate. In fact, I'm entirely open to *all* possibilities.' There was a buzz of excitement. He turned in a circle, giving each group eye contact. One pack of girls blushed under his gaze. 'It's just that it's been very stressful for me these last few months. I'm sure you all understand.' There were frantic nods of agreement. 'Your excellent work here is to be applauded and, naturally, I unequivocally admire your dedication to finding answers that will benefit us all.'

'You wouldn't be patronising us, now, would you?' Crank sneered.

'Not at all. Where would we be if we all stopped believing?'

Stuck in a Journey time warp?

'What do you want from us?' snipped Crank, rocking on his heels. 'As you can see, we're very busy prototyping space solar power technology.' *What, with a handful of foil pie dishes and a canteen of cutlery?*

'Of course you are. I won't keep you from such important work.' Okay, so even I smelt a whiff of condescension. 'I've come here because I – we – need your help.'

That perked up the crowd no end. 'How so?'

'I believe you had a visit from PC Payne yesterday and she will have explained that a valuable classic car that belonged to my uncle was stolen from our garage.'

'Hmm, she might have made reference to such an offence.'

'Well, the car actually belongs to us – myself, Sunny and two friends. We've been working hard for that reward and now someone has stolen it.' Murmurs of sympathy rippled across the marquee. 'However, we do think we know where it is being kept. We've informed the police, but have been told they can't respond until next week. We have reason to believe the car is to be moved again tomorrow so,' he paused, 'we plan to go tonight and retrieve what is rightfully our property.'

Crank made a point of looking at his watch. '*And?* What do you want *us* to do about it?'

'We need your help,' Gil repeated. 'The car is being stored in a farm about five miles from here. The engine isn't working, so we intend to push it, but we need as many people as possible to assist – to take it in turns to move the car. But we also need people with torches at the back to warn other drivers and some with torches in front to light the way.'

Crank folded his arms and scowled. 'You're asking if my

conference delegates would be willing to commit this unlawful act – to steal a car?'

'It's not technically stealing,' Gil said.

'These are vulnerable young people,' Crank continued. 'You have no right coming here and exploiting the good nature of these students. I think you should leave now.'

'Would you mind if I just asked?' Gil appealed.

'I've asked you politely. Now *go!*'

'Please?'

Crank stepped forward, his arms wide in an attempt to sweep us out of the way. As we turned to leave, Gil threw aside his good manners. 'Is anyone able to help rescue our car this evening?' he pleaded. About twenty hands shot into the air, followed by a *Please pick me!* wave.

Crank surveyed the scene with disdain. 'Seems like you haven't disillusioned the *entire* assembly. Well, perhaps those interested in what Mr McIntosh has to say could congregate over at that side of the marquee.' Half the crowd scrambled to its feet and trotted behind us. Gil took centre stage as he outlined his plan to their excited faces.

'This is all too much!' Blossom wailed as she cradled her tea. The packet of party rings she had brought lay untouched on the kitchen table.

'I know,' Mavis concurred. 'Talk about "What A Difference A Day Makes". I can barely keep up with events.'

'So let me get this straight,' Blossom said, holding her head. She had only just emerged from her tent following yesterday evening's Norwegian karaoke. The tourists had been mightily impressed when Blossom had belted out all the words to 'Take on Me'. 'So

Ambrose slept in a field and overheard these two thugs talking about the stolen car?'

'Correct,' I nodded.

'And now you've been over to the campers and they're going to assist you, Gil?'

'That's right.'

'Even though you said you didn't believe any of their ET stuff?'

'Apparently so,' Gil confirmed. 'I obviously underestimated their dedication to the cause.'

'Hmm. And now your Uncle Clyde wants to sell this cottage?'

'Yep,' I said, cracking open the biscuits.

'Oh dear. But what will happen to you, Mavis? What was he thinking?'

Mavis sighed. 'I've no idea what's been going through his crazy mind.'

'But, Mavis, perhaps you've misconstrued the situation,' Blossom argued. 'You never know! What if your son has invested in a gorgeous wee bungalow with roses round the door and en-suite bathrooms where you can both live on the ground floor?'

'*Blossom!* Don't be a twat all your life,' Berta said. 'This is Clyde we're talking about. Now, I know you've never met him, but let's just say there's as much chance of that happening as Ambrose's father having preserved a spare bedroom in the hope that one day his long-lost son will knock on the door.'

'Oh,' she said, deflated. 'So what's the plan for tonight? Shall I come too?'

'Yeah, if you want,' I said. 'I think we'll need as many folk as possible. We're meeting at the bottom of the road at eleven o'clock – should be dark by then. The Wankers have offered to take us along in their cars.'

'*Sunny!*' Gil objected. 'We can't really call them that now they're on our side.'

'There are no sides,' I pointed out. 'Only geeks. And they're always in the wrong.'

'Ooh, this is quite daring!' Blossom breathed. 'Should I be wearing a black balaclava?'

'Why would you possibly go on a camping holiday with a black balaclava?' Berta gaped.

'I was being figurative.'

'Were you? Not stupid, then?' Berta said, munching on a pink ring.

Chapter 29

Ambrose, although anxious to embark on the next stage of his journey, had agreed to share a last supper. Shame it was only Quorn shepherd's pie – hardly robust fuel for a growing lad who didn't know where his next meal was coming from. Maybe he had a plan to splurge some of the fundraising money on sirloin steak and chips. I knew I'd be tempted. Romilly provided the lame excuse that, apart from the fact that she barely tolerated being in the same town as raw meat, it wouldn't be fair on Larry if we were to tuck into minced lamb. Larry had pricked up his ears hopefully at the mention of his name, even if we *were* dreaming of sinking our chops into his chops.

'Here's to Ambrose!' Gil toasted with a bottle of beer.

'Oh, I can't believe you're leaving us forever,' said Blossom tearfully.

'Forever is a long time, like,' Ambrose said. 'Once I get to Cornwall I will be texting you with my progress, sis.'

'Will you? Oh, please do. Maybe I could come and visit you.'

'Er ...'

'More pie, Ambrose?' Romilly offered.

'Lush.'

'So what are your thoughts?' Gil asked. 'You're going to head down south?'

'I guess I have to, my man. I've no idea if my dad's still there but he was from that area and said, like, he was going home. It's a starting point, innit?'

'Will you be okay?' I asked.

'For sure.' He nodded. 'The hardest thing is ...'

'What?' Blossom prompted.

He swallowed his mouthful. 'My whole life I've grown up believing I was from a Rasta family. It made sense to me – gave me an identity I could hang on to. I mean, I thought I *felt* different from everyone else because I *was* different. It made me sort of special. And now ...' He shrugged. 'If I'm just like any other white dude then what am I doing with this?' He yanked off his knitted beanie and threw it on the floor. His dirty blonde dreadlocks flopped into his eyes. 'I'm no more bloody Rasta than you is!' He stabbed at his food, keeping his head down.

Blossom tugged the bonnet out of Larry's teeth and handed it back. 'Ambrose, you *are* a very special young man – and don't let anyone else tell you otherwise.'

He wiped his face with a sleeve.

'I know you won't want to think about this now,' Mavis added gently. 'But you *can* make your own future. Look at me. I grew up in a family where I was expected to leave school and take up office work. Filing and typing and goodness knows what else. But as a young girl I discovered maths and found my first love. For all the war years I spent at Bletchley Park, entrenched in codes and ciphers, my family thought I was secretary to a civil servant. They never knew. Ever. But *I* knew. And I was doing what I loved. And you'll realise that that is what's important, Ambrose. Know who you want to be.' She patted his hand. He kept his head down as a tear plopped on to his plate.

'So,' Berta said, breaking the silence. 'Please tell me that's apple crumble in the oven.'

'Actually it's rhubarb cobbler,' Romilly replied.

'It's a pudding with custard. That's all I need to know.'

After our meal Ambrose rose from the table and zipped up his hoodie. 'Well, I best be off.'

'Can't you stay for one more night?' Blossom pleaded. 'Then you can set off in the morning.'

'No, I worked out cadging a lift seems to work better in the evening,' he said. 'Maybe folks want some company or somethink.'

Blossom hugged him so tightly Berta and I were forced to release her grip.

'Good luck, Ambrose,' Gil said, shaking his hand.

We eyed each other from a distance. 'Be seeing you, Miss HY.'

'Take care, Ambrose, and I hope it all works out for you.' I saluted as he left the kitchen for the final time.

'Such a lovely boy.' Blossom trumpeted into a hankie.

'You lot better get organised,' Mavis interrupted. 'Romilly and I will do the washing-up.'

'Some people will do anything to get out of Grand Theft Auto,' said Berta.

By eleven p.m. a sizeable group had gathered at the foot of Crackers Track. Clyde's truck remained abandoned on the verge, Archie having secured more comfortable accommodation under canvas. I had taken Blossom's comments to heart and wore a scarf round my face. Berta had pulled on a baseball cap and tied a bandana over her mouth. Gil was sporting one of Romilly's Vegetarian Society T-shirts on his head, intending to pull it over his face should anyone approach. *If in doubt, blame it on the lentil-lovers.* I found it hard to comprehend as, one by one, the campers appeared in their fancy-dress attire. Okay, so I could accept the disguise or camouflage offered by Princess Leia or Doctor Who, but did we really need two frigging Daleks?

We stuffed as many bodies as possible into each vehicle, Lieutenant Ripley installed in the lap of Agent Scully, Chewbacca crushing a Skywalker. Gil left in the first car and we followed in a circus convoy. Although we had made plans with about twenty volunteers this afternoon, it seemed the illicit adventure had attracted a larger majority. Perhaps it was the lure of the greasepaint. Crank remained elusive. Or envious of Gil's influence, I hoped.

As we neared the farmhouse, the cars slowed down and pulled up by the side of the road. Grey clouds occluded the moon, leaving the countryside in shadowy darkness. There were no streetlights, only distant stars shrouded behind mist. I struggled to see my hand in front of my face – goodness knows what level of vision the masked heroes had. We clambered out of the vehicles and the drivers headed back to camp, having served their country.

'Gather round,' Gil whispered. It was hard to take him seriously with a Brussels sprout T-shirt on his head.

'Golly, I need a wee!' Blossom confessed.

'Get a grip,' muttered Berta.

'So,' Gil continued in a hushed voice, 'it looks as though there is a short driveway up to the house and there are two possibilities to the right where the car could be hidden. I suggest you lot split up and guard either side of the road while I go with one other person to check out the garages.'

A show of hands went up.

'Chewbacca, come with me. The rest spread out. We'll be back in a wee minute.'

'Don't say, "wee"!' Blossom protested.

Gil tutted. 'Who's got the tools?'

Star Trek's Scotty stepped forward, toolbox in hand. 'Aye, captain! You should find everything you need in there.'

'Thanks,' Gil said drily. 'Now keep watch.'

The sideshow dispersed without a word into the darkness as Gil and his hulking partner tiptoed up the drive. A lone owl hooted from a field. It was difficult to make out anything other than two dark shapes as they moved from one outbuilding to the other. We heard a soft clunk, then the doors of one garage opening. Gil crept back to our huddle.

'It's there!' he whispered triumphantly. There was a quiet murmur of approval. 'Now, we want to exit as quickly as possible, so can I suggest I take the ten strongest people first? We can rotate later along the road but for now we need absolute stealth.'

The crowd jostled around until a group of ten moved forward. 'That's not fair!' Sarah Connor griped under her breath. 'I can take on Tom Baker any day of the week.'

'Piss off!' said a lanky lad in a knitted scarf.

'Luke, you agree, don't you? I'm much stronger than he is.'

A pale bloke in a monk's habit shrugged non-committally.

'Look, you'll all get your turn,' Gil reassured them. 'If you're so keen, why don't you close the doors behind us while we move the car?'

'Humpf!' Sarah moaned, following the group.

Gil pointed to the daintier version of Princess Leia. 'I think you should steer the car. Sunny, can you stand at the farmhouse door and keep watch up there?'

'Huh?' I panicked, thinking it's always the lookout that gets shot first.

'Come on,' he urged. I felt Berta prod me in the back.

'But ...'

'But *what*?' he demanded in a fierce whisper.

'I'm not armed.'

'Here, take this.' Sarah Connor passed me a spare automatic rifle. 'Don't worry – it's not real.' She smiled.

'Shouldn't I be *more* worried it's not real? I'm not sure how effective plastic guns are in combat.'

I stalked up the drive as Gil's posse inched their way in the blackness towards the furthest garage. After a few minutes had passed, the bonnet of the car appeared at the entrance. Princess Leia gripped the steering wheel, buns hard, her face set in concentration. The twenty-legged force leant on the boot, creeping the Jaguar down the drive. Hovering as near to the house as I dared, my eyes darted between car and building. I was pinning my hopes on it being either uninhabited or at least temporarily unoccupied. There was certainly no obvious sign of life. No light. No sound.

No such luck. *Boom!* An outside light illuminated the drive as though it were early morning on a bright summer's day. The silhouetted carnival halted mid-parade. The back door slammed open and a gruff voice shouted, 'Oy! What the hell's going on here?' A white-haired scruff of a man in a grubby vest and long johns emerged from the door, wielding a golf driver. He wasn't exactly adhering to the dress code for a midnight round of golf. Brandishing his weapon of choice, he barked, 'I *said*, "What the hell is going on here?"'

'Okay, let's all just calm down.' Gil stepped out from behind the car.

'Hang on a minute.' The old boy shuffled back into the house, returning with a pair of bent glasses perched on his nose. 'That's better. Now, where are you taking my car?'

'*Your* car?' I heard Berta mutter from the gloom.

Gil held up his hands. 'My name is Gil McIntosh. We've come from Crackers Cottage over near Bonchester. Look, can't we discuss this civilly?' He approached the house, holding out a conciliatory hand.

'You're marching around my property at night, stealing my vehicle, and you want to sit down and have a nice wee chat over a coffee?' the owner growled.

'I'm sorry,' said Gil. 'But this car actually belongs to my uncle Clyde. I have the car documents. And look.' He dangled the car keys in the beam of the intruder light.

The ancient golfer squinted from the doorframe. '*Who* did you say you are?'

'Gil. Clyde's nephew.'

'Clyde Davidson?'

'That's right.' Gil smiled. 'Do you know him?'

'Oh, aye, I ken him alright. But this makes no sense.' He scratched his crotch in bemusement. 'And *where* did you say you've come from?'

'Crackers Cottage. Where Clyde lives.'

'Aye, that's right. And *what* did you say you lot are doing?'

'We're retrieving Clyde's car. We're going to push it back to his cottage where it belongs. If you don't mind me asking,' Gil risked a swipe with the club, 'how is it in your possession?'

The grubster shrugged. 'I got a call the other day from Clyde.'

'But he's in hospital,' Gil objected.

'Aye, son – if you'll let me finish. I got a call from Clyde from the hospital. He said to me he was worried about the Jag being left out in the garage while he was laid up. He asked me to borrow my pal's tow truck and move the car to here where it would be safe.'

Gil let out a hollow laugh. 'And I'm guessing he told you specifically what night to move the car?'

'That's exactly so. He said make sure it's moved on Wednesday evening and apparently someone's coming on Saturday to move it again. That's not you lot, is it? You're a bit early!'

'No.' Gil sighed.

'So Clyde's your uncle, eh? How's he doing?'

'He'll be a hell of a lot worse by the time I get my hands on him,' Gil growled.

'*Shit!*' I cursed from behind the door. The pensioner jumped in fright.

'Help-ma-Boab! What are you doing sneaking up behind me like that? Who are you?'

'I'm Sunny. And yes, I'm Gil's sister. And yes, we're taking back this car. Come on, everyone, let's get this party started!'

'But ... but what will I tell Clyde?'

'Tell him what you like!' said Gil. 'Tell him we're on to him, the conniving bastard!'

'Eh? But he's just a poor old man lying in hospital with busted bones.'

'Don't you believe it,' I snapped.

The man stared open-mouthed as the OOOWU crowd began pushing the car down the drive. He glared at Chewbacca, shouting, 'You're an ugly bugger!'

'That's done it,' someone warned.

Chewbacca took long menacing strides towards the house, removing the hairy head. Her dark hair stuck to her sweaty face as she towered over him. 'Like to pick on girls, do you?' She snatched the golf club and hurled it into a nearby bush. He whimpered, scuttled back indoors and locked the door with a clunk. His pale face popped up at the kitchen window as we rolled away our prize. The group waiting at the foot of the drive let out a cheer. Doctor Who flourished a football clacker above his head.

Chapter 30

We made slow but steady progress along the winding country roads in eerie stillness. The fields either side were lost in a dark void. The two Daleks led the way, light emanating from their rotating domes. At the rear Sarah Connor and Lieutenant Ripley held two torches each to warn approaching vehicles. Despite the late hour there were a surprising number of cars passing. God knew where they'd come from or where they were heading. I assumed many were revellers weaving their way back from the pub based on the number of blasts on the horn we received and shouts of 'Move over, morons!' and the ever-original 'Show us yer tits!' One carload of male teenagers shrieked abuse out of their window but, when forced to slow down to overtake, crapped themselves when Chewbacca hammered on their rear window. Gil rotated the muscle fairly, but when we reached Bonchester Brae it was all hands on deck and a backbreaking effort was required to shove the reluctant Jaguar against gravity.

'Haven't you lot got access to any rocket fuel?' Berta complained. 'Or, better still, one of those beam-me-up things?'

'Are you referring to a teleportation machine?' Scotty enquired.

'I'm talking about anything that will get me home to bed as quickly as possible,' she groaned. 'Would it help if I said, "Beam me up, Scotty"?'

'Not at all,' he replied in a monotone. 'That's actually a misquotation and was never even uttered in a single episode of *Star Trek*.'

'Well, excuse me!' she said, out of puff. 'My mistake – I must have been thinking about a completely different shite programme.'

'Language, Berta!' Blossom admonished. 'Some people might take offence at that.'

'I do apologise to everyone!' Berta announced. 'Sorry *Star Trek* is shite.'

As we summited the hill and began the steep descent, we were forced to walk backwards, halting the car's slump into free fall. Without warning the Daleks stopped walking and the cavalcade concertinaed.

'*Whoa!*' Gil commanded, holding up his right hand. Our party came to a standstill a few feet away from an articulated lorry parked in the road with hazard lights flashing. The driver's door was open but the driver was nowhere to be seen.

'Strange,' Gil frowned. He climbed into the driver's cab and back out again. Murmurs of bemusement rippled from the front to the rear of our cortège.

'Shhh!' he hushed us. We held our breath. Then – yes – a muffled noise. A cry?

'Help!' a voice shouted. 'Over here!'

'You half, guard the car,' Gil said, splitting the group. 'The rest, follow me.' He edged towards the voice from the darkness, scanning the hedgerow with his torch.

'Down here.'

We congregated in a row, our torches directed towards the ditch that ran alongside the road.

'Holey moley!' a man protested from the ground, shielding his eyes from the blinding lights.

'Everyone else put your torches down,' Gil instructed, keeping his concentrated on the man, who lay crumpled in the ditch, covered in mud.

He gazed up at us in confusion, specifically at the two Daleks, who had their death-ray plungers trained on his chest. 'Where in *hell's name* am I?' he cried.

'Near Bonchester Bridge,' Gil said. 'Outside Hawick.'

'Thank God for that,' said the stranger in relief. 'Hang on, though – what *year* is it?'

'Twenty thirteen,' Gil said. 'Don't worry – you haven't died and gone to Pinewood Studios. Are you the driver of this lorry?'

'I am. Ronnie's the name.'

'Okay, Ronnie, can I ask what you're doing down there?'

'You can. I'm embarrassed to say that I stopped the lorry, thinking I was in the middle of nowhere, to have a … well, let's just say I've drunk a lot of coffee today. I nipped pretty quickly behind the lorry, not noticing the bloody great trench here. When I think back to how long it took them to forge the Channel Tunnel, and here in Scotland you have ditches you could drive a ruddy steam train through. Think I've sprained my bleeding ankle or something.'

'Where're you from?'

'Ashford, mate. Look, sorry about the jibe but I've been lying here for ages. Every time a car goes past I shout, but no one wants to stop. And to make matters worse, I still need a bloody pee!'

'Ooh! So do I!' Blossom cried.

'Are you going to help me up or what?' he implored.

'Okay, you heard the man. Watch your step – that's a pretty deep ditch. Let's help him out,' Gil said. 'Daleks, keep your lights focused down here.' They shuffled forward, their domes whizzing in excitement. We hauled Ronnie to his one good foot and dragged him towards his cabin.

'*And* I've lost my bloody phone,' Ronnie complained. 'It must have fallen out my pocket.' We lifted him up into his cabin. He winced with every movement.

'Can everyone have a look for Ronnie's phone?' said Gil.

'I'm not going to be able to drive,' Ronnie muttered. 'But I'll need to stay with my cab until my pal gets here. I better give him a call. You don't think the police will swing by if I stay on the verge?'

'I very much doubt it,' said Gil. 'But if you want to get out of here I guess we can put you in the back of our car and unload you at Bonchester?'

'Thanks, mate, but I don't trust the locals with this lot.' He nodded to his freight. 'No offence.'

'None taken. We're no more local than you are.'

'Found it!' Agent Scully yelled, hurrying forward to hand the phone to Ronnie.

'Cheers. Hey! Aren't you—?'

'Nearly but not quite.'

'You're a dead ringer, though. Right, well, I suppose I'll be holed up here until my pal arrives.'

'When do you reckon he'll get here?'

'Oh, by about Monday,' Ronnie said, shaking his head. 'Knowing my luck.'

Ronnie tooted his horn as we continued on our way.

By the time we arrived back at Crackers Cottage and had manoeuvred the car into its resting place, we were stumbling along like Neanderthals. Gil stood at the garage door, shaking each OOOWU by the hand, personally thanking each one for their contribution.

It was two a.m. when Berta and I collapsed into our bunk beds, too exhausted to even joke about the night's events. That would have to wait until tomorrow. Even the moment when we approached the sporadic farmhouses leading into Bonchester and Chewbacca came face to face with a farmer who was doing Christ knows what in his field at that time of night. To describe his reaction on confronting a six-foot talking bear was just too good to cover in the few seconds it took for us to plummet into sleep.

Chapter 31

It was Saturday afternoon before my eyes flickered open with resentment and immediately I felt something was missing. As Blossom would say, 'Something beginning with M'. My longing for Mathew was stronger than any Scotch pine. I needed to see him – and soon. Despite his indifference towards holding hands with me in public (or private) and his belief that hugs were as necessary as suggesting to Lady Gaga that she ought to express herself more, I suspected he was missing me too. His last message had indicated, without using those actual words, that he wanted me home.

'Berta, we need to go home,' I announced to her sagging bottom.

'Thank fuck for that! When?'

'Let's get some breakfast and see who's around. I'm going to tell Gil.'

'Go, sister!'

By the time Berta and I had washed, dressed and made coffee, Mavis, Gil and Romilly had progressed to lunch. As I sat facing the kitchen window with a clear view of the track leading to the main road, it did not escape my attention that a steady stream of cars was trundling in both directions.

'Hey up! There's trouble at t'mill. What's the story?' I asked.

'You'll be delighted to hear that last night, apparently, a community nurse was making her way home after her evening shift in Bishop's Itchington when she observed a strange pink light hovering in the sky. This was followed by a smallish flash of light that streamed across a nearby copse,' Gil said, squeezing lemon juice on to an avocado.

'Uh-huh,' I said. 'Bishop's what?'

'Itchington. It's in Warwickshire.'

'And?'

'And Paul Crank has declared it a "hot spot". So they've upped sticks and are on their way.'

'Just like that?' Berta said.

'I thought you'd be pleased.'

'I couldn't give a flying f—'

'*Berta!*'

'I couldn't care less what that lot get up to. I just thought they'd be a bit more strategic in their planning. Didn't think they'd up and off at the first whiff of a flying saucer.'

'To be fair, this type of credible sighting doesn't happen very often. At least, not in the UK.'

'And hardly ever in Bishop's Itchington,' I added.

'Oh, here's someone now,' Mavis warned. We heard a rap at the back door. They all looked at me.

'Really? Still me?' I pushed back my chair and opened the door. Paul Crank was positioned outside in full metal jacket. He even paraded a tin helmet and ammunition belt.

'Been called up?' I enquired.

'You could say that,' he clipped. 'Want to get there before the trail goes cold.'

'Quite right. These extraterrestrials can be flighty buggers.'

'One of these days,' he fumed, 'you will see. The whole world will see.'

'But in the meantime we're all blinkered. Is that what you're implying?'

'Keep your eyes open,' he said. 'You never know what you might see when you're not looking.'

'O-*kay.*'

He handed over a shoebox filled with cash. 'Here. I'm sure you'll find that's what we owe you.' I stirred the grubby notes with my fingers.

'It's all there,' he barked.

'And what about the site? Is everything away?'

'If you find so much as a single match or used tea bag, be sure to bring it to my attention.'

'So that's Gil off the hook now, is it?' I checked. 'You're done with us?'

'I didn't say that.'

'But—'

'But what? We helped you retrieve your property, didn't we? I think we're quits as far as obligations are concerned. However, Gil remains a "person of interest" to us and that's unlikely to change in the near future.'

'Whatever.' I sighed.

'You're lucky,' Crank threw out as he turned to leave.

'How so?'

'Being Gil's sister.'

'Yeah,' I nodded. 'Every day is a joy. Maybe that's what I'll call my next book.'

He frowned and climbed into the idling minibus. Blossom waved goodbye as the circus left town. 'Now I'm the only tent left,' she wailed, standing alone in her lilac wellies.

'Come and have some lunch.'

'Listen, Sunny,' said Mavis, fretting. 'Gil's been telling me about what happened last night. I am *mortified* by Clyde's behaviour.'

'It's not your fault,' I said, handing Blossom a coffee.

'Oh, but it *is*! I brought him up to be better than this. Do you really think he arranged to have the car moved so you'd believe it was stolen and wouldn't be expecting any payment?'

'It certainly looks that way. Sorry, Mavis,' I said. 'I mean, the fact that he gave his crony strict instructions for which evening to move it, knowing we'd all be occupied.'

'But then that *is* my fault!' Mavis said, tears welling. '*I* told him all about the fundraiser. It was my "loose lips" that sunk the ships.'

'Don't beat yourself up about it.' Berta shrugged. 'You didn't know what scumbag plans he was going to make.'

'And we have to take some responsibility too,' Gil said. 'I mean, he probably thought the Jag wasn't worth that much and it was only because we made such a big thing of it that got him thinking it might actually have some value.'

'Well, he's in for a shock when he finds we've taken it back,' I remarked.

'And I've arranged for a tow truck to transport it up to a garage in Edinburgh where they can fix it up for us.'

'Good.' Mavis nodded. 'The car belongs to you. Do what you want with it.'

'So,' said Blossom, 'this Clyde fellow manipulates you lot into coming down here to renovate his cottage only for you to discover he has conned you into making his home more marketable. And then he offers you the Jaguar in exchange for payment, subsequently staging a theft so he doesn't actually need to give you a penny.'

'I guess that about sums it up,' I agreed.

'Not quite,' said Gil. 'Sunny, we haven't even got you up to speed on our encounter last night.'

'What do you mean?' I quizzed.

'Had a call from Police Scotland this morning, looking for our dear uncle. Apparently, the trucker we rescued from the ditch was diverting through the Borders in the early hours with a special delivery of 'procured' games consoles.'

'Shit! No wonder he didn't want to leave his lorry.'

'Yep. Seemingly Clyde had arranged a meet through a contact he'd hooked up with in the ward.'

'He really is a case, that uncle of yours,' said Berta.

'I can't believe it!' I exclaimed. 'Only he could use a broken hip as a way to score a bit extra on the side.'

Mavis wept over her cheese toastie. 'Where did I go wrong with my Clyde? He used to be such a lovely little boy. All blue eyes and chestnut ringlets. I think the years spent on his own have made him very selfish. Maybe I should have insisted I move up sooner.'

'In my experience ...' Blossom began.

'Oh, here we go. The world according to Oprah,' said Berta.

'It sounds to me like this poor chap Clyde is just crying out for help,' Blossom said thoughtfully. 'Think about it. He asks his mother to move up from England to be near him. He reaches out to *your* mother – a long-standing friend. Then he invites you all to stay at his house for a holiday ...'

'Hmm, it hasn't exactly been a *holiday*.'

'Even so – can't you see? He is a man wretched with loneliness who has come to a point in his life when he needs his family around him. I saw it all the time at the care home. People who hadn't spoken to relatives in years suddenly felt the need to atone.'

'Atonement?' Berta scoffed. 'He's got an awfy funny way of showing it.'

'He needs forgiveness, not your anger.'

'Bloody hell, Blossom, whose side are you on?'

'If it's sides you—' I stopped mid-sentence as a car engine reverberated outside. Mavis peered through the window.

'Looks like Tam's taxi.'

Stepping into the front yard, I found Tam holding the passenger door open while Clyde swore loudly. 'Oy! Give us a hand, will you?' Clyde bellowed. I shouted for Gil, which brought everyone except Mavis running out of the house. Gil wrestled his arms round Clyde, hauling him to his feet as Blossom provided extra support. They hobbled awkwardly towards the door. Clyde used them as crutches as he hopped over the threshold into the kitchen.

'Daddy's home,' I whispered into Larry's ear. '*Baaa*,' he acknowledged.

Romilly retrieved a clear plastic bag from the boot. It contained his worldly belongings and half a dispensary of drugs.

'That's twenty quid,' Tam announced with a sour grimace, holding out his hand. I paid him from the shoebox.

'Get us a decent coffee, then,' Clyde ordered as we sat in silence round the kitchen table. 'You lot don't look too pleased to see me. Not got a kiss for your favourite son, Ma?'

'What are you doing home?' Mavis asked.

'Oh, that's charming, that is! I get taken to hospital with *two* broken bones, get myself rehabilitated – no thanks to the so-called nurses – and when I *do* get back on my feet you demand to know why I'm back in *my own* house.'

'Here's your coffee, sir.' Blossom smiled and gave the mug a stir. 'I'm Blossom, by the way. I've been camping in your field at Camp Crackers and it's just been fabulous fun. I *love* your wee site and my friends here have taken me to their hearts and I know they think you're a bit of a curmudgeonly old soul but I think you're sweet. I believe we're going to be the best of friends too. I bet you've got lots of really interesting stories to share.'

Berta snorted into her mug.

Clyde's mouth opened but no words came out. Eventually he exploded. 'What in God's name are you on about, lassie? Camping in my field? Are you *mad*? Someone give me a fag – I'm gasping for one. That bloody prison wouldn't let me smoke anywhere.'

'Then now's as good a time as any to stop,' Mavis snipped. Clyde glared around the room, sensing a less than favourable welcome.

'What? What have I done?'

'You know, Clyde, I really don't know where to begin.' Gil was seething. 'Perhaps we could start with how you contrived to have us spend our summer holiday refurbishing your cottage. Then we could move on to your exploitation of our goodwill so you could increase the value of your home – which you then put up for sale, effectively making your own mother homeless. Let's move on to the classic car, promised to us in lieu of payment, only to be snatched back once again to profit your own situation.'

'And don't forget your other insane notion to turn your empty field into a camping site,' I chipped in. 'Thanks for *that* warning!'

'Ah,' he muttered under his breath. 'So you know.'

'Yes, we know,' said Gil. 'We know all about your scheming and plotting and capitalisation on our good nature.'

'Not to mention dabbling in stolen goods,' added Berta.

'You really have been an unprincipled villain,' Mavis added.

'I'm sorry to say we're related. These kids have worked their socks off for you to get this place in order and make you a bit of extra money from the field, and look at how you repay them.'

'But …'

'But *what*?'

'I was worried sick,' he mumbled. 'The house was falling apart and I didn't have the money to make it alright for you, old woman. I was worried something was going to go wrong with you. You're not exactly a spring chicken.'

'*Clyde!*' Gil protested.

'I didn't know what to do. I thought if I did the cottage up and sold it, maybe we could move into somewhere a bit more suitable. Maybe pay for a wee holiday – somewhere flat so I could push you in your wheelchair. Where is your wheelchair, anyway?'

Mavis rose from her chair slowly and, propping herself against the table, stood beside her gaping son. She gave him a sharp rap across the ear.

'*Aya!*' he objected. 'What was that for?'

'Why didn't you just talk to me? We could have worked it all out.'

'Well, I didn't exactly plan on Missy here pushing me over.'

'I did *not*—'

'Let it go, Sunny.'

'I was right, though!' Clyde thumped his fist on the table. 'This has happened and now how am I going to take care of you?'

'Take care of *me*?' Mavis protested. 'It'll be *me* looking after *you*!'

'How? What about the shopping and cleaning and cooking? Who's going to look after both of us?' Clyde despaired.

'Me,' Blossom offered in a small voice. 'I could be your carer. I'd love to. That's if you're willing to give me a chance?'

'Blossom?' I said, surprised. 'What about your job in the care home? I thought you loved it?'

'I did,' Blossom agreed. 'But if you recall when I arrived, I was sad to say, "I *have been* working in a care home". Unfortunately, after I karate-chopped Mr Grosvenor in the treatment room it was made very clear to me that I wasn't welcome back.'

'But that's not fair,' said Romilly. 'Legally unfair, in fact.'

'I know, but maybe it's time I moved on. I used to be a healthcare worker for a family in Kirkton, which I *adored*. Helping people at home is my *thing* – if you'll have me, of course? We could try it out for a few weeks, anyway.' She held up her crossed fingers.

'Are you sure?' Mavis beamed. 'That would be just splendid!'

'Aye – splendid,' Clyde echoed.

'Does that mean we can stay here?' Mavis asked hopefully.

'Humph. I'm going to have a wee rest on my own settee. Someone pass me my walker.'

Clyde struggled to his feet and limped through to the living room as Gil held the door open. A few minutes later we heard a shout from next door.

'What's he done now?' I groaned as we piled into the living room. Clyde held the prized remote control aloft. 'That is one fan-bloody-tastic TV! Jesus! I am *never* leaving this house. Damn it, I'm never leaving this *room*!'

Chapter 32

'Where are my hair straighteners?' Berta yelled through the bathroom door. 'I can't find them anywhere!'

'Get a bloody move on, woman!' I bellowed back. 'There's only one bus to Edinburgh from Hawick on a Sunday and I sure as hell am not going to miss it. What did you bring hair straighteners down here for, anyway?'

'Guys prefer it when my hair looks like dry spaghetti rather than wet.'

'Check under the bed.'

'Found them!'

'Come on!' I called, bumping my rucksack down the stairs. 'Tam's waiting outside.'

'Enough of the racket out there!' Clyde roared. 'Can't a man get peace to watch the footie?'

'Bye, Clyde,' I said, patting him on the head. 'It's been a pleasure.'

He grunted. 'And tell that flower-lassie she needs to empty my bottle.'

'Blossom's her name.'

'If you say so.' His eyes never shifted from the multiplex screen.

I hugged Blossom at the back door as she wiped tears from her eyes. She really did smell of strawberries. 'It's been so lovely meeting you all. And thank you for giving me this opportunity. I'll look after them both like my own.'

'Thank *you*, Blossom.' I smiled, sensing an escape to the real world within reach. 'And don't let His Lordship get away with anything. Have you moved your stuff into Gil's room?'

'Yep.' She grinned. 'Now that Archie's scarpered too I've put the laundry on myself.'

'God, I'd forgotten about Archie! That's terrible,' I exclaimed. 'Where did he go?'

'Oh, he buggered off as soon as the Yo-Yos started packing up. You know he made enough money to buy a brand-new iPhone, so he was pretty chuffed.' I hunkered down and rubbed my face in Larry's thick wool as he watched me with mournful eyes, probably wondering whether the new girl would be as generous with her buttered toast.

Mavis clasped me with both hands. 'I'll miss you, Sunny. In fact I'll miss you all.'

'Take care!' I waved, squashing into the back of the taxi with Gil and Romilly. Berta grinned smugly from the front seat.

'Look after each other!' Mavis called, blowing a kiss. As though flagging down a passing cruise ship, Blossom waved madly until we disappeared round the corner.

Tam ambled through the village and over the river. Winding down the window, Berta whooped, 'Bye, Bonchester! Thanks for having us!' Tam muttered under his breath about city twits. He left the houses behind, dawdling through the country lanes as though out for a Sunday drive. Okay, so he *was* out for a Sunday drive, but I had a boyfriend waiting in Edinburgh who was gagging for my return.

As soon as Tam pulled into Hawick the four of us sprinted to the bus just as the driver moved into first gear. Gil hammered on the tri-folding door until the driver scowled and released it with a reluctant hiss.

'Where have you lot been?' he grumbled.

'To hell and back,' I snapped, climbing aboard.

'So did you miss me?' Mathew fished.

'Miss you? If hacking my arm off would have got us home any sooner I'd have borrowed Gil's reciprocating saw,' I replied, gulping my vodka.

'That bad, eh?' Mathew grinned.

'You have no idea how good it feels to sit in a normal pub with you and have a normal conversation. And not have to sleep on a mattress stuffed with gravel or be woken by Berta's grunting. Then have to get up before noon and entertain the paying public with historic tours, mountain hikes and creative writing.'

'Sounds like you had a ball,' Mathew smirked.

'I'm sorry, but I can only think of a rude response so I'll say nothing.'

'Okay, well, while you're saying nothing let me tell you how much *I* have missed *you*.' Mathew smiled, squeezing my hands. 'Life is definitely not the same without you.'

And, hearing those words, just might have made the last two weeks worth it.